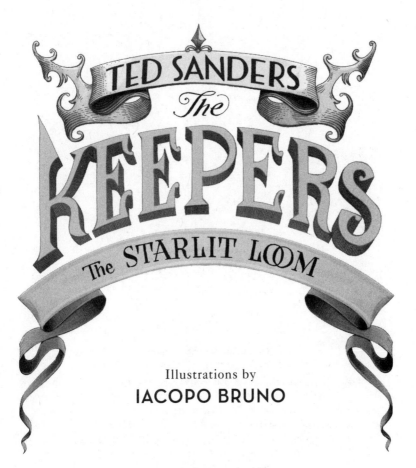

TED SANDERS

The

KEEPERS

The STARLIT LOOM

Illustrations by
IACOPO BRUNO

HARPER
An Imprint of HarperCollinsPublishers

ISBN 978-0-06-227591-2

Typography by Carla Weise

18 19 20 21 22 PC/LSCH 10 9 8 7 6 5 4 3 2 1

First Edition

For the entire Mulholland gang,
in all their noisy glory

I couldn't ask for a better family.

Your children are not your children.
They are the sons and daughters
of Life's longing for itself. . . .
You may house their bodies but not their souls,
for their souls dwell in the house of tomorrow,
which you cannot visit, not even in your dreams.
— KAHLIL GIBRAN

Let your soul stand cool and composed before a million
universes.
— WALT WHITMAN

CONTENTS

Approaching Thunder

THE WAR PARTY *3*

IN THE PIT *19*

THE EMPATH *44*

THE FATES OF THE UNCHOSEN *58*

TANGLED UNIVERSES *81*

RESCUED *89*

APPROACHING THUNDER *99*

EARTHEN SKY *120*

The Corners of the Earth

THE GREAT COUNCIL *141*

THE SAME FIRE *165*

WHAT COULD HAVE BEEN KNOWN *176*

THE FADED *209*

Through the Mothergate 223
The Starlit Loom 249
A Great Need 276
A Refusal Refused 297
Seven Minutes, Six Days 308

The Sending

Uroboros 343
Memories 358
A Traveler's Tale 372
The Story Told 392
The Answers to Everything 409

Epilogue

The Boy Who Knew Tomorrow 421

Glossary 425

PART ONE

Approaching Thunder

CHAPTER ONE

The War Party

TRAVELING BY MAL'GAMA AT NIGHT WAS ALMOST ENOUGH TO make Chloe forget everything.

Not that she wanted to forget. In fact, she was annoyed that so much of her anger had slipped away—anger about the Warren, her home and sanctuary for these past few months, now invaded and conquered by the Riven. Anger at Joshua, whose fault it sort of was and who was maybe a traitor. Anger at Isabel—that was a given. Anger at Mr. Meister and Brian and Sil'falo Teneves and the rest of the Wardens, who had hidden the wretched truth about the Mothergates all this time.

It had only been a day since the Warren had fallen.

A day since she had learned she was going to die.

But up here, Chloe found it hard to cling to that anger. It was well past midnight. The mal'gama sped through the darkness, a thousand feet above the open farmland of Illinois, carrying its small crew of Wardens. All around them, the night sky was a black dome of unbroken cloud. Somehow it seemed right that there were no stars, since Horace wasn't here to name them. Chloe was glad he'd stayed behind. It was safer for him back at Ka'hoka, a sanctuary deeper and better protected than the Warren had ever been. The thought made her almost sleepy, him being safe.

And it didn't hurt that the mal'gama itself, a massive carpet of small soft stones, cradled Chloe as it flew, undulating like water. The front edge of the mal'gama had formed into a kind of a prow, so that the wind barely licked at her short black hair. The overall sensation, she realized, as she fiddled with the Alvalaithen hanging from her neck, felt a little bit like going thin and diving into the dark earth, soaring through solid ground, as only she could. Except that here she was not in control. And although she hated to admit it, not being in control right now was . . . nice.

She supposed Dwen'dailen Longo, the Altari warrior, was in control. That was nice too. The mal'gama wasn't Tan'ji, and so it didn't have a Keeper, but Dailen wore the ring that controlled the huge Tanu. Did that make him the pilot? The dog walker? Flying carpet wrangler? She'd been watching the young Altari, to see what he did, but he didn't do much. Maybe the mal'gama had a bit of a mind of its own. All Chloe knew was, they were going fast. Fast was good. The faster the better.

This was a rescue mission. Allegedly. And Chloe had to

admit that the rescue team she was a part of was definitely badass, even if the word "team" made her gag a little. Besides herself and Dailen, five other Keepers rode the mal'gama now, all of them Wardens. They were headed back to Chicago to try and save those who had been captured by the Riven in the raid on the Warren. They were going to find Mr. Meister, for sure. And possibly Joshua too, whether he wanted to be saved or not. And maybe Isabel—her mother.

Even if the word made Chloe gag a little.

If her mother was even alive.

Most of the Wardens' Council was here, with their towering bodies and their powerful Tan'ji. The hulking Go'nesh carried his blue-bladed staff, the Fairfrost Blade, whose every swing left a swath of impenetrable ice hanging in the air. Okay, not quite ice and not *quite* impenetrable. But bitterly cold and brutally dense, as Chloe knew all too well. Beside him, dark and surly, Ravana wore her faultless wooden bow over her shoulders. Named Pinaka, it was as thick as a man's arm and three times as long. And off to Chloe's side, exasperatingly beautiful Teokas had her . . . whatever it was. Some kind of bracelet. Thailadun, she called it: the Moondoor. She'd shown it to Horace, but Chloe had no idea what it did, and it was nagging at her. Whenever Chloe glanced over at Teokas now—a painfully graceful silhouette, a magnet for anyone's eyes, her long legs dangling over the edge of the mal'gama—it seemed Teokas was looking back at her.

Gabriel was here too, the tallest of the humans, though

still dwarfed by the Altari. He sat with Dailen, well back from the edge, the Staff of Obro across his lap. The staff was the only cure for Gabriel's blindness, and a temporary one at that, but he would never use it here. Not when calling forth the humour that gave him sight meant blinding everyone else.

Gabriel and Dailen were talking animatedly in low voices, even laughing now and again. Other than Chloe, Gabriel was the youngest here, five or six years older than she was. And as far as she understood it, Dailen was not much older than Gabriel, in Altari years—he was a kind of teenager himself. Barely an adult, anyway. But because the Altari lived much longer, Dailen was closer to eighty than eighteen.

The final member of the party sat with Gabriel and Dailen, mostly silent. Mrs. Hapsteade bent over her own lap, tiny and dark, her prim black dress piled around her. Every now and again she muttered something quietly to Dailen. Unlike the others, Mrs. Hapsteade hadn't come to fight. Her Tan'ji was no kind of weapon; it was useful only in identifying the powers of new Keepers. But she had insisted on carrying the Tanu that told them where to go, a compass whose red needle pointed straight at Mr. Meister.

Before being captured, he'd swallowed a small Tan'kindi called a backjack, and as long as it was inside him—no matter where the Riven might take him—this compass would track him down. The others assumed the old man must still be in the Warren, deep under the streets of downtown Chicago. But Chloe wasn't so sure. If she were the Riven, she would have gotten Mr. Meister out of there quick. The Warren might have fallen, but she suspected it was still full of traps, and Mr. Meister certainly knew them all.

But whatever. Wherever the compass took them, that's where they would go. Chloe was ready. She was ready because she had no idea what else to do.

And she had to do *something*.

The mal'gama rippled beneath her, pulsing. Teokas walked along its very edge, coming toward her, the green stones shifting under her graceful steps. She was small for an Altari, only seven feet tall or so. Watching her move, it occurred to Chloe that Teokas wasn't as old as Chloe had thought—again, for an Altari. Older than Dailen, but younger than her splendor and confidence made her seem. Maybe a hundred years old? It was hard to guess, to say the least.

Teokas stopped beside her, gazing down over the edge of the mal'gama, looking like the sculpture of some untouchable goddess atop a windswept cliff. Or something equally daunting and majestic. Her Tan'ji, the Moondoor, hung from a strap around her wrist, a shadowed sphere as big as a plum.

Chloe frowned up at her, opening her mouth for the first time since they'd left Ka'hoka. "Will the Moondoor save you if you fall?" Chloe asked. "You seem pretty carpe diem about the whole falling-to-your-death thing."

Teokas laughed, a thick, enchanting chorus of oboes and low bells. All of the Altari had rich, musical voices, but Teokas's voice was especially full of slinky woodwinds and soft percussion. As Brian had put it, she sounded like the sultry part of the orchestra.

"It won't save me, no," Teokas crooned. "But it is hard to fall off the mal'gama." Abruptly, she took a step forward, as if she planned to walk right off the edge. With a leathery rustle, the mal'gama shifted in an instant, stretching out to catch her foot just as it alighted.

"Teokas, please," Dailen said, looking over.

"*Ji tolvë tanduvra?*" Teokas said lightly, stepping back. Chloe only understood a few words of Altari, and none of these, but Teokas was obviously teasing. Flirting, maybe.

"When do you never?" Dailen replied, and Teokas and the other Altari all laughed.

Teokas sank to the floor beside Chloe, stretching out her long form as the mal'gama rose to meet her. "What I've always wondered," she said quietly to Chloe, as if in confidence, "is whether he could *stop* it from saving me."

Chloe shrugged. "He couldn't stop it from saving me, if I didn't want him to." She blushed as the words left her. It seemed like one of the stupider things she'd ever said.

"No, I suppose not," said Teokas. "Even Go'nesh couldn't stop you." She gazed at the Alvalaithen, openly fascinated. Even in the feeble light, Chloe could see the golden rings around Teokas's dark irises, like halos. When Teokas blinked, her crisscrossed double eyelids seemed to flicker. Suddenly the Altari frowned at Chloe's Tan'ji. "Why a dragonfly, do you suppose?" she asked.

"What do you mean?"

"I'm not complaining. Our Tan'ji are what they are. But why do you suppose your Maker chose a dragonfly?"

Chloe looked down at the Alvalaithen. She didn't much like the question. Perfectly white, with intricate mazy wings, the dragonfly was precisely what it needed to be. Chloe tapped briefly into its sweet song, letting its power fill her. How many more times would she get to do this before the Mothergates died? The dragonfly's wings fluttered buzzily, blurring. She felt her body go thin, become a ghost. She kept herself afloat atop the mal'gama's rippling stones with no effort whatsoever, though she could've just as easily fallen straight through them, with nothing to stop her. Not even Dailen. After a moment, making sure everything was clear of her flesh, she released the Alvalaithen. Its song left her, and the dragonfly's wings went still.

"Wings," Chloe said. "I can fly underground."

"I know. I witnessed as much, in the Proving Room."

"Oh, but you didn't know that Alvalaithen means 'Earthwing'?" Chloe said, letting her voice bend with irony. "I could have sworn I just heard you speaking your own language."

"You did," said Teokas earnestly, as if sarcasm were so far beneath her it couldn't touch her. "But why a dragonfly, and not a bird? We are fond of birds, we Altari."

Mrs. Hapsteade's voice rang out in the dark. "A dragonfly is always a predator," she said.

"Ah," said Teokas, as if that answered everything. She

pointed at Chloe's forearm, where two dagger-shaped patches of dark skin ran from palm to elbow, front and back. "These are the scars of a predator, then?"

"You could say that," Chloe replied. She still remembered the awful burn of the crucible the day she'd gotten these scars. Certainly not her only scars, or even the worst. Still, it had been one of the two or three most excruciating things she'd ever done, extinguishing the Riven's mind-consuming flame with her own flesh and bone. Were they heading to another Riven nest even now? Would there be another crucible dog there, with its beckoning green fire?

"I know how you got the scars," said Teokas. "But you won't tell me the full story, will you? You're not a bragger."

Now Gabriel stirred. "Chloe brags *before* she does things," he said. "Not after."

Chloe found herself fighting a sudden grin of pleasure. This was maybe the nicest thing Gabriel had ever said about her.

"Confidence," Teokas sang, smiling at her. "I respect that."

"Yeah, well," said Chloe, "it's easy to be confident when you know you're going to die. Consequences schmonsequences, am I right?"

Teokas blinked at her thoughtfully, and then clearly chose to pretend she hadn't understood what Chloe meant. "I wonder if your friend Horace feels the same way. The Keeper of the Fel'Daera deals purely in consequences, after all." She shook her head as if in wonder. "My talents have to do with time too, but Horace is on another level altogether, far beyond my own."

Across the mal'gama, Ravana raised her head, watching them. Go'nesh stood beside her like a boulder. It was no secret that Horace hadn't come with them tonight because his Tan'ji, the Fel'Daera, made some of the Altari uneasy. Most of the Altari were still adjusting to the fact that the Fel'Daera still existed, since it was supposed to have been destroyed long ago. Chloe blamed them for their discomfort, but only a little—partly because Horace was better off where he was and partly because, well . . . it wasn't exactly easy, having a companion who could see the future.

Horace could only see one day into the future, sure. One day at most. And only in his immediate surroundings, look-ing through the rippled blue glass of the Fel'Daera, the Box of Promises. But to be honest, when Horace looked through the box and then told you your future, told you—just for example—that you were going to let yourself be captured by the Riven, or that you were going to surrender your Tan'ji, or that you were almost definitely going to figure out a way to survive some deadly dangerous thing you hadn't even imag-ined yet . . .

No pressure. No biggie.

Just your fate.

On a plate.

No, it wasn't always easy being Horace's friend, even for

Chloe, even though she trusted Horace with her life. In fact, she had done precisely that, more than once, and wouldn't hesitate to do it again. She trusted Horace more than she trusted herself.

Chloe looked Teokas in the eye. "Horace is on a whole other level, yes," she said.

She meant it as a dig. But Teokas gave her a warm, eager smile in return, not at all condescending. Not the knowing smirk of a grown-up, but a childish smile of enthusiasm. Chloe realized abruptly that Teokas didn't fear Horace; she admired him.

"I'm glad you have such a friend, truly," Teokas said. "We'll all have need of good friends in the days to come."

Chloe decided to stop trying not to like her.

They sailed on, she and Teokas sitting silently side by side. After a while, the glow of Chicago became plain in the northeastern sky, lighting the clouds above. Eventually the city itself came into view, a golden spiderweb of light. Or half a spiderweb, anyway. On the far side, the spray of light ended abruptly, the dark unbroken expanse of Lake Michigan stretching out to the far horizon beyond.

"About the Mothergates," Chloe said, and she had no idea why she was saying it. She had no idea what she expected Teokas to tell her.

"What do you want me to say?" Teokas said, when it became clear Chloe wasn't going to finish. "That we will survive?"

"I want you to tell me that the Mothergates have to die. Tell me that the Riven are wrong to want to keep the Mothergates open."

Teokas shrugged. "They are not wrong to want. But they are wrong to try to make it happen. If the Mothergates remain open, the entire world will come to an end."

"And you're staking your life on that."

"My life is not the issue." Teokas pointed at the sprawling city lights below. "You have family down there, I think. Will you stake their lives that the Riven are correct? That the Mothergates should be forced to remain open, and our powers allowed to live on, regardless of the consequences?" She spread her great arms wide, encompassing the city as whole. "Will you stake *all* these lives?"

Chloe glared down at the city, practically beneath them now. Her father was down there somewhere, and her sister too. She said, "I asked Falo what would happen to us Keepers when the Mothergates die. When the source of our power is cut off, and we lose our bonds with our Tan'ji."

Teokas nodded. "Vital bonds," she murmured, holding Thailadun aloft. "Bonds that cannot be safely broken."

"Falo said—and I'm quoting here—'*Some may survive.*'"

"Maybe," said Teokas. "But if the Mothergates remain open, no one will survive."

"Define 'no one.'"

Teokas fixed Chloe with her golden-green gaze. "No one you have ever known, or ever will, or ever could."

A shiver jittered down Chloe's arms, nothing to do with the sky's night air. "That's . . . very thorough," she said. "Thanks."

"The Mothergates cannot remain," Gabriel said suddenly. "The Riven cannot be allowed to save them. Mr. Meister is the Chief Taxonomer, and he knows more about the Tanu and the Mothergates than any living Keeper, except perhaps Sil'falo Teneves herself. He would never betray us, but we cannot risk the Riven learning what he knows."

"We'll save him, then," said Chloe. "So that he can die when we win this war." She meant for the words to sound bitter, but they spilled into the air like a resolution. Like a fate that had already been sealed and delivered.

"Spoken like a true Altari," Teokas said, and she laughed. "We'll rescue him to death."

They sailed into the heart of the city. Downtown Chicago rose around them like an electric forest. The tops of the tallest towers stood hundreds of feet above them, even as high as they already were. A few cars, tiny as toys, roamed the nighttime streets below.

Mrs. Hapsteade was on her feet now, peering down at the compass that would lead them to Mr. Meister. Maps were not especially Chloe's strong suit, but from what she could tell, they were headed straight for the Warren. The Willis Tower loomed just ahead, off to the left, a chunky stack of dominoes. She'd never liked the looks of it. Its two huge white antennas rose like bleached bones, towering high overhead

14

as they passed, just a block away.

"He's still in the Warren, after all," Chloe said.

But Mrs. Hapsteade shook her head. She laid a hand on Dailen's arm. "Circle east. Take us to the lakeshore."

Dailen nodded, and the mal'gama gently swerved. They sailed toward Grant Park, passing directly above the Art Institute's glass roof and then out over the harbor. Rows of pale boats bobbed in the dark water like sleeping birds. With a gesture, Mrs. Hapsteade directed them north, toward Navy Pier, where the Ferris wheel glowed, motionless, shut down for the night.

But they weren't headed there, either. Instead, with Mrs. Hapsteade guiding him, Dailen steered back toward shore, cruising over Streeterville between Michigan Avenue and the lakeshore. Everyone was on their feet now, gathered around Mrs. Hapsteade. The mal'gama circled tighter and tighter, the needle of the compass swinging. At last Mrs. Hapsteade raised her hand.

"Stop," she said, and she pointed straight down. "He is here."

The mal'gama eased to a stop, hovering. "Watch your step," said Dailen.

The stones beneath their feet rustled and began to part, like water circling a drain. A wide hole opened in the mal'gama, revealing the city below. Chloe peered through it cautiously, Teokas at her side. Far beneath them, a rectangle of dark, undeveloped land jutted out into the water, just

15

where Lake Michigan drained into the Chicago River. Lake-shore Drive was a pale golden band crossing high above the river, sprinkled with drifting cars, and in its shadow—directly below them on the dark spit of land—a great round hole yawned. A perfect circle a hundred feet across, black as pitch.

"There," Mrs. Hapsteade said, pointing.

Chloe stared, hardly able to believe it. "The hell pit?" she said.

The hell pit was a notorious eyesore in the city. Years ago, there had been plans to build an enormous skyscraper here, one of the tallest in the world. But no sooner had the hole been dug for its foundations than the project was abandoned. The hole was never filled. It had been here for as long as Chloe could remember, plainly visible from above on Lakeshore Drive. The city had made an effort to disguise the hole—small hills had been built beside it, and trees now grew in the surrounding empty lot. But the pit was still there, barred by only a stout chain fence around the edge. Inside the pit, Chloe knew, the walls of the hole were lined with rusted steel girders. She had no idea how deep it went.

"You know this place?" Teokas asked.

"I mean, everyone knows this place," said Chloe. "Kids tell stories about it. But no one actually goes there. It's off-limits."

"In other words," said Dailen, "just the sort of place the Riven would love."

The mal'gama swirled, becoming whole again. Smoothly

Dailen steered them back out over the harbor, dropping low once they were in darkness. Then they came back ashore, skimming the water. They passed beneath the Outer Drive Bridge, a hulking rusty skeleton, out of sight of the traffic that crossed above. The mal'gama slid stealthily over a metal retaining wall at the shoreline and a white concrete fence beyond, settling into a shadowy patch of scrubby green between Lakeshore Drive and some apartment buildings to the west. The hell pit lay just a few hundred feet ahead in the darkness. Chloe's heart began to pound. What would they find below?

Dailen removed the ring that controlled the mal'gama and handed it to Mrs. Hapsteade. She gave him the compass in return. *"Du'gara jentro,"* she said, shocking Chloe a bit. She had no idea the woman could speak Altari.

Dailen bowed low. *"Ji mogra jentro duvra."* He reached down to clasp her hand. *"Dak'fol ka laithen,"* he added solemnly. *"Tel tu'vra fal raethen."*

"Tel tu'vra fal raethen," Mrs. Hapsteade repeated.

And though Chloe didn't know the words, she recognized the ritual at once, and knew what they were saying.

Dak'fol ka laithen. Fear is the stone. *Tel tu'vra fal raethen.*

"May yours be light," Chloe whispered.

Teokas nodded, her eyes shining. "May yours be light," she said.

"They won't be expecting us," said Gabriel, thumping the ground with the tip of his staff. "Not so soon, and not here."

Go'nesh stepped off the mal'gama. He hefted the Fair-frost Blade, big as a stop sign. "They certainly won't be expecting *me*," he growled, his voice rumbling like a platoon of bass drums. He looked down at Ravana. "It feels good to be out. Good not to hide."

Ravana unlimbered her mighty bow, nodding. She pulled back on its thick string, testing it. For a moment a bloodred bolt of fire appeared, fuming in the dark. She eased up on the string and let it fade. "Good indeed," she said.

"It's time, then," said Dailen, and suddenly there were two of him. Then four, and then eight, their little band effectively tripling. "Let's go get our friend," all the Dailens said together.

Chloe grinned, drinking deeply from the Alvalaithen's song, letting herself go thin. Nothing could stop her, nothing could touch her. She looked around at the band of warriors with her now, mighty and magical.

"Now this is what I'm *talking* about," she said.

CHAPTER TWO

In the Pit

Although he had been brought here wearing a blindfold, Joshua knew exactly where he was.

The Riven who had hustled him out of the Warren on Dr. Jericho's orders apparently hadn't realized that it was pointless to blindfold him. Dr. Jericho, who knew better, hadn't bothered to stop them, laughing as he watched.

Despite not being able to see, Joshua had tracked the brief journey from the Warren in his mind. He knew they'd traveled almost exactly one mile east-northeast—traveling mostly underground before climbing up into the cool nighttime streets of the city for a few blocks. A dozen Riven traveled with him, slinking through the dark, forcing him onward. Several small Ravids were among them, hissing and popping in and out as they teleported, jumping forward like water striders flicking across the surface of a pond.

Joshua hadn't needed to smell the water to know that they'd brought him to the lakeshore, just beside the Outer Drive Bridge. He hadn't needed eyes to remind him that there was a huge round pit here, the leftover of some giant skyscraper that had never been built. Three Mordin, ten feet tall and stinking of brimstone, had brought Joshua deep into the great pit—carrying him at one point, as they climbed downward. A screeching doorway, a series of damp tunnels and stone stairs, and finally they'd removed his blindfold, here in this large dark chamber lit dimly with sickly brown lights. How deep they had come, Joshua couldn't say, but despite the blindfold he could have plotted his current location on a map to within just a few feet.

Not that it mattered. Yes, he could track himself through space just as well as Horace could track himself through time. It was a talent Joshua used to be proud of.

But not anymore.

There was so much to worry about, so much to feel terrible about, that Joshua's brain had gone numb, unable to decide even where to start. The secret location of the Warren had accidentally been revealed by Joshua himself when one of the Riven's Auditors got inside his head, inside the Laithe of Teneves. The Warren had been invaded not long after, and had fallen.

During the attack, Mrs. Hapsteade had been forced to destroy many of the Tanu there, so that the precious devices wouldn't fall into the hands of the Riven. Ingrid, the former

Warden turned traitor, had been freed to join the Riven once more. Unbelievably, Mr. Meister himself had been captured, his leg broken. And as for Isabel, Chloe's mother . . . it wasn't clear yet what had happened to her when the Riven had stormed across the Maw and into the Great Burrow. Joshua could barely poke at his hopes when it came to Isabel. She'd done some good, yes, but also so much bad. Did he hope she was dead? Captured? Suffering? Escaped? Joshua had no idea. It wasn't his place to hope.

Worst of all—though it was hard to explain *why* it was the worst—the Riven hadn't taken the Laithe of Teneves from him. For some reason, they had let Joshua keep his Tan'ji.

He hated to think what this might mean.

The Laithe hovered beside him now, a perfect globe of the earth, alive with rippling water and drifting cloud and green forest. A meridian encircled it, a flat copper hoop inside which the globe floated, like Saturn inside its rings. With the Laithe, Joshua could have chosen any location on the planet and then—by tearing loose the meridian and spinning it wide open—created a portal to that location. A doorway. A gateway to anywhere on earth. An escape.

Not that he could have escaped. Not likely. The Riven hadn't taken the Laithe, no, but they hadn't left him alone with it either. The Mordin that had brought him here were still with him. Like all Riven, they were pale skinned and beady eyed, like ghoulish humans. They had long ghastly limbs that folded and unfolded like the legs of insects. The

Mordin were hunters, taller than regular Riven, at least twice as tall as Joshua himself.

Two of the Mordin guarding him, Joshua had decided, were lazy and careless—obviously delighted that the secret sanctuary of the Wardens had been conquered, and feeling pleased with themselves. They sat on the floor, leaning against the wall, talking back and forth in low, harsh whispers. But the third Mordin was sharper, quieter, crouching warily and watching Joshua with a keen black stare. He reminded Joshua of Arthur the raven, gazing at some suspicious object.

And these three weren't the only guards with him in the cold stone chamber. There was a fourth, the worst by far—busy with a prisoner all its own.

The golem filled one side of the room, a glistening hulk as big as a bus, made entirely of shining thumb-sized stones. Hanging open like the mouth of a cave, not bothering to disguise itself, the golem pulsed slightly with a faint rattle, as if breathing. Inside it, Mr. Meister hung like a tiny doll, his arms and legs buried in the golem's grip, only his chest and his white-haired head hanging free. Unlike Joshua, the old man had not been allowed to keep his Tan'ji. He was still alive, so the instruments must still exist—but stripped of his red vest and his glasses now, Mr. Meister looked small and blind, completely helpless.

In the several hours since they'd been here—maybe even a full day?—Mr. Meister hadn't spoken a word. He hadn't so much as looked at Joshua since first laying eyes on him back at the Warren, after they'd been captured. And that was fine with Joshua, because the expression on the old man's face as he realized Joshua hadn't escaped had been . . .

Bad. Worse than disappointed.

He looked . . . frightened.

Joshua hadn't even known Mr. Meister could *be* afraid.

I tried, Joshua had wanted to tell him. And it was true. Or at least, it was true that he'd tried to save the Laithe of Teneves. He'd tried to push the Laithe through its own portal, his grand plan once he'd realized the Warren was lost. He would send the little globe through the portal he'd opened into the green forest near Ka'hoka, two hundred and fifty miles away. He would protect the Laithe by sending it far away, into the hands of his friends, the other Wardens who had already escaped. He would protect those friends, too, by surrendering himself to the Riven, powerless and pointless. He'd already done so much harm.

But his plan had failed. He hadn't even known enough about his own Tan'ji to know that the plan was doomed, that the Laithe didn't work that way. The globe wouldn't go through the portal without him. And now Joshua was captured, and the Laithe too. He'd failed in every way possible. Everything was ruined, all thanks to him.

Suddenly Mr. Meister lifted his head. *"Kro'gesh jian tu,"* he said, his hoarse voice echoing in the hollow chamber. For a

23

moment Joshua thought he was speaking nonsense. But then one of the lazy Mordin laughed, and replied in the same dancing, hissing language.

"*Gosht kota,*" he said, still laughing. "*Jian kell jo'thra tendu.*"

"*Kal nadra!*" the sharp-eyed Mordin snapped.

The lazy Mordin fell silent, but went on chuckling softly to himself.

"What's happening?" Joshua asked. "What's he saying?"

The sharp-eyed Mordin stood slowly, like the growing shadow of a winter tree, and slid toward him.

"Nothing meant for your ears, obviously," he said. "Isn't it strange that when your friend finally speaks, he chooses a language you can't understand?" The Mordin glanced over at Mr. Meister, whose head was hanging limply again. "Perhaps he has nothing to say to you. Not anymore. After all, you're one of us now."

"I'm not," Joshua said, his face flushing.

The Mordin held up a long, gruesome finger, wagging it. Joshua noticed he wore a large black ring with a twisted bloodred stone. "I was there when we took the Warren," the Mordin said. "I saw your portal. You could have escaped with the other Tinkers, but you didn't. You chose to stay with us." His voice was light and jingling, maddening.

"That's not what I—" Gritting his teeth, Joshua turned to Mr. Meister. "I tried," he said.

"Save your breath, Joshua," Mr. Meister replied. "Don't listen to their lies."

"Lies?" said a new voice, billowing through the chamber like a black curtain, splendid and fiendish. Joshua froze.

Dr. Jericho strode elegantly out of the darkness, taller than the other Mordin by a foot at least. The sharp-eyed Mordin stepped back from Joshua alertly. The two guards sitting on the floor scrambled to their feet. Dr. Jericho ignored them all, gazing at Mr. Meister. "The Chief Taxonomer dares to accuse *us* of lying? He whose very purpose is to hide the truth from his so-called friends? How terribly rich."

One of Dr. Jericho's forearms was wrapped tightly in scarlet, and Joshua remembered the snap of bone as Neptune had plunged into the Mordin from high above, in the battle on April's roof. The memory, and the sight of Dr. Jericho wounded now, brought him a stab of satisfaction.

But it quickly faded. A thin golden light seemed to shimmer and shift in the hallway behind Dr. Jericho, buried in a massive moving shadow, coming closer. Footsteps dragged heavily across the stone floor. The Mordin hadn't come here alone.

An enormous figure shambled into the room, stooping as if carrying a great weight. Even bent over as it was, it stood half again as tall as Dr. Jericho. Mr. Meister let out a gasp of surprise, sending goose bumps up and down Joshua's arms. The new arrival was a Riven, but not quite a Mordin, despite the huge size. This was something else.

Wide pale eyes, empty and unfocused. Ashen, drooping flesh, like an abandoned snakeskin. Slender arms that

25

reached all the way to the floor. Hands that were almost creatures unto themselves, as broad as school desks, with fingers a foot long or more.

Worst of all, the creature was shirtless, and a large oval stone was buried in the sagging flesh of his chest—a Tan'ji. This was the source of the faint golden light Joshua had seen, somehow familiar. The stone glowed like the dim reflection of the sun on cloudy waters.

"Let me introduce you to Grooma," Dr. Jericho said. "Keeper of Aored. He is *Dorvala*." He turned and looked Joshua in the eye, obviously wanting to make sure that Joshua understood the word. "A Maker."

A Maker. The same as Brian. That was why the creature's Tan'ji looked so familiar—the oval stone buried in his chest was a Loomdaughter, just like Tunraden, but even larger. *Aored*, Dr. Jericho had named it. With it, this massive and miserable Grooma had the power to shape the Medium, to create new Tanu.

Mr. Meister looked grim. Not afraid, exactly, but . . . resigned. Watching his face, Joshua slowly pieced together a worrisome thought. Makers were extremely rare. Only nine Loomdaughters had ever been made, and many had been destroyed. Every Tanu that ever existed had been created either with the Starlit Loom itself—the very first Tan'ji—or with one of the Nine. Brian, therefore, was one of the greatest secrets the Wardens had. Surely the Riven guarded Grooma just as carefully. The fact that Dr. Jericho was revealing the

Dorvala now, letting Joshua and Mr. Meister see Aored . . .

It couldn't mean anything good.

"Are you frightened?" Dr. Jericho asked Joshua, strolling over to him, bending down like a giant mantis.

"Yes," Joshua said. His eyes drifted to Grooma, lurking hugely in the shadows.

"How strange it must be for you. Thrust into a war you barely understand, mere days before it will be won."

"Or lost," Mr. Meister called out.

"Do not be afraid of Grooma, Joshua," Dr. Jericho murmured, almost sweetly. "Instead, fear the man who calls to you now. Fear the lies that spill from him like breath." He spread his great hand against his own chest. "I will tell you no lies. I will tell you the truth."

"I don't believe you," Joshua said. "I won't."

"What cannot be denied *must* be believed," said Dr. Jericho. "And even Mr. Meister will not deny what I tell you now, though he never had the courage to tell you himself."

"Tell me what?"

"Do you know why we fight, Joshua? Why we Kesh'kiri— the Riven, as you call us—battle the Wardens at every turn?"

"I don't care why," Joshua lied.

Dr. Jericho went on as if he hadn't heard. "The conflict is a simple one. The Wardens believe that the Mothergates are fated to die. They guard the Mothergates, refusing to heal them, refusing to keep the source of the Medium alive. The Wardens are determined instead to perish alongside the

Mothergates—to wither away as the Medium ceases to flow and the bond of every Tan'ji breaks forever, dispossessing us all." He leaned down into Joshua's face. "We Kesh'kiri, on the other hand, recognize that the Wardens are fools." Then he grinned, baring tiny white teeth as sharp as glass.

Joshua held his breath. Was it true? Were the Wardens going to let the Mothergates die? He looked desperately to Mr. Meister. A soft raspy sound drifted from the old man's chest.

He was laughing.

"Fools," Mr. Meister muttered, shaking his white head.

Dr. Jericho's grin faded. He turned to the old man. "Fools indeed," the Mordin sneered. "Deny it, then. You Wardens are nothing more than jailhouse guards, the Mothergates your prisoners."

"I do not deny it, Ja'raka Sevlo," Mr. Meister said. "But the Mothergates cannot be allowed to live."

"Says who?" Dr. Jericho insisted. "The Keeper of the Starlit Loom, Watcher of the Veil? Sil'falo Teneves, your precious high priestess?"

"I've seen the signs with my own eyes," said Mr. Meister. "The way we twist the Medium—"

Dr. Jericho sprang at the old man, freezing Joshua's heart. The Mordin reached the pulsing canopy of the golem in three mighty bounds and thrust a great finger into Mr. Meister's face. "I do not twist the Medium, Tinker," he snarled, his voice like a lion's roar. "You are the abomination, not I."

Mr. Meister scarcely flinched. "If the Mothergates remain open, disaster will befall us all."

"What disaster?" Joshua asked. He realized he had scooped the Laithe out of the air, pressing it against his belly.

Dr. Jericho straightened and stepped back. "Fairy tales," he crooned, all honey and music again. He spun elegantly, his eyes dropping onto the Laithe. "Let us speak of the true disaster that awaits if the Wardens get their way. Have you yet been severed, Keeper?"

Joshua shook his head. He'd seen Isabel sever other Keepers plenty of times, and it looked awful. He'd only been a Keeper for a couple of days, but already it was almost impossible to imagine losing the bond he had with the Laithe. Although severing was temporary, when you were severed long enough, you became dispossessed, the bond permanently broken. The Laithe would be lost to him forever.

And honestly, he wasn't sure he cared what came after that.

"The Kesh'kiri can't survive being severed for more than a few moments," Dr. Jericho said. "Such is our dedication to our instruments." He rolled his shoulders and bent his neck this way and that, stretching gruesomely. His joints crackled and popped. Joshua knew that Dr. Jericho's Tan'ji was fused into the flesh between his shoulder blades, half buried in his spine the same way Aored was buried in Grooma's chest. Raka, Dr. Jericho called it, a gleaming blue shaft that was the source of his powers as a Mordin. With it, Dr. Jericho could track down Tan'ji from miles away.

"Yes, we Kesh'kiri will perish first," Dr. Jericho continued, "but even you Tinkers won't survive when the Mothergates fail. Your instruments will cease to function. The bond will break, and you will die. That is the true disaster." He rolled his shoulders one last time, as if working out a kink, and then spread his arms. "But do not fear. The Mothergates can be saved. *We* can be saved. And I have figured out the way."

"How?" Joshua asked, and while he wasn't sure what made him say it, he heard the desperate hope in his own voice.

"It does not matter what you do. We cannot be saved," said Mr. Meister.

"Spoken like a true believer," Dr. Jericho replied.

Mr. Meister scoffed. "Keeping the Mothergates open does not fix the underlying danger. It only allows that danger to live on. But even if this weren't true, forcing the Mothergates to stay open is beyond the talents of your Dorvala here."

Dr. Jericho glanced back at Grooma, who seemed too dull to even notice he was being talked about. "You make an excellent point," he said. "And that is the goal, is it not? To find the three Mothergates, and ensure that they do not fail? Yet Grooma's skills are limited, and Aored is among the weakest of the Loomdaughters." He tapped his chin thoughtfully, putting on a show, as if he did not know what to do.

Mr. Meister said nothing. He glanced at Joshua, his face rigid. Apparently it was true—the Mothergates were dying, and the Wardens were letting it happen. They were *fighting*

30

to let it happen. But why? What disaster would come if the Mothergates stayed open?

"I spent the day exploring your Warren, you know," said Dr. Jericho. "An astonishing place. So many treasures. And still so much still left to explore!" He shook his head sadly at Mr. Meister, clicking his tongue—*tsk-tsk*. "Such a shame you didn't keep your stolen hoard better protected."

"There's nothing you could have found in the Warren that can help you keep the Mothergates open," Mr. Meister said. "Nothing. Whatever your foolish plans, you can't succeed. Too much stands in your way, and you don't have enough time."

"Perhaps you are right," said Dr. Jericho, biting his thin lips as if feigning dismay. "Time is indeed short—less than a week, I am told."

Joshua went cold. Only a week before the Mothergates closed forever. He clung to the Laithe like a life preserver, too frightened to say anything, too bewildered to know what to believe.

Dr. Jericho stood motionless for several seconds, seeming to consider Mr. Meister's words. Then he stirred abruptly, uncoiling like a spring, throwing a fist resolutely into the air.

"If our time is so short, let us begin at once!" he crowed, grinning. "Our foolish plan begins now. As your good friend Horace might say, what better time than the present to change the future?"

He pointed at the two lazy Mordin near the entrance and barked a harsh command at them. They bowed and loped clumsily from the room. Grooma watched them dully, scratching with one dreadful hand at the flesh around Aored.

Dr. Jericho held out his good arm and snapped his great fingers—a crack like a whip that split the air, painfully crisp. *"Golm'ruun,"* he demanded. The sharp-eyed Mordin hurried over to him, tugging the bloodred ring from his finger and placing it in Dr. Jericho's hand. Dr. Jericho slipped it onto his own finger, turning back to face Mr. Meister.

On the instant, the golem roared to life.

The river of rock buried the old man, engulfing him as it plowed forward like a cloud-shaped train. It barreled right up to Dr. Jericho, dwarfing him, becoming a tornado that shook the ground, filling the air with thunder. Grooma straightened, his dull eyes widening. He slapped his huge hands over his tiny ears and took a step back.

Gradually the golem began to slow and subside, and Mr. Meister emerged from its peak, spit out slowly by the golem until only the bottom half of his legs remained buried. Mr. Meister teetered and heaved for breath, held captive high overhead. A trickle of blood ran from the edge of his disheveled white hair down his wrinkled cheek. He clutched at the knee of his broken leg, grimacing.

"Sticks and stones," Dr. Jericho murmured, watching, hefting his own scarlet-clad arm. "Open your eyes, Taxonomer. Look at Grooma. Look at Aored."

Mr. Meister opened his eyes, gazing icily over Dr. Jericho's head at the hulking Dorvala beyond.

"I said Grooma's skills are limited," Dr. Jericho explained. "I did not say he had no skills. He specializes in matters of the flesh—Tanu made from living things."

"That is forbidden," Mr. Meister rasped.

Forbidden. Suddenly Joshua remembered Ethel, the hedge witch, and her Tan'ji Morla. Morla wasn't an object, but an animal—a tortoise, alive and miserable, tied to Ethel the same way the Laithe was tied to Joshua. The memory made him sick. His mind reeled, filling with all sorts of horrible things Grooma might do to Mr. Meister, at Dr. Jericho's command. His chest seized up.

But instead, Dr. Jericho only laughed. "You have no grounds to tell me what is forbidden, Tinker. In my world, you yourself are forbidden." He sighed, shaking his head. "And some of what you have done is not just forbidden, but unforgivable." He clenched his fist and the golem rolled forward, bringing Mr. Meister down until he was face-to-face with the Mordin. Joshua managed to catch a breath.

"I met your Dorvala," Dr. Jericho purred. "Brian, Keeper of Tunraden. He is powerful. I believe he could repair the Mothergates, if he put his mind to it. Such a shame we could not persuade him to aid us."

"Brian would never join you," said Mr. Meister.

Never, Joshua wanted to add, but he couldn't find his voice.

"No," Dr. Jericho agreed. "Other than his wild excursion earlier this week, Brian marches tamely to the Wardens' tune."

He leaned in closer still, hands behind his back. "That's how you prefer your Dorvala, I believe. Housebroken. Obedient. Rebellious only in the mildest of ways."

Mr. Meister jerked his chin toward Grooma, standing mutely behind Dr. Jericho. "As do you, it seems."

"We would never have denied Grooma his right to Aored, no matter his nature. But you Wardens see things differently, don't you? When it comes to Dorvala, only the tamest recruits will do."

Mr. Meister stiffened, but said nothing.

"And no wonder!" Dr. Jericho continued. "Because of your outrageous belief that the Mothergates must not be allowed to survive, you could never risk recruiting a Dorvala who might disobey you. If a Keeper like our friend Ingrid defies you, it is a matter of little consequence. But if a *Dorvala* defies you, rejecting your stories of disaster, refusing to accept your insistence that she must die . . ." Dr. Jericho raised his eyebrows high, shaking his head ruefully. "She might repair the Mothergates to save herself. To save us all. And that is a risk you simply could not take."

Still Mr. Meister didn't reply, his eyes locked on the Mordin's.

"In fact," Dr. Jericho said, "hypothetically speaking, if a child came to you with the potential to become a Dorvala, you might reject her if she were too wild. If she were too fiercely independent to march in lockstep toward the doom you've devoted yourself to."

"The doom that awaits us all," said Mr. Meister.

"You make my point for me," Dr. Jericho said smoothly. "With fears as strong as yours, what would you do if a child appeared on your doorstep, burning with the power to become Dorvala, but full of anger and defiance? If you had an unclaimed Loomdaughter in your collection, would you even let such a candidate lay eyes on it, lest she claim it? Wouldn't you deny her the opportunity of the Find?" He leaned in close, peering into Mr. Meister's face. "Or would you do something even worse?"

Off to one side, the sharp-eyed Mordin shuffled slightly, furrowing his brow, apparently as confused as Joshua was. What was Dr. Jericho driving at?

The golem shifted abruptly. Joshua jumped. The massive Tanu bottomed out and slid apart, catching Mr. Meister by an arm and a leg on each side and spreading itself slowly, as if it meant to rip the old man in two. Mr. Meister threw his head back, bellowing in pain.

"Stop!" Joshua cried.

Dr. Jericho ignored him. "I know what you did," he said, leaning in closer than ever to Mr. Meister, whose face was a grimace of pain. The Mordin bared his teeth. *I found the kaitan.*

Mr. Meister squeezed his eyes closed.

Kaitan. Joshua had heard that word before. Something Brian had said to Isabel—that the kaitan, whatever it was, had wounded her. Isabel wasn't a Keeper; she was a Tuner, a powerful one, able to manipulate the Medium in certain ways. Although she wasn't Tan'ji, and had no instrument of her own, she could use special Tanu called harps to twist and bend the Medium, which was what gave her the power to sever and cleave. Horace's mother Jessica was a Tuner too, but Isabel was far more powerful.

Or at least she had been.

And now all this talk of Dorvala, and rejecting their claims. The mysterious kaitan. Puzzle pieces began to slide sludgily together in Joshua's mind.

"Wait," he said aloud, hardly aware he was speaking. "Wait."

"The stink of old evils still seeped from the machine," said Dr. Jericho. "Too faint for me to identify, but one of my brothers had the necessary skills. From the residue of the kaitan, he put together a violent tale of woe. Two young girls, years ago, on the cusp of the Find. Placed into the kaitan together, along with the unseen instruments that had drawn them to you in the first place. And then . . ." He swept a flat hand through the air like a knife, so swiftly that it hissed. His tiny black eyes blazed with fury. "The kaitan ripped the power from the instruments that should have been Found, reducing them to useless rubble. Instead of being bound to the instruments they had come to claim, the girls were bound to each other, thick bands of the Medium flowing from one to the other and back again—only to be torn apart, moments later. The new bond between them was shredded, left to hang like tattered flesh, leaving the girls wounded forever. Leaving them Forsworn."

Joshua tried to swallow but had no spit. The Forsworn. That was what the Riven called Tuners like Isabel. Isabel, and Jessica—Horace's mom. These were the girls Dr. Jericho was taking about.

"Spare me your false sympathy," Mr. Meister said stubbornly. "They were Tinkers like me, weren't they? Abominations, you call us."

"We have always pitied the Forsworn," Dr. Jericho said, and for once he sounded sincere. "It is cruel to cut the tongue from a fish, even if it has no right to speak. But your other crime was greater still."

"No deed is a crime, when it preserves the greater good," said Mr. Meister. "The greater good by far."

"You sacrificed a Loomdaughter to the kaitan."

A Loomdaughter. Joshua understood now, didn't want to understand. A sound slipped from his throat, sad and croaking.

"I did," Mr. Meister said, lifting his chin. He swung his head to look straight at Joshua, unblinking. "And I would do it again. Isabel had the claim to the Loomdaughter, the most potent of all—Vishkesh, the ninth." Dr. Jericho inhaled greedily, but Mr. Meister barreled on, still gazing at Joshua. Joshua listened intently, drinking the words like poison. "When we tested Isabel—when Mrs. Hapsteade and I read the ink of the Vora in Isabel's own hand—we saw the signs. Isabel had the affinity to become a powerful Dorvala. Powerful enough to rival even Sil'falo Teneves, perhaps even strong enough to make a claim on the Starlit Loom itself. But she was wild. Stubborn and furious, sneaky and arrogant. She thought only of herself, and that made her . . . unfit. We couldn't risk that Isabel would undo everything we had worked for, once she mastered her powers and learned the truth. A truth she might not accept. We would not risk that she would find a way to force the Mothergates to stay open."

Dr. Jericho's eyes seemed to glitter. He drew a deep breath through his nose, a dreadful, jubilant smile splitting his face. He stepped back, stretching to his full height. "The truth at last," he said. Then he turned toward the dark corridor across the room. "Have you been listening, my dear?"

Silence for a moment. Joshua thought his heart might pound its way into his belly. Then a voice, a girl's voice, rang out thinly.

"She has."

Mr. Meister whipped his head around. Joshua strained to see. Two small figures, humans, emerged from the darkness of the corridor into the murky brown light, flanked by the Mordin guards from before. One of the humans was thin, with dark blond hair—Ingrid, the former Warden turned traitor. At her side, a woman shuffled as if dazed. Even in the gloom, her wild red hair seemed to gleam, a knotted nest of dark fire.

Isabel.

The golem shifted again, dropping low. Almost gently, it deposited Mr. Meister onto the cold stone floor as Isabel approached. Unable to stand, the old man lay there, looking helpless.

Joshua started toward them. The sharp-eyed Mordin stepped in front of him, blocking him with a massive hand. Isabel was powerless, anyone could see that. Her old harp, Miradel, had been destroyed—eaten whole by Dr. Jericho. The last Joshua had seen Isabel, she'd taken Jessica's harp and was using it to cleave Mordin in the Warren—dispossessing them instantly, killing them, trying to buy enough time for the others to escape. But now even that weak harp was nowhere to be seen, and Isabel herself seemed . . .

Lost. Like the shell of a body that couldn't remember its mind.

Dr. Jericho reached out for her, placing an enormous hand across her shoulders and pulling her forward. "The truth is known," he intoned. "Have you anything to say to this man?"

Isabel lifted her head to look at Mr. Meister. Her face was a mask of sadness and confusion. Her usual rage was nowhere to be seen. "You stole from me," she murmured. Her voice was like a ghost's. "You ruined me."

"Some limbs must be lost," Mr. Meister said, "so that the tree may be saved."

Isabel's eyes widened, and she drew back. "You would do it again. You would do it a thousand times. You don't even regret it."

"I lament it," said Mr. Meister. And then he shook his head. "But I do not regret it."

Isabel shook a trembling fist at him, a spark of her old fire revealing itself at last. "I was meant to be a *Maker*," she hissed.

A ripple of disgust flickered across Dr. Jericho's face, but he quickly smoothed it away. Joshua wasn't sure anyone else had seen it—Isabel definitely hadn't.

"Certain wrongs cannot be righted, Forsworn," the Mordin sang. "But there are gifts that can be given that might make amends. Gifts that will allow you to save your daughter—and so many others. Gifts that only Grooma can provide."

He guided Isabel over to Grooma. Slowly she lifted her face up along the length of the huge creature. Grooma peered down at her curiously, shifting, his sagging skin grating against itself like a rough hand against bark.

"*Che'th noldu?*" Dr. Jericho asked Grooma. "Can it be done?"

Grooma studied Isabel for a moment. Joshua knew he was seeing things the others couldn't—Isabel's wounds, the raw strands of the Medium torn apart after her ordeal in the kaitan. What must they look like? Joshua couldn't help himself from picturing innards, spilling from Isabel's belly.

At last Grooma nodded. He hummed happily, so loud and low that it rumbled in Joshua's chest.

Dr. Jericho smiled and stepped back. "As we discussed, then."

Grooma lifted his dragging arms, still gazing down at Isabel.

Aored blazed to life. Golden light swallowed the room. For several long moments, Joshua was blinded. As his sight slowly adjusted, he saw Grooma's grotesque hands moving furiously, pulling thick clinging filaments of yellow fire from his own chest. The Medium.

Aored was an oval furnace, full of golden lava. Grooma's eyes, no longer pale and blank, fixed on the stuff with dark ferocity. His fingers worked like the legs of great spiders, and between them the Medium was woven into crystalline shapes—jagged webs and looping flowers and bristling spirals of light. He let them drop down onto Isabel, where the structures clung briefly to her flesh and were absorbed, like dangling strands of honey pulled loose from the whole and left to fall back into itself. Isabel stood frozen, back arched and arms thrown out.

"You'll kill her," Mr. Meister said, and Joshua was shocked that he didn't need to shout. The storm brewing in Grooma's hands was violent and flashing, but utterly silent.

Dr. Jericho shook his head, staring hungrily at Grooma and Isabel. "No," he said. "You are blind." And then he pulled something from his pocket, handing it back to Mr. Meister. Mr. Meister fumbled, grasping.

His glasses. The oraculum, his Tan'ji. With it, he could see the flows of the Medium in ways that no one but Tuners and Makers could. As Joshua watched, the old man slipped the

41

lenses onto his nose and tipped his face up at what Grooma was doing.

His mouth fell open.

Dr. Jericho began to laugh. "The universe finds a way to restore itself. See how the fears you surrendered to all those years ago have come back to roost, to become a thing you could not have imagined. And you will thank me, when it is done."

Isabel sank to her knees. Grooma's fingers were slashing knives, jabbing needles, swooning birds. The Medium poured from them and into her body, an unending shower of lacy light.

And then suddenly Grooma grunted and staggered back, lifting his head. The light went out; the hanging strands of the Medium splashed noiselessly to the floor and vanished, plunging the room into darkness. Isabel began to keen sharply, as if in pain.

Was it done? Was it over? Joshua strained to see. But then Dr. Jericho's voice cut through the gloom, angry and demanding.

"*Den'desh?*" he barked. "*Desh'du volgra, Grooma?*"

Grooma answered him, the first words he'd spoken, his deep voice like a foghorn. "*Ji mog Altari,*" he said.

Footsteps, running. Dr. Jericho, shouting. The two lazy Mordin were anything but lazy now, hurrying out of the room, loping like giant wolves. As Joshua's eyes relearned the dark, he saw Grooma turning in slow circles, looking up at the roof of the chamber, clearly upset by something he'd sensed, some-where in the tunnels above. Or not something, but some*one*. Unexpected visitors had entered the pit.

And Joshua knew who they were. Grooma's final word seemed to burn and echo in his ears, filling him with hope and dread.

Altari.

CHAPTER THREE

The Empath

APRIL WASN'T SUPPOSED TO BE IN THIS PLACE.

And also she was.

Finding her way here hadn't been easy, but also it had. In a way, it had been *too* easy.

Here in the most remote halls of Ka'hoka, the Veil of Lura was an ocean of striped light—endless suspended waves of drifting radiance, towering above a barren seafloor. There wasn't supposed to be a way through the Veil, really, which was the whole point. The Veil was meant to hide a thing that should never be found, but April had found it again, all on her own, buried in the folded light.

The Mothergate.

It stood before her now, a yawning black abyss lit with slowly streaking stars. She could not have said whether the Mothergate had size, or shape. There was no size here. The gate was enormous, something she could have swept into her palm. Through it, she could sense the other two Mothergates, fabulously distant and immediately nearby. Through it, she could sense . . .

Everything.

She laid two fingers against her left temple, pressing the silver curls of the Ravenvine against her flesh. Through her Tan'ji—which she wore constantly, tucked snugly around her ear—she could share in the unshareable. If she'd thought she'd understood what it meant to be an empath before, she now knew that she'd understood nothing. She could listen at the doorways to other minds, yes, but some minds were off-limits. Or so she'd been told. In the outside world, she could only listen to the minds of animals, their thoughts coming to her through the vine. She'd gotten so good at it that sometimes she felt like she could almost *become* the animals she encountered, letting their thoughts run wild through her own—their emotions, their senses, their memories. Meanwhile the minds of humans, and Altari, and even the Riven, were forbidden to her.

But not here. Here nothing was forbidden. Even if none of it made sense.

The Mothergate spouted a weeping river of thought, pouring through the vine and into April like wind through a tree, rattling her, threatening to tear her down. She couldn't understand any of it, not really. She felt certain specific things, absolutely—there were stubborn eddies in the flow, for example, knotted and troubling, and thoughts slipped from these patches, catching in her mind. *Undone and again. Here and then. There and now. Over and after, undone and redone.* They repeated themselves like chants, strange and familiar, flickers of clarity. But everything together was all too much— too strong, too wide, too deep, as if everyone and everything that had ever lived were speaking at once, and their voices had become a great chorus. A chorus too grand for the singers themselves to ever hear.

Except for April.

This was the river that poured from the Mothergates. This was the Medium. But not really a river, April learned as she listened. More like the bloodstream of the universe itself, its pulse ten million hammers striking ten million anvils. With each blow a new hammer, a new anvil, more beats, more voices, more threads, more story. She heard everything. She heard nothing. She realized she was crying. Her tears were in the story too.

"One could drown, could they not?"

April spun around. Sil'falo Teneves stood there, awash in the slowly sweeping light of the Veil, like a sunken statue. The Altari gazed at April as if she had been watching her all along, as if she had been here even before April arrived.

April started to wipe away her tears, but then didn't bother. Like so much in this place, Sil'falo Teneves, Keeper of the Starlit Loom, was a twisted skein of contradictions. Distant and present, young and old, monstrous and exquisite, frightening and comforting. She stood there as if made of marble, long hands folded, the great oval pendant around her neck so black that it gleamed with unlight. April and the others had discussed this pendant before, whether it could be some kind of link to Falo's Tan'ji, the mysterious Starlit Loom. Every Keeper could instantly recognize a Tan'ji when they saw it, and this pendant definitely wasn't one, but still . . . there was something powerful about it, magnetic. The same kind of pull pouring now through Falo's gaze. In each of her dark eyes, the peculiar halo unique to the Altari blazed like the corona of an eclipse.

"Could I?" April managed to ask. "Drown, I mean?"

"It has happened," said Falo, her beautiful stillness flitting instantly into graceful motion. She glided up next to April. "When other empaths, weaker than you, have followed the song of the Mothergate into the Veil. When they have lingered too long, listening."

April turned back to the Mothergate, its endless depths. "What is it? That song? It's the Medium, I know. But it's . . . more."

"You said it yourself, when you first came here yesterday. It is everything."

"Life," said April simply.

"The echoes of life. The felt presence of every mind everywhere. We—and every living thing—are the witnesses that give shape to the universe, simply by being alive, by seeing what we see. And the universe *knows* that it is seen, simply by becoming what it becomes."

"And the Mothergates?"

"Through the Mothergates, we are witness to that becoming."

April actually laughed out loud, a giddy burp of joy that was uncomfortably close to a giggle. Falo's words were absurd and circular, water spiraling around a drain but never going down. And yet April understood them completely.

"The universe is every story, braided into one," April said dreamily, the words blooming in her mind like unexpected flowers. "And through the Mothergates the universe is telling that story back to us. The power of the Medium is the power of that telling."

Now it was Falo's turn to laugh. Their laughter also belonged to the story, a tiny thing—like the faintest curve of shine on the surface of a single drop of water, falling somewhere-sometime in a downpour a million miles wide, a million years long.

"Yes," Falo said. "Thank you. In all my days of trying, I have never said it quite so well."

"You're being kind," April said. "I know there's more to it, layers I don't understand yet." She looked up at Falo. "But if it's a story, the book is closing soon. The Mothergates are dying."

"Yes. The story will go on, of course, but the telling will soon fade from our hearing. As if a window where we've been eavesdropping is about to close."

Falo let the words hang in the air, clearly expecting April to ask the obvious question. The Mothergates would close soon. The Medium would cease to flow. And when it did, every Keeper would be severed, dispossessed—a condition most Keepers couldn't hope to survive for even a single day. But April believed the obvious question had been asked and answered, yesterday when she and Horace and Chloe first stood before the Mothergate. She believed in the answer Falo had given.

Some may survive.

"I've been trying to hear," said April quietly. She pointed to the Ravenvine, buried in her auburn hair. She tapped the tiny black flower that hung suspended just at the entrance to her ear. In this place, so close to the source, her Tan'ji was aflame with power. But not power enough. "I've been listening to the Mothergate, but it doesn't make sense. I suppose I'm just not strong enough."

"No one could ever be so strong."

"Not even you?"

Falo's eyes widened, the Veil's light swooning across them. "I am not an empath," she protested. "I am a Maker. I feel the Medium the way a child feels cloth. I can fold it and shape it and tie it, yes. I can measure its strength and grain. Meanwhile, in this place, you can feel the rub of every fiber in every thread, tangling with their neighbors near and far, up and down along every endless length. Here at the very source of the Medium, the Ravenvine lets you hear things no one else can. Not even me. But you could never hope to understand it all."

April shrugged. She wasn't sure she even wanted to understand it all. Still, she'd come back here, hadn't she? She let the Mothergate's symphony flow through her for several moments, basking in it, letting its power take her breath away. "Anyway, I do understand *some* of it," she said after a while.

Falo looked down at her sharply. "Is that so?"

"Tangles, you said. I feel them. Knotted-up messes, clumps of contradiction and repetition, and they're sort of . . ." April held out her hands, curling her fingers into spread claws, twisting her hands together, trying to describe it. "Ripping at each other. Pulling themselves into each other. Like bugs in a spiderweb, wrestling themselves to death, and taking the web with them."

Something desperate seemed to tremble in Falo's eyes as she listened to April speak. Some kind of dread relief. Like she knew everything April was telling her, but had never had someone else say the words to her.

"Yes," Falo said. "And these tangles are the danger. They will be the death of everything we know."

"But not if the Mothergates close," April said, surprised she didn't feel more fear. "The tangles wouldn't even be there if we couldn't sense the Medium, and the only reason we can sense the Medium is because of the Mothergates. So when the Mothergates close, the danger will go away. Is that right?"

Falo knelt swiftly and grasped April's hands, her long fingers swallowing her arms up to the elbow. "Yes," she said. "Yes, precisely right. And soon the Mothergates *will* close. It won't be long now."

"It was never long to begin with," April said, turning to watch the Mothergate, feeling woozy from the relentless flow of the Medium that poured from it. So much time and space. So many minds. She gestured at the looming black mass, pulsing beneath the light of the Veil. "This was just a moment. The Mothergates. The Tanu. Just a moment in the grand scheme of things."

"A moment that now must end," Falo said, nodding. "Are you afraid?"

"No," said April. "Or yes. Will you tell me what the tangles are?"

"Why?"

"Because they're . . ." And what were they? *Next and again. Everywhen at once. Everywhere here.* "I was going to say familiar, but that's not quite right. It's more like . . ." She cocked her head at Falo. "Do Altari dream?"

Falo nodded. "Often, and deeply."

"Have you ever dreamed about someone you know—a friend or a brother or something—but then when you wake up, you realize that in your dream they had the body of a stranger? Strange voice, strange face. But in the dream, you knew absolutely who they were?"

"I have had such dreams, yes."

"Well, these tangles I'm feeling through the Mothergate—they make me feel like I'm outside a dream like that. Except I never actually *had* the dream. When I listen to those tangles, I hear things I know I ought to recognize, wearing disguises I never saw through."

Falo leaned closer, her smooth, ancient face alight. "This is precisely the manner in which other empaths have drowned. They lingered before the Mothergates, struggling to hear that which they were too frightened to understand. But you are made of sterner stuff. What do you know, April Simon?" Falo held up a finger as long as a painter's brush. The rings inside her eyes contracted, thickening intensely, darting toward the tip of the Ravenvine at April's temple. "Do not listen. To listen is to be awake outside the dream. In this place, our *lives* are the dream—the dream of the universe. Tell me what you know."

April tried to pull herself away from the Ravenvine, to quiet the roar of voices in her head, the pulse of a witnessed universe full of life. It was like trying to shut down a waterfall. *Promises unmade. Paths untaken. Matter into matter. One or another or another.*

Falo squinted at her. "You said you weren't afraid."

"To be fair, I also said I *was*," April replied. She lifted her eyes high into the Veil, letting the sight of it help quell the raging river of the Medium in her head.

When April still didn't speak, Falo said, "Is your mind not your own?"

"I'm trying to let it be, if you'd just give me a second."

But Falo wouldn't let up. "When you heard those tangles through the Mothergate, what named shadows walked that dream? I believe you know. What do those tangles make you think of?"

"The Fel'Daera," April blurted out, and then she slapped her hand across her mouth. What was she saying? Horace was her friend. The Fel'Daera had saved her life. And Falo herself was its Maker.

"I don't know why I said that," April said. And she didn't. She hadn't even thought it, really.

But it wasn't wrong.

Falo's expression didn't change. "You are an empath," she said. "You have tasted the mind of the universe, and the Fel'Daera, it seems, weighs heavy on that mind. But not just the Fel'Daera, I think." She nodded, urging April to go on. April slowly lowered her hand. The Ravenvine was silent at last, her thoughts her own once more.

"Horace," she said. "And Chloe too. The Alvalaithen. Joshua and the Laithe. You and Gabriel and Brian and Mr. Meister. Every Tan'ji, all of us and our instruments." She hesitated. *Undone and again. Here and then.* "The Fel'Daera," she said one more time, and she shrugged an apology she wasn't sure Falo needed.

Falo released her hands and stood swiftly, rising high into the light of the Veil. Her face was kind. "You are not the most powerful empath I have ever met," Falo said. "But you are perhaps the wisest."

April chewed her cheek, considering. "I can live with that. But I still don't really get it . . . the tangles, the knots. What does it have to do with—"

"There are layers you don't understand, you said. It is time for you to understand them." She turned her back on the Mothergate and began walking away.

April hurried after her, heart fluttering. And although she'd wandered for what felt like a mile trying to find the Mothergate in the first place, now she took no more than ten steps before she found herself stumbling out of the light and into the vast stone chamber deep behind Falo's quarters. The Veil of Lura loomed behind them, a brilliant rippling curtain, stretching wide and high to walls and a ceiling April could not see.

The shock of leaving took April's breath away. "That was fast," she said, trying to sound at ease.

"It was what I wished it to be," Falo said with a shrug.

A rattling croak greeted them, rolling across the stone. With heavy thrusts of his great black wings, Arthur lifted off from the floor a hundred feet away and flew at April, squawking softly. She smiled as the raven approached, opening the vine to him. The bird's thoughts sprouted easily in her mind.

Welcome. Friend. Happy.

April didn't so much hear these things as feel them, as though they had come from herself. A swell of wetness rose in her eyes. Arthur's thoughts were so simple and clean— tidy little gifts compared to the torrential consciousness that poured from the Mothergate. She wallowed in them gladly.

Happy. Friend. Food.

"You waited for me," she told him as he swooped in to land on her shoulder. The raven shuffled, digging his talons into the leather shoulder perch Brian had made for her. Her head received only a mild battering from Arthur's clumsy wings as he got situated, a soft clunking she felt both in her skull and—through the vine—the bones in her wrist and fore-arm that matched the bones in Arthur's wings. He plucked lightly at her hair with his thick beak, the heavy ruff of feath-ers around his neck puffing slightly.

April could sense that Arthur had been worried. She kept his presence low in her mind, lest his worries bubble up into her own. Even so, she picked up a memory of the bird watch-ing as Falo had stepped into the Veil, mere seconds after April herself had gone in. Through the bird's keen eyes, the Veil was a suspended silver rain shower, rippling but never falling. April couldn't help but wonder how she had managed to find the Mothergate so easily within it. Had Falo helped her? Or had something about the Veil changed?

Arthur bobbed his head, getting ready to speak. April knew what he would say before he said it. *"Foood,"* he croaked hopefully, and the Vine added more: *Please. Want. Love.*

"I'm out of food," she told him. "Soon."

He couldn't completely understand her, of course. The vine was a one-way street. *"Fooood fud-fud,"* he said, bouncing up and down.

"I agree," Falo said, eyeing the bird. "Let us find bread, and fruit. Perhaps Horace will be hungry too."

April looked up at her. "We're going to see Horace?"

She must have sounded alarmed, because Falo said, "Of course. He is your friend. Do not imagine anything has changed because of what you heard through the Mothergate today."

April shook her head, embarrassed to have felt even a trickle of hesitation. Horace was her friend, and Chloe too. She was also embarrassed to remember that Chloe was off on a dangerous rescue mission at this very moment, headed back to the city to rescue those captured in the Warren. And yet she'd barely given Chloe—or Gabriel or Mrs. Hapsteade—a thought in the last hour or two.

"Nothing has changed," April said firmly. "I'm just trying to imagine what you're going to tell him."

"*Tellim*," Arthur gulped. "*Tellim*."

"You have questions, he has questions," Falo said. "Many of the answers are the same."

"Are you going to convince him that the Mothergates have to die?"

"Does he need convincing?"

April shrugged. She and Horace and Chloe had spent the evening discussing the revelations of the day before. Not only were the Mothergates dying, but the Wardens were fighting to make sure they did. They were fighting to ensure their own doom. It was a lot to swallow, and April was having an easier time with it than the others.

"Horace trusts you," April said. "But he's not exactly what I would call . . . a man of faith."

"His is a logical mind," Falo said. "And that is all for the best. I will explain everything, and he will know it for the truth." She smiled thinly down at April, her face full of old sadness. "After that, the only faith he'll need is faith in himself."

CHAPTER FOUR

The Fates of the Unchosen

HORACE WASN'T HAPPY HE'D BEEN LEFT BEHIND. HE'D BEEN complaining about it, or more like pouting and fretting, for two hours and forty-seven minutes—in other words, ever since Chloe and the rest had left Ka'hoka for the city, in search of Mr. Meister. Brian had been trying to cheer up Horace by reminding him that Horace hadn't just been left behind, but distinctly *uninvited*.

"Being left behind means you're useless," Brian had argued. "Being uninvited means you're scary."

"What if I don't want to be scary?" Horace asked.

Brian shrugged as if the question were utterly pointless. "What if *I* don't want to be handsome?" he countered.

Horace eyed Brian. His thick glasses, strangely cat-eyed. His pale skin and scrawny arms. His shaggy brown ponytail. Like the rest of the Wardens, Brian had been given some human clothes, and he now wore a sagging T-shirt on which he'd drawn a frantic-looking horse head. Beneath it he'd written:

THE END IS NEIGH.

"My point is," said Brian, when Horace didn't respond, "sometimes we just are what we are."

"Some of us more than others," Neptune remarked. She was floating upright near the high ceiling, examining a lofty bookcase full of Altari books, big as briefcases. These were the first words she'd spoken since drifting in an hour before.

Horace and Chloe had been given this room when they first arrived at Ka'hoka, each of them taking one of the two absurdly huge Altari beds, twice as long as Horace was tall. When the others from the Warren had shown up, telling their terrible tale, April had joined them here, claiming a space in the bed next to Chloe in some kind of unspoken girl pact. Neptune and Gabriel were bunking in the room next door, and Brian had a room to himself farther down the hallway, where he could work in peace with his Tan'ji, Tunraden. Mrs. Hapsteade and Horace's mother, meanwhile, had been spending most of their time with Sil'falo Teneves in her quarters, closer to the Veil of Lura and the Mothergate hidden within.

Having his mom here—never the clingy type, but certainly never cold either—was a blessing he could hardly endure. Some moments she would move desperately, pleasantly close to him, and others she would step firmly away. She was being the perfect mother, basically, under circumstances he could hardly imagine. But her presence *forced* him to imagine. And when he started to wonder too hard about what she was going through, here at the end of things . . . his brain sort of seized up. And she, of course, seemed to know this too.

At the moment, though, he was distracted from worrying about his mom—or wondering what his dad might be doing or thinking right now!—by fretting over Chloe. So far, Horace had resisted the urge to look through the Fel'Daera to see whether—or rather, *when*—Chloe would return. He ached to try, the Fel'Daera like a nagging pet at his side, stewing in its pouch. It was almost certainly safe to look; after all, the rescuers were long gone, and none of them would know what he had seen. The greatest lesson he'd learned about viewing the future was that the very act of viewing *changed* that future. The act of opening the box was itself a link in the chain of events that led into tomorrow. Horace had learned to say as little as possible about what the box revealed, so that his companion's future decisions wouldn't be colored too heavily by what he said. At the moment, of course, he couldn't have told Chloe what he saw even if he wanted to. Even so, he wouldn't let himself open the box now, to look through the rippling blue glass. He knew full well why he'd been unwelcome on the rescue mission. The Fel'Daera's powers—*his* powers—were frightening.

They were especially frightening to the Altari, most of whom had only recently learned that the Fel'Daera still existed. Sil'falo Teneves, its Maker, had long ago told the Wardens' Council it had been destroyed. Some of the Altari didn't seem troubled by discovering the truth now—Dailen, for instance, and especially Teokas. Others were wary, like Go'nesh and Ravana, who seemed much more interested in straightforward warrior stuff than the brain-bending, will-testing challenges of the Fel'Daera. But it had been Mal'brula Kintares, head of the Council and perhaps the Fel'Daera's smallest fan, who had forbidden Horace to partake in the rescue mission. The fact that Brula wasn't even going to be there didn't seem to make a difference to him.

And so Horace had stayed behind. As had April, who'd drifted away to explore Ka'hoka a couple of hours ago, and hadn't yet returned. She'd endured more than most of them in the past several days, and since arriving in Ka'hoka had been strangely and peacefully distracted . . . almost otherworldly. No one had even suggested she might go with the others to find Mr. Meister.

It was less clear to Horace why Neptune hadn't gone along, though. She was deeply devoted to Mr. Meister, and to Gabriel, and Horace would have thought she'd fight to be included. But in fact, she'd refused to go.

As Horace watched Neptune now, wondering, she twisted in the air, her long cloak flaring. "Someone's coming," she said. "Two humans and an Altari." Her Tan'ji, the Devlin tourminda, not only gave her the ability to ignore the effects of gravity, but allowed her to sense the gravity of nearby objects—larger ones, anyway, like people and cars.

A moment after she spoke, the huge door opened. April came in first, Arthur on her shoulder. Sil'falo Teneves followed, looking frighteningly regal as always. She carried a basket as big as an oven, a dog-sized loaf of bread sticking out of the top.

Horace's mother came in last of all. Horace blinked; she was still a startling sight in this place. She belonged here, of course—sometimes she seemed to belong here more than Horace did—but she was just so . . . *Mom.*

The best mom, sure, no doubt about it. But it was like Horace had to look at her for several moments each time he saw her, looking past the momness he'd known all his life, to see the woman and girl who—he had recently learned— had known about the Wardens since before he was even born. She'd held the Fel'Daera as a teenager. She'd seen the Starlit Loom, something even Mr. Meister had never done. She was kind of a legend.

She made a goofy face at him as she came in and mouthed a single word, rubbing her belly: "Cheeseburger."

Horace stifled a laugh. Altari food was good—especially the bread—but a cheeseburger sounded delicious on a whole other level right about now.

April clambered onto the bed beside Horace, nodding a distant hello without really looking at him. Arthur hopped down from her shoulder and plucked at Horace's sleeve. Falo set the basket on the table and turned to Brian.

"Have you finished the jithandra?" she asked him musically. Her tone, though kindly, clearly suggested she wasn't asking out of simple curiosity.

"I'm like . . . *this* close," Brian said, holding his hands a yard apart.

For reasons Horace didn't fully understand, Mrs. Hapsteade had asked Brian to remake Mr. Meister's jithandra. All Wardens carried a jithandra, a small crystal that glowed in darkness, its color directly linked to the nature of each particular Keeper's power. Horace's was deep blue, and Chloe's was red, while April's was forest green. In addition to providing light when it was needed, a jithandra served as a kind of personalized key, granting passage through certain doorways and obstacles in the Warden's strongholds.

When he was injured in the Warren, just before he was captured, Mr. Meister had apparently destroyed his own jithandra instead of letting it fall into the hands of the Riven. Now Mrs. Hapsteade and Falo wanted it remade.

"Have you encountered a difficulty?" Falo asked. "May I be of assistance, one Dorvala to another?"

"I mean, it's just a jithandra," Brian said, blushing. "I've done it loads of times. But this one's tough. That ink sample Mrs. Hapsteade gave me is pretty dried out. Mr. Meister must have written it like a hundred years ago."

"Surprising," said Falo, "since the Vora it was written with

63

didn't even exist a hundred years ago."

Brian looked at Horace. "Notice Mrs. Hapsteade's Tan'ji can't be a hundred years old, but Mr. Meister himself . . . ? Maybe."

"Just make the jithandra," Neptune said sharply, high overhead. "So it'll be waiting for him when he gets back."

"But when he gets back," Brian said, "he can use the Vora to write me a better—"

"Just make it," Neptune repeated.

"Neptune needs a new jithandra too," April said unexpectedly. "I smashed hers in the Warren."

"Why?" said Horace.

April didn't look at him. She still hadn't looked at him this whole time, in fact. Instead, she peered up at Neptune, as if unsure whose story this was. "It was in the Gallery," April said.

The Gallery, a mysterious corridor deep in the Warren, was filled with doorways that only appeared when the light of certain jithandras fell upon them. Without the proper light, the doorways simply did not exist.

"The door—" Neptune began, and her voice cracked. She turned back to the bookcase again, hiding her face. She cleared her throat and tried again, her words squeaky and hoarse. "The door to Sanguine Hall needed disappearing. The Riven were coming, of course. The golem was . . . it almost made it into the Gallery, while I just stood there keeping the door real, my jithandra shining all over the place."

Suddenly Neptune fell. She dropped ten feet, her cloak billowing. She bounced high off the bed below, shaking it so hard Brian nearly toppled over. Arthur fluttered noisily into the air, chattering. Neptune sprang into the middle of the room, hanging for the tiniest extra beat at the peak of her jump—enough to make Horace blink—and then she landed lightly on the floor between the two beds.

"Napping," she said thickly. "Wake me when everyone gets back." And then she swept from the room.

"It's not about the door," April said, once she was gone. "She tried to slow Mr. Meister when he fell, but she couldn't quite manage it, and then he . . ." She trailed off.

"We heard the story," Brian said tersely, sliding from the high bed onto the floor. "Broken leg. Golem. Captured. I don't know that we need the details." He paused and then shot an apologetic look at April. "Not that I'm trying to be a jerk about it."

April shrugged. "It's okay," she said. "We're all stressed. The end is neigh, right?"

Brian plucked at his shirt, turning to Horace. "See? She gets it."

"I got it," Horace said. "I just didn't think it was funny."

Brian sighed and looked down at himself. "What's *really* funny is, I've never even seen a horse. Not in real life."

Horace's mother stepped forward and laid a hand on Brian's cheek. "Don't be sad, Keeper," she said. "Horses aren't that great."

Brian nodded. "I appreciate you maligning an entire species to make me feel better," he said, and sighed again. "I guess I'm going to go work now. Don't talk about me when I'm gone."

Falo smiled. "What else is there to talk about?"

"I honestly don't know," Brian said, sweeping his gaze around at them and letting it land on Horace. "But it sure feels like you're going to talk about something."

Beside Horace on the bed, April shifted uncomfortably. Horace suddenly felt very nervous. Brian waved good-bye and slipped out of the room, closing the huge door behind him.

Falo and Horace's mom took seats on the bed opposite Horace and April. No one spoke for a while, as Falo broke into the bread she'd brought—spicy and hearty. There was fruit, too, and a pitcher of icy-clear water. They ate in silence, Horace's nervousness growing by the second, until at last Falo—after downing a pear in two delicate bites—said, "April has been to the Mothergate again."

"Oh, yeah?" Horace said, not sure what that had to do with anything, but thinking maybe it had to do with everything. He glanced at April and she nodded, still not catching his eye.

Falo said, "She has questions whose answers, I think, will serve you well in these last days." Horace's mother nibbled at a withered apple, carving off tiny bits of skin between her teeth. Falo hesitated, throwing her a sympathetic look, and then added, "Questions about the Fel'Daera."

Horace frowned. "Seems like everyone has doubts about the Fel'Daera these days," he growled, feeling a little pouty again and hating it. "That's why I'm sitting here now, instead of heading to the city with the others. Nobody trusts it. Or me, I guess."

April turned to him, looking him full in the face for the first time since arriving. "I trust it," she said earnestly. "I trust you."

"As do we all, Horace," said Falo. "But even if one trusts the Fel'Daera, and its Keeper, there are reasons to despise it."

Horace realized he had his hand atop the box. He let it slide causally away. "What reasons?" he asked.

Falo contemplated him for several moments before answering with a question of her own. "This is a conversation you wish to have?"

"It's the conversation you came here to have, isn't it?" Horace asked. "I mean, I'm not stupid."

"That is an understatement," Falo said. Her ringed eyes seemed to glow. "Let us talk, then. Let me tell you everything Mr. Meister never dared. You want to know why one might despise the Fel'Daera, even if she trusts it."

"Yes," Horace said, just as April said the exact same. Suddenly he wasn't at all sure that he did want to know.

"Very well," Falo said. "But the answer—the answer you need to hear—begins with a lesson. A lesson as big as the universe itself. Bigger, in fact." She looked alertly around at the others. "You humans are fond of money, I know. Does anyone have a coin?"

Bewildered, Horace slapped his pockets. Empty. But April produced a nickel from the folds of her dress and held it out.

"Ah, good," said Falo, nodding. "Now flip it, please."

April hesitated. "What are we deciding?"

"Nothing," said Falo. "And everything."

April glanced at Horace and then shrugged. "Okay," she said good-naturedly. "I don't believe in luck anyway." She flicked the coin expertly into the air with a soft *ting*! It spun high, winking. Arthur squawked. Horace's mind lit briefly upon the Fel'Daera, although the box wasn't particularly good at seeing the outcome of totally random events.

The coin clattered to the stone floor. It rolled a little ways and toppled over.

Falo leaned in to see. The great black pendant around her neck, an oval as big as a bar of soap, swung like a pendulum. "Tails," she said. "I believe that's the proper term. Are we all agreed—we all see tails?"

"Yes," said April. Horace's mother said nothing, her apple abandoned, her face alight with intelligence. Horace got the feeling that whatever lesson Falo was teaching them now, his mother had learned it long ago.

"Tails, definitely," Horace agreed.

Falo smiled. "And so we are all here, in this universe,

where the coin has come up tails. This we witness. *But . . .*"
She let the word hang, holding up a long, elegant finger,
ghostly as a wand. "But even as we sit here, elsewhere there is
another universe. One where the nickel came up heads. And
in that place, even now, we are all agreeing—or rather, the
versions of us that occupy that place are all agreeing—that the
coin came up heads."

"Another universe," April said, as if a question that had
been nagging her had suddenly been answered. She glanced
around the room as though that other universe might be visible, ghosted over the top of this one.

"A parallel world," Falo said.

Horace, suddenly, was way ahead of them. "The multiverse," he said hoarsely.

April cocked her head at him. "What's that?"

"It's a theory," he said, letting his mind slip into gear. "I
don't totally understand it. But basically it says we're inside
an endless multiverse, made up of an infinite number of
parallel universes. We're only aware of a single one of those
universes—the one we live in. But whenever we see something happen a certain way in our universe, another universe
is created where it happens *another* way."

"Yes," Falo said. "Reality splits, and two new realities are
created. But not just two—a new universe is created for *every
possible outcome of every witnessed event.* There is now another
universe where the coin rolled under the bed. Another where
the coin was a quarter rather than a nickel. Even a universe

where the coin landed on edge."

"Is that even possible?" Horace's mother asked. "Landing on edge?"

"Once every six thousand tosses or so," Horace mumbled, dredging up a fact he'd read once that he wasn't entirely sure he believed.

Arthur hopped to the ground. As if he understood, and wanted to try it for himself, he began fussing at the nickel with his sturdy beak.

"Okay," Horace said. "I understand the theory—sort of—but if the universe is constantly splitting into new universes, why are we *here* and not *there*?"

"We *are* there," April replied, surprising him.

"Yes," said Falo. "In fact, Horace, there would be a universe where you are asking that same exact question, but your shirt is red instead of blue."

Horace shook his head in wonder. It was one thing to imagine the idea of the multiverse, a theory that not even all scientists embraced. It was quite another to learn he was actually living in it. "And I guess red-shirt Horace thinks *he's* the real Horace," he said.

Falo nodded. "Every reality believes itself to be the true reality. And why shouldn't it? The very phenomenon of consciousness itself is created along that messy rift where realities split apart. The act of witnessing is the act of being."

Horace must have look puzzled, because his mother explained softly, "What we experience is what we are."

"Yes, precisely," said Falo. "Thank you, Jess. We *are* what we *experience*. And when our experiences diverge, so do our consciousnesses. New worlds are thus created. New selves. But one consciousness—one *self*—is not more real, or more valid, or more true, than any other."

April seemed to be taking all of this in stride. If anything, she seemed deeply satisfied. She watched Arthur silently, kicking her booted feet as they dangled from the huge bed. Horace became suddenly sure, though he could not have said how, that she was imagining a universe in which her parents were still alive. That she was picturing another April, as real as the one sitting here now, with her parents in a happier place, far away from all of this.

No one spoke for a little while. Horace swam through a stew of logic and emotion. Concepts he could barely grasp, wispy feelings he couldn't begin to name. He felt . . . small. An infinite number of Horaces, in an infinite number of universes. And not just Horaces. There would be a universe where Chloe and the others made it back to Ka'hoka safely.

There would be a universe where they didn't.

He shoved the thought from his mind, trying to keep his thoughts away from Chloe. Many Horaces. Many universes. Not just a theory, but reality.

"Although we cannot witness the multiverse firsthand," Falo said, "its existence is vital to what we do. The falkrete stones, the Nevren, the dumindar—all of these operate by exploiting certain links between universes. Indeed, some of our most powerful Tan'ji can only function by accessing the multiverse. Take the Alvalaithen, for instance. When Chloe uses the dragonfly, she is shifting partway into other universes. Universes where an obstacle like a wall—or a tree or a body or a mountain—simply does not exist. She still has to navigate between the atoms of the object here in our own universe, but the trip is greatly simplified."

"*Everywhere here,*" April whispered. "That's brilliant."

"I vote we *don't* tell Chloe that's what she's doing," Horace's mother said.

"Seconded," said Horace. He'd long ago accepted that Chloe vehemently did not want to know how the dragonfly worked. She was convinced her mastery of her Tan'ji depended on instinct, and that too much knowledge would spoil it.

Falo waved a pale hand. "I'm simplifying the matter a bit. I'm not ashamed to say that the details of the Alvalaithen are beyond me, and the truths I do know are not really mine to tell. I am not its Maker." Her eyes lit on Horace, as if incidentally. Her gaze was like an open door.

Horace hesitated, then pulled the Box of Promises from its pouch at his side. "But you *are* the Maker of the Fel'Daera."

"I am," Falo said solemnly, her voice thrumming.

"And the multiverse has something to do with how it works, doesn't it?" asked Horace.

Horace couldn't have said how, but the mood in the room

suddenly thickened. Goose bumps blossomed along his arms. April pressed her fist against her mouth. His mother shifted nervously and threw a worried look at Falo. Falo seemed not to notice, leaning in, her eyes locked on Horace's. Pressing her thin lips tight, she drew faint breaths through her nose over the Fel'Daera, as if she savoring the smell of it. She didn't look at it.

"What are you asking me, Keeper?" she said low. "What is it you think you wish to know?"

A curl of sickness rolled through Horace's gut. After he had first come through the Find, when the Fel'Daera was still new and overwhelming, Mr. Meister had offered many reassurances about Horace's newfound power: *You do not control the future; you do not create it; you are not responsible for whatever the future might bring.*

But the old man was a deceiver. Had he deceived Horace about the Fel'Daera?

"There are many universes," Horace said, pressing forward cautiously. "Each universe has a different future. Each one takes a different path."

"Each path *is* a different universe," Falo clarified. "Each time there is a splitting, a new universe is created." She held out her hand, palm up. "Consider a bare tree," she said, and then something incredible happened.

A tree made of golden light grew from her hand. It rose and spread, its bare branches forking and bending. It grew two

73

feet high, wondrously complicated and real, but shimmering like the sun on water. Its roots wrapped around Falo's hand as if gripping her tight.

April clapped softly. Beside Falo, Horace's mom sat watching with obvious delight. This was the Medium, of course, and his mom could feel it in a way that Horace never would. It was only the second time he had even seen the Medium; apparently making it visible was a trick only Makers like Falo and Brian could manage. But where was Falo's Tan'ji, the Starlit Loom? How was she doing this?

"Forgive me the fireworks," Falo said. "I am only trying to illustrate a point. Imagine that the trunk of the tree is the present. As we move into the future, up the tree, each branching represents a splitting, the creation of a new universe. These splittings happen because events have happened in slightly different ways."

"Heads instead of tails," Horace said.

"Yes. Note, though, that these future universes used to be a single universe. They all share the same history, up until the split." The trunk pulsed and glowed. "Every time a split occurs, a new path is created. A new universe. And so the tip of each twig on this tree is a different possible future, a future that we here in the present might eventually end up in." Swiftly, a wave of twinkling lights swept over the crown of the tree, thousands of sparkles illuminating the tips of every twig. "Each twig, in fact, is effectively a different universe, even though they all began in this one."

"So it's kind of like the tree of life," Horace said. "Like whales, for example. Even though we see a bunch of different species of whale now, we know that long ago they shared a common ancestor."

"Precisely," Falo said. A single path grew bright inside the tree, rising from the trunk and following the bends of a particular series of branches out to the very end of a single twig. The path burned for a moment, and then went out. Now another path lit up, following a different series of branches and ending in a completely different place. "Like species, some universes are very different, because the path they used to share split a long time ago," Falo said. "But others are quite similar, because the split happened only recently." The very end of the current path shifted slightly, somewhere along the last few bends, so that it remained mostly the same but ended on a different twig a short distance away.

Horace reached out for the tree. He thought Falo might stop him, but she didn't. He stuck his finger into the trunk of the tree, right beneath the first branching. The Medium swirled and danced around his fingertip. He was surprised to feel nothing.

"So I'm here in the trunk," he said, "and I open the Fel'Daera. The box then shows me one possible future, one possible path—"

"One potential universe, yes," said Falo, a new path lighting up from trunk to twig as she spoke. "An extension of the universe we occupy in the present—a particular future universe where only certain things have come to pass."

Horace was getting it. It definitely helped to think of it as tree. A single branch splits to become two, with each branch having no knowledge of the other except for the past they once shared. And the branching went on and on and on . . . forever. A Horace on every branch. A Fel'Daera on every branch. As his brain clutched at the notion, he began to feel tinier than he had ever felt before. Tinier, and more full of wonder.

But there was a problem.

"Okay," he said slowly. "I get that the box shows me a particular path into a particular future, like the paths you're making now. But you're just choosing a path at random, for show. In real life, who decides which path the box shows me?"

"Not you," his mother said suddenly, sharply. Her voice had the tone of a bear protecting her cubs.

Falo dropped her hand. The tree swirled with a flourish and vanished into sparkling dust. "That is correct," she said. "The only decision you make, Horace, is whether to open the Fel'Daera in the first place, and what your state of mind is when you do open it. Consider this, as an example: the Horace that opens the Fel'Daera in fear is already in a different universe than the Horace who opens it in anger. They are already on different branches. Therefore the futures the Fel'Daera reveal to them will also be different."

Horace digested the thought for a few moments and decided that this, after all, wasn't so different from what Mr.

Meister had told him after the Find. Opening the box was the first step toward the future the box then showed him. And yet . . . there was something new here. Something troubling that he couldn't quite put his finger on. That tree. All those branches, most of them dark.

At last he said, "But what about all those other universes the box *doesn't* show me? All those other paths, where other things might have happened?"

Even as he asked, Horace wished he could take the question back. His mom—his own *mother*—hung her head as if she could not bear to look, or even listen.

But not Falo. She let her deep eyes drop onto the Fel'Daera, just for an instant. Then she looked back at Horace and said clearly, "The other paths are extinguished."

"Extinguished," Horace repeated. The word didn't even start to make sense to him until he said it out loud. He tried to breathe. "You mean *destroyed*?"

Falo tilted her head as if reluctant to agree. "Erased," she said. "Absorbed. They expire to make fuel for the one future you then witness."

"Fuel," he said dumbly. The box was a sinking anchor in his hand. Hot ice.

April cleared her throat. "I wonder if you could show us, Falo," she said. "I'm not sure I totally understand."

Falo held out her hand again, and the glowing golden tree grew anew. "When the Keeper of the Fel'Daera looks through the blue glass, the Fel'Daera devotes itself completely to a

77

single path. One particular future." Right on cue, a fresh glowing path appeared within the crown of the tree, leading jaggedly all the way from trunk to twig. "Every branch and stick that does *not* lie along that path is absorbed. As these other paths disappear, the desired path becomes thicker. Stronger."

Her words came to life as she spoke. The darker outer branches on the tree began to crumple and fade. They receded like melting snow, like rotting flesh. As they did, the chosen path Falo had illuminated grew stronger and brighter. The other branches continued to shrivel out of existence, seeming to feed the thickening central path. At last nothing was left but a bare crooked stick, with no branchings whatsoever. It looked like a wound. It looked powerful, and cruel.

"This is what the Fel'Daera does," said Falo. "It consumes the many unchosen paths to strengthen the single path that remains."

"The willed path," said Horace thickly, staring in horror. "But why do those other paths need to be destroyed?"

Falo made a fist. The jagged, branchless tree evaporated in a cloud of drifting sparks. "Not destroyed. Extinguished. Swallowed. The proper word is—"

"But those paths," Horace interrupted. "Those universes. They never really existed in the first place, right? They aren't real."

"What does it mean to be real?" Falo said, her voice infuriatingly calm. "Is the future real? Is a forgotten memory real?"

"You know what I'm asking you," Horace said. "I'm asking you if there are things that would exist—could exist, should exist—if not for the Fel'Daera. Universes that would exist if not for me."

"Yes," his mother said abruptly, practically spitting out the word. Then she softened, and said it again. "Yes, Horace. They would."

"Your mother is correct," Falo said. "The unchosen paths *do* exist, in a manner of speaking. But the moment you crack open the Fel'Daera, those possibilities . . . give way."

"But why?" Horace pleaded. "Why did you make it do that?"

Falo sighed. "Without that fuel, the visions of the Fel'Daera would be no better than a guess. A roll of the dice." She nodded at the floor, where the nickel still lay. "The flip of a coin. Without the energy provided by this sacrifice, the Fel'Daera could not see tru—"

"Stop," Horace said. "Just stop." *Sacrifice.* Horace glared at Falo, at her magnificent, horrible hands. The branchless tree burned in his vision, and a thousand furious demands rumbled like bees in his head: *a destroyer of universes . . . how could you make this thing? . . . who do you think you are? . . . what gives you the right?* But none of them made it to his tongue. Instead his thoughts tumbled, tussling and buzzing. He looked down at the Fel'Daera, at the elegant, shimmering wings of its lid. He very nearly opened it, thought he might vomit if he did. He tried not to think of the hundreds of times he'd opened the box before now. Countless futures, erased.

He felt himself splitting in two again. To question the existence of the Fel'Daera was to question the existence of himself. The box belonged to him, and he belonged to it. All those universes, snuffed out . . . but then again—were they really real? Did they even truly exist yet?

And then *again*:

Did he care?

If the box was monstrous, was he willing to be a monster?

~~~

CHAPTER FIVE

Tangled Universes

HORACE TURNED MISERABLY TO CHLOE—BUT NO. CHLOE wasn't here. She was out doing terrible things, dangerous things, straddling universes. Here was only April, a perfectly decent friend gazing at him now with her perfectly sensible face, a perfectly reasonable furrow in her brow. She wasn't going to spew any venom on his behalf, wasn't going to smack him loose from his dismay, wasn't going to bristle so fiercely that there was no room for anything else.

But then April said, looking him straight in the eye, "You look mad. Do you think there's a universe where you're destroying the Fel'Daera right now?"

It was nothing Chloe would have said. But it was every bit of cold water Chloe could have mustered, and then some. He actually gasped. He pressed the box to his chest.

"I'm not mad," Horace lied. He searched inside himself for

a better word. "I'm ashamed." Still he clutched the Fel'Daera. Shame, yes, but also a nasty trickle of something else. He recognized it the same way he recognized that he would never—could never—destroy the Fel'Daera. That this little box, his Tan'ji, should have the immense power to erase entire universes . . . with it came a sliver of something that had to be called pride.

His shame grew deeper still.

"The Fel'Daera's best Keepers have always felt shame," Falo said. Her face was calm as ever, full of open light. Horace got the sense that she knew precisely what he was feeling. And maybe she did, through the bond of lavro'dorval between Maker and instrument. He resented her for it, just a little.

"Don't you feel ashamed too?" Horace accused. "You're the Maker."

"When I first realized how I could create a Tan'ji that saw the future truly, I had shame. Deep shame, and sorrow. But I also had great need."

"What need?" asked Horace.

"There were specific dangers that have since passed—"

"What dangers?" Horace interjected. Falo ignored him.

"—but broadly speaking, our need then was the same as it is now. To prevent the Riven from finding and repairing the Mothergates."

"The Mothergates. Right. And they're about to die, taking us Keepers with them." His mother let loose a soft grumble of worry and tucked her chin against her chest. Horace wouldn't let himself pause. "So why bother telling me this now? It's like . . . a guy is falling from a building to his death, and on the way down someone leans out a window to tell him he's a terrible person."

His mother slid nimbly to the floor and crossed to Horace, climbing up on the bed beside him. She lifted his hand from his lap and held it, squeezing it. Her grip was warm and strong.

Falo watched her. As far as Horace was concerned, his mom was the best mom possible, but somehow in the light of Falo's steady, maternal gaze, she looked like a child. Falo shone with frightening wisdom and endless care, as if she had given birth to the very idea of motherhood itself.

"She worries," Falo murmured, turning to Horace. "She is well aware of the fate we Keepers will face if the Mothergates die—of the fate that may await her only son. And yet we intend to let the Mothergates fade away. Have you not wondered why she is not more angry?"

"Don't speak for me, Falo," his mother said.

"You're a Tuner," Falo told her. "You know the dangers of keeping the Mothergates open as well as I. Tell your son. Tell him what we face."

"Don't say I'm not angry. I didn't ask for any of this."

"You are not so angry that you cannot accept the truth," said Falo. She leaned toward Horace again. "Tell me, Keeper, have you heard of thrall-blight?"

Thrall-blight. Horace's queasy gut gnawed at him. He'd first heard the word from Dr. Jericho. "When I don't follow the future the box shows me, I feel sick." Dr. Jericho had told him that the awful sickness spread outward from Horace into the Medium, all the way to the Mothergates themselves. Was it true? Were the Mothergates dying because of the Fel'Daera, and Horace?

Falo said, "Thrall-blight is an affliction that strikes the Keeper of the Fel'Daera when he rejects the universe the Fel'Daera promised him."

"Mr. Meister told me the Box of Promises makes no promises."

"He was being kind. It's more truthful to say that the Fel'Daera makes no promises its Keeper cannot break."

"Fabulous," Horace said. "So okay . . . tell me what thrall-blight is. I suppose when I reject the future the Fel'Daera showed me, I'm destroying yet another universe. Is that why I feel so crappy? I'm killing the universe the Fel'Daera promised me?"

"No," Falo said. "That universe remains, even if you reject it. Somewhere, another Horace did not reject it, and still walks the willed path. What you feel, rather, is the rebirth of universes that were extinguished when you opened the Fel'Daera."

Horace actually rocked back, stunned. "But that seems good. Why does it feel so bad?"

"Because you are treading ground you were never meant to walk," said Falo. "Doing work meant to be done by the multiverse itself, in a manner of speaking."

"So it's my fault," Horace said. "This . . . sickness the Mothergates have. It's because of me, and the Fel'Daera, and thrall-blight."

Falo's brows went high and her eyes slid closed. She shook her head as if she did not know how to explain to him everything he'd just gotten wrong.

"A dying thing isn't necessarily sick, Horace," his mother said. "The sun dies every day."

April, silent for several minutes, suddenly spoke. Her voice was hollow, far away. "I can explain it to you, Horace," she said. "Or at least, I can explain what I feel." She pointed to the Ravenvine, peeking out from under her auburn hair. Falo nodded her encouragement. "The Mothergates are temporary," April said. "They are . . . fleeting, actually, in the grand scheme of things. Like the eyes of a sleeping giant, cracking open for just a second. They'll close again. But while the Mothergates are open, the life force that creates new universes is spilling through them into our world. The life force of the universe itself. *All* the universes. And when it spills into our world, it becomes something we can twist and bend."

"The Medium," Horace said.

April nodded. "But the more we witness it—the more we *use* it . . ."

As she trailed off, Falo picked up the thread. "There are things that are not meant to be known. Bridges we are not meant to build. Yet through the Medium, through the Tanu, we reach out to other universes. We may slip between

85

universes, like Chloe. We may, like Neptune, borrow the laws of physics from another universe. We may live in another universe while we die in this one, like those that have sacrificed themselves to the Nevren. We may extinguish other universes, Horace Andrews, or even bring them back to life. And even if we do none of these things, we seize hold of the consciousness of the multiverse every time we use a Tanu. This in itself is not bad, but in all these cases, we tie our universe to another, and another, and another. We bind things that are not meant to be bound."

Horace realized he was holding his breath. "Not meant by whom?"

"Consciousness has one rule," Falo said. "Time moves forward. And as time moves forward, everything expands—knowledge, self, space."

"Why?" said April.

Falo looked surprised by the question. "Because if things do not expand, we do not *become*. And becoming is what consciousness is all about. We are not unmade; we are *made*."

"Then why is it not okay to expand into another universe?" Horace said.

His mother hummed, pleased with the question. She squeezed his hand, which she'd been holding all this time, and then let it go.

"Because then we are no longer ourselves," said Falo. "No longer individuals. The mind of the multiverse is all-encompassing. It is the same mind in every universe. But the individual minds that live *within* the multiverse—yours and mine, and the minds of every living thing—*are confined to the universes in which they live.* They are the building blocks of the multiverse itself, and the multiverse depends upon them not to stray."

"But we Keepers," said Horace, grasping it at last, "we stray."

"Yes." Falo scooped out a huge handful—an Altari handful—of spicy bread from the loaf sitting on the bedside table. She crushed it between her fingers, working it into a large pile of tiny crumbs, and then scattered the crumbs across the floor, thousands of amber specks against the gray. "The multiverse," she said. "Each crumb a universe unto itself, each universe expanding. And of course, the entire multiverse itself must expand, too."

She leaned down, stooping between her long legs like a mantis, and drew a circle in the middle of the mess, isolating a little island of crumbs. "If it has not occurred to you, recognize now that the Tanu do not exist in every universe." She pointed at the little island. "Here are the universes where the Tanu exist. Our own universe is one of them. Like the rest of the multiverse, this group of worlds should be expanding. But it is not. Because of the Tanu, these universes are entangled. Tied to one another. Overlapping, interdependent, jostling each other. This section of the multiverse cannot expand. Instead it struggles, like an insect caught in a web of its own making." For some reason, she glanced at April.

87

"Tangles," April said again, firmly this time.

"Yes. And eventually . . ." Falo encircled the little island of crumbs with her huge nimble fingers and crushed it, flicking the crumbs away, leaving a huge patch of empty space. "The tangles become so knotted that the mind of the multiverse will cease to know this part of itself. It will no longer understand the witnesses within, witnesses that give it life. It will no longer understand the difference between those witnesses and itself. And when that happens, our universe and thousands of others—every universe where the Tanu exist— will be destroyed."

—⟋⟋⟋—

CHAPTER SIX

Rescued

THEY WERE COMING. JOSHUA COULD HARDLY DIGEST THE thought.

Somehow they'd found him, and Mr. Meister too.

The Altari were here.

But before Joshua could even think what it might mean, sudden music filled the chamber—the wavering strains of a flute, sweet and somehow cunning, playing a tune that was not a tune. The notes seemed to reach for Joshua, to enter not just his ears but his skin, his very flesh.

Ingrid stood by the doorway with Dr. Jericho, playing her white flute, sending the awful, beautiful music down the hallway and out in to the passageways beyond. Her Tan'ji gleamed in the darkness like a bone.

Ingrid's music was a way of seeing, somehow—Joshua knew that much. If anyone was within earshot of the flute's tune, Ingrid would know they were there. But *who* was there? Joshua had never even seen an Altari, the mysterious beings who lived in Ka'hoka. They were the lost brothers of the Riven, and their sworn enemy, too. He now knew that the Altari, along with the Wardens, were fighting to let the Mothergates die. But he still didn't understand why. Was April helping them? Did she know? What about Horace and Chloe? Were his friends here with the Altari now, attempting a rescue?

And if so, had they come for him, or for Mr. Meister?

Joshua caught his breath. The sharp-eyed Mordin had left his side, and was standing now with Ingrid and Dr. Jericho. Grooma was still gazing mutely at the ceiling, clearly shaken by the presence of the Altari somewhere above. Isabel, all but forgotten after Grooma's weavings were interrupted, was a heaving lump of cloth and red hair, collapsed at the Dorvala's feet.

And Mr. Meister was on the move.

The old man was taking advantage of the distraction, inching his way across the floor toward Joshua. The golem off to his left just sat there, a mindless pile of stone, Dr. Jericho's attention elsewhere.

Ingrid dropped her flute. Her grasping song fell away. "Grooma's right," she told Dr. Jericho. "Altari—several of them, two levels up. And humans too. They know we're here." She hesitated, and then added, "Gabriel is with them."

Dr. Jericho growled angrily. He barked something to the

sharp-eyed Mordin, who nodded and galloped down the hall-way after the others.

Mr. Meister kept creeping closer to Joshua, clutching his broken leg. His eyes were wide and wild now behind his glasses. He silently mouthed a single word at Joshua, his teeth glinting.

Open.

The Laithe. He wanted Joshua to open a portal. But there was no chance. The moment Joshua began to use the Laithe, steering the surface of the little globe down onto some safe place—Ka'hoka, maybe?—Dr. Jericho would sense it. Besides, the Altari were coming. He shook his head at Mr. Meister, hugging the Laithe, but the old man kept crawling toward him, nodding.

"They have warriors," Ingrid was saying. "One has a bow, and another—"

"Ravana," Dr. Jericho said. A name, apparently. He cocked his head at Ingrid. "How many did you say there were?"

"At least a dozen Altari."

"No," Dr. Jericho said. "Not a dozen. Far from it. Young Dailen is here, I'm sure of it. And he is only *one*, at the end of the day."

Suddenly Joshua heard the sounds of distant battle. The Ravids screeching. grunts and shouts. A steady twang like a great string being plucked, and now a scream.

Dr. Jericho laughed. "The Ravids have found them."

Ravids. The hissing, screeching little monsters. The

91

Wardens had barely managed to escape from them in the Warren.

Mr. Meister was just twenty feet away now. Close enough so that if Joshua opened a portal, the old man might be able to reach it and crawl through. But Joshua would have to be *fast*. Faster than he'd ever been.

He laid a hand on the meridian, the flat copper ring that encircled the Laithe. A silver slider straddled it, in the shape of a dozing rabbit. Once the globe was focused in on the exact location he chose, and the Laithe was torn loose, Joshua could make the rabbit run, letting the meridian spin beneath its feet, opening the portal wide. He looked down at the tiny earth in his hands, at North America and the Midwest, a swath of green brushed with imperceptibly drifting clouds. Ka'hoka was just there, near a kink in the bend of the Mississippi. Dr. Jericho was still talking to Ingrid. No one was watching. Maybe he could do it.

But did he want to?

The Mothergates were dying, and Mr. Meister was determined to see that they did. This secret, this truth, had been kept from them all. Maybe Dr. Jericho was right. Maybe whatever it was Grooma had tried to do to Isabel could fix the problem with the Mothergates, in ways the Wardens had never imagined.

Across the room, still oblivious to the creeping Mr. Meister, Dr. Jericho fished something out of his pocket. "Enough," he said. Joshua saw a glint of crimson. It was another golm'ruun, the ring that controlled the golem. Dr. Jericho lifted his hand, and off to the right, in the darkest shadows of the broad chamber, the wall crumbled and then rose again. Joshua swallowed a gasp as a second golem peeled itself away from the stone, darkness come to life. It poured forth, splitting in two briefly as it rumbled past Grooma and Isabel, like a river around rocks. Dr. Jericho lifted his other hand, and the first golem reared up. The two moving mountains flanked him like faithful hounds.

"There will be no rescue today," Dr. Jericho said.

Mr. Meister, watching, turned his eyes to Joshua once more, just ten feet away now. His face was full of horror. *Now,* he mouthed. *Trust me.*

On the instant, hardly knowing if it was right or wrong, Joshua let his eyes fall onto the Laithe. He slid the rabbit around the meridian, fast as it would go, not sure if he was even using his hands. He was the Keeper of the Laithe. As the rabbit slid, the surface of the globe seemed to spread like melting wax as the view changed. It zoomed in on Illinois, fast as a falling meteor. It was nighttime, of course, but on the Laithe it was never night. The Mississippi, on the west side of the state, grew from a thread to a ribbon to a fat snake in half a blink. The view flickered through a wisp of clouds and then the river was gone, over the western horizon. Down and down. The dots of trees became shrubs, and then Joshua was past them. A sea of green resolved into blades of grass, and he was there. A crooked stick lay in the meadow, close enough to touch. The rabbit had come full circle, back to where it had started. It sat alert now, ears erect, eyes wide and blazing blue, ready for the portal to be opened.

Dr. Jericho was already whirling toward him, bellowing. Mr. Meister lifted himself onto his hands, grimacing, his legs dragging. Joshua ignored them both. He tore the meridian free. The globe became a sphere of featureless yellow light in his hand. As he set the meridian in the air, where it hung like a picture frame, Joshua willed the rabbit atop it to run—*fast, fast*. Its feet became a blur, hurtling. It rode the meridian as the copper ring spun beneath it, and as it spun, it grew—no, it *exploded*—opening faster than it ever had before. It slammed fully open with a heavy thump, eight feet wide, and became a window. The green meadows of Ka'hoka lay beyond, dark and empty.

The very instant the portal was open, Mr. Meister clutched at it. His fingers passed through and he gripped the edge of the meridian. Dr. Jericho was sprinting toward them, howling, his sharp tiny teeth bared. The twin golems roared forth beside him.

"The truth," Mr. Meister said to Joshua, and with a grunt he hoisted himself through the open portal. He rolled clumsily into the grass, two hundred and forty miles away, just as Dr. Jericho lunged forward and swiped at him with his huge sharp fingers, catching nothing but air.

Dr. Jericho straightened, heaving, glaring through the portal at the old man. The Mordin obviously wanted to go

94

after him, but knew Joshua might trap him on the far side—or worse, slam the portal closed while he was passing through it. Joshua astonished himself, thinking these thoughts. But watching Dr. Jericho hesitate now gave him the strength to think them.

"Go ahead," Joshua told him. "Leave this place. See if you can get back. I don't know how those rings of yours work, but I'm pretty sure you can't control the golems from across the state."

As if in reply, the golems swirled around the little scene, becoming a massive stone tornado, surrounding Joshua and Dr. Jericho and the portal. The Mordin just stood there, seething. Through the portal, Mr. Meister lay gasping, looking blind. From the other side, Joshua knew—since Joshua and the Laithe were here and not there—the portal was just a hollow ring, the meridian hanging empty in the air, revealing nothing and leading nowhere. Joshua reached out with his thoughts, asking the blue-eyed rabbit to run back. It ran swiftly, the portal closing. The meadows of Ka'hoka winked out, replaced by the tumbling avalanche of shapes, until the meridian was back to its normal size, no bigger than a dinner plate.

Still Dr. Jericho didn't move. The swirling golems ground slowly to a halt, looming all around them as if Joshua and the Mordin stood in the bottom of a dark well. Cautiously, Joshua reached out and plucked the meridian from the air. He looped it back over the yellow globe of the Laithe, and the blue-and-green living earth faded back into view.

Dr. Jericho reached out, striking like a snake. He grabbed Joshua by the throat, hauling him from the ground. The Laithe slipped from Joshua's grip, left to hover bobbing at his side.

"The Altari," Dr. Jericho growled. The stench of brimstone poured from his mouth. "How did they find us?"

Joshua grappled with the Mordin's huge hand, choking. "I don't know," he gasped.

"Is it you? Were you left behind in the Warren on purpose—some kind of beacon the Wardens could track?"

Joshua's vision began to dim. "No. I stayed on my own. I don't know how they found you."

And he didn't.

"You heard the truth tonight," Dr. Jericho snarled, pulling Joshua even closer, their noses practically touching. "You'll die if the Mothergates are allowed to fail. The Taxonomer has been lying to you all. Why did you let him escape?"

And then Joshua saw a startling thing, deep in the Mordin's dark eyes, on the edges of the black rage that burned there. It was in his voice too, Joshua realized. A shiver of something unsteady and unfamiliar.

Fear.

For all his taunting and raging, all his awful threats and sinister plans, Dr. Jericho, Ja'raka Sevlo, was afraid.

He didn't want to die.

Joshua's realization must have bled onto his face, because

Dr. Jericho drew back angrily. Then the Mordin released him, practically tossing him aside. Joshua fell heavily to the floor, clutching at his throat.

Dr. Jericho clenched his fists, and the golems that surrounded them parted. In the room beyond, Ingrid and the sharp-eyed Mordin stood there watching, full of alarm. Past them, Isabel had risen onto her haunches, still trying to catch her breath. Grooma had wandered away from her, Aored glowing dimly in his chest, his blank eyes still on the chamber roof.

"They're coming closer," Ingrid called. "The Ravids—"

Dr. Jericho held up a hand, silencing her. Faintly, through the rattle of the golems, Joshua could hear the battle still raging. Coming closer. Something or someone roared furiously—an Altari? And then a familiar tearing sound, like a giant sheet of paper being torn in two.

The Humour of Obro. Gabriel *was* here.

"You heard the truth tonight, Joshua," Dr. Jericho repeated, his voice low and full of sullen rage. "And here is another."

He clasped his hands together. The golems to either side of him surged forward and became one, like two flocks of birds mingling into a single massive cloud, big as a building. The huge new mass began to ripple and heave, assuming the loose shapes of predatory beasts, shifting swiftly from one colossal form to another, suggestive but never explicit—a shape like a tiger, a dragon, a wolf, a raptor—pulsing and rippling with power. Each one seemed to seethe with the desire to crush and kill.

Dr. Jericho looked back at Joshua. "You live because we need you. I freely admit it. But the so-called friends who come for you now?" He smiled his savage smile and spoke slowly, seeming to taste each wicked word as it left his mouth. "Them I *do not need*."

CHAPTER SEVEN

Approaching Thunder

THE CONCRETE TUNNELS BENEATH THE HELL PIT WERE DARK and silent. The Riven were here, all right—Chloe could smell the brimstone, but it was faint. This place wasn't a nest. A nest meant a crucible dog, and a crucible dog meant hypnotizing green fire, sulfurous and maddening. This place, with its abandoned man-made corridors, smelled mostly of mold and wet stone and stale water.

And yes, brimstone.

Chloe had pulled out her jithandra, setting it aglow. It dangled from the chain around her neck, a shining red crystal set in a silver flower. The Alvalaithen hung just above it, looking bloody in the red light, its wings a fluttering blur that filled her with song. She was ready for anything. They were all ready.

Dailen led the way downward—the real Dailen, or at least

the original Dailen, the one who held the compass that would point them to Mr. Meister. Chloe couldn't see the young Altari up ahead because Gabriel was next in line, carrying the Staff of Obro, and he'd released the humour. The humour, a featureless gray cloud on the inside and a terrible place to be, couldn't been seen at all from the outside, appearing instead as a wrinkle of unsight. Chloe's eyes slipped queasily across it whenever she tried to look straight ahead, so she kept her gaze elsewhere. The rest of the group walked with her, including seven other Dailens, each identical. They were all Dailen, all the same consciousness, all aggravatingly handsome. Beautiful, actually, even if Chloe hated her mind for conjuring up the word. It was easier not to think it, though, with Teokas gliding effortlessly at her side, *beyond* beautiful.

Behind them, Ravana held her bow at the ready, and giant Go'nesh had his Fairfrost Blade. These two had also revealed their jithandras, and their light mingled with Chloe's—somber bronze from Ravana and a bluish silver from Go'nesh. The Altari's jithandras were larger than those from the Warren, and set in a cluster of bare black branches, but they seemed to work the same. The light of the three jithandras cast dozens of shadows along the smooth walls, as if a horde were passing. Chloe wasn't much for teams, but right now she felt pretty fierce, pretty happy not to be alone. This was a proper war party.

"Don't look at Thailadun, by the way," Teokas said suddenly. She wiggled her hand, indicating the mysterious Tan'ji that dangled from her wrist. "I'll try to be careful when I unveil it, but you should make an effort not to look."

"Why?" Chloe asked. "Will I turn to stone or something?"

Teokas shrugged, somehow managing to make the gesture look flirtatious. "Not permanently," she said, her voice like silken petals. "But it's not fun."

Chloe was mulling that over when the seven Dailens, who'd been marching in lockstep, suddenly stopped all in the same instant. If he wanted to, Dailen could have made each version of himself do or say its own thing—his consciousness flickering from one to the next faster than the frames of a film—but Chloe gathered it was rather easier for him to not bother, to let them all move in unison as they were now.

It was also creepy as all get-out.

"Stairs," the Dailens said quietly, seven voices hissing into the hallway. Seven pairs of eyes gleamed, platinum halos shining around black irises. "To the left and the right. I can't tell from the compass which way is best."

"Let us split up," said Ravana.

"Fine," the Dailens said, and all seven of them stepped to the right in perfect synchrony. As they stepped, they doubled, and another row of Dailens materialized. Now there were fourteen Dailens in the hallway, plus the original, somewhere ahead beyond the humour. Chloe remembered that fifteen was the maximum Dailen could manage. There were sixteen flat tiles on Floriel, Dailen's Tan'ji, a segmented band he wore low around his throat. But apparently one of the sixteen copies he could make of himself—variants, he called them—had been killed at some point. And when a variant died while Dailen's consciousness was still inside, it never came back.

And neither did a tiny part of Dailen himself.

Their little band, no longer so little, briefly discussed how to proceed. In the end, Chloe, Teokas, Ravana, and eight of the Dailens took the stairs on the left. The remaining seven Dailens took the stairs to the right, along with Gabriel and Go'nesh.

The stairs were slippery, damp planks of wood. Ravana took the lead, stalking down the steps three at a time, as wary and limber as a panther. Chloe followed farther behind, among the Dailens, starting to feel impatient. Left to her own devices, she could have simply dropped down onto the next level whenever and wherever she chose, swimming through concrete and steel and wood. But the Altari seemed to have their own way of doing things, smooth and practiced, and she didn't want to bump them out of their groove.

Not yet, anyway.

She poked the Dailen in front of her, effortlessly willing her ghostly finger to jab him instead of enter him. When he turned to look at her, she said, "Are you the real Dailen?" She'd lost track in the hallway above, as they'd split into two groups.

"Absolutely," Dailen said.

"Me too," said the Dailen behind her.

Then the eight Dailens spoke one by one, whispering

a swift series of words in turn, a single word each from the front of the line to the back. The sentence swept past her as it formed: "There's no such thing as an unreal Dailen."

Several steps ahead, Teokas said, "He doesn't want us to know. If *we* know which Dailen is the original, the Riven might figure it out. We'd rather they didn't."

The Dailens nodded. "*I'm* Spartacus," they all said together.

Chloe laughed, and then frowned. Where would an Altari learn a joke like that?

They reached the bottom of the stairs. The stink of brimstone had grown stronger. The passageway opened up into a wide-open space—vast, judging by the echoes of their footsteps on the concrete floor. Exposed steel girders, thick as a man, ran from floor to ceiling at widely spaced intervals, extending into the darkness like a machined forest.

The Dailens spread out warily. They moved as individuals now, each one distinct—watching, listening, standing, creeping. Chloe thought back to the meadow where she and Horace had first met Dailen, and how he'd single-handedly—well, not *really* single, but with no one's help but his own—managed to hold off Dr. Jericho and a small army of Mordin. A rush of adrenaline filled her, and her confidence grew even stronger. They were going to wreck this place, and get Mr. Meister out of here. And maybe Joshua too, and maybe even—

Music pierced through the gloom, encasing them. A flute, distant but thickly present. Chloe clenched her teeth as

Ingrid's song crept across her skin, knowing her. Finding her.

"What is it?" Ravana cried. She swiped at her ear as if she could brush the flute's tune away. "It clings to me."

"Go toward it," Chloe said, not at all sure it was the best plan, but sure she wouldn't do anything else. "They know we're here, and they know where we are. They'll come find us if we wait. Run toward it, fast as you can—don't give them time to think."

She thought she would have to explain more, but the Dailens were already running, headed deeper into the room as fast as a horse, into the music. Ravana sprinted after them, quickly disappearing into the gloom.

Teokas watched them go. Her pretty nose was wrinkled with disgust, as if the creeping notes of the flute were like insects on her skin. She glanced down at Chloe worriedly. "Our friends have forgotten you don't have the legs of an Altari," she said. "How will you keep up?"

"How will *you*?" Chloe said, and she dove into the floor.

Dark beyond dark, and silence. The only sound came from inside her now, Ingrid's song replaced by the swelling music of the Alvalaithen, a symphony. The concrete was cool and gritty through her flesh. Chloe held her breath and willed herself forward, propelling herself through the stone. Truth be told, she didn't know how fast she could move down here. Faster than she could run, for sure, but also she believed— *knew*—that she could go faster still.

And faster still.

She pushed with what felt like every atom of her body. How many atoms? Billions, probably. Billions of billions. Horace might know. But it didn't matter—it *wasn't* matter. Not completely. The path was easy for her, as if the dragonfly gave her a way to be both elsewhere and here, every obstacle removed except those from which she could leap, onward and onward.

Chloe rose, breaching the floor like a dolphin, briefly going airborne. The Dailens thundered up ahead, and Ravana too. She was catching them. She plunged back into the cool sea of the floor, straining. More speed, a trillion tiny thrusting footholds, and then another breach. She was nearly among the sprinting Altari now. She flew on, ever faster, but when she breached for a third time, the air was filled with screeches and cries. She rolled, somersaulting. She skipped clumsily to a halt, keeping herself afloat atop the stone floor.

Ingrid's music had stopped. But around her, a battle raged.

The Ravids had found them. Dozens, it felt like, but it was impossible to count. No bigger than humans, the hideous creatures flickered in and out, fizzling from sight only to reappear several feet away, scampering on all fours and screeching with their foul, toothy mouths. The Dailens—larger by far but outnumbered—were wrestling with them, throwing them to the ground and tossing them aside, grappling at their throats.

With a *whuf*, a Ravid burst into existence right in front of Chloe. It swiped at her, screeching, but she was still thin. She felt its cold, sharp claws pass through her belly, her spine.

She stepped through the creature, whirling, letting the Ravid stagger past. Just as it spun to try her again, a great *thwang!* rang out. On the instant, a bolt of molten red, finger thick and four feet long, materialized inside the Ravid's body, protruding from its chest. The Ravid burst into flame. Panicking, it vanished with a hiss and reappeared twenty feet off, screaming and scuttling away, still on fire.

Ravana stood to one side of the fight, standing tall in the bronze glow of her own jithandra. Her attention was already elsewhere. She pulled back her great bow, Pinaka, again, and another bolt of red fire blazed to life on its string. She loosed it, and the massive arrow, like a rod of melted steel, vanished. In the same instant, forty feet away, another Ravid burst into flame as the arrow blossomed deep in its belly, flightless and faultless.

Suddenly Teokas was at Chloe's side, puffing. "Earthwing indeed," she said breathlessly.

"I can't fight," Chloe said, furious with herself that she hadn't brought a weapon of some kind. But none had been offered, or even mentioned.

Teokas laughed. "The invincible girl who thinks she cannot fight. But she cannot lose, can she?"

A Ravid materialized on their left with a soft burst. Teokas spun toward it as it leapt, raising her hand, Thailadun dangling from her wrist. Just as Chloe remembered she wasn't supposed to look at it, a corona of white light exploded from the little black sphere, stabbing at her eyes. This was the view from the backside of the Moondoor as Teokas unveiled it, and even from here Chloe felt a tiny dizzy swoon, as if she had lost a moment of awareness. Meanwhile the Ravid, caught in the full brilliance of the Moondoor like a possum in headlights, instantly froze. It hung in the air, its black eyes now utterly white.

One of the Dailens darted over to the hanging Ravid, shielding his eyes from Thailadun. Teokas closed the Moondoor, letting it go dark. Immediately Dailen grabbed the bewildered Ravid and slammed it viciously to the ground.

"You froze him," Chloe said.

"Time slows to a crawl in the light of Thailadun," Teokas said. "But there are limits." Her jithandra was hanging free now, Chloe saw. It shone like a sapphire, brilliant blue. Just like Horace's.

Ravana cried out.

Mordins had joined the battle. Six of them, two full hunting packs. One of them leapt at a Dailen who was wrestling with a Ravid, lunging for his throat. The Dailen, caught by surprise, winked out of sight. Not dead, Chloe knew. Just taken out of play before it could be harmed. Soon enough, another Dailen would split into two, and the lost variant would return to the battle.

But where was the real Dailen? And where were Go'nesh and Gabriel?

A Mordin charged at them. Teokas stepped into it and spilled the light of the Moondoor into its snarling face, freezing him.

Chloe watched the Mordin's eyes, chillingly still. If time was slowed almost to a halt for him, everything around him must seem to be moving crazily fast. Right? And what were the limits to Thailadun's powers? Obviously Teokas couldn't freeze the whole room, or she would have done it already.

Chloe's head ached trying to make sense of it. This was more Horace's territory, not hers. "I'm going down," she said. "I can't help here. I'm going to find Mr. Meister."

"You can't go alone," the nearest Dailen said.

"Pretty sure you can't go with me," Chloe replied. Briefly she released the Alvalaithen, catching her breath, and then filled herself with its song once again. She began sinking into the floor. She shrugged at Teokas, whose face looked caught between worry and approval. "Besides," Chloe told her. "I'm invincible."

Into the cold stone again. She headed downward. She quickly left the concrete behind, moving into damp, hard-packed earth. For a moment, her old fear grabbed hold of her. The earth was a bottomless sea into which she could sink. A literal world to get lost in. And truth be told, she didn't know for sure that she needed to go down to find Mr. Meister. But her experience with the Riven told her that the deeper the secret, the deeper it was buried. And so she would search. She could hold her breath for nearly four minutes, and she could fly down here. There was nothing to fear. And Mr. Meister owed her answers.

Was that why she was so determined to find him? To get answers?

And would those answers make a difference?

She kept going down. The earth grew colder. She was just beginning to think she'd gone too far, that she'd made a mistake thinking there was passageway down here or that she could somehow find it, when she plunged into open air. She began to fall. She caught herself by her still-buried feet, arms pinwheeling. She hung there upside down like a bat, dangling by her ankles from the ceiling of a wide, rough-hewn passageway. It was obviously much older than the construction project above.

She could hear the battle still raging, down the tunnel to her right. She heard an Altari bellow—Go'nesh, no doubt— and then the unmistakable tear of the humour. To her left, meanwhile, a distant light, and voices. One particular voice, angry and sneering. Dr. Jericho.

And then thunder. The earth shook. The light at the end of the tunnel was swallowed like the sun behind a cloud. Swiftly Chloe reached up into the rock with one hand and hoisted herself back into the earth, leaving only her face sticking out.

The thunder grew. It shuddered through the bedrock inside her, rattling her bones. The golem roared through the tunnel beneath her, not like a snake but like a many-limbed beast, arms and legs writhing into existence to claw at the stone, pulling the bulk forward, and then melting back the body of the thing. And the body was . . . huge. Massive. Far bigger than any golem she'd seen. It tore at the tunnel walls as it passed, leaving a trail of dust and rubble. Chloe glimpsed a flash of red, a cruel-looking crystal the size of a fish, darting through the black. The heart of the golem. But then she saw another.

Two hearts.

Two golems, moving as one. And it was headed for the battle still raging up above.

After what seemed like forever, the terrible creature was past. Dr. Jericho followed in its wake, walking alone. Biting back a growl, Chloe tucked her chin into the stone, leaving just her eyes free, hoping that the Mordin wouldn't sense the Alvalaithen. She was protected, yes, the signal of her Tan'ji masked by the time she'd spent in the guarded realms of the Warren and Ka'hoka. Still, when the Mordin passed without so much as glancing up at her, she felt a flood of relief.

Briefly, she considered following him. There were things she could do to help her friends, maybe, and the golem couldn't harm her as long as she stayed thin. But if Mr. Meister was here, he had to be in the room down the corridor, where the faint light still glowed. Him, and maybe anyone else the Riven had brought here from the Warren.

Anyone who had survived.

Staying inside the stone, letting only her face break the

110

surface, she slid along the tunnel ceiling, slid toward the light—as if she were floating on her back along an upside-down river. There were soft voices. Human voices. She drew closer.

She reached the entrance to the room, a large chamber lit with dirty golden light. She saw Joshua, the Laithe floating at his side, looking miserable. Ingrid crouched before him, murmuring in a distinctly unpleasant way, her terrible white flute in her hand.

"Where did you send him, Joshua?" Ingrid was saying. "To Ka'hoka? So he can finish the terrible work the Wardens started?"

"He was hurt," Joshua said. "You were just hurting him more. I let him go."

"Letting him escape didn't change anything, Joshua," Ingrid replied. "You haven't helped a friend, because he was never your friend. All you've done is anger those who truly want to help you."

"Mr. Meister *is* my friend. You're not."

Ingrid jabbed the flute at him. "Then why didn't you go with him?" she asked scornfully.

Joshua hung his head, looking miserable, stubbornly refusing to say any more.

Chloe could hardly believe it. Mr. Meister was gone. A stupid, aimless surge of anger filled her. She tried to quash it. She'd come here with the Altari to rescue Mr. Meister, but apparently he'd already been set free by Joshua and the power of the Laithe. Why did that make her angry? Because Joshua had done their work for them?

"You believe him," Ingrid said to Joshua, mocking him. "When he says the Mothergates have to die—that we *all* have to die—you believe that?" She flung her hand back, pointing across the room. "You saw what was happening here tonight. It'll be finished soon enough, Altari or no Altari. And when it is, you think we can't fix what the Wardens say is unfixable?"

Chloe was hardly listening anymore. Where Ingrid had pointed, a third figure she hadn't noticed stood swaying woozily. Wild red hair, an arresting but scowling face.

Isabel was here. Still alive. Chloe's own mother, back from the abyss—yet again. The sight was a shock, bringing a firestorm of emotion Chloe couldn't hope to name. She was disgusted to find in the tumult a shimmer of something like relief, and she crushed it, disgusted by it. Disgusted by the mere fact of Isabel at all.

Ingrid was pleading with Joshua now, murmuring too low to hear. Chloe slid closer, until she was directly above the girl, twenty feet below.

"This can be fixed, Joshua. She can do it. We've been given this gift, and we intend to use it. Everything will be set right."

This gift. Isabel. But what kind of gift was she, and what could Isabel possibly do? The anger and disgust brewing in Chloe's belly churned, growing stronger.

"Don't you see, Joshua?" Ingrid said. The boy was

looking up at her now, his face full of hope and doubt. "I left the Wardens in order to *save* them. I mean them no harm, believe me. I want to save them from themselves." She threw a finger back at Isabel again. "And *this*," she said, spitting the word like she was talking about something scraped from the bottom of a shoe. "*This* is the way."

Chloe let herself fall. She slipped from the ceiling like a stone, like a hawk. She descended on Ingrid, her eyes on the bone-white flute in her hand.

Chloe reached out, pouring all her focus into it. She fell into Ingrid and grabbed at the flute, willing it to go thin, willing it to go with her. In a flash, she was past, and the flute came with her. Down into the dark stone underneath, too fast to even hear or see Ingrid's reaction. She went deep, so full of rage that she thought she might heat the earth around her.

She was going to let the flute go.

She was going to leave it behind, leave it melded here in the dark ground, no longer the thing it once was, its atoms intertwined irreparably with the atoms of the earth. And what would happen to Ingrid then? Dispossession, at least. Cleaving? Would she die on the spot? It would be beyond easy, come what may.

But instead Chloe held on to the flute, hardly knowing why. She flew swiftly back up to the chamber above, bursting from the ground, still clutching the flute. She released the Alvalaithen and landed on her feet, breathing hard.

Ingrid was on her feet too, her face clouded with rage.

"Don't," Chloe warned as Ingrid took a step toward her. She wiggled the flute and pointed at the floor. "I could have killed you already. Maybe someone can explain to me why I didn't do it, but I sure as hell can't promise you I still won't."

Chloe backed away, edging toward Isabel, who was kneeling now but taking no notice of them at all.

"Open a portal, Joshua," Chloe said.

But Joshua just sat there, eyes wide, staring at Chloe. "The Mothergates are going to die," he said.

"I know," said Chloe, and a jolt of confused hurt skated across Joshua's face. Chloe continued to back away. "Open a portal, and we can get out of here. We can figure it out."

"We already *are* figuring it out," said Ingrid.

"Isabel," Joshua said, as if that explained everything.

Chloe turned to her mother. Isabel looked up at her. *Still alive*, Chloe had thought when she first laid eyes on her.

But now she wasn't so sure.

Isabel looked . . . empty. Hopelessly famished. Like a soul who had lost everything she had ever been given but still wanted more, if only to give it all away again. Like a bottomless drain into which—for no other reason than to obey a hunger that could never be satisfied—every last thing might be fed.

And then Isabel looked at her, and Chloe knew that she herself, this woman's own daughter, was one of those things.

This was not her mother. Chloe had not had a mother in years.

"Chloe," Isabel said. "You're here. You've come to see."

"I came to save people who need saving," Chloe said.

Isabel nodded eagerly. "Me too. I'll save everyone. The Riven—"

And then an enormous figure stepped out of the shadows, so large that Chloe's eyes hadn't even allowed her to see it. A Riven, standing nearly to the ceiling, with arms that dragged along the floor and sagging gray skin. Buried in its chest, like a gaping wound, was an oval Tan'ji leaking faint golden light.

The Riven's pale gaze drifted over Chloe without so much as a hint of curiosity, and then fell on Isabel. A new kind of hunger seemed to light in its face, and Isabel looked up at it.

"More," she begged, staring into its eyes. Her voice was desperate and mad, making Chloe want to vomit. "Finish me, please. Fix me, and then I can show her. I can show them all."

Chloe ran. She ran before she even knew she was running, down the tunnel the way the golem had gone. She kept running even as she realized how silly it was, this running, how beneath her—she was the Keeper of the Alvalaithen. She did not *run*.

But her mother's face. The hulking beast that stood with her, the ghastly way she'd pleaded with it, begging for more. More what? It was nothing she understood, except that she had to get away.

On and on Chloe ran, down the darkening tunnel. She heard no sounds of pursuit behind her. And then, abruptly, the world disappeared. She sprinted into a sea of gray, full of dull blank light, a blindness so complete she could not even see the tip of her own nose. She stumbled on the unseen floor beneath her and went hard to the ground. The rib she'd broken the other day bit at her painfully.

"Chloe," came Gabriel's voice, filling the humour, coming from nowhere and everywhere at once. "Are you all right?"

Chloe got uneasily to her feet, shutting her eyes against the blankness of Gabriel's humour. Better no light at all than endless unsight.

"I'm fine," she said. "Fine."

"Why are you running? Is someone coming?"

"No. I don't know. Joshua's in there, and Ingrid, and . . ." She didn't know how to say more. She wondered if Gabriel could feel the heat that burned in her cheeks now.

But instead, his voice thick with shock, Gabriel said flatly, "You have Ingrid's flute."

Chloe looked stupidly down at her hand, though there was nothing to see. Gabriel, though, could feel its every detail. She rubbed a finger across the flute, testing its smoothness. It was wrong to touch another person's Tan'ji without permission, and she hated that it felt wrong even now.

"Yes," she said. "I stole it. I was going to bury it. Meld it."

"That would have killed her."

"And so?" Chloe demanded. Gabriel didn't respond, seeming to know better. "What are you doing here?" she asked him. "Where are the others?"

"Fighting, as best they can," Gabriel said. "But there's a golem, huge and—"

"I know. I saw it."

"I came to find you," he said, "I'm not much help against the golem. We need to find Mr. Meister and get everyone out of here."

"We're too late for that." Quickly she told Gabriel what she'd overheard, that Mr. Meister had already been freed.

Silence. Through the fog of the humour, she could practically hear Gabriel thinking. At last he said, "Let us go, then. What we came here to do is done. We must return to the others. They need us."

"And what about Joshua?"

"He can't be helped," Gabriel replied. "We don't even know if he *wants* to be helped."

"Don't be stupid. He got Mr. Meister out of here, didn't he?"

"So you say. Yet he did not get himself out. Again."

"You're not serious."

"The portal was open, wasn't it? If an old man with a broken leg could get out, why not the Keeper of the Laithe himself?"

Chloe fumed, hating his logic. Hating that he was probably right. And Joshua had refused to open a portal for Chloe, even when it would have been safe to do so.

"It's not easy for a Keeper to resist what the Riven

offer," Gabriel said. "They promise survival. We promise death. Ingrid left us for a reason, you know." He paused for a moment, and when his voice returned it seemed more present than ever, leaning on her heavily from all sides. "Have you not considered leaving us yourself, since you learned the truth?"

Chloe threw up her hands. "I just learned the truth, like, yesterday!"

"And I would wager there were moments yesterday when you could not have sworn you'd still be with us today."

"A moment is a moment," Chloe said, scowling. Gabriel wasn't wrong, but . . .

Gabriel wasn't wrong.

Maybe she hadn't completely swallowed the bitter pill Falo had given her, not yet. But she sure hadn't spit it out. Because after all, the Riven were the Riven, horrible in every way, and when Chloe tried to imagine trusting Dr. Jericho, her mind simply shorted out in a fiery jolt of rage. If anyone was going to tell her what to do, it certainly wasn't going to be that ten-foot freak with the rotten-egg breath and beady eyes. Even if he promised survival. And whatever that creature was in the room back there, whatever he was going to do to Isabel, even if she deserved it . . .

Chloe squeezed the flute, then tossed it aside. It clattered to the ground unseen, the sound echoing thinly inside the gray waters of the humour.

"I'm not Ingrid," she said. "Even if I'm not sure about the good guys, I know who the bad guys are."

"But Joshua may not," Gabriel said simply.

Chloe sighed. "Get me out of here, then. Take me upstairs to the others." She held out her hand. She felt Gabriel take it, warm and strong.

"It's bad, I'm afraid," he said, leading her onward at a cautious trot. "We came in force instead of stealth, and with the Riven . . ."

Chloe scowled and started to tell him that they were a war party, that they didn't simply sneak around. But here she was, the girl who walked through walls, buried in a cloud meant to hide everything from anyone.

And she said nothing, instead promising herself that she would find a way. She would turn stealth into force. She'd done nothing here tonight, saved no one.

But that was about to change.

CHAPTER EIGHT

Earthen Sky

GABRIEL LED CHLOE THROUGH THE TUNNELS, QUIETLY NARRAT-
ing the way, still holding her hand. He led her around a bend
or two, or so it seemed, and then up a slick, steep slope. Chloe
knew Gabriel couldn't see anything outside the humour—and
was utterly blind without it—but he had perfect knowledge
of everything inside it. He guided her surely, confidently, no
doubt knowing she hated it in here. He knew well enough not
to bother asking her why she didn't simply leave him, traveling on her own by way of Alvalaithen.

Chloe didn't want to be alone.

Somehow she found it easy not to think of Isabel. Much,
anyway. Instead she thought of her sister Madeline, and her
father. How when Isabel had disappeared all those years ago,
her dad had raised them on his own—badly, at times, but at
least he'd been there. And where was he now? Mrs. Hapsteade

had assured her that he'd gotten safely away from his room in the Academy, above the Warren, when the Riven attacked. Chloe wondered when she would see him again. She wondered if.

Gabriel tugged at her hand, startling her. He pulled her down to her haunches.

"We're here," he said.

For a moment Chloe thought they were too late. It was utterly silent. But then again, no sound could pierce the humour from the outside. They could have been inside a hurricane and neither of them would have known it. And now she realized—the floor was shaking beneath her feet.

Chloe nodded. She took a great breath and drank from the Alvalaithen, filling herself with its song.

"Show me," she said.

Gabriel squeezed her hand and let her go. "Tell me what you see," he said.

The humour parted.

Into a hurricane.

The great golem she'd seen below was everywhere, swirling madly across the wide-open concrete floor, clanging against the tall steel columns. It moved so swiftly, so massively, that as it swung its mighty limbs about they hissed audibly through the air. A few limp Mordin and Ravids lay strewn here and there, but others were still fighting. A handful of Dailens grappled with them, now winking out of sight, now doubling. The Ravids screeched. The Mordin roared.

She heard an Altari bellowing faintly. Chloe took another step into the room, awestruck.

Dr. Jericho was here, his back to her. He fought savagely with a pair of Dailen—now just one, now three. The bristles on the Mordin's spine had pierced his clothes, and his face was the monstrous visage Chloe had seen in the meadow, his true face, one he wasn't bothering to disguise. She saw more clearly now that he wore two of the golem's rings, one on each hand. He steered the huge, doubled golem about even as he fought, clearly directing its wrath where he could, letting it thunder on its own when he could not.

Beyond him, Ravana stood inside a transparent sphere, ten feet across and shining with light. A smallish stream of the golem circled it, pounding. The sphere was a dumin—a shield so strong, Chloe knew, that even the golem couldn't hope to break through it. But apparently Ravana's arrows could. The grim Altari fired her bow, again and again, into the swarming mass of the golem. Wherever the fiery bolts struck home, a cluster of the golem's chunks turned to hot coals and shattered, crumbling to ash. But it was far too little, far too slow, handfuls shoveled from a mountain. And the dumin was only temporary. How much longer would it last?

Go'nesh was faring better, swiping at the creature with great swings of the Fairfrost Blade, dancing deep into its thickest midst. Teokas and one of the Dailens moved with him. The Dailen had a phalanx, a wandlike Tan'kindi that

122

fired a great blast of force. Whenever he fired it, with a huge crack that slapped the air, stones went flying as if struck by a great fist. But no sooner had they scattered than they swirled together and surged forward once more.

Go'nesh was scattering stones with his blade, too—by the bucketful. But even better, buckets more of the relentless black bits were frozen inside the great curtains of glistening blue the swinging blade carved into the air. A gleaming sequence of these swaths crossed the room like painted memories of the battle Go'nesh had been waging, huge and beautiful arcs that took Chloe's breath away—boomerangs, corkscrews, sails, scythes. The golem knew well enough to avoid the blue curtains, cold as they were. At nearly absolute zero, Chloe imagined the curtains might shatter any stones that touched them.

Still, the golem managed to pour through the gaps, reaching for the Altari inside. Teokas was flashing the Moondoor at it wherever it got close, and when the ghostly white light fell upon the stones, the golem's grasping limb became a statue, if only for a moment. Dailen fired the phalanx at them when he could, blowing them back.

Chloe couldn't breathe. The scene before here was maybe the most magnificent sight she had ever seen. Magnificent and horrible. And if Horace had been here . . .

What would *Horace* have seen, through the Fel'Daera? What could he have told them about how this great clash would unfold? Because as mightily as the Altari battled the golem and the Riven now, as boldly as they fought and as beautifully they moved—like gods out of a storybook—they were losing.

Horace should have been here. Horace could have told them. The Altari were mighty, yes.

But so was Horace. And so was she.

She backed into the humour. Silence swallowed her.

"Tell me," Gabriel said. "Your heart is pounding."

And it was pounding. No doubt Gabriel could feel her pulse in her neck. But not from fear.

"Get outside," she told him. "Keep Mrs. Hapsteade safe. No need to hurry, but she'll be unprotected in a minute or two. Wait for me there. I'll bring the others."

"But what about—"

Chloe left him. She strode boldly into the room. She pulled her jithandra from her shirt and let it blaze. It burned like a ruby on fire.

Dr. Jericho turned, spotting her at last. His beady eyes locked on to hers, and his face became a crumpling fist of rage.

A huge swath of the golem swirled furiously toward Chloe, curling and rattling, deafening. It poured into her body, hammering at her—cold angry bees swarming in her flesh. It couldn't touch her, no one could. Not even Ravana's bow, not even the blue blade of Go'nesh. She kept walking. But now the golem began to tear at the ground beneath her as she walked, ruining the path in front of her, cracking the concrete under her feet and pulling up chunks of it, now great slabs of it, snapping and twisting the buried rebar there like the bones of a corpse. Soon there was nothing to walk on, but Chloe kept walking. Or not walking. She hovered inside the very flesh of the golem itself, the atoms of her body finding purchase in the golem's thick earthen sea. Or earthen sky. Maybe it didn't matter—matter was matter. She was the Keeper of the Alvalaithen, the Earthwing. This was like nothing she'd ever done before, like swimming in a deadly current, but the current couldn't touch her. She didn't want it to. One of the golem's hearts flashed past her, a vicious crimson fish.

She knew what to do. She knew how to do it.

She went up. The golem rose with her, still trying to crush her, its blind and pointless rage of course belonging to Dr. Jericho. He wore the rings. She ascended through the tornado of the golem, glancing back one last time at her brave companions fighting below. She reached the ceiling of the great room . . . and kept going. She left the swirling body of the golem behind, accelerating now. Upward and out. Stone and clay and dirt and grass and then—open air. City sounds and light. She was traveling so fast she shot high into the air, and as she peaked she thought for a moment she might hang there, or that she might keep going, just because she could. But there was something here she had to do. She let herself land in the grass, searching.

The mal'gama was a lumpy green hill, buried in shadows.

125

A small figure in a black dress stood atop it, staring, and then began running toward her.

Chloe met her halfway.

"What's happening?" Mrs. Hapsteade said. "Where are the others? I felt a tremor."

"I'm handling it," Chloe said.

"They have a golem?"

"That would be an understatement."

"What about Henry? Did you find him? What about Joshua?"

"Mr. Meister's gone," said Chloe. "Joshua saved him. He's safe—at Ka'hoka, I think."

Mrs. Hapsteade sank onto her knees in the grass.

"I need the ring," Chloe said, and she held out her hand.

"What?" Mrs. Hapsteade said.

Chloe tipped her chin at the slumbering mal'gama. "The ring," she said again.

It took her a moment, but then Mrs. Hapsteade shook her head. "No. Let me steer it, we'll take it through the halls and we'll—"

"No halls. I'm taking the short route."

Again Mrs. Hapsteade hesitated. Her eyes slid from confusion into dubious wonder, and then into a quiet resolve. Or surrender. Or disappointment. It didn't matter, as long as she gave Chloe the ring.

Mrs. Hapsteade slipped the green-stoned ring from her

hand. Taking it, Chloe slid it onto her own finger—it was big for an instant, but then suddenly it wasn't. But Chloe didn't bother to think about that for more than a second, because the mal'gama was in her mind.

The mal'gama was alive. Or not alive, but like a living extension of herself, one that could never disobey her, but that also had a mind of its own. She hurried over to it, clambering onto its furry green stones. She could feel herself walking, could feel the mal'gama responding to her movement. Taking a seat in the very middle of it, she silently asked the mal'gama to ripple, and it did, rocking her. She wanted it to lift her, and it rose into the air, cradling her gently. She didn't know quite how she was doing it—a simple matter of asking, or desiring. A laugh popped out of her. She felt the mal'gama's weight, its strength. It was mighty. Its might was her might. It wasn't the fierce machine the golem was, no, but it was just as strong. Maybe stronger. Dailen had showed her and Horace how strong, the first time she rode it. She was taking that strength now.

And Dailen had showed them another thing. How the mal'gama's stones were chiseled flat on every surface. Though far more complicated, they could stack like cubes. Perfectly. They could *tessellate* like cubes—that was the word Horace had used—into a perfect solid, with no gaps between them.

And that's what Chloe needed.

She drank deeply from the dragonfly, going thin. She

lifted her eyes to Mrs. Hapsteade, who was watching her intently from the grass.

"Do you think I can do it?" Chloe asked her.

"I am beginning to think you can do anything," Mrs. Hapsteade replied.

Chloe laughed again. "I can't see the future," she said. "But I'll meet you there."

"May yours be light," said Mrs. Hapsteade.

"Tel tu'vra fal raethen," Chloe replied. And then she gathered the mal'gama to her, bringing the stones into her body and stacking them. They rustled, strangely warm, somehow soft but diamond hard. She asked them to tessellate and they did, locking together so tightly that Chloe could only tell them apart at the level of molecules.

They filled her. The world went dark. But still she kept gathering, and through the ring she could feel the mal'gama taking shape outside her, encasing her. The mal'gama felt like an extension of her own flesh, in a way, and she wondered if this was what the Ravenvine was like for April. Swiftly the mal'gama became a solid mass, an uninterrupted monolith, as big as a whale, however big a whale was.

When it was done, when the mal'gama was packed as tight as it could go, Chloe forgot the ring and reached for the dragonfly instead. She reached out into the stones that surrounded her. She willed them to go thin, letting the Alvalaithen's song flow into them. She could do this, she knew. She'd done it to Horace—made him go thin and pulled him through the

128

supposedly impassable shield of a dumin. The mal'gama was bigger than Horace by far—she didn't even want to *know* how much bigger. She just had to know she could do it.

Slowly the mal'gama became a ghost. Stone by stone, out from Chloe at the center. She pulled hard at the Alvalaithen, pulling its power through her and out into the mal'gama, its song swelling and spreading. Her body ached with the effort, her mind growing blank to everything else. It helped that the mal'gama was utterly uniform, every atom the same. Even as she did it, she knew she could never have managed it if it had been even a fraction more complex than it was.

But somehow, through luck or talent or sheer will, she managed it. The mal'gama was a phantom vessel, no more solid than air.

And it was hers.

Down, she thought.

They went down. Into the ground, through soil and rock. The mal'gama moved sludgily at first but quickly picked up speed. Meanwhile Chloe did her best to stay motionless inside. She wasn't propelling herself now. She was inside the mal'gama, and the mal'gama was inside the earth, a nested vessel that the ring allowed her to steer. She could not bother to wonder if she'd ever done anything like this this before, or if she would ever do it again. The effort was outrageous, an unaskable thing. She had to hurry. Down and down. Concrete and steel. Damp ground.

And then, startlingly, she was there. She felt it through

the mal'gama's ring before she felt it in her own flesh. She brought the ghosted mass down into the great room with the tall metal columns, where she'd left her friends. The mal'gama brushed heavily against the steel beams, coming apart at the edges. The moment she felt its mass come entirely free from the ceiling above, she pushed its stones from her flesh, letting the mal'gama spread, coming undone and releasing her. When the last stone left her, she felt the mal'gama go solid once more. She sank from it, falling through it, and landed hard on the concrete floor below.

Her arrival—their arrival—brought the battle almost comically to a halt.

The giant golem seemed to pause and rear back, a cloud of suspended malice. Go'nesh stood among the exquisite chain of curtains he had carved, the Fairfrost Blade hanging motionless over his head, tearing at Chloe and the huge mal'gama she had brought here.

And then the golem attacked, a tidal wave. She met it with the mal'gama effortlessly, and the collision was like two trains colliding. The golem was faster, but the mal'gama was strong, yes. Dailen had showed her how strong. He had taken the heart of the masterless golem whose ring Chloe had destroyed in the meadow. He'd taken that heart and laid it down in the mal'gama's grip.

The mal'gama had crushed it into powder.

This was why she had brought it here.

But the mal'gama wasn't meant for fighting. The battle was desperate and clumsy, like trying to run on stilts. Had she been anyone other than who she was, Chloe would have been flattened in an instant, because in order to keep the mal'gama moving—searching for the golem's hearts—she couldn't keep it solid. The golem wormed its way through the cracks of the mal'gama, slick and writhing. It tore at her again, fuming and pounding. And though it couldn't harm her, the golem's assault distracted her, blinded her. She willed the mal'gama to keep fighting, to keep searching, to keep the bulk of the golem at bay, but above all to find the bloodred crystals swimming somewhere inside it. They had to be destroyed. Over the terrible din, she could hear Dr. Jericho roaring thinly. It was him she was fighting, him she had to defeat. But she could barely think, the golem an angry, clattering cloud, literally in her head.

And now Go'nesh was at her side, swinging his blade, battling the golem back. Teokas appeared an instant later, throwing the light of the Moondoor. The Dailen with the phalanx joined them, blasting holes in the golem as it circled.

And then she had it. Through the body of the mal'gama, through the ring, she felt one of the golem's hearts slashing past. She clenched her fist reflexively, willing it to bear down.

The fiery heart imploded audibly, crumbling into red ash.

On the instant, half of the black stones surging about them dropped out of the air like black hail, clattering lifeless to the floor with a great crash. One half of the great twinned golem was dead. Chloe caught sight of Dr. Jericho now, through the thinned arms of the beast that remained. He roared in anger, ripping one of the black rings from his finger and flinging it aside. The other Riven cried out now too, and some began to turn and run.

Go'nesh surged into the belly of the remaining golem, swinging his Tan'ji with brutal, musical grunts. Ribbons of blue sliced at it, captured it, shattered it. He was heading for Dr. Jericho. Chloe brought the mal'gama together over his head and beat back the golem with him, grasping at the golem's flesh and crushing huge bites of it in the mal'gama's irresistible grip.

"Ji'an fura!" Go'nesh bellowed. He swung the Fairfrost Blade down like a hammer at the golem, swinging it so hard it plunged into the floor. The floor cracked asunder, crumbling around the sickle of frozen blue that bloomed inside it. Go'nesh swung at the blue arc, and shockingly it shattered beneath the new one that now formed, spraying bits of itself across the room like blue meteors. Some of them struck a nearby Mordin, and it clutched its face, screaming, fleeing. *"Ji kentu, Raka!"* Go'nesh shouted. *"Tu'landa mi gom'ra."*

Chloe brought great fists of the mal'gama down on either side of the raging Altari as he stormed onward toward Dr. Jericho, shaking the floor like it was made of paper. Her muscles burned, and her teeth ached from grinding.

Dr. Jericho just stood there, heaving. He cast his angry eyes about the room, at the thousands of dead golem stones scattered everywhere, at the cracked floor and crumbling ceiling, at the dozens of Riven lying helpless all about. Then he stood tall and lifted a hand, pointing at Chloe through the wreckage, through the thinning boughs of the golem.

"You are the progeny of your own savior, Tinker," he snarled, "though you do not yet know it. Do not bother to come and thank me when it is done." Then he smiled his savage smile. "I will come for you."

He turned, and ran. The golem withdrew, swirling, after him. The few Riven remaining—those still able to walk—followed him into the darkness and out of the room.

For a moment, Chloe thought she would go after him. She would muster the mal'gama again and take it down to the chamber where she'd left her mother. She would rescue that woman from the terrible beast that loomed over her, even though Isabel was beyond saving. She would save Joshua too, even if he didn't want to be rescued.

But the will wasn't there. Nothing was there. She collapsed, and the world seemed to go away. For a moment she thought she had fainted, but no—it was just this new quiet, the golem no more than a distant rumble now. She tried not to think about where it was going, about who waited for Dr. Jericho in the tunnels below. She tried not to think about whether it was right to go after Isabel, or right to never try again.

A Dailen knelt in front of her. He cupped her chin. Chloe held out her hand, the one with the mal'gama's ring. "I can't do it anymore."

"You don't have to." The Dailen took the ring from her finger and placed it on his own, where it fit him perfectly.

"There was a creature, down below," Chloe began. "Huge. He had a . . ." She circled her hand over her chest, trying to indicate what she'd seen. "And my mom—" She choked on the word, unable to go on.

"Your mother is here?"

Chloe squeezed her eyes shut. A trickle of stupid water ran down her cheek. "No," she said, waving the truth away. What even was the truth anymore? "But Mr. Meister escaped. Joshua got him out."

Concern swam briefly in his golden-ringed eyes, but then he nodded. "I assumed as much," he said, and he pulled the silver compass from his pocket. This was the real Dailen. Or they were all real. Did it matter? It did matter. He was so pretty, even now. "The needle won't budge," he said, showing her, "no matter how I move. Wherever he is, he's far from here."

"Ka'hoka."

"Let us find out." And then he picked her up. Chloe caught a glimpse of Floriel, his Tan'ji, peeking from under his high collar. Two of the black slabs that hung from the necklace had gone stark white, the golden symbol that adorned them erased. Permanently erased. Only thirteen now. Chloe realized she was crying.

"I think we helped," she tried to tell him. "The rescue—I don't think Joshua would have had a chance to do it if we hadn't been here."

Dailen smiled. "And if *you* hadn't been here . . ."

But if he ever finished the sentence, Chloe couldn't say, because she sagged into an exhaustion she'd never felt before—not even after crawling from the burning wreckage of her own home, or being severed for a full day. Everything that happened next became a blur.

The mal'gama, easing slowly upward through the maze of hallways with the Altari. Their brave little band—so much smaller now—emerging into the bottom of the hell pit, under the city sky. Rising up to gather Gabriel and Mrs. Hapsteade. Climbing into darkness and wind.

They flew on for however long it was, away from the city. Chloe lay on her side, her cheek pressed against the blanket of the mal'gama. At some point she looked up, suddenly startled by a memory she didn't have.

"Where's Ravana?" she said.

But Teokas only stroked her hair. "Shh," she said. "Rest now." And she hummed a tune so lovely and strange that Chloe knew she would always recall never being able to remember it.

Hours later, or minutes, or days, the mal'gama brought them down onto thick grass and a grove of quiet trees. Chloe didn't want to move. Her bones hurt, and her head was milk.

The stars were out now. They had always been out. The clouds had found another place to sleep. Her father lifted her again easily, tall and strong. Or no, not her father—Dailen.

A man with white hair was here. Sitting in the grass. Chloe blinked at him, utterly lost, until at last a sliver of her senses came back to her. Mr. Meister. Ka'hoka. They had come back, and so had he. Joshua had let him come here.

Mrs. Hapsteade hurried over to the old man, crouching down at his side. They murmured quietly to each other. His glasses glinted in the dark. Somehow, he'd gotten the oraculum back.

"You've traveled far to find me," Mr. Meister said. "By the Loom, I am glad you've returned."

"And you, Taxonomer," Teokas said kindly, squatting before him and bowing her head. "How badly are you hurt?"

"No worse than I was, in the body. But I—" He spotted Chloe.

Chloe slapped Dailen's chest, fidgeting softly. Gently Dailen lowered her to the ground. She stood before Mr. Meister, her legs trembling.

"My mother," she said.

"I saw her," he said. "Please forgive me."

"What did they do to her?"

"Something that should not have been," he said. "My own ill deeds come back to haunt us. Please forgive me." Then he seemed to gather himself, and he looked around at them all.

"I must speak to Sil'falo Teneves," he said. "A fiendish

deed is under way. Your arrival in the city tonight interrupted it, but only temporarily. I fear that deed will soon be done." He kept his voice firm, but his eyes were wild and frightened. "And when it is, our long vigil may collapse. The end of everything, as we feared, may well be at hand."

PART TWO

The Corners of the Earth

CHAPTER NINE

The Great Council

THE PROVING ROOM WAS PACKED. HORACE WASN'T PARTICU-larly happy about it. And judging by the look on her face, Chloe was something far less than happy. Not even angry—which, for her, sometimes *was* a kind of happiness. She looked sort of broken, to be honest, her eyes focused inward in a way Horace had never seen before, sad and weary and . . . else-where. He knew she had fresh new scars from what she'd done the night before. Scars he couldn't see.

Though daylight never reached the buried halls of Ka'hoka, the lights that ebbed and flowed with the cycle of the sun indicated that it was early afternoon. Even without them, Horace knew it was just past 12:34. A rather likeable time, on any ordinary day.

Today was not one of those days.

The entire Wardens' Council was here—all except

Ravana, fallen in the battle. Her chair at the Council table was left empty, and Go'nesh sat beside it, looking huge and desolate and grim. Teokas was as beautiful as ever in a gleaming white robe, but her face was dark with sadness. Judging by the wardrobe choices Horace had seen today, white was a color of mourning among the Altari. In fact, someone had given Chloe a white flower shaped like a star, and she'd tucked it into her thick black hair. It made Horace's stomach flutter, for some reason.

The rescue party had returned in the early morning hours, bringing Mr. Meister with them. The old man's leg was broken, but somehow he was still wearing the oraculum, his Tan'ji. Horace could only assume that his other Tan'ji—as well as the polymath's ring, which gave him the unusual ability to bond with more than one instrument at a time—were lost forever.

Once Chloe was alone in the room she shared with Horace and April, she hadn't wanted to talk. It was clear she was bone weary. But when she learned that Falo had spilled secrets while she was gone, she had insisted on hearing them. Horace and April told her some of what Sil'falo Teneves had revealed, as simply as they could. Not everything. Not the bits Horace couldn't yet bring himself to say out loud—the bits about the Fel'Daera.

They explained the multiverse. They told her why the Mothergates had to die, about the many universes that would be utterly destroyed if the Mothergates remained open, including their own. Chloe had brooded through the explanation, listening intently but not asking a single question. When they were done, she'd simply said: "I just need to know what I'm fighting for. Now I know."

Then she'd laid back in the bed and closed her eyes, the Alvalaithen gleaming faintly at her throat. A few minutes later she said softly, "I didn't save everyone."

"Who didn't you save?" April asked her.

"Lots of people. Somewhere between three and infinity, apparently. I guess you'll find out more tomorrow."

And now it was tomorrow. Since waking, Horace had learned what Chloe had done the night before, in the tunnels under the hell pit. He'd never liked that place, and wasn't at all surprised to learn that the Riven lurked beneath it. But the story he heard about Chloe—not from Chloe, naturally, but from Dailen and Mrs. Hapsteade—was utterly shocking. Almost beyond belief. The tale had been floating through the halls of Ka'hoka all morning, spreading in tones of wonder. Taking charge of the huge mal'gama, and making it go thin. Bringing it down through the solid earth to save the others. It frightened Horace a little, the kind of fear that pulled him closer to her instead of chasing him away. Maybe *that* was why his heart was fluttering.

But when he'd tried to mention the mal'gama to Chloe, she'd said, "I *believe* in what *happened*, Horace. And I could never tell anyone a story that would make them understand either one of those things. Not even you."

It was as mysterious a thing as she could have possibly said. April seemed to understand it completely, but Horace still hadn't puzzled it out. But maybe he didn't have to. Maybe he just had to accept it.

Here in the Proving Room now, many eyes were on Chloe. But even more were on Mr. Meister. It was his story everyone had come to hear. Mal'brula Kintares sat next to him at the Council's table, frowning like a Scrooge. Horace wasn't sure Brula could help it—he even frowned when he smiled. Falo and Dailen were here too, and every single one of the human Wardens. Horace, Chloe, April, and Brian sat together in a row, and Gabriel and Mrs. Hapsteade sat in front. Neptune sat alone, away from the others, rooted firmly in her seat. And there were two or three dozen more attendees, too, mostly Altari. Though far from the entire population of Ka'hoka, it was still quite a crowd. Seats had been brought in to accommodate everyone, with the humans' legs dangling from the tall chairs.

Up front, a low, wide bowl sat before Brula—his Tan'ji, named Veritas. Anyone who told a lie while gazing into its smooth green waters would find that the lips of their reflection would refuse to move. Brula would sense it. Horace wondered if Brula had any plans to make use of Veritas today.

But the first order of business, apparently, was to honor Ravana. Go'nesh rose, bowing to her empty seat. Then he sang, low and slow, his voice so deep it rumbled in Horace's chest.

"Ji'ro kothra do Ravana,
Ravana kothru nahro du.
Tel ji'ro dansu fal ka raethen."

The gathered Altari sang the last line back to him in unison: *"Tel ji'ro dansu fal ka raethen."*

"Light," Chloe murmured sadly.

"What did you say?" Horace asked. But Chloe only shook her head.

Go'nesh sat heavily. Brula bowed to him.

"Thank you, Go'nesh," Brula said. "We must now speak of our vigil, here at the end of things. We do not ask if we are still one. We are here. We do not sunder."

The crowd then took up the words. "We do not sunder," the Altari intoned meaningfully. Heads nodded earnestly all around the room. Wise, sad eyes. Committed eyes. Not for the first time, Horace considered what it would be like to have lived with the truth of the Mothergates all his life. Maybe that was why the mourning of Ravana had passed so swiftly. Nearly everyone in the room was a Keeper, every one of them likely to die once the Mothergates closed for good. Nonetheless they were here, fighting to ensure that the Mothergates did close, for the sake of billions of others, billions of billions, who would never even know the sacrifice that had been made. But this morning, wandering the halls of Ka'hoka with the new knowledge Falo had given him, Horace had come to understand that the Altari did not see it as a sacrifice. Most of them, anyway.

Instead, they saw it as a way of righting a wrong they themselves had created. Tangles between universes, created by the Tanu they wielded. A vast patch of the multiverse, forced to forget itself. There was a duty to correct it.

Dailen had put it to him best, just that morning. "Whether the Mothergates stay or go, either way, we die," he'd explained. "Do we force multitudes of innocents to go down with the ship we ourselves set afire?"

"But what if you're wrong?" Horace had countered. "What if the ship isn't on fire?"

"We are not wrong," Dailen had replied, touching his collar. "Floriel herself admits it. And to deny what our Tan'ji tell us is to deny ourselves, is it not? To deny it, is to be one of the Riven. That is what makes them who they are."

Horace reached out for the presence of the Fel'Daera now, unsure whether he could feel the tangled sickness of the Medium. The Fel'Daera itself wasn't sick, no. It was as magnificent as ever, a beacon of pure and astonishing function, powerful and true.

But he now knew that it left a trail of fire in its wake that burned as bright as any Tan'ji that had ever been made. There were wrongs that had to be righted. And if he had to die, he would not die until they were.

Mr. Meister began to speak. He looked tiny at the table beside the Altari, particularly since he could not stand. And without his red vest, he hardly seemed the man he had been before.

"Thank you for gathering here, my friends," he said. "Many of you have already heard pieces of the tale that unfolded last night. I come before you now to tell you my piece, a piece that has dire consequences for us all. Last night I learned that our vigil is in danger." He cleared his throat, clearly nervous. "The Kesh'kiri have a Dorvala, and—"

Brula cut him off. "This we already know," he said. "The Keeper of Aored, the third. Hardly a danger. No Dorvala so weak could ever hope to delay the deaths of the Mothergates."

Mr. Meister nodded in acquiescence. "Your wisdom shines," he said. "I saw as much myself. But the Dorvala has a talent—this I also saw." The old man paused, as if speaking the next words would pain him. "He is a flesh-weaver."

Brian, sitting next to Horace, inhaled sharply. In the audience behind him, faint noises of disgust and dismay erupted.

"They call him Grooma," Mr. Meister called out. "He is adept at weaving the medium into flesh and bone, at making Tanu out of living beings. A forbidden practice, yes, but . . ." He trailed off, clearly finding it difficult.

"Tell the tale, Henry," Mrs. Hapsteade prompted.

Mr. Meister cleared his throat. "More than with ordinary Tanu, the power of a Tanu made from flesh is dependent upon the nature of that flesh—the nature of the vessel into which the Medium is woven."

Brian was leaning forward in his seat now, straining to hear. On Horace's other side, Chloe had barely moved.

"And therein lies the danger," Mr. Meister continued, "because the Riven have in their possession—they have taken into *captivity*—a very powerful vessel indeed."

Suddenly Horace understood. Tingling dread crept from his chest down his arms. He looked at Chloe again, and her eyes darted at him briefly. She knew this story already—had perhaps even witnessed it herself. He pushed his foot gently against hers. She kicked it away.

"Her name is Isabel," Mr. Meister said, confirming Horace's worst fears. "She is a Tuner . . . a very powerful Tuner. When the rescue party arrived last night, they interrupted Grooma at work on Isabel. I witnessed this work with my own eyes." He pointed to the oraculum, almost apologetically. "With Grooma's help, the Riven seek to turn Isabel into something that has never existed. There is no word for what I saw being done in the pits of the city last night. If Grooma succeeds—and I have no reason to think he will not—Isabel will become an instrument unto herself, an instrument powerful enough to force the Mothergates to remain open."

A voice from farther back in the room spoke up, thin and reedy. "Her body will be her Tan'ji? Is that what you're saying?"

"Isabel will not be Tan'ji," said Mr. Meister. "Nor a Tuner, either. She will be a new thing. Consider the talents she already had. Consider the—" He squeezed his eyes shut and swallowed. "Consider the wounds left by the kaitan when she was made a Tuner, from which the essence of that talent still drips. Grooma aims to stitch those wounds, to turn them round upon themselves, to create a knotted nest of power within Isabel herself. She will need no harp, no instrument. She will be immune to severing, to cleaving, to dispossession. But above all, she will have the strength to make happen that which must not happen."

"Isabel is a powerful Tuner, you say," said Brula now, glaring at Mr. Meister. "How powerful? What would she have been, if not for the kaitan?"

Mr. Meister lifted his head high, trembling but defiant. "A Dorvala."

A Maker. Isabel. The room broke into talk, shouts and murmurs, musical sighs of disbelief. Horace looked over at Chloe, alarmed. She sank deeper into her seat, refusing to look at him. Farther down the row, his mom sat like a statue, but her eyes were wide with shock. She'd been in that kaitan with Isabel, all those years ago. Tuners were always made in pairs. His mother would have become an empath, like April—though far weaker—but apparently she had not known the truth about Isabel.

Abruptly Neptune got up from her seat. She walked instead of floated, pushing hurriedly down the row past Horace. Mrs. Hapsteade watched her silently, and Gabriel twisted the Staff of Obro between his hands. Neptune swept stiffly from the room.

But no one else even seemed to notice. Horace struggled

to listen as the room teemed with argument, as Mr. Meister explained his reasons for turning Isabel into a Tuner when she could have become a Dorvala instead. She was uncontrollable, he argued—full of rage, sure to reject the truth about the Mothergates when it was finally revealed. How could a person like Isabel be asked to accept that the Mothergates must close, and that she herself must die in order to save countless universes? Some Keepers were willing to accept the truth about the Mothergates, and some were not.

Horace knew in his heart that Mr. Meister was right. Isabel was not. How could he have handed such a person the power to force the Mothergates to remain open?

But then again, how could he have done what he did?

Chloe murmured under her breath, so low Horace had to lean closer to hear. She said, "If *I* had come to them with the potential to become a Dorvala, instead of what I am, do you think Mr. Meister would have put me in the kaitan too?"

"You're not your mother, you idiot," he said, surprised at the sudden anger that flared up inside him.

And to his even greater surprise, Chloe laughed.

Falo spread her arms. So regal did she look, so full of wisdom, that the hubbub in the room died down at once.

"Friends," she said. Her voice filled the Proving Room like a peaceful wind, like the scent of sleep. "Fellow Keepers. We can lament the actions of the Chief Taxonomer endlessly, if we so desire. We can imagine we would have done differently in his place. We can conjecture, I suppose, where we would now stand had he not done what he did." She bent her head, seeming to pity the crowd. "We can wonder if we would still be standing at all. But that is not the issue before us. What is done is done. There is a question before us now, the gravest question we have ever faced." She leaned into the room, her face like a vengeful angel. *"What do we do?"*

"We must stop her," Go'nesh growled at once. "But this is an enemy I do not know how to fight."

"The question," Teokas said, "is how Isabel might proceed, once the powers you describe have become real."

"They may be real already," Mr. Meister interjected. "She will need a day or two to recover once the weaving is done, but our time is short."

"All the more reason to ask, then," said Teokas. "What will Isabel do, and how do we stop her?"

Falo tapped her chin, seeming to ponder the question deeply. "To actually weave the knots that would keep a Mothergate open, I believe Isabel would have to be standing in front of that Mothergate. Do you agree, Keeper?"

Horace elbowed Brian gently. It was him Falo spoke to now, her gaze finding him in the crowd.

"Oh!" Brian said, looking up, clearly shocked to be asked. "Well, if *I* were trying to force a Mothergate to stay open, I'd need to see it, yes. But I mean . . . I'm not exactly super awesome."

Horace leaned into him. "That's pretty much the opposite of what you said about yourself the first time I met you," he whispered.

Brian shrugged and glanced at Chloe, still sagging blankly in her chair. "I was trying to exude confidence," he whispered back.

"I don't know that I qualify as *super awesome* either," Falo said. "But I could not force a Mothergate to remain open without standing directly in its presence. And if we two Dorvalas cannot do it, we must hope Isabel will not be able to, either."

"But that means she has to find the Mothergates first," said Dailen. "She'll never manage it in time."

"She already knows where they are," Horace's mom called out. "Or at least, she can feel them calling. *I* can feel them. I've always been able to feel them, ever since—" Her eyes flicked to Mr. Meister. "Since I was young."

Horace thought back to that day in his kitchen at home when his mother had revealed her powers. It felt like years ago. She'd mentioned the Mothergates and had pointed straight at them, even straight through the center of the earth, to the far side of the globe. She had pointed unerringly in the direction of Ka'hoka, he realized now, long before Horace even knew Ka'hoka existed.

Horace cleared his throat. "Where are the other Mothergates, exactly?" he asked.

Brula scowled. "The location of the Mothergates is a secret only—"

"Australia," Falo said, cutting him off breezily. "One of them is in Australia, deep in the central highlands. The other is in Crete."

For some reason, this news hit Horace like a splash of cold water. The Mothergates were real, of course—he'd seen one—but somehow knowing that the other two were in actual places, places that could be traveled to and named, made the entire endeavor seem suddenly concrete. No longer an imagined thing unfolding in imagined places, but a real thing happening now, even if it was happening in places that were far away. Australia. And Crete—that was an island, he was pretty sure, somewhere near Greece.

Suddenly a terrible thought occurred to him. "Joshua," he said out loud.

Falo nodded. "Yes. With the Keeper of the Laithe under their sway, opening portals at their command, the Riven will be able to take Isabel to the Mothergates in no time at all."

"We don't know that Joshua is under their sway," April said, sounding distressed.

"We don't know that he isn't," said Gabriel. "But we do know that he is there, and not here."

Horace, regretfully, was inclined to agree with Gabriel. "Okay," he said. "But locating the Mothergates, getting to those locations—that's one thing. Actually standing in front of them is another. Aren't all the Mothergates buried safely away like the one here? In an Altari stronghold, protected by the Nevren? And what about the Veil of Lura?"

"Isabel can't be severed, Horace," his mother reminded him gently.

"Correct," said Mr. Meister. "And the Nevren is no obstacle to those who cannot be severed. In fact, if Grooma succeeds in planting the flows I saw him weaving last night . . ." He trailed off, shaking his head.

"As for the Veil of Lura," said Falo, "it no longer protects the Mothergates as well as it once did. Just as the sun turns red when it sets, revealing itself in a way it had not during the day, so too the Mothergates are revealing themselves now in their final days. Those who are most sensitive to the Mothergates' presence—Dorvalas, Tuners, empaths—may find themselves no longer hopelessly lost within the Veil. They may enter it and, with patience, find the Mothergate within." Her gaze seemed to light upon April. "Indeed, some have already done so."

Suddenly Chloe shot to her feet.

"Is this a game?" she demanded. Heads turned to look at her. A murmur went through the crowd. Horace heard whispers: *lai'theldra, mal'gama, Alvalaithen.* Everyone had heard the story of last night. Chloe seemed oblivious. "All these things you're saying—it's like everything's conspiring against us." She chopped her hand through the air, once for each obstacle they faced. "The Mothergates can be found. Isabel can fix them. Joshua can take her to them. The Veil can't stop her. Are you sure the universe doesn't *want* us to fail?"

Falo and Mr. Meister exchanged a look. Before either of

them could speak, though, Teokas rose elegantly from her seat.

"The universe wants nothing, Chloe," she sang. "It seeks order because it *is* order. And the Mothergates bring disorder."

Now it was Falo's turn to stand. She rose to her full height, the golden rings in her dark eyes glinting warmly as she surveyed the room, turning her gaze to Chloe.

"You say everything conspires against us," Falo said. "But it does not. *You* are here, the Keeper of the Alvalaithen. April is here, the Keeper of the Ravenvine. Horace, the Keeper of the Fel'Daera. If I were one of the Kesh'kiri, knowing all of this, I would feel the universe was conspiring against *me*."

Horace ignored the new buzz of talk that rose at the mention of the Fel'Daera. "Why?" he said. "What's so great about us?"

"Yeah," said Brian, jerking a thumb at Horace. "What's so great about these guys?"

Falo smiled at them. And in that smile, Horace understood. Falo already *knew* how they were going to stop Isabel. This was all a show—an attempt, maybe, to further strengthen the resolve of the citizens of Ka'hoka, here in the final days.

Sure enough, Falo began confidently ticking off points on her long fingers. "One, we must listen to the Mothergate here in Ka'hoka. It is the strongest of the three, and will be the last to die. Through it, a keen ear will be able to detect when the other two Mothergates are entering their final hours—or, more crucially, when an attempt is being made to repair them.

155

April Simon, will you stand with us? Will you listen, and warn us if such an attempt is being made?"

April stood. The Ravenvine glinted beneath the curtain of her auburn hair. "I'll try," she said. "You know I will."

Falo nodded. "Two, we need someone who can face Isabel without fear. I have heard of the devastation she sowed among the Riven, cleaving them one by one with nothing but a harp in her hands. And soon she will be more powerful still. As mighty as Go'nesh is, however nimble Dailen may be, no matter how cunning Teokas, we cannot send such warriors to face an enemy who would strike them down at will. We need to send a warrior that Isabel cannot *bear* to strike down. A warrior she does not truly want to defeat."

Chloe just stood there, her face practically on fire. The wings of the dragonfly were a blur. At last she threw her hands up in defeat. "I'm already standing, okay?" she said. "But I think you're overestimating the motherly love here."

Falo shook her head. "I think not," she said, even as the gathered Altari in the room were grasping what Chloe had just revealed. The big new baddie in town was her mother. Low cries of concern erupted, whispers of sympathy. Horace thought he heard someone crying, a sweet melodious croon.

Chloe spun round on the crowd. "Oh, shut up, please," she snarled. "Yes, Isabel is my mom. No, we're not close. If she's too sentimental to stop me, I promise the feeling is not mutual. And if you're feeling the urge to send me your condolences, sorry—you're like seven years too late."

She whirled back around, arms crossed furiously.

Brian whistled low.

Falo nodded at April and Chloe in turn. "One and two," she said gladly. "A sentinel. An invincible warrior." Horace's heart pounded. He was next, he knew. But he had no idea how, or why. "And now three," said Falo, ticking off another finger. "We need someone who can get us to the other Mothergates at a moment's notice, remote though they be."

"But that's Joshua," Horace protested. "Not me."

"It *is* you," Falo said. "We have no instrument like the Laithe. We cannot open a portal to anywhere we wish, and step through. But we do not *need* to go anywhere we wish. We only need to go to the Mothergates. And so we can, Horace, with your help."

"I don't understand. What does that have to do with the Fel'Daera?"

"We say there are three Mothergates," Falo explained, "as if they were three separate doors. But really they are more like cracks around the edges of a single great doorway. If you enter the Mothergate here in Ka'hoka—"

"*Enter* the Mothergate?" said Brian. "You mean actually go inside?"

"It is more like going *out*side," said Falo, "but yes. I have done it. Quite foolishly, as it turns out, but I have done it. And if you can navigate the space beyond, you will find yourself able to exit through another one of those cracks, through one of the other Mothergates."

For once, Horace found that he had no clear frame of reference for what Falo was describing. None at all. Was it like a wormhole through the Mothergate? Or like teleporting from one falkrete stone to the next? "You said it was foolish," he said. "Why?"

"Within the Mothergates, time is . . . slippery," Falo said. "It is unhinged from the flow of time we experience outside it."

Now Horace began to grasp it. Sort of. Maybe the Mothergate *was* like a wormhole after all. Falo didn't need the Fel'Daera—she needed his talents when it came to measuring time. "How slippery?" he asked. "How unhinged?"

"Very," said Mr. Meister. "And unpredictably so. Others have entered the Mothergate besides Falo. Some never returned. Others stepped out of another Mothergate halfway across the globe in mere moments, but came out madly insisting they had been trapped inside for decades. Still others took decades to reappear, but came out feeling as though no time had passed at all."

"I lost three years to the Mothergate," Falo said. "Three years that passed in an instant."

Horace and Brian exchanged a look. Like Horace, his friend was clearly enlivened by the sheer science of the thing, but he was frightened by it too.

"They want you to do *what* now?" Brian asked him.

Horace stood up. He pointedly did not look at his mom, still hovering in the doorway. "So if I'm understanding you correctly, you need me because I have a perfect sense of time." He blushed to hear himself say the word "perfect," but it wasn't wrong. He'd always been good at knowing what time it was without looking, and since becoming the Keeper of the Fel'Daera, he'd gotten even better. Absurdly better. These days, his internal clock was accurate down to a fraction of a second. "You think I can escort people safely through the Mothergates."

"No," Falo said, startling him. "I do not."

"Oh, *snap*," Brian muttered.

"Forgive me," said Falo, "but one does not make an instrument like the Fel'Daera without having a decent sense of time herself. Time *and* space. Thus my arrogance, entering the Mothergate. And yet I lost three years."

"We are not certain you can do it yourself, Horace," Mr. Meister explained. "But we believe that you can, given the proper tool."

"What tool?"

"You may not remember it, but when you first came through the Find, I gave you a watch. A rather nice watch. To help you keep track of time while using the Fel'Daera."

"That watch?" Horace said, his heart sinking. He might never lose track of time, but he was constantly losing track of *stuff*. "I don't know what happened to it. It turned out I didn't need it."

Mr. Meister waved his hands. "Certainly you did not. Do not trouble yourself. The watch is unimportant. But when I gave it to you, I told you—"

159

"You told me there was only one clock that was really suitable for the Keeper of the Fel'Daera," Horace said, the words coming back to him in a blaze.

Mr. Meister's eyes lit up. "Yes!" he cried. "Just so. A timepiece unlike any other." He hesitated, glancing up at Brula before continuing. "The astrolabe."

Brula thundered to his feet. "No," he declared. Beside him, Go'nesh had gone stiff, and even Teokas looked troubled. Brula pounded the table. "Never again."

"It is the only way," Falo said.

"Then there is no way," Brula replied.

"What is your worry, Brula?" asked Falo. "That Horace will become another Samuel? That he could do such harm, even if he wanted to, here at the end of things?"

Horace hardly listened to Brula's sputtering response. His head was swimming. He had never heard of Samuel before, but he knew at once who he must be.

The last Keeper of the Fel'Daera.

Horace had been hearing whispers and hints about the Fel'Daera's last Keeper ever since the Find. Something had gone wrong, he knew, though no one would tell him what.

And what did it have to do with the astrolabe? As far as he knew, astrolabes were ordinary human devices. Amazing devices, actually, but still made by human hands. Humans had been making them for centuries. He'd even held one; his science teacher, Mr. Ludwig, had one in his collection. Astrolabes were usually disks, or rather a stacked series of disks, that showed the movement of the planets and the stars throughout the year.

Horace raised his hand, interrupting the argument that now flowed freely at the Council's table. "Explain, please," he said firmly. "Not about Samuel. He's not the Keeper of the Fel'Daera anymore. I am." Beside him, Chloe grunted in approval. "But tell me about the astrolabe."

"The astrolabe is a Tanu," Mr. Meister said. "A Tan'kindi, but it works better in the hands of some than others."

"Better!" Brula snorted.

"And what does it do?" Horace asked. "It keeps time, but obviously there's more."

"The astrolabe does not merely keep time," Mr. Meister explained. "It does that, yes, and in the centuries since it was made, it has not lost or gained even a fraction of a second. In fact, it cannot *be* inaccurate, because it moves in accordance with the planets themselves."

"I haven't lost a fraction of a second either," said Horace, tapping his head. "In fact, I'm getting more accurate by the day."

"The astrolabe is grounded in a way that you can never be," Mr. Meister said. "In fact, some have argued that the astrolabe *makes* time."

"That's ridiculous," Brian blurted out. "Time is an illusion created by our consciousness."

"Oh my goodness," April murmured.

"Then think of the astrolabe as a kind of consciousness,

if you like," said Mr. Meister. "But the point is not to debate how the astrolabe functions. The point is, it *does* function. It anchors itself to the flow of time as it is observed here on earth. It cannot be slowed or sped up, even by relativistic means."

"You're losing the slow kids," Chloe muttered.

"He means it always keeps true time," Horace said. "Absolute time. Even inside the Mothergates, where time is slippery."

"Just so," Mr. Meister said.

Horace hadn't felt this good in days. Not because he super liked what he was hearing, or some of the things that had been hinted at, but because this was the sort of problem his mind was built for.

Brian obviously felt the same. "What if you put it in a rocket, at near-light speeds?" he asked Horace excitedly.

"He's saying it would still keep earth time," said Horace. "Right?"

"But that's impossible. Would the rocket even go? Would the astrolabe stop it from accelerating?"

"*That* would be impossible. What would be the mechanism that would negate that force? If the astrolabe can never—"

Horace stopped, a sudden thought occurring to him. He looked back at Mr. Meister. "Has anyone ever tried to send the astrolabe through the Fel'Daera?"

Brula grimaced. Mr. Meister's eyes got even wider behind

the oraculum as he gazed at Horace appreciatively.

"It has been attempted," Falo said.

"By Samuel, I guess," said Horace. "And?"

"And it cannot be sent, as you seem to have surmised already," Falo replied. "It cannot travel into the future because it is too grounded in the present."

Horace reasoned it through, letting his love for the logic of it push aside all his troubled questions about Samuel. He was even able to pretend that there wasn't a whole audience of Altari watching and listening now, some of whom were no doubt hostile to the Fel'Daera, and its Keeper.

"So let me see if I understand," he said after a few moments. "You want me to take the astrolabe into the Mothergate. You think I can make it through to one of the other Mothergates without getting lost in time, because the astrolabe is grounded in the present, here on earth as we know it."

"Precisely," Mr. Meister said. "Excellent."

"But if the astrolabe refuses to be sent through the Fel'Daera," Horace said slowly, "how can you be sure it will let itself be taken into the Mothergates?"

He caught a swift tiny movement from the corner of his eye. Down the row, his mom was pumping her fist, looking quietly proud.

"That is precisely the point," Falo said. "An unsteady hand would not be able to take the astrolabe into the Mothergate, because they would be stepping onto a slippery slope for which they were not prepared, and which the astrolabe would reject. But your hand is steady, Horace Andrews. You are a Paragon. I would not send you into the Mothergate alone, but with the astrolabe in your hand, I am confident you can make it. You, and anyone traveling with you."

"Okay," said Horace simply. "Okay then." He'd heard enough. Big, burly questions still simmered at the edges of his thought, but at the center of himself he felt nothing but a cool slab of determination. Fascination. A sense that this was the proper path. He tried not to suspect that this willingness might be partly because of one small detail—no one had told him he would actually need to use the Fel'Daera. But maybe it didn't matter. "So . . . where is this astrolabe?"

His confidence sagged almost at once when he saw the look that passed between Mr. Meister and Falo, a reluctant glance of doubt.

"Oh my god," said Chloe, watching them.

"It's not here, is it?" Horace said. "It's in the belly of some terrible beast we haven't met yet, isn't it?"

"Not exactly," said Mr. Meister. "It is safe, in a manner of speaking. It remains where it has been these many years, where we intended it to remain safe forever. Behind the blue door, in the hall of the kairotics. In the Gallery."

"The Gallery," Horace said stupidly, unable to get a grip on the name.

"Back home, Horace," Mrs. Hapsteade said. "Back home . . . in the Warren."

CHAPTER TEN

The Same Fire

JOSHUA WOKE FROM DREAMING OF GROOMA.

He tried to grab hold of the dream as it slipped away from him, so that he could tell someone about it—although who would he tell? But the more he grabbed, the more it slipped away, and the more it slipped away the more he remembered that some of his troubled memories hadn't been dreams at all.

The last twenty hours or so had been hazy and terrible, full of terrible things. This new place Dr. Jericho had brought him and Isabel to—a set of abandoned concrete silos along the Chicago Sanitary Canal, four and a half miles southwest of the pit by the lakeshore—was an altogether different place. There were far more tunnels, tunnels beneath tunnels, and more Riven. This was a lived-in place, one of the Riven's nests. It smelled terribly of brimstone.

And this morning, though Joshua still wasn't sure what

had been a dream and what had been real, Grooma had finished the work he had started the night before. Dr. Jericho had made Joshua watch, again, and he would never forget the sight. Golden strands of the Medium dripping like streams of molten snowflakes into Isabel's body. Clinging to her, disappearing into her flesh. And she'd been ready for it. Asking for it, desperately. It felt like it took all day, and near the end she'd started screaming. Screaming with an awful grin on her face— or had that been only in his dream? And then it was done. She'd become whatever it was Grooma had made her. Some kind of harp, maybe, an instrument only she could control.

She'd collapsed then, carried limp and laughing from the room by a hunchbacked Mordin. Now she slept, and according to Dr. Jericho might sleep another day at least, recovering from what had been done to her. The *miraculous* thing that had been done, according to Dr. Jericho.

And then she would fix the Mothergates.

Joshua rolled over on the thin mattress he'd been given, licking his lips. His mouth was dry and tacky. The Mordin standing guard grunted at him and looked away. The shining globe of the Laithe floated just above the bed, the blue-eyed rabbit asleep atop the meridian. The Riven still hadn't taken the Laithe from him, despite what he'd done for Mr. Meister, but they'd been guarding him more carefully. The room he was in was far from a prison cell—it didn't even have a proper door, just a wide opening that led into the tunnels beyond—but there'd been a Mordin at his side every second since arriving. In fact, usually there were *two* Mordins. One of them had slipped away.

"Where's your friend?" Joshua asked, surprising himself. The sick rags of his dream, and the memories tangled inside it, had him feeling antsy.

"Ja'raka Sevlo asked to be informed when you were awake," the Mordin said flatly, and then he blinked, slow as a frog. "You are awake."

Moments later, Dr. Jericho himself arrived. He dismissed the guard and set a huge tray on the ground. Water, and food— an orange, and a kind of stringy dried meat that smelled of pepper. Joshua didn't touch the meat, but drank the water until he thought he'd burst, then broke into the orange. Dr. Jericho sat in a chair opposite the bed, watching him silently.

"Where's Isabel?" Joshua said at last, breaking the silence. Juice trickled down his chin.

"Sleeping. I told you. She is well, but it'll be another day before she is . . . herself."

"And what about Ingrid?"

"Ingrid will be busy tonight, introducing us to her old home. The Warren is full of secrets, you know. And Ingrid has the answers."

"The guard said you wanted to know when I was awake. Was it so you could bring me breakfast in bed?"

Dr. Jericho smiled. "It's nearly evening. This is dinner." His smile widened. "You seem . . . different tonight. Bad dreams?"

Joshua dropped his eyes, concentrating on the orange. It was sour. He poked the Laithe gently. It drifted a few feet away, then circled back round toward him. "I know you're letting me keep the Laithe so I'll start trusting you," he said.

"Is it working?"

"Not likely. It just confuses me."

"The feeling is mutual, then. You are a confusing child." Dr. Jericho studied Joshua for a moment and then said, "You were a Lostling when we first met. I thought I could help you master the Laithe, even though the Laithe was thrust into your hands instead of allowing itself to be Found." He shook his head. "But you do not need my help. The way you opened the portal last night, so swiftly, allowing the Taxonomer to escape. Perhaps it was the great need of the moment, as you saw it. Perhaps your petty doubts were crushed by fear. Either way, it is clear—you are no Lostling. Not anymore."

Joshua tried not to be pleased. It wasn't easy, because he knew the Mordin wasn't lying, for once. He knew it with a bone-thickening sureness. He had found the meadow in Ka'hoka and opened the portal to it in . . . what? Three seconds? And with nothing but the power of his mind. It was a far cry from the first time he'd opened a portal, when he'd had to spin the meridian by hand.

"You want something from me," Joshua said. "Something about the Altari, and the Mothergates."

"Yes."

"But I don't like you."

Dr. Jericho laughed, a rain of tinkling glass. "How is that relevant?" he asked. "I don't particularly like you, either. It does not matter whether we like each other or not. What matters is that we share a common goal." He beamed down at Joshua. "We want to *live*." Now he leaned in close, bending like a snake. "Don't you want to live, Joshua?"

Joshua didn't answer. Of course he wanted to live.

"Yes," Dr. Jericho said, straightening. "You do. Life is good. And how strange to think—if the Mothergates had died even a week ago, you would have felt nothing. A bit of sadness, perhaps. You were not yet a Keeper, not yet through the Find. But now—thanks to Isabel—you are Tan'ji. Now your very survival depends upon the continued existence of the Mothergates."

Joshua reached out and cupped the floating Laithe with his palm. The world in his hand, a map and a doorway to anywhere. Everywhere. Would he go back and surrender it, if he could? Would he erase this incredible thing, this sense of belonging—of *being*?

He didn't know. And not knowing scared him.

"Why are the Mothergates dying?" Joshua asked.

"Neglect," Dr. Jericho said bitterly. "Misguided faith. The Altari believe the Mothergates' sickness must run its course, come what may. But tell me, Joshua, if a loved one was ill, would you not want to cure them?"

"Yes," said Joshua.

"Of course you would. It is strange, then, what the Altari

169

do—what they do *not* do." He shook his head sadly. "Therefore we must do it for them."

"You mean Isabel must do it."

"Yes. She is our only hope. A lucky find. A lucky day, and just in the nick of time."

"You hurt her. She was—" Joshua stopped himself. *Had* she been screaming?

"Surely you too have been hurt, one way or another, attempting to master the Laithe? No greatness comes without some form of agony." Dr. Jericho uncrossed and recrossed his long legs, like some huge and gruesome cricket. "Yes, I want something from you, Joshua. We need *you*. We need the Laithe. Isabel cannot cure the Mothergates without your help."

"I don't have anything to do with that."

"You do. Before the Mothergates can be fixed, they must be found. Isabel knows where they are, but getting there is another matter. They are scattered around the globe. Our time is short, and we must move fast. And no one can move faster than the Keeper of the Laithe."

"But I'm a Warden," Joshua said, not really sure it was true, trying out the sound of it in his mouth. "And you're a Riven."

"Enemies, on the face of it," Dr. Jericho agreed. "But we have a saying, we Riven: 'Two sticks at war may yet feed the same fire.' It means we will work with our enemies when the situation demands it. But if our enemies refuse . . . ?"

Dr. Jericho lifted his head to the open doorway and barked out a command. Joshua heard nothing, but after a moment a faint green light began to dance along the walls of the tunnel outside. The light grew stronger, and now footsteps slid heavily closer. Closer still. The sulfur stink of the Riven grew painfully sharp. The green light brightened, dazzling. A shadow moved within it.

And then a great hound filled the doorway, as big as a bear. Joshua reared back, clutching the Laithe. But it wasn't a hound, really—it was some horrible form of Riven, walking on all fours, with bulging eyes and a crooked neck. It stank of brimstone. The creature was bent painfully beneath a huge metal cauldron half-buried in the flesh between its shoulders, shaped like a twisted, grasping hand. This was the source of the green light, which burst forth from a brilliant carved flame inside. Or was it a flame? It didn't flicker, didn't sway, but seemed made of nothing but light and heat. And the light . . . it beckoned faintly to Joshua, inviting him. He refused to move.

Dr. Jericho was studying Joshua's face closely. "What do you see?" he asked, almost eagerly.

"I see . . . a beast, carrying a green flame." The creature shifted, took a step into the room. It bared a row of large, sharp teeth. Its fingers, adorned with long, thick claws, dug at the floor. The green light it spilled was like an ocean, warm and familiar.

"Behold the Kolfirin," Dr. Jericho said. "He carries the

crucible. Does the crucible's light not call to you?"

It did. And it made Joshua feel slightly dizzy, but also . . . special. Privileged to see this thing, to know this light. He tried to shake the thought away. "It does. Sort of. But . . . I'm not going any closer."

Dr. Jericho leaned back smiling, as if greatly satisfied. "Nor am I." Dr. Jericho waved his hand. The Kolfirin growled, lowering its thick, flat head. Joshua stiffened. But then the beast backed out of the room, leaving them, its heavy feet dragging through the tunnel, taking the green light with it. Joshua's head cleared.

"The Kolfirin is a useful annoyance," Dr. Jericho said. "But it won't be useful with you."

"Why not?"

"Because you have already decided you will help us."

"No, I haven't."

"If you truly wanted to resist us, you would not even have been able to speak in the light of the crucible. For ourselves, and for our friends and allies, the crucible's light is a beacon of fellowship and mutual protection. But for those who resist us, it is a bond of an altogether different sort. Our enemies are compelled by the light, drawn closer and rendered . . . harmless."

"I'm not harmless," Joshua said, trying to sound brave. He didn't think Dr. Jericho was telling him the entire truth about what the crucible did to the Riven's enemies, but whatever it truly was . . . it hadn't happened to him. The thought made him sick. *Had* he already decided he would help?

"No indeed, not harmless," Dr. Jericho said. "Nor are you spineless. When we took the Warren, you stayed behind instead of escaping with your friends. Last night, you allowed Mr. Meister to escape, but again did not follow him. When young Chloe showed up, she asked you to open a portal, but you refused."

"I wasn't refusing," Joshua said. "I just . . ."

"Didn't," Dr. Jericho finished.

Joshua realized he was breathing hard. He watched the Laithe spinning slowly beside him, swirls of white cloud drifting over the Atlantic like cotton candy, quilts of light sparkling atop the blue water. It wasn't right, everything Dr. Jericho was saying. Joshua didn't think he *belonged* with the Wardens, that was the problem. He didn't think he deserved them.

But then again, they had lied to him.

"Tell me why the Altari think the Mothergates have to die," he said.

"Why should I tell you a fairy tale, when—"

"Because it's a fairy tale my friends believe in," Joshua said. "My real friends."

Dr. Jericho sighed. He considered the Laithe for a long moment and then spread his arms in resignation. "Very well. Your . . . *friends* . . . believe that our Tan'ji are poisoned. That all the Tanu are twisted, the Medium itself a river of corruption. They believe this poison flows from our instruments and into the very fabric of the universe itself." He pressed his ten fingertips into his own chest, indignant. "They believe that we Keepers, by the very act of using the powers our Tan'ji grant us, are bringing about the end of the universe." He looked at the Laithe again, cupping his great hands toward it as if it were a baby, a flower, a pure and precious thing. "This magnificent creation—your Tan'ji! Poison? Evil? A claw through the heart of the universe itself?" He shook his head sadly. "I do not believe it. I believe the Mothergates are sick, yes. I believe the Altari have witnessed this sickness, and in their foolish pride, blamed themselves. They believe *they* are the cancer, and that death is the cure. But death is no cure." He raised a long arm and pointed it out the doorway. "The cure lies just down the hallway, sleeping. And when she awakes? She will fix us all."

Joshua listened to every word. He really did. And what now to believe? None of the Wardens had ever told him not to use the Laithe. Nobody had ever said anything about poison. But even if Dr. Jericho's version of the story were half true . . . it made no sense that the Mothergates couldn't be fixed. It made no sense that the Laithe had to die. Not this perfect thing. And he had only just begun.

"Isabel can fix it?" he asked softly.

"If you take her where she needs to go, yes."

"And when she wakes up, we'll start? We'll see if she can do it?"

"We will see. *You* will see."

Joshua felt sick and giddy, the brimstone still biting at his

174

nose. "You can't hurt my friends. I mean it."

Dr. Jericho leaned back, frowning like he was deeply offended. "On the contrary. I am trying to *save* your friends."

Joshua nodded. Isabel was strong. Isabel was smart. Maybe she knew things no one else knew, even the fabled Sil'falo Teneves.

"Then let's save them," he said.

CHAPTER ELEVEN

What Could Have Been Known

SANGUINE HALL WAS EMPTY. HORACE DIDN'T KNOW IF THAT WAS a good sign or bad.

Dailen had warned them that there would likely be guards here at the rear entrance to the Warren, the very path the Riven had taken when they had invaded two nights before. Here at the far end, the wall was in ruins where the golem had torn it apart to let the Riven inside, a frightening display of power. But now there were no guards, and Dailen wasn't even here to discover that he'd been wrong.

The Altari was outside, just the one of him, waiting with the mal'gama in one of the Wardens' cloisters. The cloisters, secret walled-off spaces scattered throughout the city, had doorways that led into the tunnels underground—tunnels that, in this case, fed eventually into Sanguine Hall.

Horace had walked the route only once before, and April

never, but Gabriel obviously knew it well. He led them surely through the passages—the sewers and the old freight tunnels, relying on the thin, unseen layer of the humour leaking from the tip of the Staff of Obro. It was just the three of them. Unlike the rescue attempt at the pit, the mission to return to the Warren and recover the astrolabe was all about stealth.

Falo had forbidden Chloe to come, and Horace was worried that his friend hadn't put up more of a fight. He suspected that Chloe's miracle with the mal'gama had taken more out of her than anyone knew. Gabriel was an obvious choice to come instead, and Horace all but *had* to come—he carried the blue jithandra whose light would reveal the door to the hall of kairotics, where the astrolabe would be found.

As for April, her powers complemented Gabriel's beautifully. With the Ravenvine, she had the unique ability to see and hear what was going on outside the humour, even while she was buried blind and deaf inside it with everyone else, undetectable. The problem was, she could only do that if there were animals outside for her to listen to. And there would be no animals in the Warren. Not even bugs. Bringing Arthur the raven had been out of the question, given that they were traveling by mal'gama. She wasn't willing to cage him for the three-hour trip, and he couldn't hope to keep up with the mal'gama on his own, even if he wanted to.

And so instead, after they'd risen through the horrible Nevren called Goth en'Sethra, leaving the deep halls of Ka'hoka behind for the evening meadows and ancient hills of the Cahokia Mounds above, Horace, Dailen, and Gabriel had witnessed a bizarre sight. April on her knees, jar in hand, combing the twilight grass.

Capturing crickets.

"Explain it to me again," said Dailen, watching her. "The bugs speak to you?"

"Not exactly," said April patiently. Dailen was one of Horace's favorites, thoughtful and decisive, but today Dailen was having trouble with his memory—he'd lost two variants in the battle the night before, and hadn't yet recovered. April said, "I can see what they're seeing, hear what they're hearing. Crickets have excellent hearing, but it's a little weird to tap into. Their ears are in their front legs."

Horace watched, fascinated. April scrambled nimbly, her hand darting, scooping up the crickets with a preternatural precision only an empath could have managed.

"But won't they be noisy?" Horace asked. The evening air was filled with the insects' loud chirps.

April lunged, snagging another cricket out of midair. "That's why I'm only taking females," she said. "Girls don't chirp."

After another minute or two, April stood up, screwing the lid onto the jar. A scrambling black mass teemed inside it, two dozen crickets or more. Dailen frowned down at it heavily.

April shrugged. "Portable spies," she said.

"She's going to bug the place," said Horace. Nobody laughed. He didn't blame them.

And now they were here, April still toting her silent jar of crickets, the Ravenvine glinting faintly under her hair. Only to find that Sanguine Hall was unguarded. Apparently they wouldn't need the humour yet, much less the Ravenvine.

But Gabriel was cautious. "The Riven are undisciplined," Gabriel said. "Especially in the wake of a victory. It's very possible there will be guards here when we try to leave. And if our presence is detected, it wouldn't be hard for them to close off this exit entirely."

"We could find out," April suggested. She turned to Horace, her eyes dropping pointedly to the Fel'Daera at Horace's side. "Horace could tell us if anyone's going to show up."

"No," Horace said. He was here for one reason only; to open the door to the astrolabe. He expected April to argue with him—Chloe certainly would have—but instead she just nodded.

"Because of what Falo told you," she said.

"Because of what I know now, yeah," Horace said impatiently. "Can't you just scatter some crickets around? Then when we come back, they'll be here, and you can listen to them from the other end of the hall. Make sure the coast is clear."

April looked down at the jar, full of the popping black bugs. "But they're feeling hoppy."

Horace was confused until he realized she hadn't said happy. "They won't stay put, you mean." Suddenly an idea began to percolate.

"Not for long, no," April said. "I brought the crickets more to release them while we're in the humour, so that they'll hopefully jump out and give me eyes and ears. They're not going to just stand around. They're not cows." She sighed and chewed her lip—not in a worried way, but in a word-choosing way Horace knew well. "Listen, Horace," she said slowly. "It's up to you to decide when to use the Fel'Daera, or if you ever use it again. But I just want to suggest that maybe this situation is exactly the kind of thing the Fel'Daera was made for."

"I have no idea why the Fel'Daera was made, and neither do you," Horace said testily. Then he took a deep breath, holding up his hands by way of apology. "Look. I'm not going to check the future. But maybe we can fix this another way." He turned to Gabriel. "How long will it take us to find the astrolabe?"

"That's up to you," said Gabriel. "Twenty minutes, I should think. We won't want to linger."

"That's too long," April said, hefting the jar. "Crickets, not cows."

"So we'll make it short," Horace said. He slipped the Fel'Daera from its pouch. With his thoughts, and with practiced ease, he reached for the silver star on the side of the box. Twenty-four spokes around a black center. Right now, precisely ten of the spokes were bright silver—the breach was set to ten hours. If he looked through the box, that's how far into the future he would see.

Or send.

Swiftly he closed the breach, and the sun began to go dark, spoke by spoke. He closed it down easily under an hour, the last silver spoke darkening at one end. He didn't actually need to watch the spokes—he wondered briefly if it was a cosmetic touch Falo had added just for flair. He asked the breach to close to twenty minutes, and it did. Once it was there, he set the breach in place, like closing a valve. All the spokes were dark now, except one-third of the very first one. The whole process had taken just a couple of seconds.

"There," he said. "Twenty minutes."

April was frowning, clearly unsure what he was planning to do. And was it a stupid plan? April was right—checking Sanguine Hall in the future was exactly the kind of thing the Fel'Daera was good at, to see if their escape route would remain clear. But if he did that . . .

Horace frowned up at Gabriel. "How come you never told me about Samuel?" he said. He tried to sound causal, but listening to his own voice echoing softly in the hall, he sounded grim.

Gabriel turned his sightless gaze toward him. "I never met Samuel. He was gone before I was born."

"But you knew about him. You knew the story."

"Bits, yes. This is not the place to tell it."

And it wasn't, obviously. But Horace hadn't come here to use the Fel'Daera, and holding it now made it impossible not to think of the boy—or man?—who had held it last.

"Tell me one thing," Horace said. "Tell me the shortest version you know."

Gabriel considered a moment. He tapped the Staff of Obro against the ground. "This is the short version: Samuel wanted to fix everything. He reasoned that if the problem was caused by the tangles between multiple universes, the fix was simple. Let there be only one universe."

Horace almost dropped the box. One universe. One future. One willed path. A single future, constantly known, and all the others erased. "But he couldn't do that, could he?"

"The doing of an impossible thing is never the danger," Gabriel said. "It is the trying." He nodded in the direction of the Fel'Daera. "I listen well, Horace. I know things Mr. Meister thinks I do not. I know why you are afraid to use the Fel'Daera now, and I respect those fears. But the time for such fears is long past."

Horace opened the box, being careful not to look inside. "Thank you," he said. "But that's not for you to decide."

He thrust the open box toward April. "Here. This is the best I can do."

"I don't understand."

"Crickets. We'll send the crickets. They'll arrive right before we come back, and they won't have time to scatter far. You'll be able to listen to them, right here."

Gabriel started laughing. Not in a mean way, Horace thought. Meanwhile April pressed the jar of crickets to her belly.

"That's so . . . strangely brilliant," she said.

"I think that's maybe my specialty." He blushed as he said it.

"And they'll survive?" she asked.

"Yes, but . . ." Horace reasoned it through, thinking back to the nights with Rip van Twinkle, the firefly he'd sent through the Fel'Daera, several nights in a row. The little bug remained the only living thing Horace had ever sent traveling, and he had retired in good health. "But I think you will *not* want to be in the heads of these crickets when I close the box."

"I think you're right," April said. Still frowning faintly, she unscrewed the lid of the jar and tipped it into the Fel'Daera. Four or five crickets tumbled onto the smooth blue glass, skittering. One of them hopped out before Horace got the lid closed. And when it closed, the familiar tingle shivered up his arms. They were gone.

"Twenty minutes," he said.

April fiddled her fingers at the floor. "And then it'll rain crickets."

"It sounds lovely," said Gabriel. "Let us go."

They walked slowly through Sanguine Hall. The golem had torn at the walls in its frenzy to get to the Wardens, and the floor was coated in grit and raw chunks of rock. As they walked, Horace began to notice shining bits of metal strewn among the debris, tiny carved blades like serrated scimitars. Thousands of them.

The sa'halvasa. A Tanu like the golem and the mal'gama, the massive cloud of tiny, scythe-winged creatures had once been the protector of Sanguine Hall. There was no Nevren here like there was at the Warren's main entrance, but the Wardens—Mr. Meister, to be honest—foolishly thought the sa'halvasa would be enough. Having survived the sa'halvasa himself, Horace could understand why. The little scythe-wings fed on the energy of Tan'ji, descending in a swarm on any Keeper who tried to make it through the corridor. And if you panicked—if you even moved—they would cut you to ribbons. Horace reached up to touch his cheek, where his own hard-earned cut was still healing. But now the fearsome sa'halvasa was dead, destroyed in a furious battle with the golem.

When they reached the hall's end, they stopped and sent a second batch of crickets through the Fel'Daera, at April's suggestion—the range of the Ravenvine was limited, less than a hundred feet or so. Then they stepped through another massive breach in the stone, more of the golem's handiwork, and onto a precarious ledge over a narrow shaft. One of the Wardens' warm amber lights burned gently from the ceiling overhead, spilling a spiral of soft illumination into the pit below. Scarcely wider than a man, but well over a hundred feet deep, the shaft descended into darkness. A wrought-iron ladder that Horace remembered well clung to one side. At the bottom of the shaft lay the Gallery, and within it, the entrance to the hall of kairotics.

"We don't know what's down there," Horace said.

"Let me go first," said Gabriel, reaching out with his staff to find the ladder.

"No, let *me* go," April said. She unscrewed the jar of crickets and reached out over the ledge, sprinkling it gently. Three crickets tumbled free and dropped into the darkness below. Her eyes went hazy and distant.

"Whoa," she said. "It's weird to be falling off a cliff and not be freaking out about it. It's kind of nice—not that I've ever fallen off a cliff." She jumped a little, her eyes widening. "Okay, they're down."

"Did it hurt?" Horace asked.

"Not remotely. I see the doorway to the Gallery. Or what used to be the doorway. It's just another hole now." A wrinkle of dismay swept across her face. This was the door she had closed on Mr. Meister after he'd broken his leg, leaving him to the golem. Horace knew it wasn't a pleasant memory.

April rubbed her arm. "I'm sorry I'm not better at this, you guys. I was nervous about coming back here, and I should have practiced more. This ears-in-my-elbows thing is pretty weird." She flexed her arm, and her jaw for some reason. "I hear Riven down there, in the Gallery. I'm not sure how far."

"Keep listening," Gabriel said. "Let us head down."

One after the other they descended the steep ladder that led down the shaft. Going down was much easier than up, much to Horace's relief, though the rungs were still painfully far apart.

As they climbed, the smell of brimstone grew strong,

and Horace could hear the Mordin now himself, talking and laughing in low tones somewhere in the Gallery. They dismounted at the bottom, into a pile of rubble. Now Horace saw the opening the golem had torn through the wall into the Gallery. The Mordin weren't close, but it was impossible to say how far, or whether they were the only Riven that lay ahead. Dumping a cricket or two into her hand, April crept to the opening and tossed them through. One of them began to chirp rhythmically, making them all freeze.

"You brought a boy," Horace whispered.

"I can hear that, Horace," April hissed back.

They listened, waiting, the chirping of the cricket like a tiny alarm. "The Mordin are off to the left," April reported. "They're not paying any attention. Not yet."

After twelve tense seconds, the cricket stopped.

"Okay, go," April said gruffly. "Go now."

Gabriel gathered them together, holding the Staff of Obro in front of him. "Stay close," he said. "Stay low. I'll keep you hidden."

And then the humour enveloped them.

Horace was used to the humour by now, and it had saved him more than once, but he still dreaded it. Sightless gray, and sounds drifting as though they were underwater. He trusted Gabriel, and Gabriel's perfect knowledge of everything that was happening in the humour, but even the Keeper of the Staff of Obro had no idea what was happening beyond its borders. In a battle, Gabriel could throw the humour wide, enveloping the hapless enemies within. But now the goal was to keep the humour small, and to trust that the Mordin outside wouldn't see the slippery wrinkle that indicated its presence.

They crept into the Gallery, Horace struggling to find purchase through the rubble on feet he could not see. He kept a small, firm grip on Gabriel's shirt, letting the Keeper lead. Behind him, April clung steadily to his other hand.

Gabriel guided them into the Gallery, which was a long corridor stretching left and right. They found the far wall and pressed themselves against it.

"I can't tell what's going on," said April. "My crickets are like . . . looking at a wall or something. I can hear the Mordin still, but I can't tell where they are. I need another cricket." Through the humour, Horace heard the jar cracking open. "They call me the Cook County cricket flicker," April murmured. Then a soft *tik*, crisp and sharp. Horace pictured the cricket appearing out of nowhere, tumbling into the Gallery. "Okay," April said. "Oh god."

"What is it?" said Gabriel.

"There's a Mordin right outside. He saw the cricket. He's looking at it. He's looking around."

Suddenly a strong arm wrapped itself around Horace's shoulders. He cried out.

"It's only me," said Gabriel. "Get close. Get tight. I'm making the humour as small as I can." Gabriel squeezed, crushing Horace against another body. April. Her hair caught in his mouth. He tasted grass.

"Stay still," Gabriel said. "April?"

"He's still looking. He's coming closer—" Suddenly she spasmed violently. She gagged, grunting, and then started to groan.

"What happened?" said Horace.

"He stepped on the cricket. Killed her. While I was in her head. Oh my . . ." She gagged again.

"Sit tight," Gabriel said. "Be calm."

But April obviously wasn't satisfied being blind. The jar opened again, and there was another soft *tik*.

"Okay, better," April said. "Oh, that was bad. That's never happened to me before. I felt my guts, like, squish—"

"That's okay," said Horace. "Just tell us what's happening."

"The Mordin's already moving on. We're good. And we have a useful cricket. She's looking down the hallway. Those Mordin I heard talking are headed toward the Maw. They're leaving the Gallery. And so is the cricket killer."

"Good," said Gabriel. "Tell me when we're clear, and I'll take down the humour. Then Horace can use his jithandra to find the door."

"How will I know where to find it?" Horace asked.

"Remember that the door is not really a door," said Gabriel. "It is the *idea* of a door, and therefore it has no absolute location. But it always exists somewhere within the Gallery, and once the light of your jithandra falls upon it, it will reveal itself."

"Wow, okay," Horace said. "And then I just . . . have the idea of opening it?"

April laughed, but Gabriel made no sound.

"Uh," Horace said. "Because it's . . . you know . . . the *idea* of a door?"

"It opens like an ordinary door," said Gabriel flatly.

"Okay," Horace said. "Got it. And once we're inside, how will we find the astrolabe?"

"If Mr. Meister did not tell you precisely where to find it, you'll have to search. You'll find all sorts of Tanu related to kairotics—to the altering of space and time—but I doubt if anyone's been in there for months. Most of the halls in the Gallery are a mess. No one has had the time to catalog the inventory in years. You may have a hard time finding the astrolabe, but Mr. Meister would not have put it in a careless place."

"You're talking like you're not coming in there with us," Horace said.

"Are we in the clear?" Gabriel asked, not bothering to reply. "Are the Mordin gone?"

"Yes, we're clear," April said. "Are you coming with us?"

The humour came down with a soft ripple. The long hall of the Gallery stretched out to the right and left, dark and empty. Horace pulled his jithandra from his shirt, letting its blue light spill into the black. He was hoping he'd get lucky, that the door to the hall of kairotics would be right here. But no doorway appeared.

April turned to Gabriel. "Are you coming with us?" she asked again.

"I am not. There is another item here Mr. Meister wants me to retrieve."

"What item?" Horace asked. "And from where?"

"It has no name. I expect to find it in Brian's workshop."

April pursed her lips mischievously. "Will we get to see this mystery item?"

Gabriel turned his milky blue eyes toward her, seeming to look right at her. "I do not expect to be able to hide it from you," he said. And with that he vanished. Horace's eyes slid over the spot where Gabriel had just been standing, refusing to see the humour that cloaked him now.

"I thought we were done with mysteries," Horace said.

"It wouldn't be the Warren without mysteries," April replied.

By silent agreement, they turned and headed deeper into the Gallery, away from the Maw and the Great Burrow beyond. As they walked, the blue light of the jithandra shone along the walls. But there was nothing. Only stone.

And then, just as Horace was about to suggest they would have to double back, a doorway appeared, materializing out of nowhere. A towering slab of metal, with a heavy handle nearly at eye height—made for Altari, of course.

With a nod to April, Horace reached out, heaving. The handle turned with a soft screech, and the door opened onto blackness. Inside, the light of the jithandra was swallowed

190

completely, illuminating nothing.

"How is this supposed to work?" Horace said.

"Maybe we have to go in," April suggested. "Maybe the room won't reveal itself until the door is closed. It's just the idea of a door, remember?"

Horace didn't like it, but it made as much sense as anything else. He stepped into the blackness, April at his side. The door swung closed behind them, trapping them in the utter dark. Caged in a void. Horace's claustrophobia swelled up viciously. His heart swooned and pounded. He groped madly for the door.

And then the room slowly bloomed to life. A pleasant light swelled, faintly blue, revealing a round room with a domed ceiling rising high above. A great stone hawk was set in the dome's peak—a leestone. The sight was a comfort, but right now Horace was far more comforted to see that the tall metal door was still there behind them.

"Wow," said April. "Really wow."

The place was packed. It reminded Horace of nothing so much as the House of Answers, but far less organized. No labeled bins here, just shelves and tables piled high, stacks of oddments, like a magician's garage sale gone mad.

April didn't hesitate. She waded right in and began digging around. Horace wandered in more slowly, surveying the mess. A glorious mess. He ambled along a stretch of dark cubbies and high shelves. They were packed with all manner of timepieces and other unrecognizable Tanu, from the mystifying to the merely odd, from the exquisitely pristine to the plainly busted.

An hourglass filled with black sand. The sand was gathered in the top chamber, pressed to the top, defying gravity. Horace itched to turn it over, but didn't dare.

An orrery, a mechanical model of the solar system, with a glowing sun at the center. It wasn't to scale—with a golf-ball sized sun like this, the earth should have been smaller than a period, and at least a dozen feet away. Neptune—the planet—should have been somewhere at the opposite end of the Warren, near Vithra's Eye. But these inaccuracies were easy to overlook, because this orrery had no arms. The planets floated in their orbits around the fiery sun with no support whatsoever, each of them spinning slowly. It reminded Horace of the Laithe.

Leaning against the wall, a grandfather clock, clearly broken, its pendulum standing loose by its side. Inside the bob of the pendulum was another tiny clock, with a minuscule pendulum of its own.

A small brass top, standing upright atop a concave slab of glass. It looked motionless, but when Horace bent to get a better look, he realized the top was spinning. It balanced on a small spherical tip of gleaming red, like a ruby. He glanced over at April, who was rummaging swiftly but methodically through a massive set of tiny drawers that resembled a card catalog. Open, peek, and close. Open, peek, and close.

"Hey," she said as she pulled out a glass sphere about the

size of a baseball from one of the drawers.

Horace went over. Could this be the Altari version of an astrolabe? But no. Instead, inside the sphere, a tiny tree was growing before their eyes, sprouting branches and leaves. As they watched, a single flower bloomed on the tree and slowly became a fruit, plump and purple. The fruit ripened and dropped to the ground, and began to rot. The leaves of the tree browned and fell, and the tree withered. It toppled over, splintering, turning to dust. Within moments, where the fruit had fallen, a new sapling began to grow, starting the cycle again.

"What would even be the point of something like this?" Horace asked, awed but confused.

"Beauty is its own reward, Horace," said April, her face alight as she watched the tree begin anew.

Horace blushed. "I didn't mean it like that."

"I know," she replied. "I'm just saying, it's important to appreciate the beautiful things. Especially now." To Horace's surprise, she tucked the everlasting tree into a pocket of her dress and then flicked her fingers at him, shooing him away. "Go find the whatsit. Gabriel will be back soon."

Horace went on searching, growing more nervous by the moment. What if they couldn't find the astrolabe? He encountered a magnifying glass as wide as a hula hoop, a toy train on a track shaped like a figure eight, a splendid dollhouse that looked disconcertingly real, a pile of broken pottery shards. He reached for the shards, curious. As soon as his hand got near, they sprang to life. In a flash, with a soft earthy rustle, they assembled themselves into a tall flask. Steam rose from the top. Horace pulled his hand away. The flask crumbled to pieces once more.

"What will it look like, again?" April called.

"Like a disk, probably."

"Like a watch?"

"No, it won't have hands. I don't think. But it'll have markings around the edge."

April turned toward him, arm outstretched. "Like this?"

In her palm lay a gold disk two or three inches wide. Horace hurried over.

The astrolabe.

Horace took it from her and held it close. This was nothing like Mr. Ludwig's astrolabe. Or it was, but far more beautiful, infinitely more complex. This one had multiple layered plates, each one made of thin, sweeping arcs and carefully crafted curves, so that he could see the other disks beneath. Each plate was made of a different material—gold, silver, a white that looked like porcelain, a rusty red metal Horace couldn't identify. The back plate—the mater, Horace thought it was called, upon which the celestial sphere was engraved—was made of obsidian, with golden arcs carved precisely through it, a warped spiderweb.

April bent over it. "Don't tell me you understand that."

"I'm supposed to, aren't I?" Horace said. "But no, I don't. Not most of it, anyway."

194

"And it tells time? But how?"

"I don't really know," Horace admitted, peering closely at the intricate device. "I'm not even sure it's working. Or maybe I have to *make* it work?"

And then abruptly, silently, the astrolabe's many plates began to spin.

Horace almost dropped it in surprise. But he kept watching, and slowly certain things began to make sense. The earth's horizon and the stars above it. He recognized many of them by names—Altair, Deneb, Polaris. And now planets, Venus and Mars, and Jupiter too. The white plate was for the moon, he realized now, and it spun round swiftly, carrying a tiny white disk that waxed and waned just like the real moon.

"You're seeing this, right?" Horace asked April.

"I'm seeing it," April said, her voice breathy with wonder. "But I have no idea what I'm seeing."

"It's setting itself," Horace said. "It doesn't make time, like Mr. Meister said. It's setting itself to here and now."

"To you, you mean."

Horace's eyebrows went up. He'd been thinking about the astrolabe since leaving Ka'hoka, bothered by what he'd been told. The problem was there was no such thing as absolute time. Time was *always* relative—depending on speed, on gravity. Depending on the observer. And yet Mr. Meister had said the astrolabe couldn't be sped up or slowed down.

"To me, right," Horace said softly. "Me here and now."

"It's like your pet watch."

The spinning plates of the astrolabe began to slow, zeroing in on the present like a missile. *Summer . . . July . . . mid-month . . . a Monday . . . late evening . . . ten thirty-two . . . seventeen seconds.* The astrolabe seemed to settle Horace's hands, becoming heavy, finding the precise time down to the millisecond—down to the microsecond, levels where time's march was a blur, even to Horace. The motion of the plates resolved, locking to the flow of time as Horace was experiencing it. Most bizarrely of all, all the while, the Fel'Daera seemed to resonate with the astrolabe happily, to gather the astrolabe's groove like a kind of lullaby, an immovable comfort. And Horace himself felt . . .

Sure.

"What's happening?" said April. "I feel like something's happening."

"Nothing," said Horace. "I don't know. It's good. This is good."

"Can it get you through the Mothergates?"

"Yes," Horace said, not even caring that he had no idea what the inside of a Mothergate was like.

"Then let's go. Gabriel should be back now. Where are we on cricket time?"

Horace found the time effortlessly. "Fifty-seven seconds until the first batch. One minute forty-six seconds until the second, at the top of the shaft."

"Perfect," April said.

Horace put the astrolabe in his pocket, where it sat like

a stone. They went to the door, opening it cautiously. Somewhat to Horace's surprise, the Gallery's long hallway was right there.

"We're clear," April said, her eyes far away. They let the door shut behind them. Horace dropped his jithandra back into his shirt, snuffing out its light. The door vanished.

They hurried quietly down the hallway, back to the opening to Sanguine Hall. As they approached, April said softly, "Oh! And there's Gabriel. You know, I'm beginning to think crickets are underrated."

Horace saw nothing, but April walked confidently over to a patch near the crumbled wall and stuck out her hand. Her hand disappeared in a ripple of shadow. A moment later, with a soft tear, the humour came down, revealing Gabriel, dark and silent.

"Well met, Keepers," he said.

"You made it," said Horace. "Did you find what you were—"

Suddenly April lurched at Gabriel. Fervently she bent in front of him, practically sniffing him up and down like a dog. "What is that?" she demanded. "What do you have?" She put her hand to her temple, pressing the Ravenvine against her skin.

Horace was at a loss. "What are you doing?" he asked.

April ignored him. She slapped Gabriel's chest. "What *is* *that*?" she hissed. "It's . . . terrible. It's a terrible thing that's been done. Why do you have that?"

Gabriel looked stricken. "I'm sorry," he stammered. "Mr. Meister warned me, but I did not think—"

"It's alive," April said. "And not alive. I need to see."

Horace watched, bewildered, as Gabriel revealed a rod, long and thin. It glinted faintly. April grabbed it from him and whirled away. She fumbled in the collar of her dress, freeing her jithandra. As its mossy green light poured into April's hands, Horace saw.

A transparent cylinder, a foot long and two inches thick. Inside it, a fish, black as coal. Or something like a fish, almost an eel. Finless and thin, the black fish nearly filled the cylinder. It swayed gently, pulsing, as if swimming in an endless current. It was alive in there, with no room to even turn around. Horace stared, hardly believing it.

He had seen this before.

April gazed at the fish, silent. Horace thought she might be crying. He had first laid eyes on the fish the day he became a Keeper, in the House of Answers, where the fish had been offered to him—or at least, he thought it had. It had been in the *Of Scientific Interest* bin, along with the Laithe of Teneves, and the Fel'Daera itself. He'd forgotten it in the rush of the Find that came right after. But as Horace looked at the fish now, the same swell of pity that had risen in him that day rose again. And whatever sick dismay he was feeling, he figured April was feeling it a hundred times as hard.

"So old," April said. "A thing can't be this old. And what is it . . . how is . . . ?" She whirled back to Gabriel. "Explain this.

I can't hear it properly. Is it the glass? It's *thinking* something. But why can't I hear it?"

"I do not know." Briefly Gabriel touched two fingers to the corner of one milky eye. "I cannot see it, Keeper. I have only been told that it is alive."

"Alive," April muttered. "Not alive. Something in between. Why would you do this thing?"

"I did not. And would not. It is fleshwoven, and that is forbidden."

"Oh, but you'll just keep it around anyway. You'll go on a secret mission to get it back." She thrust the cylinder at Gabriel, striking him in the belly. He took it from her, gently.

"It was Sil'falo Teneves who asked that it be retrieved," Gabriel said. "This Tanu is ancient, older than Falo herself."

"Is that supposed to be reassuring?"

"April," Horace said, not at all sure what to say.

She turned to him. "I mean, am I supposed to be reassured by that?"

"You're supposed to be upset, just like you are. But I don't think Gabriel knows any more about the fish than we do. And it must be important somehow, if Falo wants it."

"So I am told," Gabriel said. "But I do not know why. I am not even sure that Falo knows why."

"You're bringing it back with us," April said. "It'll be riding with us."

"Yes."

She nodded. She wiped at her face. She dropped her

jithandra back beneath her collar, as if she didn't want to be seen. "Fine," she said. "Fine. But just know that it's talking to me, okay? Or trying to. I'm not even listening, and it's talking to me." She poked herself in the temple. "And as soon as we're out of here, I'm taking the vine off."

Gabriel bowed slightly. "Every Keeper does as every Keeper must." He hesitated a moment, and then said, "I'm sorry, April."

"We've got to go," Horace said. "The crickets are back. Not cows."

April shook herself out, like she was shaking off a dream. She smoothed her dress briskly and then stepped past them into the bottom of the shaft. When she reached the ladder, she glanced back. "Tangles or no tangles, did you ever think maybe the Mothergates should die anyway?" she said. And she put her foot on the ladder and started to climb.

And then she stopped.

"Wait," she said. "Wait." She hung there, her head cocked. Without even seeing her eyes, Horace knew she was listening through the vine. Was it the fish again?

"There's something above," she said. "In Sanguine Hall. A bad smell. I think it's brimstone." She dropped to the floor, coming back to them, her eyes hazy. "Mordin. Two full hunting packs, at least. And there's a . . . bear? A wolf? It's carrying a bright light. And wait . . ."

Horace looked up. At the top of the shaft, a trickle of green light danced across the ceiling.

"A crucible," he whispered.

And then something worse. Music, pouring down from above. It crept across his skin like fingers.

Ingrid's flute.

Gabriel grabbed Horace's hand. "Run," he said. "Out the front."

Horace snatched up April's hand. The jar of crickets slipped loose. The humour bloomed from Gabriel's staff and erased the world just as the jar shattered on the ground.

They ran.

"Out the front?" Horace said into the gray, as Gabriel dragged them on. He led them at a quick trot, knowing that Horace and April would struggle to sprint full-out while blind. "Through the Great Burrow? But aren't there Riven there?"

"Judging by the sounds I heard earlier, yes. Plenty. But no Ingrid, and no Kolfirin."

"The crucible dog?" puffed Horace, struggling not to stumble. "But you can protect us from the light. You've done it before."

"Ingrid knows we're here," said Gabriel. "Even if we got past them, there would be a pursuit. One we would not escape. There's only one way we can separate ourselves from the Riven now, and it's through the Great Burrow."

Vithra's Eye. The Nevren. If they could get across the water, the Riven would be unable to follow.

They ran. They were running blind, Horace knew, Gabriel unable to see what lay ahead of the humour, and April all out of crickets. But Horace trusted Gabriel to take whatever cautions he could.

"Stay tight," Gabriel said. "Watch your step." Horace knew they were now navigating the narrow bridge that crossed the deep chasm of Maw. Nerve-racking, but at least the Maw's raging wind couldn't be felt in the humour.

"Steps," Gabriel said a half minute later, and they began mounting the Perilous Stairs. Horace's legs burned. Behind him, judging by her grip, April seemed to be moving strong. If anything, Horace felt like he was slowing the group down.

And then a growling roar filled the humour. A Mordin. Gabriel yanked his hand away, and there was a brief, distant scrape of scuffling feet. Then a howling, angry scream, suddenly cut off.

Someone lifted Horace's hand again. "Watch your step," said Gabriel. "I'm told it's a long way down."

Up they went until at last they reached flat ground. Gabriel steered them sharply to the right. "Wall," he said, releasing Horace. Horace let go of April and felt for the wall. He slumped against it, heaving. From here, he knew, it was a straight shot through the stone forest of the Great Burrow to the shores of Vithra's Eye.

"This won't be easy," Gabriel said. "I know my way, every inch of it, but—"

April's voice popped out of the gloom. "Bird," she chirped.

"What?" said Horace.

"Birds, I mean," said April. "Outside the humour. They're here. They're alive."

She must have meant the birds from Mr. Meister's office. Somehow some of them were still alive—much to the Riven's dismay, no doubt.

A hand swatted at Horace, grasping. April. He took it. "Left!" she cried. "Go left."

They sprang from the wall and hurried on, with April and her birds as guide, half sneaking and half running through the Great Burrow. From the sound of it, the Riven were everywhere. Horace was almost glad he couldn't see it. Twice he heard the distant hiss and pop of a Ravid materializing somewhere in the humour—the Riven knew they were here. But Gabriel kept them safe.

"Rocks here," said Gabriel. "From when the keystone collapsed. We'll have to climb."

The collapse of the keystone, Horace knew, had been the Warden's last defense against the invading Riven when the Warren fell. And judging by the huge pile of jagged rock he clambered blindly onto now, it had been a mighty collapse indeed.

They made it over the top. Horace fell and scraped his arm, but April's firm hand pulled him to his feet. They stumbled on until Gabriel brought them to a halt.

"They're coming," he said heavily. "Some of them are already in the humour. The water is just ahead. Step out and start across while I hold them back."

"But what if there are Riven on the other side?" Horace cried.

"There aren't," April replied, chin tipped into the air, her gaze foggy and faraway. Horace was dumbfounded for a moment, and then he remembered. The owls of Vithra's Eye. What they knew, April knew. And they knew the way ahead was clear.

Horace squeezed April's hand, and they stepped out of the humour together. Horace yanked his jithandra free, stepping up to the water's edge. Behind them, the great rockfall at the mouth of the Great Burrow was unseeable, hidden behind the wrinkle of the humour. Horace turned to the dark water, hesitating.

Only a Warden could cross Vithra's Eye. But Horace had never done it alone. The Nevren that lay waiting for them over the darker waters had been too powerful for him, too debilitating. But not today. He dipped the glowing tip of the jithandra into the pool. Immediately the water began to gather and rise around it, seething, becoming solid. It turned blue and slick. He stepped onto it, testing his footing, sliding the jithandra farther out. The path held, and grew.

"Let's go," he said.

They went, April clinging to his shirt. The path extended, the water firming itself for their passage in the wake of the jithandra. It wouldn't last forever, this path. Just long enough to let them through.

But what about Gabriel?

They'd made it about twenty feet, the blue path already dissolving back into water behind them, when the humour came down with a roar. There was Gabriel, and a crowd of ranging, groping Riven—Mordin and Ravids alike. Now they saw Gabriel, and turned to him. The Mordin bellowed.

Gabriel ran for the shoreline. But he couldn't see. Two Mordin charged after him, gaining ground fast.

"Here!" Horace cried, and Gabriel veered toward his voice. At the water's edge, he leapt. A Mordin swiped at his feet, knocking him askew. Gabriel careened through the air, pinwheeling, clinging to his staff. He landed hard on his knees at the back of the blue pathway, falling, his legs sliding into the water. He cried out in pain, clinging to the slippery blue surface. April reached down, grappling with him, pulling him aboard.

Gabriel's pant legs were in tatters. The brown skin beneath shone with blood. "Go on," he gasped. "On."

Horrified, Horace pressed on, dangling his jithandra, carving the way across the dark water. A Ravid suddenly popped into existence at the back end of the trail, mere steps behind Gabriel. An owl darted in from the darkness, swooping at it, screeching. The Ravid stopped to fight back, snarling, and as it did the blue patch it was standing on dissolved, dumping it into the water. The Ravid screamed, splashing, and then vanished with a hiss, reappearing on shore. It danced and howled with the other Riven gathered there. Behind them, Horace saw Ingrid emerging from the Great Burrow at a run. Behind her, a sick shimmer of green light began to grow.

Horace turned his back on them, and on the green light of the Kolfirin. His jithandra plowed through the water. A moment later, a coldness began to clutch at him, though it wasn't cold at all. The Nevren.

And then suddenly he couldn't feel the Fel'Daera. It was gone from him, all gone. He was nothing without it, but he made that nothing keep walking, still dangling the jithandra. And whose jithandra was it? What was the point? He had lost something, something important he could not remember, and he did not want to be without it. Not ever. He did not want anything anymore.

Angry cries, far behind now. But he didn't care, whoever it was. There was no caring. Anger couldn't touch him. The only thing was to walk, into or away, it didn't matter. Just walk.

And then warmth. The cries fading now. And suddenly the Fel'Daera bloomed to life again as the powerful river of the Medium once again began to flow. Horace took a great breath—Horace, yes, Keeper of the Fel'Daera. He began to cry.

Behind him, he heard April gasp, and then an exhausted sigh of relief from Gabriel. They were through, all of them. The far shore of Vithra's Eye was ahead, deserted. Horace could just make out the three archways that stood here, leading up and out, one of them to the Mazzoleni Academy directly above. And owl swept past them, hooting softly. The blue path continued to seethe and grow, until at last they stepped ashore.

Horace collapsed. He extinguished his jithandra and fumbled to pull the Fel'Daera from its pouch. He cradled it to his chest. He felt the astrolabe brooding steadily in his pocket.

"You did it," April said, gasping down at him, hands on her knees. "We did it."

"Barely," said Horace. "It would have been better if we'd known. Better if I'd seen what was coming."

April shook her head. "Maybe if you'd seen, we wouldn't have done it at all."

But that was not how it worked. The Fel'Daera found a way. Or no—it *showed* a way, and then it was up to Horace to make it work. He was a Paragon. There was no obstacle that he should not be able to overcome, once it was known.

But it had to be known, whatever the price.

He said none of this to April. "Maybe," he said simply. "Maybe." And he could see by the look on her face that she knew what he meant.

Gabriel was looking back across the water, where the Kolfirin's green light still shone faintly—too far to enchant them—and the Riven's howls still echoed.

"They'll come around, eventually," he said. He pointed his staff in the direction of the archways looming before them now. "But I know a way out. Let us get back to Dailen. Let us get back to Ka'hoka."

"And then what?" April said. She looked down at Horace. "Then what?"

Horace got to his feet, slipping the Fel'Daera into its pouch. "Then we fight again," he said. "That's what we do now. We fight until we're done."

CHAPTER TWELVE

The Faded

APRIL STOOD DEEP IN THE SWAYING SEA OF THE VEIL OF LURA. The Ravenvine was wide open, and through it poured the vast song of the multiverse, a knotted and beautiful hurricane blasting from the furnace of the Mothergate.

There was nothing wrong here, not yet. Or at least nothing wrong that was new. The tangles were still there. Maybe they had grown, or maybe April was just getting better at hearing them. *Many into one. Rules of broken rules. Threads into threads.* It was clearer than ever that too many melodies had been combined with no thought at all for the larger harmonies. Too many stories twisted into a single telling, too many windows open where walls should have been. None of this alarmed April much. The multiverse was self-correcting, because what could not be corrected was simply removed. The removal *was* the correction.

And soon the Medium would be removed, once the Mothergates had closed. Everything would be fine then. You could not tangle what you could not touch.

April had slept soundly after returning from the Warren, a deep sleep pebbled with dreams of marvelous clarity. She didn't believe in dreams as portents—dreams were stories the mind told itself about the past, not the future. She dreamed about Horace and Chloe, about Gabriel, about the Fel'Daera. About the Mothergates.

About the fish, of course.

That fish. April didn't know where it was now. With Falo, probably, or Mr. Meister. At first, when she'd heard it speaking to her in the Warren, she'd hated it. Using the Ravenvine was like opening a door, and while it wasn't always easy to keep that door closed, she didn't really want it to be closed, most of the time. Her willing curiosity kept it open, a sort of invitation. But when she'd first sensed the fish in the glass cylinder, she'd felt something different. Not a passive mind waiting to be witnessed, but an active presence, demanding to be heard.

And what had she heard? She had no idea. Mostly just that insistence. And it wasn't that the fish had known she was there, not at all. Rather that the fish had been . . . what? Broadcasting? Something like that. A living beacon, trapped in glass, forced alive by the power of the Medium. The glass itself was a kind of barrier, she thought, clouding what little she could hear. But inside it, she knew, the fish had been thinking its tormented thoughts, waiting to be heard, for centuries. There was no desire there; it was just a fish. But there was purpose. Nothing *but* purpose, in fact.

There was a reason this terrible thing had been done, a reason dear to whoever had done it. In her dream, the fish had been a cold forest, April lost inside it. It swam though a harmless sea of broken glass worn smooth by ceaseless tides. In the forest, in the distance over the treetops, a thin trail of smoke had endlessly risen. She'd known absolutely that it came from some promised homestead, some comforting shelter, if only it could be found.

But dreams weren't portents, no. Definitely not. They only seemed that way because sometimes buried intentions tested themselves in the mind during sleep. If things came true later on, it wasn't because you dreamed so well. It was because you listened to your mind imagining what you might do.

And April always listened.

The listening she did now, though, had nothing to do with the fish. A sentinel, Falo had called her, and that's what she was being. It was true that she could feel the Mothergates closing, moving slowly toward a moment she couldn't precisely predict. Three days? Four? Through the Mothergate here in Ka'hoka, she could hear the other two—a kind of whistle in the river of story, like a window closing on a howling wind. She knew by now that one would close before the other, though she couldn't say which, and that the Mothergate she stood in front of now would close last of all, just as Falo had claimed.

As for the other thing she was listening for, she had no doubt she'd know it when she heard it. She even had an idea what it might be like. If Isabel managed to reach one of the other Mothergates, and began to weave the flows that would force it to remain open—not against its will, exactly, but against its *need*—

"Do you think she can do it?"

April spun around, craning her neck. The voice had come from above. Neptune hung overhead, sitting crisscross applesauce, high among the rippling waves of the Veil.

"Hey," April called up to her.

"Hay is for horses," Neptune said, and then huffed a shallow laugh. "The end is neigh."

Through the vine, April quieted the roar of the Mothergate to a babble. "Are you asking about Isabel?" she said. "You must have been reading my mind."

"I was there in the Proving Room yesterday. I heard what Falo wants you to do." Neptune drifted lower, her cloak billowing softly. "I still remember when Isabel severed me, when she was just a Tuner. When she had Miradel." She shook her head. "She did things to the flows in my Tan'ji that were . . . very surprising. Astonishing."

"I'm familiar," said April. She watched Neptune carefully. The things she was saying about Isabel sounded an awful lot like compliments. Like admiration. Neptune hadn't been the same since the fall of the Warren, and April had assumed it was because she was worried about Mr. Meister. But now Mr. Meister was back, and Neptune hadn't brightened, hadn't found her old sharp shelf. She seemed . . .

Sad. Lonely. Uncertain.

Like your average teenager, maybe, but . . . April knew something had changed, or was changing. Or was about to change.

"When you ask me if she can do it," April said, "I have to wonder what you mean."

Neptune laughed. "Do you?" She rolled onto her belly in the air. "They say that empaths become empaths not because they love animals so much, but because they understand things. Human things. People."

"But I do love animals," said April. "And I don't feel like I understand people at all."

"I don't think anyone who's met you would agree with that second part. You're very soothing. I've never been soothing, myself. How are you so soothing?"

April shrugged. She'd never been called soothing before. And people were an absolute mystery, as far as she was concerned. "Maybe . . . ," she began, trying to form an idea on her tongue. "Maybe it's because I really don't understand people, and so I end up giving them a lot of room. More room than I even give animals, which is a lot, I think. And maybe people find that room soothing."

"That makes sense," said Neptune. "But also you understood me, when I asked if you thought Isabel could do it. I think you understood me very well."

And April was pretty sure she did. "You want to know if Isabel can actually fix the Mothergates. Not just force them to stay open, but *fix* them. Fix the medium. Fix the Tanu."

"See, this is what I'm talking about. You do understand." Neptune sighed and did a slow somersault. "The Riven don't believe there is anything to fix. They only think the Mothergates need to remain open."

"But that's wrong. I can feel the tangles. I can feel the danger."

"I believe you," Neptune said. "I never didn't believe it. As for fixing those tangles, Falo claims she herself can't do it, and I believe that too. But Isabel is becoming a whole new thing. Even Mr. Meister said so. And maybe that whole new thing can *do* whole new things. Things we thought were impossible."

April didn't answer right away. A queasy nervousness nibbled at her gut.

Because Neptune was wrong.

And it occurred to April suddenly—standing here in the Medium at its source, listening to things the girl high overhead couldn't begin to imagine—that maybe April knew better than anyone how tainted and tangled the Medium truly was. How big the crumpling patch of the multiverse had become. It occurred to her that maybe not even Falo knew as much as April knew now. For Falo, it was faith stacked atop rumors stacked atop facts. A precarious pile, but not wrong. For April, meanwhile, the tangled multiverse was the story she was living in now. The life that belonged to every branching version of herself, in every snarled universe. The song that played in her head when she went to sleep.

But these weren't easy things to say. They wouldn't be easy for Neptune to hear.

"Did Falo part the Veil for you?" she asked Neptune, keeping her voice light. "Is that how you got here?"

"No. Falo doesn't even know I'm here. It turns out she was right about the Veil, and the Mothergates—the Veil isn't hiding them very well anymore. The Mothergate has tremendous gravity. You probably can't tell. But to me, it feels much more massive than it is. Or I guess it actually *is* much more massive than it *looks*. It feels as big as a building to me. Bigger. Bigger than the Willis Tower. I've felt it before, when Falo brought me through the Veil, but now I can feel it even from the outside. I came straight to it through the Veil just now." She furrowed her brow down at April. "Did you think I ought to be asking permission before coming here?"

April didn't. But her nervousness was bubbling a little harder now. She scarcely knew why, and she hated the feeling. She shook her head. "I don't believe in permissions," April said honestly. "Not for this. Not now. If you need to be here, you should be here."

Neptune laughed softly. "There you are again, giving me

room. And I do feel soothed."

Something fell to the floor beneath Neptune with a barely audible *plip*. And again. Neptune rolled onto her back, hands on her face. She was crying.

"Are you okay?" April called softly.

Neptune wiggled her head. Her body shook.

"I can leave, if you like," said April.

Neptune flapped an impatient hand. "Like that wouldn't just make me feel worse. You're actually *doing* something here. I'm just . . . moaning into the void." She folded her legs beneath her again and sank slowly toward the floor. She let herself drift until she was just a few inches off the ground. April sat in front of her, folding her hands in her lap.

"You went back to the Warren yesterday," Neptune said.

"Yes."

"The Riven are there now. I hear they brought a crucible dog in, which means they're turning it into a nest."

April hesitated, waiting. What was it Neptune wanted to hear? What could April possibly want to tell her about what she'd seen and heard and smelled through the vine, through the animal witnesses left behind in the Warren? Crumbled walls, sooty fires burning, the Wardens' own belongings tossed from their dobas like trash. Cruel taunting chants being sung, vile-looking words carved into stone, precious looted Tanu in the hands of the Riven. She hadn't even told Horace or Gabriel about these things.

"I don't want to know, do I?" Neptune said.

"That's not for me to decide," said April. "Are you asking?"

"I'm not asking if you're not offering," Neptune said. "Besides, it doesn't matter." She gazed into the Mothergate. A curling wave of the Veil swept past, throwing muted shadows. After a minute Neptune said, "You also didn't really answer me when I asked if Isabel could fix things. And I'm not dumb. I know what that means." She nodded at the Ravenvine in April's hair. "The patient is inside you. And if you say the only cure for what ails the universe is to let the Mothergates close, I believe you. I already believed it, I think. I just didn't *want* to—and I've wanted to less and less with every day that's passed, now that it's becoming real. But somehow you make it okay to believe. Easier."

"I haven't even really said anything," April pointed out.

"Well, April, maybe that's just the magic of you."

"I don't believe in magic," said April, watching the lights streak through the darkness of the Mothergate.

"Me neither," said Neptune. "And I'm totally floating right now."

They laughed. They watched the Mothergate. The Veil rippled around them, a blown curtain over an unseen moon.

"I've been thinking about stopping," Neptune said after a long while.

"Stopping what?"

"*Stopping,*" Neptune said, and she tossed something onto the floor, a tiny pointed dagger of a stone—her Tan'ji. She fell onto the ground, still seated but swaying, looking suddenly heavy. Her hair lay strangely flat. Her cloak hung limp.

April held her breath. She looked down at the tourminda, the little stone that let Neptune fly. *Stopping.*

"I wouldn't be the first," Neptune said. "Far from it. There are faded walking these very halls. And the faded will survive when—"

"Faded?" April asked. "I don't understand."

"All I have to do is . . . stop listening. I'll drift away from my Tan'ji, from its powers. The bond will thin. And eventually my Tan'ji won't be mine anymore." She poked at the tourminda. It tumbled over like a dead thing.

"But how can you just stop listening?" April said. She was as conscious as ever, here in this strange sad moment before the Mothergate, of the Ravenvine burning with power along her skin, bringing the Medium's song into her ear. "I feel like I could stop breathing before I could stop listening entirely."

"Most would say the same," Neptune said. "But my Tan'ji is nothing like yours. It's a fine thing, I suppose, and it's been in my family forever. But I feel myself drifting away already. It's not that I'm afraid to die—although I am afraid. It's more like . . ." She shrugged, looking down at the tourminda, and there was no light in her eyes at all. No love. No self. "I'm just done."

April sat silently with the words. For a moment, several moments, she wondered if this was a thing she herself could do. Stop listening. Fade away.

Survive.

But even as she rolled the thought around like a taste, like a crime or a bravery she might commit, she knew that she would not. Could not. She was not even sure that there was an April anywhere in the Medium's song that could have done it, anywhere in the tangled universes. She supposed it was terrible, in a way. A kind of failure.

But it didn't feel like a failure. It felt more like one of Horace's willed paths. A thing that not just ought to be, but *would* be.

Neptune's eyes held none of this. And that wasn't a failure either. Not in the least. Surviving never was, because the order of the universe depended upon it.

April reached out and took Neptune's hand. They squeezed each other. The tourminda lay between them. Neptune unclasped the cloak at her throat, letting it rumple to the ground.

"I think I might do it now," Neptune said. "It started on its own, but I can help it along." She squeezed April's hand again and released it.

Neptune stood up. She glanced over at the Mothergate, pointing, suggesting not just the Mothergate itself but what lay beyond it. "Does it create us?" she asked.

"No," April said. "It's the other way around."

Neptune nodded. "That's nice. It's nice of you to say that."

"It's just true."

"Then I am creating it right now." She turned to April.

She nudged the tourminda with her toe. "Take it for me, when you leave. I can still feel it, and I will for a while, but I don't mind. You take it. Okay?"

April nodded.

Neptune looked up into the Veil. "I think I'll walk now," she said, and she turned and left.

April watched her go, watched her fade into the rolling light, kept watching long after Neptune vanished in its arms.

April let the tourminda lie there. She listened to the Medium, the thick cabled story, felt the raveled knots within. She imagined she could hear all the slender threads of Neptune, somewhere within. But probably she could not. She sat for hour upon hour, learning to bear the sad strains of universes beginning to forget themselves. Not that forgetting was necessarily sad—forgetting was a way to make room for something new. A beginning rather than an end. Forgetting could be a good thing.

But not for the forgotten.

At some point she remembered the wonderful Tanu she'd taken from the Warren. She pulled it from her pocket. Inside the little glass sphere, a tiny sapling grew swiftly before her eyes, green and limber. The forever tree, Horace had called it, but that wasn't right. Each tree was a new tree. A life could never last forever, even if life itself just might. April sat with the little sphere for hours more, watching trees grow, bear fruit, and die; grow, bear fruit, and die. When she began to believe she could hear it through the Mothergate—an infinitesimal inscribed loop, a coiled and endless eddy in the story of the multiverse—she put the sphere away.

Falo brought her food. They didn't speak—not with words, anyway, not even when Falo saw the tourminda lying abandoned on the ground. Not even when April picked it up and slipped it into her pocket. They sat in silence while April ate, and later Falo was gone. April stayed, watching, listening. She might have slept, might have dreamed of Neptune fading into a future April herself might not ever see, dreamed of her brother, Derek, and poor lost Joshua and brave First Baron, and—

A bellowing groan rocked her. A low, aching cry of pain—stubborn and surprised—and then actual pain. Agony. A callous finger probing a healing wound, pulling it apart. April scrambled to her feet, hand pressed against the Ravenvine. A flood of bewildered torment poured through it, filling her.

Isabel, somewhere in some far corner of the world. Standing before a distant Mothergate, weaving the first threads of a flow meant to yank the Mothergate wide and nail it open. It felt worse than April had imagined it would, far worse. The Mothergate was groaning in protest like a great wooden ship foundering on rocks.

This was not a dream. This was happening. Dr. Jericho's terrible, brilliant plan was under way.

April tried to calm herself, every muscle rigid with pain. The Wardens had a plan too. A good one. The *only* one. Horace and Chloe.

She turned her back on the Mothergate. She gritted her

teeth against the tortured keening that billowed through her, slow as whalesong and sharp as a scalpel. Help was coming. She would bring it. Just wait. Help was coming.

She launched herself into the Veil.

CHAPTER THIRTEEN

Through the Mothergate

"IF WE DON'T COME BACK," CHLOE ANNOUNCED, "IT'LL PROBA-bly be because my mother killed us."

Beside her, Horace gazed up at the black mass of the Mothergate, clutching the astrolabe. "Let's hope that's why," he said.

Chloe let herself frown at him. She had never had a lot of control over her facial expressions—or so she'd been told—and Horace definitely deserved her most miserable frown for that comment. She'd been kidding about the mom thing. Mostly. But it was no joke for Horace to suggest that something worse might happen to them as they prepared to step into the depths of the Mothergate. Horace caught her frown but only shrugged at her. He was barely sorry.

Falo stood beside them, her tall shadow seeming to dance as the Veil of Lura slid over her. "You will come back," she said. "A Paragon of the Fel'Daera holds the astrolabe, and a Paragon of the Alvalaithen goes to meet her mother. A mother who wants nothing more than to see her daughter safe."

Another frown, then, just for Falo. Falo saw it too, but didn't even have the decency to shrug.

April seemed the most nervous of all, but Chloe wasn't exactly sure where her worry lay. She'd sounded the alarm, alerting them that their greatest fears were coming true. With whatever awful power Grooma had given her, Isabel was attempting to repair one of the Mothergates. Horace and Chloe were going to stop her, in some remote Altari stronghold halfway around the world. In Crete, apparently.

"Where are we going again, exactly?" Chloe asked.

"Nlon'ka," Falo said, the word falling out of her lips like a rock into water. "Though it was once a great Altari city, Nlon'ka is now all but abandoned. The Nevren keeps the Riven out, but since Isabel isn't a Keeper, she likely faced no resistance when she made her way through the Veil to the Mothergate hidden there."

"And once we get there, our plan is to . . . what, exactly?" asked Chloe. Not that she hadn't been thinking of a plan. But planning wasn't exactly a strength of hers. In fact, sometimes she thought her greatest strength might be *not* planning.

"Stop her," said Falo. "Use your powers. Use whatever you can. But do not underestimate the power of words. Isabel is likely to be alone, which means she'll have no Riven whispering into her ear. Because Joshua cannot open a portal into a location underground, he would have brought Isabel—and any Riven that accompanied her—close to the entrance of Nlon'ka. But Isabel would then have had to pass through the Nevren within Nlon'ka to get to the Mothergate. No Riven could have come with her."

"Why won't she be expecting us?" Horace asked. "Doesn't she know that the Mothergates are actually . . . gates?"

"Travel through the Mothergates is rare," Falo explained. "True accounts of such travel have been told only in whispers, and those whispers have faded into rumor."

Horace studied the Mothergate. "Time is slippery inside," he said. "The astrolabe should fix that. But won't space be slippery too, then? Once we're inside, how will we even know where to go? And how will we get there?"

"Once you are within, you must get to the other Mothergate at once," Falo replied.

That was no kind of answer. "Will we see it?" Chloe insisted. "Is it empty in there?"

"Quite the opposite," said Falo. "But I won't describe what you must witness yourself. Stay together, and stay true to the astrolabe. Get to where you need to go, when you need to get there. And remember that travel inside the Mothergate is not like travel in the outside world. You must travel with your thoughts, not your body."

"No cabs, then," Chloe said. "No escalators."

"That is beside the point," said Falo. "The exit you seek might seem near or far. That distance is an illusion. You might envision yourself walking to it. The walking, too, is an illusion."

Chloe turned to Horace for help, but he hardly seemed to be listening, still fixated on the Mothergate.

Falo tried again. "When a conscious mind enters the Mothergate, the Medium within presents itself as a kind of stage," she said. "Many stages, upon which all the stories of the multiverse are being told. You must be one of those stories."

"I've got a story," Chloe said, not at all liking what she was hearing. "Once upon a time, we made it through the Mothergate. The end."

Falo spread her elegant hands. "That should suffice."

"Oh my god," said Chloe. "Horace, are you hearing this?"

"I think I understand," April said cautiously. "The thread of the story begins here, and it ends in Nlon'ka. The path between them—through the Mothergates—is the story of how you got there." She wrinkled her nose. "But the path doesn't matter. Inside the Mothergates, the path doesn't exist, only the story. And the story is in your mind."

"I don't know if anybody's noticed," Chloe said, "but I *do* things. I'm not a storyteller."

"You're not a storyteller, no," Horace said suddenly. "But I am."

Chloe waited for him to explain, feeling angry and—okay—maybe a little bit panicked. Horace wasn't a storyteller. Horace was . . .

And then she realized he had one hand on the Fel'Daera.

He shrugged at her. "What we're talking about isn't so different from looking into the future, is it? Two ends of a thread. A story in between."

"You can't use the Fel'Daera to get us there," she said, not knowing at all if that was true.

"I'm not talking about using the Fel'Daera. I'm talking about using the thing that makes the Fel'Daera work for me. A willed path. A story I know the beginning and the end of, but nothing in between."

"Yes," said Falo, beaming down at him. "Let there be nothing in between. Go now. Get there fast. Stop Isabel however you can." She stepped back, gesturing to the Mothergate.

"We're going," Chloe growled, furious that her usual reckless confidence wasn't catching fire like it normally did. She still wasn't sure she understood, wasn't sure she *wanted* to understand. She blamed Isabel for the messy doubts that were clouding her now, and she was pretty sure the woman deserved it. "I never said I wasn't going."

And then Horace took Chloe's hand. "Do you feel that?" he asked her.

For one stupid moment, Chloe thought he meant his hand, and how just the feel of it—maddeningly—crumpled her doubts into a tiny, tossable ball. She sort of hated that he seemed to know it.

But then she felt something else. Something steady and firm, pulsing out of Horace and into her. And whether it was some strength of his, or the Fel'Daera's, or the heavy grounded sweep of the astrolabe, it didn't much matter. She still wasn't catching fire, no, but she felt suddenly calm and sure. She felt, weirdly, like an arrow nocked and drawn in Ravana's bow. Maybe that was fire enough. Horace would take them true—where and when they needed to go.

And the rest would be up to her.

She squeezed Horace's hand as hard she could, wondering if she could hurt him. Just a little.

"Don't mess this up," she said. "We're supposed to be the heroes, or something."

Horace laughed and drew her tight to his side. And then either she took the first step or he did, and they walked into the Mothergate together without saying good-bye.

A yawning, endless sweep of gold, as blank as the humour. A blast of sound like a vast wall of glass breaking into silence as they passed through it.

They emerged into a kaleidoscope.

Falo had said the space inside the Mothergates was far from empty. It turned out that was an understatement.

They found themselves adrift in a sea of colliding, overlapping worlds. Chloe thought immediately of sea ice, broken and jagged and piled high upon itself, pushed together in grinding heaps by relentless tides.

Distant mountains groaned into the sky and then toppled. A forest, or something like a forest, rolled over like a breaking wave, all around them. A great stretch of liquid—an ocean?—filled and drained. Phantom buildings materialized out of thin air, only to fold beneath other structures demanding the same space—normal earth-type buildings, yes, but also buildings that were utterly strange and foreign. Alien. Towers of glass looming overhead, chunky works of stone, great flat expanses that looked alive but had obviously been crafted. Streets and paths and bridges presented themselves, then bent out of existence. Entire cities drifted past them, surrounding them, and then were swallowed as new landscapes arose. The sky filled itself with earth, and the earth broke apart. The ground split beneath them into rivers of red. Everything was here, piled high and buried deep, ever shifting.

None of it touched them.

The only thing missing was life itself. Just as Falo had promised, they saw no one in any of the storyscapes that churned around them like the dreams of giants. Even so, everything they saw seemed to hum with consciousness, intention, history. This was the witnessed multiverse—or all its ghosts, anyway—gathered and compacted like snowfall into an ancient glacier, grinding slowly and endlessly past.

Behind them—except there *was* no behind here—a white fracture like a forgotten patch of canvas seemed to yawn. A crack. Rivers of this tumbling world poured into it, vanishing. It didn't matter, Chloe knew, because there was always more, always emerging, stage after stage.

This blank patch was the crack they'd just come through. The Mothergate. How long ago? It could have been ages, here in this place. Or it could have been less than a second, but ages outside. She turned to look at it again, but now the patch was gone, a golden hill of head-high grass swelling in its place. Chloe panicked for a moment, remembering that Falo had said she'd lost three years when she'd come through the Mothergate.

But then she flexed her hand, squeezing. Horace squeezed her back. And now she saw him, Horace as he was just a minute ago, Horace as he always was.

Or no. Horace as he would be. Horace as he *could* be. Changing and changing, always staying the same. His face shifted like a gallery of pictures—Horace as a child, an old man, a young man. Horace on this path or another, subtle changes to his skin and hair and color. A scar here, an alarming gauntness there, a cheerful glow or a stoic sadness. All of it melding, fusing, fluttering past, a parade of every possible Horace that could be, or maybe was. But on every face, the same look of awe as he gazed back at her. His dark brown eyes—always the same eyes, whatever happened to the rest of him—roved her face with wonder.

"How do I look?" she asked him, and was surprised to find that her voice could be heard.

"Strong," he said. "Frightening." He watched her. He changed and stayed the same, just as she was too. "Beautiful," he said.

And she didn't even care that he was saying it.

At last she tore her eyes away, turning to the madly

churning worlds around them. "I feel like the brochure didn't really do this place justice," she said.

"Not remotely," said Horace. He looked down at his feet. "There are currents tugging at us. Do you feel them?"

Chloe didn't.

"Flows of time," he explained. "Fast and slow, pushing and pulling." He opened his mouth and lifted his briefly bearded chin. A dwindling sun roared past above them, turning swiftly red. "But it's okay." He raised his hand, still clenched around the astrolabe. "We're a rock."

She nodded at him, grateful and proud. "There are other doors here, Horace," she said, putting words to a thought that was only now forming. "A million doors. Billions. I can feel them."

"Mothergates, you mean?"

"No, not like that. It's like . . ." But there were no words. Chloe didn't even understand how she knew these doors were there, shining in the seams between the colliding realms that convulsed around them. Something in her flesh knew these doors. Or whatever passed for flesh in this place. Something about being the Keeper of the Alvalaithen. Her flesh told her that there were passages everywhere, paths she could take. It felt like there were different possibilities for nearly every atom in her body. It was frightening, invigorating.

"We don't need those doors," Horace said.

"I know," Chloe lied. "We need to get to the other Mothergate."

231

Horace smiled. "And since our need was so great, we did manage to get there."

A vast and gentle herd of sand dunes rolled past them like a pod of dusty whales. They melted away, scattering into whispers and revealing a city of green stone. The city was already before Chloe's eyes. It was nothing special, this city, just another stage. But there—or here, rather—she suddenly saw another slash of vacant space. Part of the same door they'd come through before, another crack of light around its edge. A sky of purple clouds dripped slowly into the discolored crack like paint, fading into absence.

"The Mothergate," she said. "You did it."

Horace laughed. "I guess I did. Are we ready?"

But being ready had been part of the story from the start. No sooner had he spoken than they fell into the crack, or the crack fell upon them. A blinding white cosmos, another shattering wall of sound.

They stumbled out into a dark sea, solid unchanging ground beneath their feet. They were through.

But they'd emerged into a lightning storm.

Jagged streams of golden light surrounded them, streaking past. Chloe swore she could hear thunder booming, and the crackle of electricity. But the storm was silent, and now she found her bearings. These were Isabel's flows, weaves of the Medium, hurtling into the Mothergate they'd just left, trying to pin it wide open. There were colors laced in among the gold. Colors that didn't have names, colors Chloe had seen before, watching Brian work with the Medium back at the Warren. Horace couldn't see the colors, she knew, and with that thought, her rage finally kindled, blessedly. She could only see the colors because she was the daughter of a Tuner, of a would-be Dorvala.

Isabel's daughter.

Abruptly the storm subsided. The streams of light vanished, revealing the deep, rippling ocean of the Veil. The Mothergate stood atop a low raised platform, surrounded by a wide circle of broad steps, descending in every direction. This was Nlon'ka.

And there was Isabel.

Her mother stood alone, at the bottom of the steps, hands hanging slack at her side. Her wild red hair was drawn back tight behind her head, revealing a face that Chloe knew mostly from her dreams, from a few worn photographs, from a handful of gut-twisting hours over the last several days. That face had always been wild, always fierce, too uncomfortably like Chloe's own.

But now it had changed. Isabel's eyes had gone deeper into the wild, into something closer to madness.

"Chloe," Isabel said, her voice full of wonder.

Chloe couldn't speak. Not yet. She looked back at the light-streaked black chasm of the Mothergate, memories of the jumbled landscapes within still clinging to her like dreams.

Her gut heaved at what she saw now. Partway around the edge of the Mothergate—though it wasn't even meant to have an edge—a gruesome stretch of flowing gold swept out like a curtain blown in through an open window and frozen in place. Although it was thick where it emerged from the black, it thinned as it rose high into the air above, dwindling into a hundred zigzagging fingers, each one like a ragged row of hasty stitches. Colors bled from between each stitch, crimson and rust and scarlet and mahogany and a thousand other shades of red-but-not-red. This was how Isabel was doing it. Peeling away sheets of the Medium as it flowed through the Mothergate and sewing it to the very fabric of this world. Chloe didn't need to be a Maker to know that this was wrong, that it was violent beyond reason, that it was the work of a desperate hand unable to do anything else.

And that it would work.

If Isabel finished the job, the Mothergate would be splayed open like a gutted carcass, unable to close.

Chloe wanted to puke.

"Chloe," Isabel said again. She sounded grateful now, happy to see her. As if there could ever be a universe where that would be a thing.

Chloe turned.

"You came through the Mothergate," said Isabel, shuffling closer. "You came to see how I'm doing it. I'm fixing it."

"No, Mom," Chloe said, the first time she'd spoken the word without venom for as long as she could remember. Her rage was a coiled tiger. "You're not fixing it. And that's not remotely why I'm here."

Isabel's brow wrinkled in confusion. "They've tricked you," she said, as if she was gravely disappointed. "The Wardens have you believing that the Mothergates can't be fixed."

"And the Riven have you believing that you're something you're not. That you can do things that can't be done."

Isabel sank into a cloud of outrage. Her eyes flicked to Horace, like she was just now seeing him.

A moment later, Horace crumpled to the ground.

"Stop," Chloe said calmly, though her insides were a melting vat of fury. Horace was severed, mumbling incoherently with empty eyes, cut off from the Fel'Daera. Chloe took a step forward, edging toward Isabel. "Let him go."

"You came here to stop me," Isabel said. Shadows deepened in her face. "You don't have the first idea. Do you know what I endured to get this power? To do this thing?" She flung a hand at the Mothergate, at the stitched patch of the Medium splayed out like a stretched hide.

"I know some of it," Chloe said. "I know what Mr. Meister did to you, and what you might have become if he'd let you."

"Then you know what kind of man he is. What kind of monster."

Chloe took a deep breath. Still she kept walking. "I know he did the right thing."

Isabel gasped as if she'd been slapped. Behind her, Horace groaned.

"Look at what you're doing right now," Chloe said. "Look

at what you're doing to the Mothergate. This won't fix anything."

"I'm saving you," Isabel said. "I'm saving it all."

"You're not saving anyone. And I don't even remember asking you to save me anyway."

"That's what a mother does. She does things that shouldn't need asking."

Too much. Too outrageous. A flood of heat rushed up Chloe's neck into her head. "Is that why you—"

Chloe stopped herself, holding up her hands and looking down at her feet, refusing to let anger carry her down the path she needed to walk now. She inched closer to Isabel, keeping herself steady.

"Do you remember that night on the pier?" Chloe asked. "With the Riven? You told the Auditor you were no mother of mine." Chloe was trembling now, her hands aching to ball into fists. "But you *are* my mother. Not the mother I wanted, no, and probably not the mother I deserved. And maybe I don't know much about it, but it seems like mothers can never forget the ways they've wronged their children. I hope you never forget."

She stepped up to Isabel. Here in front of the Mothergate, at the Medium's source, the Alvalaithen's music was an easy, forceful song. She only needed the tiniest sip. Chloe sank slowly into the ground, looking up at her mother. She sank in to her knees. She hung there effortlessly, hovering.

"Does this look familiar?" Chloe said. "It should. This is

how I was when you severed me that day. The day that made you leave."

Isabel stared at her, rigid with horror. Chloe thought she could see the memories flickering in her eyes.

"It was an honest mistake," Chloe said. "I know it was. You couldn't control the harp, and . . . and *I would have forgiven you.*" She felt the truth in her own words, and the confusion that came with them. "But then you left us. That was how you fixed it then. Instead of giving up the harp, you left."

"Mr. Meister—"

"Let Horace go," Chloe said quietly. "Let him go, or I'll release the Alvalaithen. I'll meld myself right here, right now, and I won't get out this time. Let him go, or there won't be anything for you to save."

Chloe felt the cold stone in her legs, in her bones, broken so badly all those years ago. Maybe she meant it. She thought she probably did. She let herself sink deeper, up to her waist.

"Let him go," she said again.

Neither of them breathed. Chloe let the wings of the Alvalaithen slow, its song fading. She felt the faint bite of matter inside her flesh.

At last Isabel stepped back, tearing her eyes away. Back by the Mothergate, Horace took a great gasping breath.

Chloe shot to the surface, finding solid ground beneath her feet again. She turned and hurried back to Horace, kneeling beside him. "You okay?" she asked.

"I'm fine. Fine. How did you—"

"They lie, you know," Isabel called out. "Mr. Meister and all the rest. They lied to me and they're lying to you too. Have they told you about the Fel'Daera? How it's to blame for all of this?"

"Is that what Dr. Jericho told you?" Chloe asked. Everyone was a liar. Everyone told stories, or hid them. But no one more than Dr. Jericho.

"I tuned the Fel'Daera, remember?" said Isabel. "And Tuners know things about the instruments they touch. Things even their Makers don't know."

"So you're the expert, then," said Horace.

"I tuned it when no one else could. Not even Jessica could do it—not even your own mother, Horace Andrews."

Horace clambered slowly to his feet. "To be fair," he said with a little shrug, "she wasn't my mother yet. She might have tried harder if she'd known."

Chloe thought her heart would burst with pride.

"It's because of the Fel'Daera that the Mothergates are dying," Isabel insisted.

"Nothing you're saying makes sense," Horace said reasonably. "The Mothergates were an accident from the start. They were never meant to last. And while they've been open, we've each grabbed the power and the knowledge pouring out of them and twisted it all up. Tangled universes together. The Fel'Daera has done that, for sure. I know that now. But so have all the other Tanu. Even the Alvalaithen. And if we don't

238

let the Mothergates close like they're supposed to—"

"Lies, lies, lies!" Isabel shrieked. "You think you know everything. Just like the Fel'Daera's last Keeper."

"You knew Samuel?" Horace asked calmly.

Isabel recoiled in surprise. It was obvious she neither knew the name nor expected that Horace would know it.

"I didn't have to meet him to know him," she said. "I scraped all his evil out of the Fel'Daera when I tuned it." She shook her head. "I should have left it twisted, full of all of his arrogance. Full of all the damage he'd done."

"Horace is the Keeper of the Fel'Daera now, not Samuel," said Chloe.

Isabel pointed at him. "But Horace carries the astrolabe, doesn't he? Just like the last time."

Now it was Chloe's turn to be surprised. How Isabel knew that Horace had the astrolabe, Chloe couldn't have guessed. She willed herself not to react. "We had an important date to keep," said Chloe. "With you."

"Horace is your friend, and that's why I'm sparing him, but you need to know. When I tuned the Fel'Daera, it was full of death."

"Death?" Chloe scoffed, trying to laugh. "What death?"

But beside her, Horace was silent.

"Horace knows what I mean," Isabel said triumphantly. "Sil'falo Teneves would have never sent him to see me on a day like today without telling him herself. Wouldn't it have looked bad for her if the truth had come from me?"

More lies. More stories. "What do you know about the truth?" Chloe demanded.

Isabel started to answer, but Horace cut her off, staring the woman right in the face.

"The Fel'Daera destroys universes," he said.

The words hung there for a moment. Chloe snatched the silence away. "Don't be silly," she said. "That's not tr—"

"It is," Horace said. "That's how it finds the future. It erases all the other possible futures that might evolve from the present. It . . . consumes all those possible paths to feed the one path that then happens. The willed path."

"Future universes that might evolve," Chloe repeated, grappling with this news. "The Fel'Daera *eats* them?"

"Basically," Horace said, still pouring his brick-wall stare into Isabel's wild eyes.

Chloe took it in, thinking hard. The multiverse thing wasn't exactly beyond her, not at all, but it was not something her brain liked to wrestle with. Or maybe it was her heart that didn't like it. April's heart was loose enough to encompass all the other universes ever, it sometimes seemed, but not Chloe's. And now Horace was talking about other *future* universes. Other *future* paths.

She watched him. She could tell by his expression and his voice—a kind of steely certainty that was pleasant to witness, in small doses—that he'd been working through this. He'd clearly *already* worked through it, in fact, without ever telling her. They'd spent the entire day together. Not a word. And while part of her was irritated that Horace hadn't told her how the Fel'Daera did what it did, another part of her was glad he hadn't.

Because honestly?

Chloe did not give a crap.

These were future universes Horace was talking about. People and places that didn't even exist yet. If the Fel'Daera wanted to chow down on a future universe with a future Chloe in it, in order to save the *present* universe with the *present* Chloe in it . . . well . . . munch away. Munch away all day.

But she said none of this to her good friend now. He didn't need to hear it. She took him firmly by the elbow.

"It's not your fault," she told him.

"It doesn't matter," he said.

"It matters to you."

"If you're looking for fault," Isabel said, "there's plenty to go around. Beginning with Sil'falo Teneves herself. She's the Maker. She created an instrument that's done more damage than any hundred instruments combined."

Horace rounded on her. "Really?" he said. "I tell you what. How about we test it out?"

And he pulled the Fel'Daera from its pouch.

Chloe had seen him do it a hundred times, but watching Horace now as he prepared to look through the blue glass—grounding himself in the present, awash in a focus so deep and devoted that it had to be called selfish—Chloe understood without question that she would never admire anyone as much as she admired this boy. Her knees nearly buckled beneath the weight of her certainty. Horace was terrified. Anyone could see that—or *she* could, anyway, plain as day. The future universes she could so easily dismiss were poisoned thorns in Horace's belly. And he was going to do this anyway.

Horace opened the box with the familiar flick of his thumb, just about the only thing he ever did that could ever be called graceful. He lifted the box to his eyes, to Isabel.

He watched. No one spoke. Chloe felt unreasonably giddy as Isabel squirmed grimly under his gaze. She actually took a step back. But there was no hiding from the Fel'Daera. Horace watched her for several seconds, then turned to face the Mothergate. He studied it through the glass, silent and sturdy. They stood there for what felt like forever. Horace's lips parted; it was so quiet Chloe heard it happen. What was he seeing? The Veil tumbled over them like night endlessly chasing day.

At last Horace snapped the box closed. He slid it back into the pouch.

He turned back to Isabel. "You have three minutes," he said.

Chloe could practically see the woman choking back the urge to ask Horace what he'd seen.

"It's not a toy you've got there," Isabel said.

"That's good, because I'm not playing," Horace replied.

And then, strangely, Isabel's mad, clouded eyes seemed to

clear, just for a moment. As she looked at the two of them, her face wrinkled with a sadness that couldn't have been feigned. "You chose which stories to believe," she said. "And I've chosen mine. I know in my heart that you're wrong about the Mothergates, but either way, one has to wonder why Falo did what she did. Why she allowed herself to bring a thing like the Fel'Daera into the world."

Chloe looked at Horace. He shifted uneasily. For the first time since Isabel had unsevered him, a shadow of doubt seemed to fall across him.

"Tell me why, then," said Horace. "I suppose you know that, too."

"Don't misunderstand me," Isabel said. "The Altari always have the same reasons for doing what they do. Arrogance and ambition. Never stopping to wonder if they should, once they started wondering if they could. It's not about why Falo did it. It's about why she didn't stop herself."

"We're done here," Chloe announced, unable to listen to any more. "Your time is almost up. Go back to your friends, Mom."

Isabel flinched from the word. "I'm not finished," she said, but she could not quite avoid looking at the Fel'Daera.

"You are," Chloe said. "Leave this place and try again. There are two more gates. Maybe you'll get lucky. But if you come back here alone, I'll come back too. And I'll come back with an Altari army so big you'll never be able to cleave them all before they swarm you."

Isabel looked down at herself. She clenched and unclenched her fists, as if testing her strength. "You'll never hear me say Falo is a fool," she said. "I know she sent you here because you were the one person I wouldn't cleave dead on the spot. But she's underestimated me. She underestimates what Grooma did to me." She laughed. "I'm still weak from the weaving, you know. Truth be told, I can barely stand! I'm here now only because that Mothergate behind you is about to die. The few stitches I managed to get in place won't hold. But like you say, there are two more gates. And tomorrow I'll be stronger." She lowered her chin and smiled, her red hair like demon fire. "You have no idea how strong."

She lifted her hands. Swirls of the Medium began to rise around her, like blades emerging from the floor. They spun swiftly into a cyclone with Isabel at the center. Chloe refused to step back. The song of the Alvalaithen roared inside her like a sea. Horace didn't budge either. He'd seen this through the Fel'Daera, no doubt. His expression didn't change.

Around Isabel, the Veil began to flutter. Its light began to bend into her cyclone, drawn like water to a drain, like smoke to a fan. Up and up the spinning funnel of golden blades went, faster and wider, and as it spun, the Veil was drawn inexorably into it and torn to shreds, howling like a banshee wind. In just a few shocking seconds, the vast ocean of light was gone. The chamber they stood in was now revealed, looking naked and vast, a great blue dome three hundred feet wide and a hundred feet high.

And they weren't alone. Halfway to the edge of the room, a small figure got awkwardly to his feet, watching them, seeing them for the first time now that the Veil was gone. A small blue sphere floated at his side.

"Joshua," Chloe breathed.

"Yes," said Horace. He'd already seen Joshua through the box. Seen and said nothing.

"Should we call to him?" she asked. "We need to take him. He needs to come with us."

Horace only shook his head.

And then Joshua was the one that called out. "Horace!" he cried, not waving, his tiny fists clenched at his sides. "Chloe?"

Chloe's heart broke a little bit. Something about her name coming out of that boy's mouth as a question. Just a little boy, really. A little boy far beyond his depth.

Isabel flung a hand at Joshua, almost casually. Joshua fell to the ground, severed. Chloe started to take a step forward. But she knew she wouldn't. Knew she didn't.

"He's mastered the Laithe," Isabel called back, her voice echoing up and around the empty dome. "He's helping me. He doesn't want to die."

"Nobody here wants to die," Chloe said.

"You say that like you believe it," said Isabel. "Tell me this, then. When I stop the Mothergates from closing, and you're still alive, will you thank me?"

Chloe found a way to laugh. She almost had to laugh not

to cry. "When the Mothergates are gone, and I'm dead, will you realize how crappy a mother has to be to ask her daughter a question like that?"

Isabel turned away. She went to Joshua, muttering something to him, and the boy got slowly to his feet. He glanced down at the Laithe for a moment and then tore the meridian free. A second later, a wide, round portal sprang to life. A single Mordin stood on the far side, gaunt and powerful and unmistakable, turning to look at the portal as it formed.

Isabel took Joshua's hand and roughly yanked him through the portal to where Dr. Jericho stood waiting. As Joshua passed, taking the Laithe with him, the image through the portal winked out. The empty ring of the meridian hung there for a moment, shimmering, and then shrank out of sight.

Chloe breathed, hardly daring to imagine what Isabel was telling the Mordin now.

"The Mothergate is closing," Horace said softly.

Chloe turned to look. Isabel's unfinished stitches were tearing free. The pinned swaths of the Medium were shrinking back into the black. The Mothergate itself seemed to be pulsing, the streaks of light within it slowing.

"It's happening," she said.

"Yes. Let's stay and watch. We'll leave before it's gone."

The suggestion was a surprise. They needed to get back. But then she realized that the box must have shown Horace that they would stay. And if they didn't . . . thrall-blight. Denying the future the box revealed was the surest way to speed up the collapse of the Mothergates. And what if all the Mothergates closed while they were inside? On the heels of that thought, it occurred to Chloe that the Fel'Daera must have also shown Horace what they could *not* stay to see—the death of the Mothergate itself.

"How long?" she asked him.

Horace lifted his brow and pursed his lips, like he didn't know. But then he said, "One minute, eight seconds."

"It's fighting what Isabel tried to do," Chloe said as another wide stretch of stitches gave way, and more of the Medium snapped back into the quivering Mothergate.

They stood and watched. Chloe felt nothing through the Alvalaithen. The Medium would still flow as strong as ever, she knew, pouring with even greater force through the two Mothergates that remained. Still, she'd thought she'd feel *something*.

"Tell me we shouldn't have bothered trying to save Joshua," Chloe said.

"You know I can't do that. I can only tell you we didn't. And anyway, I thought you said he didn't even want to be saved."

Chloe sighed, aggravated. She had said that, and meant it. Maybe it didn't matter. What did it even mean to save a Keeper, when the Mothergates were about to die?

And what did it mean not to bother?

"I'm just saying," she said. "If Joshua's there at the next Mothergate . . . before you open the box, you need to know that I want to save him. Remember."

"Okay," Horace said. "I won't forget."

Just a few of Isabel's stitches remained. The Mothergate seemed to grow blacker still, vibrating. At its fringes, it began to roll in on itself, as if its outermost reaches were becoming solid and breaking apart, falling into the abyss. It was thickening faster than it could be swallowed. The gateway was closing. And now Chloe could feel it, a thinning in the hurricane force of the Medium as it usually was, so close to a Mothergate. Horace could feel it too, she was sure. She should have been frightened.

"It's time," Horace said a few seconds later, taking Chloe's hand. "We need to enter while we still can." The Mothergate continued to fill itself, becoming a jagged monolith, a scar of bristling stone. The Medium slowed to a soft breeze.

"So this is what winning feels like," Chloe said.

"I guess it is," Horace replied.

And then they stepped into the trembling, collapsing black together.

CHAPTER FOURTEEN

The Starlit Loom

It was 1:46 in the morning. Horace hadn't slept. Sleep wasn't coming anytime soon. His mind wouldn't let it.

Chloe and April lay in the next bed over. April was snoring loudly but peacefully, like a trilling bird. Meanwhile Arthur, an actual bird, had settled quietly into a roost atop a bookshelf across the room. Chloe was curled atop the bed beside April, motionless, eyes closed.

He watched her, thinking of where they'd been together earlier that night—into the Mothergate, where Chloe had been . . . every Chloe ever. And him every Horace. It was a thing they should not have been asked to do together. A thing he would never surrender, not in a million years.

Horace held the Fel'Daera in his lap, feeling strangely rested, full of an energy he had no right to. He was waiting. He had been waiting for one minute and forty-seven seconds.

At seven minutes, on the dot—on the tiniest fraction of a dot, thanks in part to the incredible accuracy of the astrolabe—a traveler would arrive. April's nickel. The nickel that Falo had flipped for them, when telling them about the multiverse. Horace had been sending it through the box for the last fifty-one minutes. Sending it, watching it arrive, and sending it again. Wondering. Experimenting. Seven sendings so far, with the breach set at seven minutes. And every time the nickel had arrived.

But how?

And more importantly, why did it ever *not*?

He set the Fel'Daera on the bed and stood up, thinking, trying to let a completely unexpected thing come into his mind. Something . . . unpredictable. He let his thoughts roll for two full minutes, and then an idea came to him. A random idea that he was sure had not entered his mind yet tonight.

He began to do jumping jacks—the worst exercise ever invented, particularly for the less coordinated. He flailed his arms and legs, struggling to make them work in unison. Once he found some kind of rhythm, he made the peace sign with his hands as he jumped—another random thought. And a bit after that, he started smacking his lips very softly, like a fish—*pok* . . . *pok* . . . *pok*. And then he crossed his eyes. He kept jumping, smacking, doing all of it at once. He was pretty sure he was doing a thing no one had ever done before. He was pretty sure he looked like an idiot.

"Horace." Chloe's voice floated dryly to him in the dim

light. Horace startled awkwardly to a halt, blushing.

"Yeah?" he said, puffing softly.

"What the hell are you doing?"

"I'm . . . experimenting."

"Night experiments again," she said. "With the Fel'Daera. Meanwhile I'm trying to pretend to be asleep."

"I know."

"I'm pretending not to know that you're doing crazy things."

"I appreciate that."

She sat up, her feet dangling high above the floor. "I don't understand what you're doing, but there are better ways to wake a person, if you need them," she said. She looked right at him, obviously not mad, waiting for him to explain.

But he couldn't explain.

She stepped into the silence he left hanging there. "Is it the Mothergate?" She fiddled the fingers of one hand at her own face, and with the other did the same at his. "Not the stuff we saw inside, I mean. I mean the dying."

He knew what she meant. There was no way to talk about what they'd seen inside the Mothergate, and also no need. There would never be a need. But it wasn't the death of the first Mothergate that was troubling him, either. That was a trouble so huge he could barely even see it, much less talk about it.

When they'd returned with the news that the first Mothergate had collapsed, it hadn't been news at all. Not to Falo

251

and April, anyway. The two of them had felt it, of course—April through the Ravenvine and Falo through . . .

Through what? Through the Starlit Loom, it had to be, even though the mysterious Tan'ji had not been revealed. By now Horace assumed the Starlit Loom just wasn't a thing anyone ever got the chance to see, even though his own mother had seen it once, long ago. Held it, even. Horace wasn't offended, exactly—there was no reason for Falo to reveal the Starlit Loom. Least of all to him.

The closing of the Mothergate hadn't been news, no, but Falo had asked a dozen questions about Isabel's attempts to force it to remain open. She listened to their descriptions of Isabel's crude and violent weavings, and agreed that what she'd done had probably hastened the Mothergate's death—but only because Horace and Chloe had interrupted her. Unable to finish her terrible work, Isabel had sped the inevitable process along, as the Mothergate recoiled from what she was doing. But if Isabel had been allowed to finish, Falo felt sure, what should have been inevitable might have become impossible. She seemed more convinced than ever that Isabel, with her terrible new powers, had the ability to pin the Mothergates open, no matter how primitive her weavings might seem.

And Isabel was only getting stronger.

Now they were waiting. Falo and Chloe were confident that after this first failure, the Riven would wait before sending Isabel out again. She'd been temporarily weakened by the weaving she'd endured at the hands of Grooma, and weakened further still by her efforts at Nlon'ka. They couldn't afford to send her until she'd gained the full strength promised by what Grooma had done—not unless the next Mothergate was truly on the verge of collapsing. Falo had told them all to get some sleep while they could, and April was definitely taking advantage of the opportunity.

But here were Horace and Chloe, awake in the middle of the night, talking. Again.

"It's not about the Mothergates," Horace said to Chloe. "It's the Fel'Daera."

"Because of what Falo told you? About the box feasting on other futures?"

Horace grimaced. "That's not . . . can we not use that word? Feasting?"

"Horace, I know it's not the best news. Not the best story. But maybe—*maybe*—you're worried about harming things that don't even exist."

"It's not that simple, Chloe. The future . . . those other universes . . . it's complicated."

Chloe let out a sigh that was more of a growl. "I know. It's so complicated, I'm not even convinced we're supposed to be thinking about it."

"If we weren't supposed to think about it, we wouldn't be Tan'ji."

She went quiet for a minute, letting April's snores fill the room. Then she said, "I'm not really feeling the need to talk

253

about it, but I can't stop thinking about when we stepped through the Mothergate. What we saw there. Do you think there's a universe where there's a Chloe who never Found the Alvalaithen?"

"I don't know," Horace replied. "I suppose there might be."

"Do you think she's as awesome as I am?"

When Horace didn't answer right away, considering it, Chloe said curtly, "She's not, Horace. You're supposed to say she's not."

"She's not. Of course she's not. How could she be?"

With a soft pop, the nickel reappeared in midair, glinting. Chloe jumped. The nickel fell noisily to the ground. April grunted softly.

On the instant, there was a soft musical knock at the door—*tap, tap, tap-tap.*

Now it was Horace's turn to jump. Arthur rustled too, letting out a babyish chirp. Before they could say anything, Sil'falo Teneves glided into the room, a towering angelic ghost. "You are awake," she said softly to Horace, her matter-of-fact tone suggesting it was a thing she'd already known. Had she felt him using the box?

"I couldn't sleep," Horace explained.

"The heavier the burden, the busier the mind." She glanced at the nickel lying on the floor, heads up. Then she waved a long, pale hand, beckoning him. "Join me, Keeper. There are things I would tell you."

Horace didn't even think to ask what kind of things. He

grabbed the Fel'Daera, slipping it into its pouch.

Chloe hopped down from her high bed. April snorted in her sleep again, but didn't stir. "I'm coming too," Chloe said.

Falo's brows lifted high. "Are you?" she said melodiously, and it was impossible to say whether it was a challenge or genuine curiosity. She turned and swept from the room.

Chloe followed her into the hall, Horace right behind. Falo was already far ahead, and they hurried to catch up. Ka'hoka was murky and empty at this time of night. Their footsteps rang out sharply in the shadowed, hollow quiet.

"Ours is a secret world," Falo said after a while, her voice like sudden moonlight on dark water. At first Horace thought she meant Ka'hoka. But quickly he realized she meant more than that. She meant the world of the Keepers, the world of the Tanu. "Secret upon secret," Falo sighed. "We have kept them even from ourselves." She glanced down at them from her lofty height, a look of warm guilt on her face. "Perhaps you have noticed."

"Never crossed my mind," said Chloe innocently. And then she said, "Oh, wait . . . you mean all the *lying*. The whole thing where no one told us we're going to die, that all the universes might explode, et cetera. Yeah, I did notice that."

Falo laughed, a quick staccato of soft drums. Chloe scowled. Falo said, "I make no apologies. One of the Mothergates is already gone, and the time for secrets is over. Even here at the end of things, when some might argue such things do not matter, I think it is important that you know everything.

Therefore, I am going to share one of the last secrets with you now."

Horace caught his breath. "And what secret is that?" he asked.

"It is time for you to learn why I created the Fel'Daera, Horace. Time for you to understand why I dared bring such a thing into the world."

Chloe stopped walking. Her face went slack, full of doubt, as if realizing she should not have come along. But even through the sudden pounding of his heart, and without missing a step, Horace reached back and took her hand, pulling her gently forward. Her hand was cool and strong. They walked this way for several moments, hand in hand, not talking, until at last by some unspoken agreement, they let go of each other.

Horace felt unreasonably calm. He had been told many things about the Fel'Daera—that it was a mistake, that it was supposed to have been destroyed, that it had been created for a singular purpose, that it was never meant to be used as Horace had been using it. But now he was here with the Maker herself, and she had the answers to everything.

They wound through the deserted halls of Ka'hoka, headed for Falo's quarters, or perhaps the Mothergate itself. They slipped into the familiar rough stone passage and across the vaulted hall beyond, through the gleaming white doors, tall as a two-story building. The Medium, barreling even more thickly from the nearby Mothergate now that only two remained, poured through the Fel'Daera into every nerve in Horace's body.

Falo led them through the domed sitting room of her quarters, deeper into her home. A new corridor, this one lined with birdcages. Horace had to laugh—it was just like the tunnel of birds at the House of Answers, dozens of cages holding hundreds of birds. Except that while the birds at the House of Answers had been flitting and noisy, these birds were utterly silent and still. As tiny as mice, and colored like the sea— every shade of blue and green—they watched Horace and Chloe with bright black eyes, without a single peep.

Falo led them past without comment, around two more turns, and at last they came to a large, low room—low by Altari standards. It was brightly lit and smelled faintly of sawdust and spice.

This room, too, had a familiar feel. Tables and workbenches, almost at eye height on Horace, were crammed tidily with all manner of oddments—reams of fabric, slabs of wood, tools both ordinary and bizarre. A set of enormous chisels, big as baseball bats. A carving knife the size of a small sword. Panes of glass slotted into a storage bin, every imaginable color. A jar full of feathers, all shapes and sizes, some as long as Horace's arm. A pyramid of small, perfect cubes that looked disturbingly like flesh. On the floor, a round pool of placid neon-green liquid. And books, everywhere, filling the shelves that lined the wall, lying about on every surface. Horace glanced at the page of a large red book as he passed.

There was a drawing of a skeletal hand—an Altari hand, with its thumblike pinkie and its extra finger joints. Beneath it, a dense paragraph of text in a flowing, angular language.

This was Falo's workshop. Not so different from Brian's, back at the Warren, but much neater. Falo kept walking, on to the far end of the room. There, a perfectly round doorway, wide as a train tunnel, opened into a chamber suffused with deep blue light. Horace and Chloe exchanged a look. Brian's workshop had its own quiet chamber at the back—an almost sacred place where Tunraden sat on a stone pedestal, where Brian could open it to the power of the Medium, weaving thick golden strands of it to create Tanu.

Chloe mouthed words at Horace now: "The Starlit Loom." He nodded. They followed Falo through the door and into the placid blue light beyond.

Sacred, yes. The chamber was as round as the doorway, and had that same faint electric smell Horace remembered from Tunraden. The Medium felt especially thick here; this room must have been particularly close to the Mothergate.

In the center stood a pedestal made of wood. It looked like a squat, sturdy tree, with stubby branches. And then he realized it *was* a tree, or a part of one, only it was upside down. These weren't branches, but roots—and yet the tree did have branches. Where the tree bore down into the floor, swallowed by the stone, it didn't truly end. The entire floor—the entire room—was covered with a thick weave of intertwining branches, spreading out from the tree, becoming its crown.

Rounded like thick snakes underfoot, and thinning into leaf-less twigs as they climbed the walls all around, the branches looked utterly real. Horace tipped his head back, his eyes darting upward along the encircling wall as the twining limbs rose, splitting into finer and finer threads, a hundred becoming a thousand becoming ten thousand becoming many more, a dizzying web of complexity, like a map of blood vessels in the body, or of neurons in the brain.

Or the multiverse.

And then a little gasp of awe slipped from his chest. High above, beyond the highest reaches of the stone tree, the ceiling of the chamber rippled and crackled. A low blue fire, or something like fire, burned there. It burned downward instead of up. The dangling tips of the small blue flames danced and rippled, sliding across the surface like leaves swirling in the wind, like butterflies swarming.

"This is where you made the Fel'Daera," Horace said, his sense of wonder threatening to drown him.

"Yes," Falo replied. "This is the Aerary." She took a seat on a wide bench that circled the room, piled with soft, somber pillows as big as Horace himself. "Now sit," said Falo. "Let us talk."

They crossed to Falo. Horace squeezed the Fel'Daera in its pouch as they passed the upside-down tree. He peeked into the tangle of its upended roots. A broad flat surface had been polished smooth there, buried in the seat of the trunk itself, exposing the looping rings of the tree. This was where it had happened. This was where Falo spun the Medium into Tanu.

But there was no Starlit Loom here. No Tan'ji at all.

Again, Falo gestured for them to sit. Horace wrestled for room among the huge pillows as Chloe clambered up beside him. He laid a hand on the wall behind them, wondering at the endless branchings of the tree clinging to the stone. Up so close, he was suddenly struck dumb by how swiftly the tree expanded. Each fork gave birth to an entire new tree, an explosion of new universes born from a single shared moment. Most of those histories, he realized, would be identical. But their futures diverged wildly, spreading farther and farther. Path upon path, tree after tree. Even so, this couldn't truly be a map of the multiverse, he knew. There probably wasn't a building on the planet big enough to hold such a map.

"Have I overwhelmed you, bringing you here?" Falo asked.

"Temporarily, maybe," Horace replied honestly.

Chloe didn't say anything, or even look over, which was its own kind of answer. Although Falo hadn't made the Alvalaithen herself, some earlier Keeper of the Starlit Loom certainly had—perhaps right here in this very chamber.

Falo said, "You were experimenting with the Fel'Daera tonight, Horace. What did you hope to discover?"

"Oh, that? I don't know. It was stupid."

"You don't strike me as particularly stupid," said Falo. "Do you spend a great deal of time doing stupid things?"

"You might be surprised," he said. "But no, it was just . . . after what you told me about how the box sees the future, I just got to thinking about how it sends things." He looked her in the eye, his curiosity reasserting itself. "And I guess I'm wondering how it isn't insane to send something through the box."

Chloe turned to him. "Insane how?" she asked sharply, her fingertips gripping the tail of the Alvalaithen.

"Well, when I look through the Fel'Daera, I see one particular future. One universe. But there's no guarantee I'll actually end up in that universe. And if that's true, isn't it dangerous . . ." He paused and glanced at the Alvalaithen. "Isn't it dangerous to send something valuable into a universe I might never find? Or even, maybe, into a universe the Fel'Daera itself might erase?"

Chloe's mouth went wide.

"Not particularly stupid at all," Falo murmured, gazing at him warmly. "You raise the very dilemma I faced when I set out to make the Fel'Daera. If an object travels into a specific future, but then you end up in a *different* future, wouldn't that object be lost forever? Stranded on some other branch of the expanding multiverse, a branch that the Fel'Daera cannot guarantee?"

"Oh my god," said Chloe. She poked Horace in the arm. "This is why you were doing those crazy jumping jacks. You were trying to create some super-weird future where the nickel hadn't gone."

261

"Yes," Horace admitted.

Chloe turned her wild eyes to Falo. "Could he have ended up in a different future than the nickel?" she demanded.

"I do not know what jumping jacks are," Falo said. "But the nickel has returned. Or rather, we find ourselves in a universe where its existence continues."

Chloe held up the Alvalaithen. "One time, we sent my Tan'ji through the box. Could I have lost it?"

If the sending of the Alvalaithen was news to Falo, she didn't show it. She said nothing at all. Instead, she unfolded her hand, and there—to Horace's great astonishment—a golden replica of the Fel'Daera swirled into existence, perfect down to the last detail. It even seemed to shimmer like the real Fel'Daera, as if the strings of the Medium from which it was sculpted, here near the Mothergate, quivered with extra life. Chloe stared with undisguised awe, letting the Alvalaithen drop to her chest.

As they watched, the double-winged lid of the phantom box swiveled open. A bolt of the Medium darted up from within, forging a twisted path. It rose three feet or more toward the fire-blue ceiling before ending in a glinting point.

"The future, as witnessed by the Fel'Daera," Falo announced. And then, beside the golden Fel'Daera: a honey-colored dragonfly, wings aflutter. Chloe scooted forward, eyes wide. Falo's mock Alvalaithen darted around the box—once, twice—and then flitted inside. The lid of the ghostly Fel'Daera swung closed, trapping it, sending it. On the instant, the dragonfly rematerialized out at the tip of the illuminated path.

"The Alvalaithen is sent into the future," said Falo. "And if that future is realized—if the Keeper of the Fel'Daera walks the willed path—all is well." She gazed at Horace. The meandering path made from the Medium hung in the air between them, crossing her face like a scar. "But we do not always walk the willed path, do we? Even the Keeper of the Fel'Daera still has free will." The twisting path shifted subtly, carving out a slightly different future than what the Fel'Daera had revealed. A flutter of nausea passed through Horace, as if thrall-blight were striking him even now. The new path now ended in a different place, several inches away. The golden dragonfly hung alone, stranded. Its wings flickered briefly, and then it winked out.

With a flourish of her hand, Falo waved away the rest of the illusion. The shining Fel'Daera dissipated like smoke. "How can any object be sent safely into the future the Fel'Daera sees?" she said. "How can we guarantee that such an object would not be lost in some parallel universe, along a future path we didn't or couldn't take? Perhaps along a path the Fel'Daera itself consumed?" She folded her long hands together and pressed them against her mouth, fixing Horace with an expectant gaze.

"You're asking me," he said after a moment.

"I am."

"But I'm not a Maker."

"True. I am the Dorvala here, not you. Yet you are a Paragon. And I must tell you, no Keeper before now has thought to consider this problem. I am curious whether you can solve it."

Horace puzzled it over. She had turned his question back around on him, and he was determined to answer it. He was no Maker, no, but he knew there was a kind of logic here, a matter of engineering.

"You solved the problem yourself, though, right?" Chloe asked Falo.

"I solved the problem," said Falo confidently. "Objects sent through the Fel'Daera can never be lost."

Horace blinked. Never lost? But that would mean every path—

Suddenly it clicked. But no—could it be possible? "The only thing I can think of," he said slowly, "would be to send the object into *every* possible future. That way, no matter which future you end up in, it'll be there."

Falo reared back and clapped her great hands in delight, three times. They cracked like whips. "Excellent."

"But that just seems—"

"Extravagant?" said Falo. "Wasteful?" She held out her hand again, and the golden Fel'Daera and Alvalaithen reappeared, replaying their pantomime. But this time, when the lid of the box closed over the Alvalaithen, a thick cloud of dragonflies bloomed high overhead. Thousands of them, too many to count, a flickering golden canopy against the sea of blue flame beyond. Crooked paths began to shoot up from the shining box in Falo's hand, like bolts of lightning in reverse. Each time one struck, it ended at a waiting dragonfly. "When you sent the Alvalaithen through the Fel'Daera, you sent ten thousand dragonflies into ten thousand futures," Falo said. "No matter which path you took, the Alvalaithen would be there." She let the show continue for several moments, a dazzling thunderstorm—bolt after bolt, future after future, and in every future the Alvalaithen was found again. Then abruptly, she waved it all away. The canopy of dragonflies dissolved into a shower of golden dust that rained down upon them into nothing.

Far from seeming relieved, Chloe looked absolutely furious. Horace thought he knew why. In her mind, there could be only one Chloe, one dragonfly. The multiverse was not a thing she was equipped to embrace, even after their trip through the Mothergate.

"It seems preposterous, I know," said Falo. "All those replications. All those versions of our instruments. But remember that such splittings, such expansions, are the very flesh of the multiverse." She turned to Chloe. "Even now as we speak, different versions of ourselves—and our instruments—are splitting off and multiplying along alternate paths we cannot see."

Chloe hugged herself angrily, as if she could prevent those splits from happening. "That is the absolute worst bedtime story I ever heard," she said.

Falo laughed. "You cannot have heard many Altari bedtime stories, then."

265

Horace was feeling for the Fel'Daera in his mind. What Falo was telling him seemed crazy on the surface, and yet . . . it was perfectly sensible. Logical. When the box sent objects into the future, it was merely following the rules of the multiverse.

"I always knew that sending things through the box was less serious than looking through it," he said.

"By far," said Falo. "In fact, though you may not have realized it, anyone can send objects through the Fel'Daera."

"I know," Horace said. "Chloe did it before."

Falo nodded approvingly. "As have I," she said, "in the years when the Fel'Daera was Tan'layn, when it had no Keeper. But only the Keeper of the Fel'Daera can *see* the future."

"Still, though . . . why did you need it to do both?" Horace asked. "I understand wanting to see the future, but why did you need it to send things, too?"

"Ah," Falo said, as if finding at last a long-sought thing. "That is the story, isn't it?" She folded her long legs beneath her like a graceful child, her gauzy white robe billowing. Her knees stuck out far to either side, her elbows jutting as she folded her hands in her lap. She became a flower, some extravagant and alien orchid. When she spoke, her voice was a celestial song.

"We are Tan'ji," she said. "Our instruments belong to us, and us alone. Yet we are not the only Keepers our instruments have ever had. Nor are we the only Keepers our instruments might have chosen, *even today*. As we speak, there are individuals walking the earth who possess the skills and affinities to bond with our instruments. Individuals who possess the ability to use the powers we call our own."

"When I first met Joshua," Horace admitted, "I thought he might try to claim the Fel'Daera for his own. His abilities are sort of like mine."

"His abilities are not quite like yours, and I doubt very much that he could have claimed the Fel'Daera—especially not when the Laithe was there for the taking. Nonetheless, the fear is a reasonable one." She pointed at the sky. "Up there, around the world, there are dozens—perhaps hundreds—who could have bonded with the Fel'Daera, or the Alvalaithen, or even the Starlit Loom. In fact, though it pains me to say it, our instruments call to those individuals even now, however faintly."

"You're not serious," Chloe said.

But this was perfectly logical too, Horace knew. After all, this whole thing had started when he himself had stepped off the bus that day on Wexler Street, for no reason he could have named. He knew now that the Fel'Daera had been calling to him.

"There is a gravity," Falo insisted. "A pull. Most of those individuals who share our abilities will never heed the call—perhaps they are too far away, or the pull is too weak, or they are not open to the same possibilities that you both were when you Found your Tan'ji. But if they *had* heeded the call, and had gotten to our instruments before us, perhaps they would have become our instruments' Keepers, instead of us."

Chloe squashed a pillow in her lap. "But they would have sucked at it," she growled.

Falo smiled. "Perhaps. We are Paragons, we three, and our abilities are rare. Nonetheless, there *are* others for whom the Fel'Daera would reveal the future, or for whom the Alvalaithen would flit its wings. That is my point."

"And so?" asked Horace, not sure what she was driving at. What did this have to do with the Fel'Daera?

"So some of those others, of course, could be Kesh'kiri."

The Riven. "That would be unlikely, though, right?" he said.

"Somewhat," Falo said. "It is rare to find Keepers for instruments like ours, especially among the Altari and Kesh'kiri. Our numbers have dwindled greatly. Most new Keepers in recent days have been young humans like yourselves."

"But some of those humans turned traitor," Horace said. "They sided with the Riven, like Ingrid."

"Unable to face the truth about the Mothergates, yes. But the Riven stole the Fel'Daera from you once before, Horace. If they had anyone who could have bonded with it, and gained its powers, Dr. Jericho would have had no use for you. They would have killed you, disposed of you, and given the Fel'Daera to your replacement. The Kesh'kiri detest human Keepers, and tolerate them only when they have no other choice." She looked back and forth between Horace and

Chloe. "The fact that the two of you were captured by the Riven, yet lived to tell the tale, means that neither of you is nul'duna. You are not disposable. There is no one among the Riven who can replace you—at the moment, anyway."

"So being nul'duna is basically . . . super dangerous, then," Chloe said.

"Oh my, yes," said Falo. "Gabriel is nul'duna, though I doubt he's ever mentioned it. And so is Dwen'dailen Longo."

"Gabriel?" Chloe said in disbelief. But Horace's mind was already moving onward.

"And what about you?" he asked Falo. "Are you nul'duna?"

Falo studied his face calmly for a moment and then said, "Not anymore."

"But you were once. The Riven had someone who could have bonded with the Starlit Loom, and used its powers?"

"Yes. For a long time. Someone with great skills. Eventually that individual was . . . dealt with. But that came later. What matters most is what I did when I first learned I had become nul'duna."

"You went into hiding," said Chloe. "Or no—if you were disposable, it wasn't really you the Riven were after."

"It was the Starlit Loom that needed to hide," said Horace.

"Yes," said Falo. "And not just for my sake, but for the sake of all. The powers of the Loom could not be allowed to fall into the hands of another."

"Because the Riven might use it to force the Mothergates to remain open."

269

"Yes."

"Is that why we haven't seen it yet?" he asked. "It's still in hiding?"

"Oh, but you *have* seen the Starlit Loom," said Falo. "Unless you are quite blind." She leaned forward intently, and for a few confusing moments Horace thought she was going to pluck the mysterious Loom from behind his ear, or tell him that somehow the Fel'Daera was the Loom, all this time. But no, that was stupid, it must—

And then he saw.

The black oval pendant around Falo's neck. It swung before his eyes, as big as a child's hand and twice as thick, gleaming and black. Or not black, not entirely. Dots of light moved within it now, tiny and faint, drifting into the depth of the thing like receding stars. It looked strangely familiar, and then Horace realized—it was like the Mothergates, black and endless, a shape seemingly carved from the universe itself.

"The Starlit Loom," he breathed.

"Hiraethel," Falo said. "That is her name." She sang the name breathily, scratching throatily across the R and stressing the long middle A—it sounded like "dear Rachel." On Falo's lips, the word was like a wind through a tall autumn meadow, like a whispered spell.

"But this . . . ," Horace began, staring. "It's not Tan'ji." Like all Keepers, Horace could recognize a Tan'ji when he saw one, as easily as he could recognize a human for a human. But this was not Tan'ji.

"Of course she is," said Falo. She reached up and cupped Hiraethel in her hand. The Loom released itself silently from the chain it hung from, as easily as the Alvalaithen. Chloe edged closer, and Falo held the Loom out for them to see. The Loom was tiny in her hand, a smooth oval slab scarcely bigger than Horace's palm. The starpoints of light within it continued to recede, on and on, mesmerizing. "Hiraethel is the first Tan'ji, the mother of all," said Falo. "She is perfect, utterly contained. She does not reveal herself unless I wish her to."

No sooner had she spoken than the specks of light in the Loom reversed course, coming closer now. Swifter and swifter. They became streaks of light, and then those streaks began to bend, veering counterclockwise. They became oval rings, stacked one atop the other into infinity, so that looking into the surface of the Loom was like looking into a bottomless well of circled light, reaching into the very flesh of Falo's palm.

And then Falo burst into flames.

Or not flames. And not exactly light, either. She became a burning flaxen thing, as if the matter of her flesh had turned to energy, slipping into the simplest version of what a living body could be. She was still Falo, still herself, and her hand still cupped Hiraethel. But skin and tendon and bone did not matter to that hand, nor to any part of her. She was all potential and purpose, idea and intent, knowledge and means—an indescribable golden fountain, flickering like a ghost, the most wonderful and terrible sight Horace had ever seen. The Fel'Daera seemed to vibrate now, basking in Falo's presence like an island in the sea that gave it shape, quivering like a heart squeezing the blood that gave it life. Horace realized that the sea of blue flame above them had turned to gold.

Beside him, a long soft hiss of air escaped Chloe. He knew she was feeling what he was feeling—that their bodies were so silly, so extravagant, so unnecessary, compared to what Falo had become. What she had returned to.

And then Falo's fingers clasped around the Starlit Loom, and she faded. Hiraethel became a smooth black slab once more. The room went dimmed and went blue again, though it had never been truly bright. Horace stared at Falo, hardly able to process her. He had seen Brian working the Medium, and been awestruck, but this . . . was something else entirely. And Falo hadn't even *done* anything.

"Honestly," Chloe said breathlessly. "I mean honestly. What the hell *are* you?"

Falo laughed, a giddy tinkle. "I am just a girl," she said merrily, and then her voice got mossy, silken. The haloes in her eyes turned to platinum. "But through Hiraethel, I become the conduit. I am the flesh of the Medium itself. I am open to the universe, and therefore whatever the universe deems possible, I can bring to bear." She lifted her chin, indicating the box still in Horace's lap. "And just so, once upon a time, I brought the Fel'Daera to life. Because my need was great."

Horace knew these last words were meant for him, a prod and a reminder. Still half swooning, he considered the Starlit Loom again, watching its pinpoints of starlight drifting ever inward. Hiraethel was still so familiar somehow, and now that he was seeing it true, its lovely curves and smooth planes, its perfect oval self—

"Oh my god," he said.

"What is it?" asked Chloe.

He understood. And this understanding was perfect. It was right. It was sensible and warm, a homecoming. "You had need," he murmured to Falo. "You were nul'duna. You had to keep Hiraethel safe."

"Yes," Falo said softly. "Above all else."

"But you couldn't risk losing her, or sending her blind. You had to send *and* see. The future had to be known."

"Wait," said Chloe. "Are you saying—"

"Open the Fel'Daera, Horace," said Falo, reaching out with the Starlit Loom in hand. "Know why your Tan'ji was Made."

Horace opened the box. The lid swung open like the wings of an imagined bird. Inside, its smooth oval walls like a coffin, like a nest, like the chamber of a heart.

With her long, delicate fingers, Sil'falo Teneves slipped the Loom into the mouth of the Fel'Daera. Hiraethel slid in perfectly, of course she did, the most perfect thing the Fel'Daera had ever allowed or ever would. The Loom filled the box like water fills a glass, like sunlight fills the day. The

Fel'Daera had been made for this, for this and nothing else. Horace swayed, flooded with understanding. The box was a peaceful ship in his hands, sure of its destination. He clung to it.

"You had need," he said again, not lifting his eyes. "Hiraethel was in danger and had to be hidden. And so you built a device that would let you hide her in the space between days. Out of time and out of reach, where no one could ever find her. Never ever. Not until she returned."

"Yes," said Falo. "And when she returned, when I could bear it, I sent her again. And again. And again. These were dark times."

Horace could scarcely tear his gaze away from the Loom, snug inside the Fel'Daera. The box seemed to be almost purring in his hands—or at least, it emanated a contentment he had never felt from it before. And he himself felt . . . old. Or wise, or something. Complete. If he closed the box now, Hiraethel would travel into the future—a mere seven minutes, the breach very narrow. It would be deeply satisfying, he knew. Like scratching an unreachable itch. But then Falo would . . .

Horace looked up into Falo's eyes. Ancient eyes, deep and lucid and utterly fearless. As fearless as the universe was boundless.

He stood. He stepped up to Falo and reached over her lap, holding the Fel'Daera out to her, the Starlit Loom still nestled inside. The box hummed in his hand, a sustained, trembling chord of purpose.

"You understand me, Keeper," Falo said. "You understand everything at last."

"I do," Horace said.

And then he closed the box.

CHAPTER FIFTEEN

A Great Need

A JOLT COURSED FROM THE FEL'DAERA AND INTO HORACE, LIKE nothing he'd ever felt before. Not a tingle, no. A freight train. Even sending the Alvalaithen hadn't been like this. His muscles seized and his body buzzed—not quite unpleasant, not quite, but bone deep and necessary. Necessary, above all else. If the urge to send the Loom had been an itch, this was like scratching that itch until it bled. He went rigid, giving in to a force he could not hope to resist. His head rocked back and he stood that way for several seconds. When at last it passed, he opened his eyes. He hadn't even known they were closed.

Chloe was already on her feet. "What did you do?" she demanded.

He'd sent the Starlit Loom traveling. He'd done what the box wanted him to do, what it was meant to do.

But what had he *done*?

Falo had scarcely moved. Horace knew her Tan'ji was nowhere right now, traveling, beyond all senses. She was severed. Yet although the light in her eyes had dimmed a bit, she was still there. Still aware. She saw him, knew him.

"I'm sorry," he said. "I don't know why I—"

"You owe me no apology, Keeper," she said clearly. Some of the music had left her voice, but she was talking. Horace had never before seen a severed Keeper actually able to utter a complete, coherent sentence. "Every Tan'ji is a temptation," Falo continued. "Yours more than most."

"The Loom was in the box, and I just . . . I had to."

"No. You *chose* to. But it is all right. I put the temptation before you, and you took it. Now you know. Should the situation arise again, in other circumstances more dire, you will know better what is it you choose to do."

Other circumstances more dire. Horace shuddered to imagine what those circumstances might be, or why he would be asked to send the Loom away.

Chloe was watching Falo with a look so fearful it almost seemed angry. It occurred to Horace that she and Falo might be the only Keepers in existence who knew what it was like to send their Tan'ji traveling through the box. Chloe almost hadn't survived it. How had Falo endured, time and time again? And not for the seven minutes she faced right now, but for what sounded like long painful hours, perhaps even full days, one after the other?

"How are you doing this?" Chloe asked her, echoing

Horace's thoughts. "Are you just . . . amazing?"

Falo laughed. "What should I tell you? That my will is so strong? Unbreakable?" She shook her head, and turned to Horace. "What about you? Are you all right? Sending the Loom is quite an intense experience, I know."

Horace was beginning to realize that he ached, everywhere. Muscles he couldn't hope to name throbbed dully. "Yes. Intense."

"Sending objects forward in time—even ordinary objects—creates a disturbance in the Medium. Like a rubber band snapping. The effect is magnified when the object in question is Tanu. But when the Loom is sent, the echoes of that disturbance—by design—resonate outward from the Fel'Daera. That's what you felt. Those echoes merely pass through you, but they take up residence in me. They sustain me while I'm severed. Not very well—it's like the smell of food when one cannot find anything to eat. But it's enough." She bent forward to look Chloe in the eye. "My will is strong, yes. I know who I am, and I do not easily forget. But without those echoes, even I could not survive the utter abyss of the severing caused by the Fel'Daera."

It sounded horrible, frankly. Horace was ashamed that he hadn't resisted the temptation to send the Loom, and ashamed again that Falo apparently hadn't expected him to resist. But even in his shame and dismay, Falo astonished him. With everything else the Fel'Daera could do, she'd built in a mechanism that would allow her to survive the long severings she knew she would have to face.

"Dark times," he muttered, repeating Falo's words of a few minutes before.

"Yes," said Falo. "Now sit. Sit while we wait for the Loom to return, while I tell the tale of why I ever wanted it to leave in the first place, all those years ago."

They sat, but Falo didn't speak right away. For a moment Horace thought she was slipping away, giving in to the void. If she slipped too far, she would be permanently dispossessed and beyond all hope.

But then she shook her head. "Dark times," she muttered again. "Ka'hoka was . . . unsafe for me in those days."

"Unsafe how?" Chloe asked quietly.

"My rival," said Falo. "The one who could have claimed the Starlit Loom for himself. He was Altari. Kathra was his name. He lived among us, here at Ka'hoka." She sighed. "Understand that not every Altari believes the Mothergates should be allowed to die. Kathra was one such. And some believe that only the Hiraethel can save the Mothergates—that only the Keeper of the Starlit Loom could contrive to keep them open."

"So what happened?" Horace asked.

"Among the Altari, when you become nul'duna, your right to your Tan'ji can be challenged by another who possesses the same affinities. Such challenges are extremely rare, and rarely honored. But when they happen, you must prove yourself."

"What, like a competition?" said Chloe. She sounded

mad, and Horace didn't blame her. No one had ever told them that a Keeper's right to his or her Tan'ji could be challenged.

"A demonstration," Falo said. "That is the purpose of the Proving Room. A Keeper who wishes to defend her right to her Tan'ji must go there and make the strongest demonstration of her power that she can. The rival does not get a chance to lay hands on the Tan'ji in question—thank goodness—but his potential is weighed against the prowess the Keeper displays. There are judges, possessing some of the same skills possessed by Mr. Meister and Mrs. Hapsteade. And if they deem the rival's potential to be stronger than the Keeper's demonstration . . ."

"So what did you do?" Chloe asked. "What was your demonstration?"

"The Fel'Daera," Horace said, sure of it. "You made the Fel'Daera."

Falo actually laughed. "Yes. My greatest creation. It took me weeks to make the vessel, a full day to sculpt the foramen and weave the Medium. Only Hiraethel could have handled the flows I wrestled with that day, flows I had scarcely imagined." She looked around the room, as if the memories of that day were emblazoned on the walls. And for all Horace knew, maybe they were. "I barely finished in time. When I brought it before the Council, the Fel'Daera was hot from the forge, humming with power. I knew I had made something earth-shattering. I had meddled with time before, in some of my earlier creations—"

280

"What creations?" asked Chloe.

"Teokas's bracelet, Thailadun," Falo said. "And a clockwork ball that was never given a name, never found a Keeper."

"I think I've seen that ball," Horace exclaimed. "It was there when I found the Fel'Daera."

"It was offered to you, yes. Your affinities demanded it. But you took home the greater prize that day. Thailadun and the clockwork ball can manipulate one's perception of time, to an extent, but the Fel'Daera was the first Tan'ji to actually encroach upon the future. It was the first true time machine."

"First and only," Horace prompted, not quite sure if this was true.

"First and *last*," Falo confirmed. She sighed again, wistful now. "I hope you won't think I am bragging when I say the Fel'Daera was truly astonishing. So astonishing that I feared my demonstration before the Council might backfire, that they might think me *too* powerful." She straightened, rearing to her full seated height and looking down at them haughtily, emanating strength and wisdom, as if the mighty Starlit Loom still hung around her neck. And then she shrugged, like a child might, slouching. "But it did not matter. Their judgment did not matter. With the Fel'Daera in hand, I could guarantee Hiraethel's safety, regardless of what they said. And that was all that mattered." She smiled. "The Council was different then, but Mal'brula Kintares was there. You should have seen his face when I opened the Fel'Daera and sent Hiraethel—sent her out of all knowing, all finding, and

281

severing myself in the process . . . ."

Falo closed her eyes. She took a sharp breath, as if in pain. After a moment, though, she opened her eyes again and fixed them with a pale grin.

"Not long now," she said.

"Eighty-seven seconds," said Horace. Eighty-seven seconds until the Loom would arrive.

"Such precision," Falo said kindly. "On that day in the Proving Room, I was the only one who knew when Hiraethel would return. I did not tell anyone. Not the Council, and certainly not Kathra. In fact, I may have implied that I could not be sure how long the Loom would be gone." Her eyes twinkled dimly. "But of course I *was* sure. Down to the second."

"So what did the Council do?" Horace asked.

"After witnessing the power of the Fel'Daera, the greatest testament to my abilities, they could hardly honor Kathra's challenge for the Loom. However, Kathra then made the argument I had feared. He said I had become *too* powerful. Some on the Council agreed with him, including Brula. Worse, my demonstration rekindled the debate about the Mothergates, and whether their continued existence was indeed the threat I knew it to be. Kathra argued that I, in my arrogance, was only hastening the Mothergates' demise. He said that if the Loom were in his hands, he could use her to repair the Mothergates safely. He claimed that they could remain open without endangering us. Some began to listen to him, and believe him."

"But he was wrong," Chloe said.

"Very wrong. I am the Keeper of the Starlit Loom, perhaps the most powerful that has ever lived. I know better."

"So what did you do?" asked Horace.

Falo didn't answer. She cocked her head as if listening to a distant sound. Horace realized what was happening a moment before it did. With a pop, the Starlit Loom materialized in the air over Falo's lap. Hiraethel fell into her already waiting hand, and Falo closed a grateful fist around her, eyes aglow.

"She returns, just as she did then," she said, pressing the Loom against her chest. "The Fel'Daera always delivers."

Horace, awash with relief, busied himself for a moment trying to imagine the simultaneous arrival of the Starlit Loom in thousands of other universes, just as the Fel'Daera promised. Was there a universe where Falo had been telling a different story while she waited? Where Chloe was a boy instead of a girl? Where Falo dropped Hiraethel as she fell? He shook his head, feeling fractured, his thoughts slipping back to the tumbling realms inside the Mothergate, where everything had been not only possible but present.

"When Hiraethel reappeared in the Proving Room the following day," said Falo, "I collected her in secret. And then I left Ka'hoka. I fled to other sanctuaries."

"What about Kathra?" Chloe asked.

"He continued to find support for his ideas, but not as much as he craved. Eventually, he realized that there was a better audience for his notions, and for his plan to take

Hiraethel from me. A better audience by far."

"The Riven," Horace breathed.

"He was a traitor," said Chloe.

"He was misguided," Falo said. "Full of fear and arrogance—as all the Riven are. But he had always been a nasty fellow. You are aware, I think, that what we now call the Riven were once Altari. A great rift grew among the Altari, long ago, between those who accepted the rising phenomenon of human Keepers and those who did not. Those who continued to believe that only Altari should be allowed to become Tan'ji rebelled. They left us, renaming themselves the Kesh'kiri, the Riven. They started along the dark path they still tread now. They blamed the human Keepers for what was happening to the Mothergates—a distant threat at the time, but one we could not ignore. And even among those who stayed with the Altari, there were many who nursed a silent, fuming resentment. Kathra was one of these. Not particularly surprising, since many in his family had gone the way of the Riven. And when he could not claim Hiraethel for himself, he joined them in earnest."

"And you took Hiraethel into hiding," said Horace.

"Yes. I truly was nul'duna, disposable. I was in great danger. We all were. Should the Kesh'kiri manage to find the Starlit Loom, I would have been killed and the Loom would have fallen into the hands of one who might have forced the Mothergates to remain open. In doing so, Kathra would have put our universe—and every universe where the Tanu exist—on the path to certain destruction, just as Isabel is unwittingly doing now."

"You stayed at the Warren, didn't you?" Chloe asked Falo. "That's when you brought the Fel'Daera there."

"I did stay there, yes. But I didn't leave the Fel'Daera with Mr. Meister until much later. I had need of it still. Even in the Warren, the other Wardens and I lived in constant fear that the Riven would discover us, and the Loom would be found. I kept myself severed as often as I could, using the Fel'Daera to send the Loom beyond reach in the space between days. But I grew tired. I could not keep it up forever. I needed a companion, one who could help me deal with the dangers the future might hold."

"The Fel'Daera needed a Keeper," Horace said.

"Yes. I could send the Loom into the future, but I could not see what that future held. I could guarantee her safety while traveling, but not when she returned. And so Henry—Mr. Meister—put out the call. It was risky, putting the Fel'Daera on display in his warehouses, hoping to attract a Keeper with the right affinities. But we had no choice. And eventually the call was answered." Falo smiled, and now her eyes truly did shine. "A girl. Not so different from you, Horace. A bit older. Elizabeth was her name."

Despite himself, Horace felt a surge of jealous rage. The Fel'Daera, taking another Keeper. And not just any Keeper, but the very first. *Elizabeth*. He tried to swallow his irritation. It was illogical, hating someone he'd never met who'd done nothing wrong.

"Once Elizabeth had come through the Find, and could see the future truly, I felt safer keeping Hiraethel with me. But not always. We had reason to fear that the mere presence of the Loom might draw Kathra near, and the Fel'Daera was powerful enough in its own right to draw its own kind of unwanted attention."

"Dr. Jericho."

"Ja'raka Sevlo, yes. He is a hunter, and like all Mordin he has a Tan'ji that helps him track down others Keepers, and their instruments."

"I've seen it," Horace said, sickened by the memory of the gleaming bulge of blue metal, embedded in the Mordin's spine.

"Dr. Jericho and I are connected, in a way," Falo said. "I have a flair for making kairotics—Tanu that alter time and space. His Tan'ji, Raka, is particularly attuned to such instruments. Meanwhile, to make things worse, the Loom called to Kathra, day and night. Therefore, Henry and I decided it would be best for me not to remain in one location. But travel was risky, of course, unless one was willing to endure the miserable falkrete stones, and so I . . ."

"You created the Laithe," said Horace.

"Yes. It was easier than the Fel'Daera, but I poured a great deal of beauty into it. It was, in fact, the last Tan'ji I ever made. After it was finished, again Mr. Meister put out the call, and again we found a Keeper—rather quickly, as I remember. Once the Laithe had been mastered by its first Keeper, we settled into a kind of routine, my companions and I. With the Laithe, we could move safely from sanctuary to sanctuary. With the Fel'Daera, we could keep Hiraethel beyond all reach, for several hours a day—all that I could endure. And all the while, the Riven searched and searched for the Loom."

"And so what happened in the end?" Horace asked. "You said Kathra was killed, or something."

"'Dealt with,'" Chloe said. "That's what you said."

Falo scrunched up her face. "Yes. Eventually, I was too exhausted to continue with our routine. Over time, the constant severing takes a gruesome toll. At one point I even considered destroying Hiraethel, and putting an end to it all—although Henry believes the Loom cannot be destroyed, and he may be right. At any rate, I did not try. Instead, we did something only mildly less desperate."

"What did you do?"

"We set a trap. Hiraethel was our bait. We lured Kathra near, and there was a battle. We knew what was going to happen, of course. Or we knew some of it, anyway. Elizabeth had seen it through the Fel'Daera, and so we made a . . ." She paused, considering the box in Horace's hands. "If you devise a plan only *after* the Fel'Daera reveals what you will do, can it rightly be called a plan?"

"Are you asking *me?*" Horace said, surprised. After all, she was the Maker here.

"I ask no one. I am merely offering a question that has no answer. Through the Fel'Daera, Elizabeth saw what we would do. And so we did. Kathra came near, in the thick of the battle. The Keeper of the Laithe had opened a portal, into a particular location chosen in advance. Kathra stumbled through the open portal . . . stumbled? Fell? Pushed?" She shrugged. "And then we closed the Laithe behind him."

Horace waited for Chloe to say something, to ask the obvious question. He realized she was waiting for him to do the same. "And where did the portal lead?" he said.

"Somewhere over the Pacific Ocean," Falo said. "Far out to sea, as far as one can go. A thousand miles from the nearest point of land."

The room fell silent. Horace tried to picture it—the round gate of the portal, hanging above an endless reach of churning water, as far from anything as could be. A long body tumbling through the portal, plunging into the cold water.

The portal shrinks to nothing, vanishes.

And then: only the empty sky, and the sea.

"You killed him," Horace said.

"Oh, yes," said Falo pertly. "Killing him was never not an option. But the way it happened . . . I sometimes think of it. He fell into a distant sea, with no hope of rescue. He drowned there, far from everything. It was a bitter end for Ja'kathra Sevlo."

Horace startled. "Wait, Ja'kathra . . . Sevlo?"

Chloe had caught it, too. "Like Ja'raka Sevlo. You're saying this rival of yours was related to Dr. Jericho?"

"His brother," said Falo.

"Wait, wait, wait," Chloe said. "So the instrument that Joshua is carrying now, while he's held captive by Dr. Jericho and carting Isabel around the world, is the same instrument that was used to kill Dr. Jericho's brother?"

"Yes," Falo said.

"And it was the Fel'Daera that revealed the plan to kill him," said Horace. "The same instrument you only made in order to prevent Kathra from taking the Starlit Loom in the first place."

"Yes," said Falo. "And in that sense, the Fel'Daera ended up doing precisely what I meant it to the day I forged it. It kept Hiraethel safe."

"More tangles," Horace murmured, trying to digest it all.

"Why are you telling us all this?" Chloe asked Falo. "One Mothergate is already gone, and the other two won't last the week. In a few days, none of this will matter. Most likely, we'll all be dead."

"If we succeed," Falo pointed out.

"But even if we fail, we'll die anyway," Chloe said. "So again, why are you telling us these things—about the box sending objects into every future, about the reasons you made the Fel'Daera, about Kathra—if death is so close?"

Falo seemed to consider the question long and hard. It

was a question Horace didn't really need the answer to. He wanted to know these things, *needed* to know them, even if he only had a few more days to live with the truth.

When Falo spoke, the words came out slowly and cautiously. "Despite my confidence—my *belief*—in what the next few days might bring, our futures are not yet forged," she said. "No one will play a greater role in forging those futures than the two of you. And I cannot place our history's end in the hands of those who do not even know that history."

"But there's a part of the history I still don't know," said Horace.

"Indeed," Falo said. "The most vital part. The part that will be the hardest to hear."

"Samuel."

"Yes." Falo sighed. "In time, Elizabeth grew older and faded. Other Keepers came and went, friends and companions. But then Samuel came through the Find, and his thinking was clouded from the start. He learned about the Wardens' true purpose from Dr. Jericho himself, before he was ready. When I told him the full tale—a tale he only half understood, or believed—he became convinced that the Fel'Daera could save us. He reasoned that if the problem lay with the tangles between universes, the solution was self-evident."

"Remove those universes," Horace said.

"Precisely. Although utterly without merit, Samuel's plan was simple: witness a single future through the Fel'Daera, thereby eliminating all other possible futures, and then walk the willed path. He believed that by rigorously obeying the Fel'Daera, he could eventually forge a path upon which the Mothergates could remain. He thought if he could force the single universe he witnessed to walk that path with him, all would be well."

"And the astrolabe?" Horace asked.

"Samuel was obsessed with sending the astrolabe through the Fel'Daera. He insisted that if he could manage to send it, it would be proof that he had achieved what he most desired. A single future, unalterable. Uncluttered by the messy possibilities of the multiverse. But his aspirations were pure madness." Falo gestured at the walls around them, at the sprawling, branching tree that crept along them. "No one can contain the unrelenting spread of the multiverse. Not even the Keeper of the Fel'Daera." She looked pointedly at Horace. "Not even a Paragon."

"You don't need to warn me," Horace said.

"Which is why I have not spoken to you of Samuel before now," Falo said with a kind smile. "His is a cautionary tale you did not need, Horace Andrews."

"But all that trying he did," said Horace. "It messed with the multiverse even more, didn't it? He made the tangles worse." He fidgeted uncomfortably in his seat. "I've heard a lot of bad things about the Fel'Daera. Isabel said it's done more damage than any other ten instruments combined."

"It depends on what we mean by 'harm,'" Falo said. "The more tangled the multiverse becomes, the more quickly the

Mothergates will close. Remember that the multiverse is self-correcting—it will not destroy parts of itself unless it is forced to, and we will only force it to if we prevent the Mothergates from closing as they should. It is true that no other instrument has done more to disturb the multiverse than the Fel'Daera—with or without Samuel. But those disturbances have only hastened the necessary death of the Mothergates."

Horace leaned in. "Did you know that would happen? When you made the Fel'Daera, did you know it would create more tangles?"

"Yes."

"But it didn't stop you," said Chloe.

"Far from it," said Falo, sounding surprised. "In fact, I considered it a benefit."

Chloe blinked. "So the dark sides to the Fel'Daera—Samuel, thrall-blight, all the rest . . . you think these are actually *good* things?"

"If they bring us closer to that which must occur, yes."

"Closer to our own deaths, you mean," said Chloe.

"Closer to a place where countless other lives are saved." Falo turned her golden eyes to Horace. "I knew what Samuel was doing. I could have stopped him, if I chose. But I did not choose to do it."

"So what happened to him?"

"He died," Falo said simply. "Through the Fel'Daera, he witnessed his own death at the hands of the Altari."

"Which Altari?" Chloe demanded.

"It does not matter," said Falo. "That particular death did not come. For the first time since becoming a Keeper, Samuel refused to walk the willed path. He rejected the path utterly, fleeing his own foreseen death. He opened the Fel'Daera again and again, seeking a different way forward. But in every viewing—hundreds of them during that final day—death came for him, in one form or another. Each time, Samuel took steps to ensure that that death could not occur. And that is how he died."

"Thrall-blight," Horace whispered.

"Yes. We felt it as it was happening—all of us. So desperate was Samuel's fear that his struggles to disobey the Fel'Daera shook the very foundations of the Mothergates. The multiverse itself felt the tremors, and the Medium roiled with poison. Indeed, Samuel's last day as a Keeper set in motion the Mothergates' final death throes. A day that we thought might not come for another century was now no more than a couple of decades away. A blink of an eye."

Horace hardly knew what to say. Thrall-blight was a sickness like no other, one he had only experienced a couple of times. It brought such horrible, novel pain that he could easily imagine dying from it. But he could not imagine what that death would feel like.

"And so the Council told you to destroy the Fel'Daera," Chloe said to Falo. "You lied and said that you did, but really you took it to the Warren. To Mr. Meister. Not long after that, my mom tuned it—getting rid of all the Samuel goo—and twenty years later, Horace came and Found it. And now here we are."

"Yes."

"But you're not sorry that Samuel did what he did," Horace said.

"Not remotely," said Falo. "If I were, I would have destroyed the Fel'Daera just as I claimed."

There was one more thing Horace needed to know. "On that final day, did Samuel know he was only bringing the deaths of the Mothergates closer?"

Falo face crinkled, looking pained. "I am not sure. He should have had the means to know, but also I . . . I did not truly want him to know."

Chloe snapped up straight. "Why not?"

But Horace was way ahead of her. "Because then he might not have done what he did," he said.

Chloe gaped. "You kept him in the dark on purpose," she said. "Just like the Wardens have been doing with us all along."

"Understand, please," Falo said. "Samuel was a Keeper. He went through the Find and was set loose with his instrument, as all Keepers are. If his later actions, however ignorant, suited my needs—the needs of us all—then who was I to interfere?" She bowed her head and ran a long hand down her ivory face. "Or so I thought at the time."

She looked sadly up at them, full of hope and remorse. "You have been a pawn in a struggle whose rules you did not know, Horace Andrews. I freely confess it. Every time you opened the Fel'Daera, every time you contemplated the future, every time you failed to walk the willed path, you brought us closer to the end of days." She shook her head. "But you are a pawn no more. You know everything now. If I've held anything back, it's only because there is so much to tell. It's easy to overlook a pebble in a rockslide."

A pawn. Ignorant. Horace knew he should have felt sick, angry. He should have been filled with a righteous rage, having been used this way. He felt that anger boiling off of Chloe now like a cloud.

But he felt none of his own.

He looked up at Falo, not at all sure what he was going to say. But then the words fell out of him, simple and right. "I forgive you," he said.

Falo clasped his hands in her own, swallowing them. Her skin was as thin as leaves. "Thank you, Keeper, but I do not ask forgiveness. I only ask that you continue the fight we dragged you blindly into. Tomorrow is another day. One of the last. Take the Fel'Daera into battle. Show the Riven what it can do—what *you* can do. There is nothing they might attempt that you cannot foresee."

Horace nodded. He would do these things, yes. He and Chloe both. Not in spite of the lies they'd been told, or the truths that they hadn't, but because these little lies and truths didn't matter anymore. Only the one truth.

The world was in danger. All the worlds imaginable, the

worlds he'd barely glimpsed inside the Mothergate, seen flickering on Chloe's unspeakable face there. And maybe there was a world where Chloe had never found the Alvalaithen, or him the Fel'Daera, and for those distant beings—and for his mother, and his father, and everyone who might survive, he would not worry about the past, or the wrongs that had been done to him there.

Only the future.

CHAPTER SIXTEEN

A Refusal Refused

JOSHUA WAS COLD. COLD IN THE BODY, YES—IT WAS COLD HERE in the nest beneath the concrete silos in Chicago, in his little room underground, with its thin mattress on the hard stone floor. But he was also cold in every other way—in his head, in his heart. He'd done terrible things. Made every wrong decision, even when he was trying to do right.

He rolled over on his mattress, hugging the Laithe. The Mordin guarding him watched him warily, but Joshua wasn't going anywhere. There was nowhere he was wanted. Not after what he'd done.

The trip to Crete the day before had been easy. A small island off Crete, actually, where there was an ancient fortress on a rocky hill by the water's edge. Only he and Isabel and Dr. Jericho had gone. Dr. Jericho had waited while he and Isabel found their way through the Nevren and into the Altari sanctuary below. Nlon'ka, it was called. Isabel had been full of fire, leading them through the vaulted hallways, following a call only she could feel, into the great striped ocean of the Veil of Lura.

Sitting by himself in the Veil had been frightening, waiting for Isabel to come back. She was supposed to be fixing the Mothergate, fixing everything. But then after a long time, when Joshua was just beginning to wonder if she would ever come back for him, she'd torn down the Veil in a tornado of golden light. Joshua had seen the Mothergate for the first time. And maybe he didn't know any better, but what Isabel had done didn't look anything like fixing. Stretched sheets of the Medium, yanked out of the black gate and covered in stitches. It looked like more torture, or a kind of prison. It wasn't what the Mothergate wanted, or needed. Anyone could see that.

And the Wardens knew it. They'd been right all along, telling the truth all along. They'd come to stop Isabel—Horace and Chloe, somehow arriving there in Nlon'ka. Joshua knew now that they'd come through the Mothergate itself, something he hadn't known was possible. And when he first saw them there, he wanted a chance to do it all over again, to take back the things he had done, even the things he hadn't meant to do. But he knew that nobody got that chance, not even Horace. Even the Fel'Daera couldn't change the past.

And so Joshua wouldn't do anything else he might regret, even if that meant doing nothing at all. Isabel couldn't weave her terrible stitches onto the next Mothergate if she couldn't get there in time, and she couldn't get there in time if Joshua didn't take her.

And Joshua wasn't going to take her. Not again. Not ever.

He had no idea what time it was. The room was lit with the same dingy light, night and day. But he knew that soon they would come for him and ask him to open yet another portal. Isabel had been exhausted after the first Mothergate, even though she'd failed. She wasn't ready, she claimed, still weary from Grooma's weavings. Dr. Jericho had promised her only another day, because the Mothergates would fail soon. Had it been a day? It felt longer, and as the time slipped past his nervousness grew. The moment would come.

And then, an hour later or maybe many more, it did come.

Dr. Jericho stepped into the room. "Ah, there is our young traveler. And his trusty Laithe. How sweet. Are we quite rested?"

Joshua didn't answer.

"How silly of me," Dr. Jericho said after a moment. "Whether you are rested or not, the circumstances call us forward. The next Mothergate beckons, and Isabel is ready."

"I don't care," said Joshua.

"Time is short, Joshua. The Wardens have already allowed one Mothergate to fail. Only two remain."

Joshua shrugged. "Maybe they *should* fail."

It was brave to be talking this way. Brave to say these things. And if it was stupid too, he wasn't sure he cared.

"Come, Joshua," Dr. Jericho said, his voice still mild but threaded with a bit of steel now. "Come and open the portal for us. We must get to Ulu'ru, and repair the Mothergate there."

Ulu'ru. That named seemed weirdly familiar, and his brain started ticking, trying to place it—literally place it, on the great atlas he carried in his head. But no. He wouldn't take the bait. "I won't do it," he said. "I'm not opening any more portals."

He thought Dr. Jericho would try to convince him. To tell him yet again that the Wardens were liars and fools, that Isabel's horrendous weavings at Nlon'ka hadn't been horrendous at all, but necessary. But Joshua wouldn't listen. He promised himself he wouldn't listen.

"Poor Joshua," Dr. Jericho began. "Poor boy. You poor, foul Tinker." He bent down close, down between his knees like a bug, his eyes glinting evilly. "We do not need you to say yes."

And then he grabbed Joshua around the waist, as if he were a toy. He hauled Joshua into the air, knocking the wind out of him. Joshua gasped for breath as Dr. Jericho carried him swiftly from the room, the Laithe following obediently behind.

Dr. Jericho barked a harsh order at another Mordin as they passed. Joshua only caught one word he recognized—"*Quaasa.*" He'd heard that word before, a word that filled him with dread, but his panicked brain wouldn't let him remember where or why.

They sped through the hallways, dirty corridors so low

that Dr. Jericho had to half crouch. He took great lurching strides, his knees brushing the ceiling, laying his hand on the floor now and again like a massive, hairless paw. They descended a flight of stairs in two huge, swooping steps, making Joshua gasp again. He heard voices in the darkness ahead, many voices, the slithering murmur of many Riven speaking.

They emerged into a large square room. It was brighter here, and Joshua realized they were at the bottom of a deep shaft that rose high overhead, into open air far above. A sickly gray light trickled down upon them. Dr. Jericho deposited Joshua onto the rough dirt floor, and the hovering globe of the Laithe swooped in beside him, spinning silently.

Riven stood all around, gruesome shadows in the sickly light, turning to look—Mordin mostly, but also an uncountable number of Ravids, fizzling in and out of sight. One small figure stood alone, in a clear space of her own, as if the Riven didn't want to get too close.

Isabel stepped into the light. She seemed ablaze with power, a golden light flickering in her eyes.

"Are you ready to open the portal?" she asked him. "We mustn't fail again."

"He refuses," Dr. Jericho said, before Joshua could even think of replying.

Isabel frowned down at him, like she felt sorry for him. Or maybe sorry for herself—like she could not understand why he didn't want to help her. "You're confused," she said. "It went badly last time, I admit that. I told them I wasn't ready.

This time will be different."

"This time won't happen," Joshua said. "I'm not going. I'm not taking you there."

She shook her head, genuinely confused. "No one wants me to save them. Am I so frightening? Are my methods so abhorrent? Would you rather die than see me succeed?"

"Leave him be," Dr. Jericho said. "His refusal is irrelevant. We do not need his cooperation, only his power. The Quaasa comes."

Footsteps in the doorway, light and calm. The Riven murmured expectantly. Joshua heard the same harsh whisper over and over. *Quaasa.*

Isabel backed into the shadows. Joshua turned just as the new arrival stepped through the doorway, and he nearly swooned. A Riven, but not at all like any of the others. Smaller than the Mordin, as tall as a man. Long hair of the palest gold, pulled back into a sharp, severe braid that hung down her back. Eyes as blue as winter ice. A red stone embedded in her forehead, pulsing rhythmically. Beautiful and horrible.

An Auditor.

Dread bubbled miserably in Joshua's gut. He should have known, should have guessed what Dr. Jericho would do. The Auditor was here to borrow and steal, to defile the Laithe.

To take its power for her own.

Joshua remembered the Auditor—or maybe more than one, since they were all identical except for their eyes—who had chased him and April into the city, and done battle with the Wardens, using all their own powers against them. The Auditor who had fought Chloe to a draw by the lakeshore, mirroring Chloe's powers inch for inch, her mind side by side with Chloe's inside the Alvalaithen, wrestling for control. Worst of all, the Auditor—*this* Auditor, actually, with the blue eyes—who had wormed her way inside the Laithe after Joshua opened a portal out of the Warren. He had tried to stop her, tried to kick her out of his mind and out of the Laithe and away from all its powers, but he couldn't do it in time. That was how the Riven had learned the secret location of the Warren.

All Joshua's fault.

And now she was here. With the Auditor's arrival, Dr. Jericho didn't need Joshua to cooperate. He only needed Joshua to stay alive, so that the Auditor could worm into Joshua's mind and bend the Laithe's power to her will.

The Auditor exchanged a few soft words with Dr. Jericho. He heard that name again—Ulu'ru. The Auditor nodded and turned to Joshua.

Joshua braced himself. The Auditor slunk nearer, moving with the grace of a dancer, so lovely. The Riven all around them murmured excitedly.

"Do you remember me, Tinker?" the Auditor said. Her voice was low and smooth and gritty, like a monstrous snake sliding over sand.

"Yes," Joshua said.

She circled him slowly, stalking like a cat. "I feel I must

thank you. Without you—without your Tan'ji—we could never have found the Warren. And now you know in truth what I tried to tell you before." She leaned in close, hissing in his ear. *"Ruuk'ha fo ji Quaasa.* All doors are open to me."

Without warning, she grasped the Laithe with a strong, elegant hand and snatched it away. Curls of revulsion smoked through Joshua's flesh at her touch, but he knew there was worse to come.

The Auditor gazed down at the little globe. It was tiny in her hands. *"Koli tantra laithe desh kali tant'ro,"* she purred. "What a marvelous world, to be full of such wonders."

And then suddenly, horribly, her mind was inside the Laithe. Her presence was like a poison, an invader. Joshua tried to fight her off, grappling for control of the Laithe. But he was too weak, and she was too strong. She shoved back so hard that she pushed him out completely, evicting him. He was severed, the Laithe lost to him. He swam senseless for a moment before regaining the tiniest fingerhold, gasping. He looked over at Isabel. She watched from the shadows, frowning faintly. Not shocked by what was happening to him, not worried about him.

Disappointed in him.

"If you will promise to be good, I will let you watch," the Auditor said. "See how I've learned from the last time we met." She took hold of the sleeping copper rabbit and began to slide it.

And though Joshua couldn't quite see with his eyes, still his mind followed what the Auditor was doing. She brought the Laithe down over the Pacific, sliding to the west and south. New Zealand came and went. Australia loomed, filling the hemisphere. It wasn't as smooth or as swift as it would have been with Joshua in control, but she was managing it. With a surge of anger, Joshua pushed at her again, but her concentration held.

"Be good, I said," she spat.

Down they went, into the central highlands of the little continent, in the Alice Springs area. And suddenly Joshua understood the name Dr. Jericho had uttered earlier.

Ulu'ru.

Down into a massive expanse of rippled red, closer and closer. And now a great shadowed form began to resolve, growing larger. Shaped vaguely like an arrowhead, it pointed almost due east. The thin ribbon of a road looped around it.

Ulu'ru. Not just an Altari name, but a name Joshua knew well. Ayers Rock, it was also called, maybe the most famous landmark in Australia. A huge monolith of red rock rising out of the plains, nearly a thousand feet high and two miles long.

This was where they were going. This was the site of the next Mothergate, in the sanctuary called Ulu'ru, no doubt deep underground.

The Auditor brought the Laithe down right atop the grooved surface of the massive stone. She stepped back and tugged at the meridian. It refused to budge for a moment, but then she had it free.

"Open, please, Quaasa," Dr. Jericho said greedily. "Open so we may breathe life into what the Wardens would let die."

Joshua felt the Auditor willing the copper rabbit to run. Grudgingly, slowly, it ran, and the portal began to widen. The tunnel of shapes appeared as it grew, a swift, unseeable flight from this place to that, hurtling over the surface of the earth. And when at last the portal opened wide, the light of the bright Australian sun and a pale blue sky poured into the room. Joshua shielded his eyes. Although it was late evening here, it was early afternoon in Australia.

Dr. Jericho began to laugh. He stepped into the sudden light. "Come now," he said, leering around at the room, his gaze settling last on Joshua. "The path has been laid, with or without you. Now it is time to go."

Joshua shook his head. "I'm not going," he said, but of course it was a pointless thing to say. He wanted to spit, wanted to vomit. The Auditor's thought still curled inside the Laithe like a tumor.

"Don't be silly," Dr. Jericho said, and he spread his arms wide, encompassing the crowded room. "We are *all* going."

All of them. A small army of Riven. But what was the point? The Mothergate would be protected deep below the Nevren, and the Riven wouldn't be able to get through.

Would they?

"I rather hope your friends will be there when we arrive,"

Dr. Jericho said. "Horace and Chloe. It will be quite the party, and you know what they say about parties." He leaned in closer than ever, grinning savagely, the sulfurous stink rolling off him. *"The more the merrier."*

CHAPTER SEVENTEEN

Seven Minutes, Six Days

CHLOE STEPPED OUT OF THE MOTHERGATE, HER HAND STILL wrapped around Horace's. The Veil of Lura rippled around them, faint and wispy. The ground beneath their feet was dry and gritty, the air chilly.

"So this is Australia," Chloe said, looking around, her voice echoing. They were in a vast stone chamber, scarcely different from any of the other chambers where the Mothergates lay hidden. "It's really good to get out in the world, see the sights, you know?"

Horace laughed, letting her go with a squeeze. "We can't say we never go anywhere."

They wandered apart, letting the strange intimacy of traveling through the Mothergate fade peaceably away. This place—Ulu'ru, it was called, home to the second Mothergate—was as empty as a tomb. April had given them no alarms, not yet, but it was Horace who had come up with the idea to get here early, before Isabel. As he'd pointed out, seeing the future wasn't a whole lot of help if you arrived in the middle of the party.

"Are you going to open the Fel'Daera?" Chloe asked him.

"I was thinking I wouldn't yet. Not here, anyway. I was thinking about what we'd do if we had no box, knowing Isabel was coming."

Chloe considered it. "Well, if we could stop her, I don't think we'd let her get anywhere near the Mothergate."

"That's what I was thinking too," Horace said. "And that means we need to find the entrance. We'll find the Nevren, and see what we see." He patted the Fel'Daera.

"And do you know where the entrance is?" Chloe asked, knowing that he didn't.

Horace shrugged. "We're probably hundreds of feet underground. Up means out, right?"

They left the Mothergate. The Veil was so thin here, scarcely more than a fog, that they had no trouble finding their way. Even when they reached the edge, Chloe could still spot the Mothergate far behind them, like a black ship out at sea.

They kept walking. Chloe sort of loved the place. Whereas Ka'hoka was all clean lines, straight corridors, and soaring planes of smooth rock, Ulu'ru was rough and meandering. The rock was reddish and coarse, and had a damp, earthy smell. The lights, too, were red, similar to the amber ones in the Warren, emitting soft swirls of drifting sparks. The place seemed larger than the Warren, but not nearly the labyrinth Ka'hoka was. In no time, following Horace's sensible idea that up meant out, they stumbled onto what was clearly the sanctuary's main passageway.

Here and there, small tunnels branched off from the main route. They passed a massive wall lined with walkways and dotted with doors—the living quarters, no doubt. But there was no one living here now.

"Why are they all deserted?" Chloe asked. "All these places?"

"It's the end of things. Some fled to Ka'hoka, I'm sure. Others just fled."

"Or faded," said Chloe.

"Like Neptune."

"Yes," said Chloe, thinking of that sad news and whether it really was sad. Neptune was free now, or would be soon. Whether it would happen fast enough to save her, no one seemed to know, not even Falo. Chloe listened to the Alvalaithen's song, a song she didn't remotely understand how to live without. "I couldn't have done it, could you?'

"No," Horace said. "But even if I could, I wouldn't. Not now. Not when we're so . . ."

"Needed," Chloe finished.

"Yes."

They walked on in silence. Up and out. They crossed a bridge above a smooth underground river, clear as glass. They passed through a honeycomb of narrow tunnels that seemed at first like an impossible maze, but was so inter-connected that every path led them through. And when they came through, they found themselves in a vast cavern, bigger even than the biggest chambers in Ka'hoka. It was alive with crimson light.

A huge mountain of fallen rock lay before them, apparently broken loose from the ceiling far above. Red boulders—some as big as dogs, some the size of small buildings—were heaped a hundred feet high, jagged and precarious and uninviting. The entire chaotic pile was alight, not just red in color but actually illuminated by some red light within, so that it looked like a chiseled mound of gigantic, glowing hot coals. But there was no heat.

"I'm checking it out," Chloe said, stepping forward.

"Be careful," said Horace. "I'd bet anything the Nevren is here."

Chloe had already come to the same conclusion. The place had that feel to it—a quiet, massive barrier, meant to deter the Riven but allow passage to those who belonged here. "I'm on it," she said.

She didn't bother trying to climb. The boulders were too huge, too sheer, too sharp. She wondered briefly if her jithandra might get her through, revealing a secret path or something. But she didn't need it.

She went thin. She didn't dare go under, didn't dare move with the speed she could have, not when she might stumble across the Nevren at any moment. Instead she simply began walking up the pile as if she were wading through thick red snow, letting her feet sink and get purchase as she trudged up the hill. Even so, it wasn't easy going. Up one glowing boulder, and down the next.

Suddenly, when she was about halfway to the peak of the pile, a creeping cold seized hold of her. She froze in place.

"Nevren," she announced. "Just ahead."

"You're sure?"

Chloe rose out of the glowing red stone she was standing in, clinging instead to its surface. She eased forward, and in just a few feet the Nevren took her. The Alvalaithen's song vanished.

She jerked back before she went any deeper. The dragonfly returned to her at once.

"Definitely sure," she said.

"This is it, then. Isabel will be coming through here."

Chloe backed away cautiously until she felt the cold no more. She looked around, picturing Isabel climbing over this mess, coming to find the Mothergate. She leaned out, pressing her hand against a nearby stone the size of a car. What if Isabel was walking on this, and then suddenly . . . ?

Drinking from the Alvalaithen, Chloe willed the stone to go thin. Since the mal'gama, she'd been practicing cautiously, and had learned more about her limits. She couldn't simply make patches of earth go thin, not when it was a continuous piece of matter. She needed chunks, discrete bits—big though those bits might be. The stone she bled her power into now was separate from the other boulders around it, and far smaller than the mal'gama.

Swiftly the stone became a ghost. It wasn't difficult, not at all. When it was nearly thin, the boulder abruptly began to shift and sink into the pile. Chloe yanked her hand back, releasing it. The huge stone, suddenly solid again, shuddered violently as it melded with the rocks into which it had partially sunk. A great booming crunch rocked through the ground and into the air above.

"Be careful," Horace called up to her.

"I don't have to be careful," she replied. "I'm the Keeper of the Alvalaithen."

"Well then, be . . . judicious."

"I think if I waited here for Isabel to come here, I could make it very hard for her to get through."

Horace didn't say anything. She knew what he was thinking, though—things she could barely bring to the surface of her own mind. Making it hard for Isabel to get through here this way very likely meant not letting her get out alive.

"Is that what you want to do?" Horace asked.

"*Is* it what I do?"

He beckoned to her. "Come down. Come back."

Unafraid of the Nevren now, Chloe slipped into the stone and flew back to Horace, cold red light flickering past her. She was down in no time, arcing from the stone up into the air, landing on her feet beside him.

The Fel'Daera was already in Horace's hands. "Do you want me to look?"

Chloe hugged herself, rubbing her arms. "Why is it so cold in here? I thought Australia was hot."

"It's winter in Australia right now. But we're in a cave. It's the same temperature all year round." He gestured with the Fel'Daera. "Do you want me to look?"

"I won't tell you yes. Only you can decide to open the box, Horace. You know that."

"But you won't tell me no."

She rubbed her arms again, then shook her head. "I won't tell you no."

Horace turned to the massive, glowing rockfall. He settled himself, his face going slack, doing that thing again. Preparing to open the box. It was a kind of meditation, Chloe had decided, and while she didn't exactly envy it, she knew it was a state of mind she'd never find for herself.

After several seconds of careful thought, Horace opened the box. He lifted it, gazing into the rockfall. Into the future. On the side of the box, the silver rays of the sun began to dim, one by one. He was adjusting the breach, moving backward in time again, looking nearer and nearer to the present.

Finally only one spoke was left. It slowly began to shrink. Less than an hour. Maybe Isabel wasn't coming at all. Maybe—

Horace inhaled sharply, and the silver held fast. A fraction of an hour. Chloe ached to ask him what he was seeing, but didn't dare.

Horace actually took a step back. He scanned across the rockfall, this way and that. Then he slammed the box closed.

"We're in trouble," he said. "The Riven are pouring through here. The Nevren isn't stopping them."

"But that's not possible."

"It happens. It will happen. I think Isabel did something. I saw her, up there." He pointed to the top of the rockfall, at what must have been the center of the Nevren. "There were flows of the Medium around her, like ghosts."

Ghosts. Chloe didn't like the sound of that. They had only recently learned what truly lay at the heart of every Nevren—a Keeper, buried underground, suspended in a state of undeath, willingly fused to his or her Tan'ji. The act of fusion created a kind of black hole from which any nearby flows of the Medium could not escape, which was why no Tan'ji would work within it. What could Isabel possibly have done to reverse such a sacrifice? She'd promised she would become more powerful, and it seemed she had.

"How many Riven?" Chloe asked. "And how long?"

"Fourteen minutes. And I don't know how many Riven. I saw two dozen, at least."

"I can fight them," Chloe insisted, knowing it was true. "I can fight them here in the rockfall. I can move underground, make the boulders go thin beneath them one by one, drop them into the earth. They won't be able to touch me."

Horace only shook his head. "But that's not what you do."

Chloe wanted to tear her hair out. The willed path. Except that on that path, she apparently didn't have the will to do what she wanted. She could fight the Riven here and win; she knew she could.

"Why wouldn't I do that?" she demanded. "It's our only chance."

"We obviously decide it isn't."

"Well, when do we figure out *another* chance, Horace? When does our brilliant plan arise?"

Horace shrugged. "Now, I guess."

"Do you have that brilliant plan yet?"

"We can go back to Ka'hoka," Horace said. "We can bring back an army. Go'nesh and Teokas and—"

"There's no army we can bring back that Isabel won't strike down. It's up to us." She pointed to the rockfall. "Why won't I do what I said I could? I'm telling you, I can stop them here. You know how fast I am underground."

Something thoughtful suddenly bloomed in Horace's eyes. "I believe you," he said. "But because you don't do it, that means there must be something that stops you from trying."

"There's nothing," Chloe insisted. "Isabel won't cleave me. This whole thing she's doing is her stupid attempt to save me. And there's nothing else I'm afraid of. Not the golem, not the Mordin, not the—"

And then she knew. There was one thing that would stop her, one thing that would give her pause.

"An Auditor," she breathed. "Did you see an Auditor?"

Chloe had battled Auditors before. She'd even killed one once, as she'd wrestled it for control of the Alvalaithen. She'd cast away the Auditor's grip on the Alvalaithen's power while the Auditor was underground. Going solid the instant she'd lost the ability to remain thin, the Auditor had died instantly.

But a strong Auditor might do the very same to Chloe.

Horace was nodding. "I didn't see an Auditor. But if I were the Riven, after what happened at the last Mothergate, I'd sure bring one now."

Chloe stamped her foot. "Dammit, Horace. It's awfully hard to be a hero, what with you flinging your logic all around like some . . . logic-pooping monkey." Chloe grabbed his hand, pulling him away. "Come on," she said. "Let's get back to the Mothergate. Whatever we're going to do, we've got to do it there."

They ran. Their footsteps echoed through the empty tunnels. Chloe was so furious—and yes, frightened—at the idea of facing another Auditor that absolutely no ideas came to her. She was stronger now than the last time, she knew that, but she couldn't be sure that an Auditor wouldn't be able to evict her from the Alvalaithen, if even for a moment. And a moment was all it would take, if Chloe was underground. What would happen to Horace then? Her worry nagged at her grumpily as they ran. By the time they got back to the Mothergate at last, she was down to the dregs of her confidence, clinging to hopes too blind to be sensible.

But at least there was this: if hope was a blind thing, the Fel'Daera was not. Horace was already taking it out as they stumbled to a halt, puffing hard.

"This time, tell me everything," Chloe said.

He shook his head. "I can't promise you that."

She scowled at him, knowing he was right. Taking direction from the Fel'Daera was like becoming a puppet. Freedom of choice wasn't free when you already knew what your choices would be.

"Tell me where everyone is, then," she said. "The Auditor. Isabel. I need to know. And Joshua too—don't forget what I said about him." A thought suddenly occurred to her, the first decent one she'd had since leaving the rockfall. The vaguest spark of an idea, but at least it was a spark.

Horace nodded. "I remember. You want to save him."

"I'm *going* to save him. Bet you anything he's not making that portal on his own this time. I bet they had to bring the Auditor in to do it." There was no real reason to think this was true, but she made herself think it anyway. More blind hope—her own personal version of seeing the future. Her spark of an idea became a tiny flame.

Again Horace prepared himself—this time studying Chloe for a moment that was uncomfortably long—and again he lifted the open Fel'Daera to his eyes. He began to walk, slowly roaming the space around the Mothergate, watching the future that would unfold here and narrating what he saw. Chloe followed him.

"Here they come," he said, sweeping his arm. "Eleven minutes from now."

"How many?"

"I count thirty Riven, at least. Dr. Jericho is right here, with Isabel beside him." He pointed to the floor. "He senses the box."

With his powers, Dr. Jericho had the ability to sense the Fel'Daera when it was open in the past—which meant that in the *future*, he was sensing Horace right now. It gave Chloe a headache to keep it straight, but for Horace it was nothing at all, as if both present and future were simultaneously alive.

Horace laughed. "He's trying to be cool about it, but he's worried."

"What about Joshua? And is there an Auditor?" Chloe dropped to one knee. Drawing lightly from the Alvalaithen, she reached into her shoe, took hold of her sock, and pulled it loose right through her flesh, through her shoe. Horace, thankfully, was too busy to notice, still choreographing what was about to unfold.

"There's an Auditor, yes," he said, walking. "And I think you're right. I think she's got control of the Laithe. She's standing over here, and Joshua's right in front of her."

319

Chloe hurried to the spot where Joshua would be. Dangling her sock, she lowered it into the ground. She buried it, leaving just the tiniest tip showing, and let it go.

"What else?" she said. "Is there a golem?"

"No golem." Horace turned back toward the Mothergate, the Fel'Daera still at his eyes. "But no Chloe, either," he said. "I don't see you."

That was good. That was right. Chloe's hope burned brighter still. It was a stupid hope, maybe, a hope for a thing that might not get them what they needed. But it was something. "I'm underground," she said.

"What about the Auditor?"

"I'll be deep. I'll be fast. Where will you be?"

He pointed. "I'm over there. I'm—"

He stopped, staring. He stood frozen for several long moments, and then snapped the box closed.

"Do you know what you're going to do?" he asked her.

"Do *you* know what I'm going to do?"

"Not at all," said Horace. "You aren't there."

"But I am. What are *you* going to do? Did you see yourself?"

"Yes." His eyes darted back and forth sharply, his mind clearly racing. "I think I'm going to do something . . . heroic."

"Define heroic. Please distinguish it from stupid."

"I think the stupid part will already be over."

"Oh my god."

"Remember Samuel?"

"Of course," Chloe said. "The wannabe. Thrall-blighted himself to death."

"Right, but before that, he kept trying to send the astrolabe through the Fel'Daera."

"Which is impossible."

"Ordinarily, yes," said Horace. "It's too grounded in the present to be sent into the future. But what if it wasn't grounded?"

Chloe squinted at him, pursing her lips. Horace was having one of those moments where he was trying to drag her into a conversation he was really having with himself. "Okay," she said, "you've obviously figured out some brilliant thing. Just tell me."

"I didn't figure it out. I saw it. Or I saw it, and then I figured—"

"Horace," she said. "Please."

He dug into his pocket and pulled out the astrolabe. He held it up like the answer to everything. "I'm going to take the astrolabe back into the Mothergate. Right now."

"No."

"Yes, and I'm going to let it align to the time in there. It's going to set itself to all the crazy flows of time inside the Mothergate, and then—"

"No," Chloe said. No way was she going to let him do this thing.

"—and then when I bring it back out here, I'll send it through the Fel'Daera. It'll work, because the astrolabe won't be set to the present anymore. It'll be set to *every* time. Every time everywhere. Everywhere the Fel'Daera sends things. It'll be ungrounded."

"That's assuming you can escape the Mothergate without the astrolabe set to *this* time," Chloe said, thrusting a finger at the floor.

"But I *do* get to escape. I come back. I already saw."

"Did you see yourself go in? Or come out?"

"No, but—"

"So check now," she said. "Convince me you do it. Then you can go."

"Chloe, you know I can't do that. It's a fool's proof."

She did know it, of course. A fool's proof was a kind of circular argument the Fel'Daera could be forced to make, and it could go horribly wrong. You couldn't ask the Fel'Daera for permission to do something, especially if you were secretly planning to do that thing no matter what the box revealed. Those desires had a way of creating a future that was easy to misinterpret—the box might give you a sign that encouraged you do the thing, but with zero actual assurance that the thing would work out. A fool's proof had sent Chloe back to her house the night it burned down, where she'd been trapped inside the flames with the Alvalaithen—her skin taking none of the physical damage, but her mind taking every bit of the pain.

"Horace, it probably won't go bad if you go back into the Mothergate, but if it does, it could go really bad."

He looked genuinely insulted. "I'm the Keeper of the Fel'Daera."

"I know. And you're a walking talking clock. But you heard Falo—she went into the Mothergate and felt like she came right back out, except when she came out, three years had gone by! Plus, if you go in there and unhook the astrolabe from the present, won't that be sort of like cutting the string of a kite? One second you're tethered, and the next you're not."

"I'll be ready for it. Look, I know it's dangerous, but I feel like you're not hearing me. I saw myself sending the astrolabe. It happens. I'm going to send it."

All that light in his eyes. He wasn't afraid. He was going to do this, and she wasn't going to stop him. "Fine," she said. "But what happens when you do send it? I mean, what's the point?"

The light suddenly went out. "I'm not sure."

"What did you see?"

"Nothing. I closed the box as soon as I realized I was sending the astrolabe." He shrugged. "I didn't want to see any further."

"And that's the truth?"

"Why would I lie?"

Plenty of reasons, actually. Most of them not so good. Her skeptical silence must have unnerved him, because he said, "Chloe, I didn't want to see. I was afraid."

"Afraid," she repeated, testing out the word. And then

she understood. "You think it could be the end. Sending the astrolabe could be the end."

He rolled his head side to side, neither a yes or a no. "I don't *think* it will be, but . . ."

"But it could be. It could force the Mothergates to close."

"It's possible. Nothing twists the Medium like the Fel'Daera. And it seems like sending the astrolabe would be a pretty big twist."

A fear like nothing Chloe had ever known seized hold of her, crushing her. She'd thought she was ready, prepared for the end. But she wasn't. Not at all.

"How much longer?" she said, gesturing to the Fel'Daera.

"Seven minutes, twelve seconds."

Seven minutes! Worst case scenario, seven minutes to live. She had to forcibly remind herself, though, that the sudden closing of the Mothergates was not the worst case scenario. The reminder didn't help.

"This is crazy, Horace," she said, trying to turn her fear into anger. "Why don't you just refuse the willed path? Thrall-blight twists the Medium too. That's what Samuel did."

But Horace only shook his head. "You've got a plan of your own. You had it before I opened the box—an inkling, anyway. Whatever it is, it's a part of the future I saw. If I refuse the willed path now, your plan falls apart too. It all falls apart."

She dropped her head into her hand, rubbing her temples. So much to consider. So much to fear. So much to rage at.

"Chloe," Horace said softly. She looked up at him. "I do

my thing. You do yours. It's not that we have no other choice, it's that we already made the choice. Okay?"

She nodded. "Okay," she said. "Okay."

"It's time, then," he said.

They went back to the Mothergate together, through the wispy remnants of the Veil. Horace still held the astrolabe in his hand. The black mass loomed and pulsed.

Horace reached for her. Cautiously he put his hand inside her chest, through the sturdy plate of bone beneath her throat. She thought she might die. He scooped around the back of the Alvalaithen, lifting it. She let him, willing the dragonfly to go solid in his palm. He held the fluttering thing, gazing at it for a moment as if astonished at what he was doing, and then laid it softly back against her skin.

"I'll be right back," he told her. "I promise."

He turned and stepped into the Mothergate. It sizzled briefly around the edges of his body as he entered, like hot oil. And then he was gone.

"Horace!" Chloe shouted. Her voice rolled into the Veil and was swallowed.

She was alone.

She just stood there, staring into the black.

And then Horace stumbled out of the Mothergate. Gasping.

Chloe actually leapt back, startled, but then her heart swelled. He was safe.

Horace's eyes, wide and searching, fell on her. He grabbed

325

her, pulling her close. He talked into her hair, his voice buzzing against her skin.

"Chloe!" he cried. "You're still here. I'm sorry. I'm sorry, are you—" He thrust her out to arm's length, looking her up and down frantically, then pulled her close again.

She just stood there, letting him hold her, arms at her sides. "That was fast," she said. She squirmed, trying to fight free. "Did you do it?"

He let her go. He looked at her like she was the one who had lost her mind. "How long was I—?" he began, and then he fumbled in his pocket. He pulled out the astrolabe and clumsily forced it into her hand. "Take it," he said. "If I keep it, it'll reset itself. Don't look at it or think about it."

Bewildered, Chloe shoved the astrolabe into her pocket. As she did, she caught a glimpse of madly spinning dials, flashing colors.

"You did it, didn't you?" she said. "How did you do it so fast?"

Horace shook his head. "Not fast. Not fast at all. How long was I gone?"

"Like, barely. Maybe five seconds."

He nodded, looking up and all around at the Veil, like he was trying to get his bearings. Goose bumps blossomed up and down Chloe's arms as understanding slowly dawned.

"Horace," she said softly, "how long were *you* gone?"

He swallowed, letting loose a hiccupping groan that was

part laugh, part cry. "Six days." He began to nod, his breath slowing. "Five seconds here . . . six days there," he said, still nodding. "But I'm back now. And you're still here. It's okay."

Chloe grabbed him. She hauled him in close, and he wrapped his arms around her, sobbing.

Six days inside the Mothergate. Six days alone in there—in his mind, anyway—but only five seconds here. Her head swam to catch up with him, to where he'd been. Six days, lost and frightened, hopelessness growing by the hour.

"It *is* okay," she told him. "I'm sorry. You must have been so scared."

He nodded into her neck, grabbing her harder. And she knew that most of his fear had been for her, not for him.

"I couldn't get out," he said. "After I uncoupled the astrolabe from the present, I couldn't tell myself the story right. I think it's because I was going back the way I'd come. The end was the same as the beginning, and I just—" He let out a great sigh, sagging in her arms. She steeled her legs for the both of them, sure he'd collapse if she let him go.

Slowly, after long moments, he disentangled himself. He stepped back, wiping his eyes.

"Oh my god," he said. "That *sucked*."

"I can't even imagine," Chloe said, and she couldn't. "But you did it. The astrolabe is—"

He waved his hands in her face. "Don't even think about the astrolabe. I'm not sure how it sets itself, or how long it'll

327

hold all the streams of time it's holding now. But yes, I did it."

"Okay," Chloe said, pulling her thoughts away. "You're amazing. You might be the most amazing person there ever was. Definitely second most, at least."

Horace laughed, his eyes beginning to clear. He was coming back to her, back to himself. Chloe shook her head, blinking away tears. "So how long until they get here?"

Horace laid a hand on the Fel'Daera, as if it could help his sense of time come back more quickly. And maybe it could, because he said, "Two minutes and twenty-nine seconds."

"Okay. That's good." She took him by the elbow, leading him past the Mothergate, to the opposite side of where the Riven would be. "I need to know how long it'll be between the moment the Riven get here and the moment you send the astrolabe."

"Fifty-three seconds," Horace said instantly.

"Fifty-three seconds. That's good. I can do that." They kept walking. Now for the next part—how far was far enough? How far was too far? "What's an Auditor's range, do you think?" she asked. "How far away would you need to be so that she couldn't take over your instrument?"

"I'd say a hundred feet, at least."

That sounded about right. "I'm doubling it," Chloe said. They kept walking until they were two hundred feet from where the Auditor would be. Chloe bent and pulled her other sock free through her shoe.

"What are you doing?" Horace asked. "Is this your plan?"

"This is my plan," she said, shaking her sock at him. "Don't mock the sock."

She knelt and slipped the sock into the ground again, but this time only halfway. She left the foot part of it above-ground, lying there like a white flag. Okay—a dingy white flag. But she could see it.

She pointed at it, looking Horace in the eye. "The second you send the astrolabe, you run for this sock. I mean the *very* second. Understand?"

"No," said Horace. "But yes."

"You're not the fastest," said Chloe, which was, to be honest, putting it rather kindly. "You're going to have to really, really run."

"I can run."

"Yeah. Well. Do your best impersonation, anyway." She took a nervous, shuddering breath, looking all around. "How long now?"

"Forty-five seconds. Let's get ready."

They hurried back to the Mothergate. Horace took up his station, right where the Fel'Daera had told him he would be. He opened the box now, holding it out. Chloe fished the astrolabe out of her pocket, its lacy dials still spinning and flashing. She laid it in the box, atop the blue glass. Horace didn't so much as look at it.

She turned away, finding nothing to say. She went out into

the mist of the Veil, where the Riven would soon be gathering. She searched until she found the tip of the first sock she'd placed, the tip of its toe barely glinting from the stone. She stood atop it. She heard distant voices now, and swift heavy footsteps. The sizzle and pop of Ravids.

"Tell me when," she said.

Back at the Mothergate, Horace nodded. "Don't forget to be awesome," he said.

"How could I ever?" she said.

The Riven were coming closer. She turned and saw them, distant monstrous shapes speeding toward them. Chloe let go of the Alvalaithen. She took a deep breath, and grabbed hold of it again, its song swelling like a choir. It would all be over fast, one way or another, but if it was going to work she'd need all the energy she could muster.

"*Now,*" Horace said.

Chloe fell. She released every last shred of the bonds that kept her afloat, all at once. She dropped into the bottomless earth. She didn't steer herself, didn't fly. She just fell, keeping her body perfectly vertical, plummeting like a stone. When she thought she'd reached two hundred feet or so, she slowed herself and came to a halt. Her heart pounded, the molecules of her blood weaving through the bedrock.

She waited. She counted down. She was no Horace, but she tried her best to keep track of the time—fifty-three seconds, Horace had told her. Fifty-three seconds until he would try to send the astrolabe.

She tried to imagine what was happening above. She reminded herself that Horace was in no danger. Not yet. The Fel'Daera had told him so. The Riven were gathering, high above her. Isabel was there, waiting to weave her terrible flows. And *directly* above her—two hundred feet, straight up—Joshua ought to now be standing, the Laithe by his side, the hated Auditor just behind him.

Twenty seconds. How fast would she need to be? Her fastest might be too fast. She didn't want to hurt him. She forced herself not to think about the astrolabe, about Horace's insane plan. Was it any less insane than hers? If both the Mothergates closed instantaneously, would she even feel it before she was severed, and her flesh went solid inside the earth?

But no time to think of that. No point. Five seconds.

Three.

She launched herself.

She rocketed up through the cold gritty ground. Not her fastest speed, no. Not quite. But fast. Up like a geyser.

She shot out of the earth, into Joshua's waiting body. He was so small, so frail. In the fraction of a second that she was inside him, she grabbed him, atom to atom, and brought him with her. He grunted, his breath leaving him. Somehow he managed to grab hold of the Laithe, and she let that come too. Faintly she thought she could feel the poisonous presence of the Auditor inside it.

They rose high into the air, ten feet. A gasp and a roar went up with them. The Veil was gone now, and ahead she caught a clear glimpse of Horace, standing by the Mothergate, the open Fel'Daera in his hand.

As she watched, he flicked the lid closed. His head rocked back violently.

The Mothergate shuddered and rumbled. It seemed to crack. He'd done the impossible—he'd sent the astrolabe. Chloe fell, unable to see more, Joshua still in her arms, still in her chest.

They went back into the earth, the dragonfly's wings still whirring. Chloe willed them forward, toward Horace and the Mothergate, and beyond. She had no idea if her time was running out.

Abruptly, another presence thrust its way into the Alvalaithen, groping and greedy, clutching at the Alvalaithen's song. It tried to shoulder Chloe aside, to wrench control of the dragonfly. For a moment, Chloe's grip slipped. The earth tore at her flesh. But the pain only fueled a welcome gout of rage, and she pushed back with all her might, forcing the Auditor out. The Alvalaithen was hers again. It would always be hers, until the end of everything.

They sped through the stone, just below the surface. Chloe found her top speed easily, pulling hard at every thread of the Medium she could muster, willing herself on. And the Medium was there. Thinner than it had been, yes, but still there. At least one of the Mothergates still held.

She breached. The air was a fury of sound, like ships crashing. She was past the Mothergate already, but didn't dare glance back. Horace should be running now. He'd better be running. She needed him; they all did. Up ahead, she glimpsed the limp beacon of the second sock.

Back into the earth, she and Joshua both. The Alvalaithen and the Laithe. One more breach, and they were nearly there. She got her feet beneath her, riding the surface to stop, just where she'd meant to end up.

She set Joshua down. "Portal. Now."

"Chloe," Joshua said. He was shaking.

Behind her, Horace was running toward them, taking great clumsy strides that somehow managed to close the distance with a speed she didn't know he had. But the Mordin were coming too, Dr. Jericho and two other Mordin out in front, catching up fast. Far behind, she could see Isabel running too, raging, bolts of the Medium pouring from her hands.

And the Mothergate. It had become a billowing cloud of stone, shutting itself down. It churned and grated, seeming to bloom into a mountain. It roared like a thousand golems, grinding and squealing, a steel avalanche in reverse.

That way was closed now. Chloe had known it would be. There was only one way out.

"Portal, Joshua," she cried. "Get us out. Get us anywhere. They're coming."

It wasn't going to work. He was too startled, too shaken. It was all going to fail. Horace was nearly here, and the Mordin not far behind.

But then Joshua astonished her. He fixed his eyes briefly

on the globe, a deep and easy mastery shining in his eyes. She couldn't see what he did—only the Keeper of the Laithe could see that—but in no time at all he'd pulled the meridian free, tossing it into the air. It blew open, becoming a round gateway as tall as a door. Through it, a rocky beach at sunset materialized—or maybe it was sunrise—with a silver sea stretching out beyond.

Horace barreled into them, his eyes wide, his mouth as hard as stone. Before he could speak, Chloe grabbed him by the arm and pulled, whirling, using his own momentum to propel him through the portal. He went through, went hard to the ground there—wherever there was—and scrambled to his feet.

Dr. Jericho roared, still coming. The bristling spines on his back had emerged, cutting through the air. A sinewy Mordin racing beside him leapt at Chloe and Joshua with a growl.

Chloe leapt too, tackling Joshua, the now-yellow sphere of the Laithe sandwiched between them. Together they plunged into the portal, a tingle of electricity passing through Chloe's flesh like a shiver. They landed painfully on the far side, Chloe's elbow cracking against a flat stone. The air was humid and warm, a salty breeze washing over her.

She rolled onto her back. On the far side of the portal, Dr. Jericho and the other Mordin flailed blindly. They couldn't get through now, couldn't even see, not with Joshua here on this side. Dr. Jericho roared at the portal, raging like a trapped tiger, baring teeth that were suddenly as sharp as knives. He pounded uselessly at the meridian with his great fists, hatred blazing in his beady eyes. Chloe found herself hoping he was thinking of Kathra, his brother, who'd tumbled through a portal just like this one to his death.

Her eyes found Horace. "It worked," she said.

"Yes."

"We're still alive. Still Tan'ji. The Mothergate at Ka'hoka is still open."

"Yes," he said flatly. He looked down at Joshua. "Close the portal, Keeper. Close it and get us home."

But Joshua shook his head. The portal remained open.

Chloe's heart froze. She'd made a terrible mistake. Joshua was going to betray them, to let the Riven through. He hadn't even asked to come here—Chloe had all but forced him.

And then she saw. Joshua wasn't refusing. He was rigid with fear, his fists clenched with effort. He stared at the portal, but not through it. Chloe turned.

Fingers of gold were creeping through the doorway from the other side, grasping at the meridian. Clutching weaves of the Medium, holding the portal open. Tiny tendrils slid into the copper rabbit atop the meridian, filling it. The portal shuddered.

"Isabel is coming," Joshua said.

And now Chloe saw her, coming closer on the other side. Even Dr. Jericho stepped aside to make way. The Medium flowed like smoke from her hands, reaching through the portal.

"Close it," said Chloe, barely breathing.

"I can't!" Joshua cried.

Horace got onto his knees before Joshua. "You can do this," he said kindly, slowly, as if they had all the time in the world. "You are the rightful Keeper of the Laithe of Teneves. Falo told me so herself."

Joshua pulled his gaze away from the portal, searching Horace's face. "She did?"

"Yes," Horace said. "You are Tan'ji. Your instrument is you. Do not ask it to close. Just . . . *close*."

"But Isabel . . ."

"Isabel is nothing," said Horace. "You think because she helped you Find the Laithe, she has some power over you? Over it?"

Isabel's woven fingers began to spread and thicken. They reached out into the air now, slinking toward the golden sphere of the Laithe in Joshua's arms. Briefly Chloe considered wresting the Laithe from Joshua's arms, burying it forever in the stony ground here. She could do it, easily. It would be fast.

"Isabel *gave* you power, Joshua," Horace was saying. "Don't you see? A power she herself will never have."

Joshua looked up at Chloe. "You saved me," he said. It sounded like he was describing a miracle.

Shame flooded her. For thinking what she'd been thinking. For not having rescued Joshua before now. For the very fact of her mother at all.

"No," she said. "You saved us. And now it's time to finish." She pointed back at the portal, where Isabel's wild face was lit with glee. Her mother almost seemed to see her, finding her across the miles, through a doorway that should not exist. "Get this woman out of your business, Keeper," Chloe said. "She's got no right to anything at all."

Joshua furrowed his tiny brow. Little fires sparked in his eyes. The tendrils of the Medium were grasping at him now, circling the Laithe, but he paid them no mind. He glared at Isabel through the portal. He opened his mouth.

"Get *out!*" he shouted.

And the rabbit began to run. It shed drops of the Medium as its legs became a blur. The portal shrank smoothly, closing like a circular guillotine, slicing through Isabel's weaves. The grasping fingers scattered and vanished like smoke, Isabel herself winking out of sight as the portal went blank. The meridian closed all the way with a hollow clang Chloe felt in her chest.

They were free. They were out.

They stood there, finding their breath. Joshua plucked the meridian out of the air and looped it back around the Laithe. The Laithe faded from gold back to blues and greens. Chloe hadn't gotten a good look at the Laithe close up before, and it took her breath away now—a true tiny earth, luminous and alive.

"You did it, Joshua," Horace said. "You did it."

"Thank you," he said politely. "But I should have done it already. I should have left with Mr. Meister." He looked up at them both, his lip trembling. "They're doing bad things."

"Yes," said Horace. "They are. But we're stopping them."

Chloe nodded at Horace, marveling at all he'd just done. All he was still doing. He grinned back at her as if he'd done nothing at all. A seagull circled over their heads, keening softly, and she tipped her head back to watch it. Out to sea, the sun was a bit higher now. Rising to make morning.

"Where the heck are we?" she asked.

"Crete," said Joshua. "I'm sorry. It was all I could think of." He pointed over the water, where a rocky island seemed to float nearby, a round, ancient-looking fortress rising from its hills. "That's Nlon'ka right there."

Horace laughed. "Wow," he said. "I feel like we were just here."

Chloe squatted in front of Joshua. "You did good. Now can you get us home?"

"Home," Joshua said, as if the word wasn't even a word.

"To Ka'hoka," Horace said. "To April and Gabriel. And Mrs. Hapsteade. And I know Sil'falo Teneves will want to meet you."

"Is Arthur there?" Joshua asked hopefully.

"Oh, yeah," said Chloe. "Not to brag, but he's bunking with us."

Joshua looked down at the Laithe, looking dubious. "And you're sure they'll want me," he said.

Chloe put a hand on his shoulder. Her throat worked painfully. "Tell you what. If anyone gives you any trouble, you just tell them . . . you're with me."

PART THREE

The Sending

CHAPTER EIGHTEEN

Uroboros

APRIL SAT ON THE FLOOR IN THE HALLWAY OF FALO'S QUARTERS, listening to the birds.

It was a welcome respite, so different from the roiling flood that surged out of the Mothergate—the last remaining Mothergate, now the only outlet for the Medium. The Mothergate had become a savage cannon of story and power and song, so loud that April could still hear it even in the farthest reaches of Ka'hoka.

She tried not to listen. She tried not to think about the Riven, either. The events in Ulu'ru, April knew, had bought the Wardens some time, trapping Isabel and Dr. Jericho in Australia with no easy way back. But eventually—soon—they would return. It definitely did her no good to think too hard about that.

She listened to the birds instead. She had no idea what

kinds of birds they were; she wasn't sure they existed in the world above. Something like sparrows, or wrens. But they were even smaller than wrens, and brightly colored. And unlike wrens—or most very small creatures, in April's experience—they were strikingly, soothingly calm. Unnaturally calm, she might have thought, on any other day in any other place. But here in Ka'hoka, on the cusp of the death of the last remaining Mothergate, their tranquility seemed utterly natural.

Falo had hundreds of the tiny birds, caged here in the hallway, and April was listening to them all, her mind open to theirs. She'd left Arthur with Horace and Chloe so that she'd be able to hear them better. There was a kind of flock intelligence at work among the little beings—not like ants, or bees, but more like a peaceable crowd of individuals, all of the same spirit. A kind of community, but without the drones. Their thoughts were simple, for the most part.

Food. Feather. Mate. Friend.

But every once in a while—and this was why she was listening—something brighter and more complicated emerged, something worth aspiring to, or being.

Joy. Yesterday. Exploration. Elsewhere.

Not that they were thinking these words, exactly. Especially that last one. It was a complicated idea, the notion that something could be different from what it was. A form of imagination, or aspiration, or longing. A kind of hope, tinted with sadness. A song of change.

And change, as April well knew, was in the air. In fact,

certain things had already changed—things she wasn't sure anybody knew about but her.

And maybe Falo.

But Falo wasn't talking.

She'd hardly talked to Falo at all, not since Horace and Chloe had gone to Ulu'ru the night before last. That night, April had wanted to stay beside the Mothergate here in Ka'hoka—to hear what she could hear, to learn what she could learn about whatever her friends might manage to do in that faraway place. But Falo had sent her away. The Altari had stayed alone by the Mothergate's side, offering no explanation whatsoever.

And Falo still hadn't explained. It was a small mystery, but a perplexing one, and April didn't like to feel perplexed. She hadn't been back to the Mothergate since.

There were other mysteries too, or maybe one big mystery with many small parts, parts that April simply couldn't piece together. She knew all about what Horace had done in Ulu'ru, sending the unsendable astrolabe into the future. She'd spent hours with Horace and Chloe since their return—and Joshua too—hearing their stories. Incredible stories, astonishing deeds. But in all their talk, April had told them nothing about the change she felt through the Ravenvine now. A change in the story that barreled from the Mothergate.

It was hard to put into words, but when Horace had sent the astrolabe, he had . . . awakened something in the multiverse. Something April couldn't name, neither good nor bad. Before that moment, the Mothergates had been closing almost as a matter of course, like a tree growing slowly away from shade into sunlight, reshaping itself in the process. But sending the astrolabe had set in motion . . . an awareness. A kind of watching. A knowing. By bringing the tangled streams of the multiverse so blatantly into this world, the Wardens' efforts to ensure the closing of the Mothergates had suddenly become a vital part of the Mothergates' own song. The story that poured from it now was rich with those efforts. The Wardens' story, in other words, was becoming *the* story.

The story would still end, of course. It was always going to end. But whereas at first that end was simply unraveling, like a ball of yarn rolling down an inevitable hill, now that end was being forged.

She'd talked to no one about the change she'd sensed, not even Falo, but there was one clear thought she'd taken away from all the turbulent tides that had poured from the Mothergate these last two days.

The multiverse was watching. It was waiting.

Waiting for them to act.

If they didn't act, nature would follow its course, and the last Mothergate would close. The tangled universes would untangle themselves and all would be well.

But in the meantime, there was a kind of pause. A lull. A breathless hanging at the very peak of a leap, where something unexpected might occur.

And April had been thinking a lot about what that

unexpected thing might be. What they might *make* it be.

She'd been thinking a lot about Neptune, too. She was still here, venturing out into the hallways at night, speaking to no one but Gabriel. April still had the tourminda, and was beginning to realize that somehow Neptune had managed to fade so completely, so quickly—in just a few days!—that she could no longer feel it. And when April looked at the tourminda now, it no longer registered as Tan'ji to her eyes.

From talking to Mrs. Hapsteade, April knew that the process of fading often took much longer than a few days. Neptune's tourminda was weak, as far as Tan'ji were concerned, but apparently the more powerful the Tan'ji, the longer it took to fade. Sometimes it took months, or even years. And when that time was over, after the bond had drifted into nothing, the Keeper was free.

Free. She hated that this was the word that came to her mind. Being the Keeper of the Ravenvine wasn't a prison. It was a privilege, or no—a responsibility. Or no. A destiny.

Not that April believed in destiny.

April sighed in frustration, letting her head fall forward into her hands. It seemed like every thought she had led into a thousand other thoughts, and so on. She couldn't keep track of them all. Her thoughts, she realized, were almost like the multiverse itself. Branching and branching and branching again.

"I see you've met my birds."

April practically jumped out of her skin at the sound of

Falo's voice. She scrambled to her feet, smoothing her dress. Her scattered thoughts fell apart like a dropped glass. "Yes," she said.

To April's great surprise, Falo lowered herself to the floor, leaning back against the wall just as April had been doing. Falo said nothing, and made no gesture, but after an awkward moment April returned to her seat, joining Falo on the floor. Even seated, the Altari towered over her, her legs too long to stretch out fully.

"I take it you've felt the change," Falo said, catching her completely by surprise.

Determined not to seem stupid, or uncertain, April answered the question the way she was sure it had been meant. She tried to say exactly what she'd just been thinking as best as she could.

"Yes," she said. "The multiverse is watching us now. It's waiting."

"It has given us room," Falo said. "Room to act."

Hearing Falo say these words filled April with a flood of almost blistering relief. Tears she didn't know she'd been making poured down her cheeks. This was the thinking she'd been wrestling with all day, dragged out into the open and shared with a wise friend.

"But why would it give us that room?" April asked.

"When it comes to the multiverse, there is no *why*," Falo said. "The multiverse is not a creature, April, no matter how alive its song may seem. The multiverse is a manifestation of what we the living choose to do."

"And we've been choosing to let the multiverse heal itself."

"To be fair, we've been poking it into healing itself."

"Poking it, right," April said. "As we tangle the universes more and more, the Mothergates will close faster to prevent those tangles from happening. But what Horace did the other day—that was more than a poke."

Falo laughed. "Yes indeed." She paused and looked intently down at April. "Being a Warden means being aware of our place in the multiverse. Not just in thought, but in deed."

Falo let the words hang, clearly not waiting for an answer, but waiting for April to absorb her words. And April tried, wiping away her tears. *"Being aware of our place in the multiverse."* Knowing the multiverse. Knowing how actions might affect the multiverse—especially if you were a Keeper, with the power to tangle universes. April nodded at Falo, willing her to continue.

Falo said, "What Horace did, sending the astrolabe, was an unprecedented physical manifestation of that awareness—a mirror held up to the multiverse itself. He showed the multiverse that we know it, that we see it. And in that mirror, we too have been seen." She shook her head and heaved a huge, lovely sigh.

April looked up at her. "You sent me away. Why did you do that?"

"I was prepared to do something I should not have done."

"What?"

"Like you said, what Horace did was more than a poke. Far more. More than enough to cause both remaining Mothergates to close completely."

April just sat there with the idea. Slowly it dawned on her what Falo had intended, why she had sent April away. The chorus of bird voices above trickled through the vine.

Hungry. Curious. Hope. Tomorrow.

"You were going to keep the last Mothergate from closing," April breathed. "You were going to weave the flows—to force the Mothergate here in Ka'hoka to stay open."

Falo sighed again, lightly this time, almost as if hearing the words spoken aloud was a relief. "Forced is a strong word. The flows I planned to weave would not have lasted—not Isabel's cruel stitches, I assure you. Even had I done it, the Mothergate would have closed in just a few days."

"I'm confused. Why would you want to keep the Mothergate open for a few more days?"

This time, Falo answered much more slowly. "First," she said, "let us gently consider where we would be right now if I had *not* been ready to do that thing." She held April in long somber stare, full of kindness and calm.

April nodded, swallowing. If the final Mothergate had closed, as Falo had expected, it would have been the end for all Keepers, then and there.

Still, she hardly knew what to say. Letting the Mothergates

close was the whole point of everything, wasn't it? And Falo was not the sort to do something so drastic without reason. It was far more likely, April thought, that Falo did not want to share those reasons with her. With anyone.

"It would have been the end we all expected, the end we've been fighting for," Falo said, seeming to read her thoughts. "But I sensed what Horace had done, and that the multiverse was taking note—that it was pausing for a moment to consider itself, and to consider this story suddenly unfolding within it. . . ." She shrugged. "I was ready to take the opportunity. Ready to step into the pause. But then I did not need to."

"Because the Mothergate didn't close. This pause the multiverse has taken—it was bigger than you thought."

"Yes."

"But if the Mothergate doesn't close," April said, "all the tangled universes will be destroyed."

"Not while the multiverse watches. Not while it waits to see what we intend. As I said, we have been given a respite. For the time being, the multiverse is not yet ready to forget this part of itself."

April wanted to ask how long that respite might be. But she was afraid that Falo wouldn't know the answer.

Falo turned to her, smiling. "You took a rather lovely trinket from the Warren, I believe. May I see it?"

Bewildered by the sudden change of topic, April barely

understood the question. And then she realized—Falo meant the tree. She pulled the little sphere from her pocket, handing it over gently.

"It's not important, is it?" April asked. "I don't know why I took it, I just—"

"Beauty is always important," Falo said, gazing at the little sphere, no bigger than a marble in her hand. Inside, a ripe purple fruit was just falling. The tree's leaves began to color, to wither and die.

"Kothulus made this," Falo said. "My predecessor. He had a flair for the profound, a fondness for the oblique. I have often wished I possessed some of his subtlety."

"You can have it back if you want," said April. She didn't think she'd done anything wrong, exactly, but it was never good to assume. "I don't even know what it does."

"It does no more than what you see, but I think you knew that already." Falo handed it back. "Keep it. It suits you far better than it does me."

"It's been comforting," April admitted gratefully. "Life and death. Renewal."

Falo nodded vaguely, as if they were discussing nothing more consequential than the shapes of clouds. "It reminds me of Uroboros," she said lightly. "The fish."

This entire conversation had April on edge—a minefield of casually dropped bombs and hints—and now she felt as though she had suddenly slid out onto a sheet of thin ice. She understood instinctively that Falo would answer any question April might ask of her now, but for April's own sake—for the sake of not slipping further, or breaking through into waters she wouldn't be able to tread—she was determined to proceed cautiously.

"You're talking about the fish Gabriel brought back," April said. "The fish in the glass rod."

"Is there another fish?"

"Not that I know of. That fish spoke to me."

"Yes, it would have," Falo agreed. "That is what it does."

"Why does it do that?"

"I do not know. It does not speak to me. Or rather, I do not know how to listen. That is for the empath to say."

"I couldn't understand it," said April. "But I know that it's old. Very old. Do you know how old it is?"

"I know what the stories say. I do not know whether those stories are true." Falo was answering the questions swiftly, as if she'd been prepared for this conversation.

"And what do the stories say?"

"That Uroboros swam forth from the Starlit Loom. The legends say that when the Loom was brought into this world, through one of the cracks between our world and all the others—"

"A Mothergate," April whispered.

"—a fish swam circles inside it, its tail in its mouth. Around and around it swam, endlessly." Falo leaned forward,

353

and the large black pendant she wore dangled in April's face. It began to shimmer and deepen. Points of light began to drift inside it.

April gaped. She knew at once she was looking at the Starlit Loom. It had been here in plain sight, all this time. She wondered if Horace and Chloe knew, and she decided that they must. A wave of awe swept over her as she gazed into the Loom, leaving her as calm as melting snow, as raw as a burn. Inside the Loom, points of light rearranged themselves, took on the shape of a long, thin fish. The fish swallowed its own tail, circling the Loom. Around and around and around.

"When the Loom was first Found," said Falo, "the first Keeper set Uroboros free. A power had been laid upon the fish, so that it could not die. It was tended to with care, kept with honor. In time, as Tan'ji were made to exploit the talents of empaths like yourself, some of them reported that the fish spoke to them. Or tried to speak, anyway. No one could understand it. Many years later—lifetimes later, when the tale I'm telling you now is all anyone knew of Uroboros—a vessel was built for it. Some say to keep it safe, some say to silence it. Some say to keep it from swallowing its tail. And there it remains to this day."

"It's cruel," April burst out. "It's a terrible thing."

Hiraethel faded back to black. The circling fish melted away. "Shall we release it, then?" Falo asked. "Break the glass?"

"No, I—"

354

"Tradition suggests that the Keeper of Hiraethel—the Starlit Loom—should be the one who maintains custody of Uroboros. But perhaps now, here so close to the end, it would be better off in your hands."

April didn't know if the offer was serious, and had no idea what she'd say if it was, so she pretended she hadn't even heard it. "If it's supposed to be with you, why was it in the Warren?"

"I took it there myself, years ago. Mr. Meister wished to study it. He had a young Tuner—a Tuner with the sensibilities of an empath—who he thought might help us unravel some of its mysteries."

"A Tuner," April said. "You mean Horace's mom, don't you?"

"I do. But now *you* are here. Uroboros speaks to you. Perhaps you should listen."

"What do you think it's trying to say?"

Falo sat up, turning gracefully toward April so that she had her full attention. She clasped April's hands, her expression earnest and pleading. "I honestly do not know," she said. "You're no fool, April Simon. You know I meant for this conversation to come to this place. But what comes *after* this place—and what you will discover there—is beyond whatever wisdom I possess. Beyond any answers that I have. Truly."

April nodded. She knew the words were true. A person couldn't stand in front of the Mothergate for long hours, as she had, without realizing just how little any one mind could know. Listening to a secret keeper like Falo—a guidance giver, a wisdom bringer—it was maybe easy to believe she had the answers to everything. But that was impossible. The universe could never be such a place. In fact, April realized now, looking into Falo's deep and searching eyes, the very existence of the universe, and the expansion of the multi-verse, depended upon a simple truth that could never change.

There were more questions than answers.

There would always be more questions than answers. Ever and forever. That was what life did.

"Take me to it," April said. "Uroboros. I want to see it." She had questions, yes.

Falo released her, nodding. "Down the hall, around the bends. In the Aerary."

April stood up. She had no idea what an Aerary was, but there would be an answer to that. An answer filled with more questions.

"And if I break the glass?" said April.

Falo shrugged. "And if you do not? What will you wonder then?"

April laughed. "You could have let me stay, you know. At the Mothergate. I would have understood."

"It wasn't about you understanding. It was about *me* understanding." Falo smiled a broad smile, so radiant that it burned countless years off her ancient face. "Sometimes a girl just needs to think."

April beamed back at her. She turned away. She went

slowly down the hallway, past the chattering crowd of birds. She did not know what she would find, and that was okay.

She laid a soft finger against the Ravenvine through her hair. And as she walked, she listened.

CHAPTER NINETEEN

Memories

It wasn't easy, waiting to die.

Horace had no idea whether having his mother beside him while he waited made the waiting easier, or even harder. He tried not to think too much about the fact that she was waiting for him to die too. Every once in a while she lifted her head, looking off into the distance with a faint frown of worry. She was listening to the Mothergate, for signs of its inevitable end. He wasn't sure she knew she was doing it.

He didn't mind. It helped that his mother wasn't the weepy sort. And of course it helped that she wasn't cold either. That would not have been good.

But most of all, right this second, it helped that she was absolutely crushing him on the chess board.

Crushing him for the third game in a row, actually.

They were in a kind of sitting room Chloe had discovered

the day before, a sacred little library space, filled with an afternoonish light. There were bookshelves and desks and chairs and sturdy stone benches filled with huge, sumptuous pillows.

And a chess board, as big as a kitchen table, with squares of shadowy black and summery blue. The pieces were absurdly large, as tall as soda bottles, carved from heavy stone. As could be expected, some of them weren't quite . . . usual. The knights were birds instead of horses, great raptorlike things. The king and queen were marvelous Altari figures, male and female, lean and elegant and strong. The rooks were cages, filled with lightless black stone—a disturbing apparent reference to the Nevren. But that wasn't the worst of it.

The pawns were humans.

And not particularly elegant humans, either. Or lean. Or strong.

"It's sort of rude, don't you think?" he'd asked Chloe when they first found it.

"It's brilliant," she'd said. "Oh my god, this is the best."

"But who even does a thing like that?" said Horace.

"Someone with a lot of confidence."

"A *jerk* with a lot of confidence."

"You should relax, Horace. It's got to be super old. I'm sure things have gotten a lot more progressive around here." She pointed to one of the pawns. "Hey, check it out. This one looks like your dad."

And now, trying to play with the pieces, distracted not so

much by playing but by losing so badly, Horace was left longing for his little wooden chessboard at home. He had been experiencing a lot of longing lately, which was only logical. The chessboard. Home. Loki the cat.

His dad.

It was hard to concentrate, for sure. But his mother seemed to be having no such problems. She hefted a feathered knight over the top of one of Horace's pawns, forking his bishop and rook. He hadn't even seen it coming.

"It's these pieces," Horace complained, for like the tenth time. "They're too big for my brain."

His mother grunted, unimpressed. "Says the kid who figured out how to send the astrolabe."

"That's got nothing to do with this," Horace said, even though it did. Being good at chess was a lot like being good at the Fel'Daera—the position of pieces, lines of influence, desired future states. So why was he playing so badly? "You're beating me without even trying," he said.

"What?" she protested. "I'm trying. I'm *very* trying." She turned and looked back at Chloe, who was sunk so far down in a refrigerator-sized pillow that only her feet were visible, sticking into the air. Her face was buried in a tall Altari book. "Chloe, tell Horace how hard I'm trying."

"She's trying so damn hard, Horace," said Chloe flatly, without looking. "You don't even know."

"See?" his mom said.

"So you're trying. Okay. But how are you . . . how can you even concentrate?"

He heard the dismay in his own voice, warped and unexpected. Apparently he wasn't as distracted as he thought.

His mother heard it too, because she sat back and watched him through the pieces, her face softening. The table was so high, and the pieces so tall, that they couldn't quite see over the tops of them, even with thick pillows to sit on. His mom snaked her arms out into the pieces and spread them, sweeping them from their positions, parting them like a sea. Horace did the same on his side, and they gazed at each other across the board.

"I don't know, Horace," she said. "I don't exactly have a lot of experience with all this. I think my brain has just slipped into . . . emergency mode, or something. Clinging-to-the-raft mode. And since there actually *is* no raft, all that energy is just . . ." She knifed her hand at the chessboard. Her eyes were suddenly puffy and red.

Horace tried to think of something to say. But only one thing came out, a simple thing. The simplest thing. "I don't want to die," he said.

His mother shook her head—a tight, violent waggle. Her mouth was steely.

"Then don't."

He took a deep slow breath, blew it out fast. "Do you know why the Mothergate hasn't closed yet? It's been almost

361

two days since the astrolabe."

"I don't know why. But I know that it will."

"And what if the Riven get here first?" said Horace. "Isabel tore down the Nevren at Ulu'ru. She'll do the same here. We can't stop her from coming right inside, marching right to the Mothergate."

"It would take a lot for her to do that."

"Well, she has a lot."

"What would you like me to say here, Horace? Look, I don't want you to fight the hand that's been dealt to you. That would be selfish, and pointless. I haven't raised you to be either of those things."

"Okay, so right back at you," Horace said. "What would you like me to *do* here?"

"The same as ever. Embrace yourself. Use your head. Be logical. Remember what you've learned."

"I've learned I'm going to die."

"And there's nothing you can do about it?"

Horace threw his hands up. "Well, sure, in fantasyland. I guess I could fade like Neptune . . . if I had even an ounce of will to do it, and years to let it happen. But that—"

He stopped himself midsentence, his mind reeling into a cascade of thoughts so intense and jumbled that there was no room for anyone else.

Faded. Years.

He lurched up from his seat. Chloe was already standing, staring, catching his mood.

362

"I need to see Falo," he said. He pointed at his mother. "Get Brian. Bring him to Falo's quarters. I need his brain."

And then he left. Chloe swept up beside him, not bothering to ask him what was going on. She knew he needed to think. They ran through Ka'hoka, and eventually into the great chamber that led to Falo's quarters, and the Mothergate. The Medium was a hurricane now, and the Fel'Daera was a furnace of power at Horace's side.

Falo was waiting for them in her sitting room, folded into an enormous chair. "Keepers," she said when she saw them. "You look . . . urgent."

"I've got a question for you," Horace said. "I don't know if you'll have an answer or not, and that's okay."

"Thank you, Keeper. I will not invent one, then."

"Is there a universe in which the Keepers do not die when the Mothergates close?"

Falo's head bobbed faintly, her lips seeming to gather the hint of a smile. "I cannot tell you there is not."

"So it's possible."

"Yes."

"Then why can't it be possible here?"

Falo smiled. "I will not tell you it cannot."

Horace's heart pounded. "Do you know how it can be done?"

"No."

But that was okay. If she'd known, she would have told them. And maybe it wasn't up to her to know. Maybe it was up to them all. "Another question," Horace said, his thoughts tumbling madly. "Where did Hiraethel come from?"

Falo waved a hand. "Elsewhere. Elsewhen."

Horace frowned. "That sounds like something Mr. Meister would say."

"If I sound vague, it's only because I know so little. The Starlit Loom came from another place, another time. That is all I know."

"But who made it?" asked Chloe.

"I do not know."

"I thought *you* made it," Horace said. "Not you personally, but the Altari. Some ancient Maker."

"The Altari did not make Hiraethel," Falo said, shaking her head. "In fact, it is far more accurate to say that Hiraethel made the Altari."

"What's that supposed to mean?" Chloe demanded.

Falo rounded on her, her face a question. When she spoke, she laid each word out slowly, like a brick in a wall. "What do you think we are?" she asked. "Where do you imagine we Altari came from?"

Chloe shrugged and shook her head impatiently, as if the question didn't matter. But Horace could see in her eyes—and hear in her silence—that she hadn't considered it before, hadn't ever stopped to wonder what the Altari actually *were*.

And neither, he realized with a start, had he. He was embarrassed to discover it. It was deeply unscientific to accept the existence of a creature like Falo without once wondering what she was, or how she had come to be. His mind still raced, going almost nowhere. He could only think of one explanation, a tough one to swallow. He was not logically predisposed to believe that aliens had come to earth, but for the moment, it was the only explanation he could think of.

"Have you ever contemplated your hands?" Falo asked suddenly, surprising him. "Look at them. Study them." She nodded, gesturing. "Go on, look at them, and consider everything they can do."

Horace looked down at his hand, flexing his fingers. Chloe did the same.

"The human hand can thread needles and tie knots," Falo said, singing the words as if they were a song. "It can pluck and crush berries. It can ball into a cruel fist or gently caress a cheek. It can plant a seed, climb a tree, tear down dead limbs. It can wield the pen or the sword, the paintbrush or the sledgehammer. Fingers can learn to read and to speak. A grasping hand can save a life, or take one."

Chloe snapped her fingers crisply, making Horace jump. She stared down at what she'd done like she'd just witnessed something utterly new. Horace himself couldn't snap, but he wiggled his fingers, one after the other, watching all his many joints flex in unspoken unison, tendons sliding beneath his skin.

"The human hand is a miracle of evolution," said Falo, "a fine machine made finer by the marvelous brain to which it is so intimately wired."

"Okay, so . . . that's cool and all," Chloe said. "Hands are rad. But what are you saying?"

"The point is," said Falo, "the human hand has evolved to be versatile. Think of everything humans could not have done if evolution had given them the hands of a squirrel, or a frog, or a dolphin."

"April was telling me about squirrel hands one time," Horace said. "They seem to have really great hands, but they don't. Relatively speaking. She said squirrels can't even touch their thumb to their other fingers."

"I do not doubt it," said Falo. "Now think on that, and on your own hands, and tell me this. What do you see in the hand of an Altari?"

She stretched out her arm, flexing her magnificent hand. Her long nimble fingers curled and uncurled with a queasy grace—an extra knuckle on every digit, a kind of second thumb where a pinky should have been. Her hands were marvels, full of a strength and agility Horace could only dream of.

"I see all kinds of things that shouldn't be there," Chloe said.

Falo let loose a small, murmuring laugh. "I do not ask you to catalog our differences," she said.

Horace looked down at his own hand again, flexing it. He touched the tip of his thumb to his pinky. "Squirrel hands," he muttered.

"What did you say?" Chloe asked.

"Our hands," he said. "They're like squirrel hands

compared to Falo's. They're not as . . . evolved." And even as he said the words, his eyes drifted from Falo's hand up along her arm, taking her in. But not the differences. Not at all. Differences were easy, the consequences of one tribe eager to distinguish itself from another.

But was Falo of another tribe? Five fingers, after all—strange though they might be. Would an alien have five fingers? Wrist, elbow, shoulder? Collarbone, throat, chin. A mouth and a nose. Two nostrils, two eyes, two ears. Everything different, yes, in ways both big and small. But the even the big differences were so small compared to everything underneath.

Everything that was the *same*.

He stared at Falo, understanding. Not an alien at all. "You're human," he breathed.

Falo broke into a radiant smile. Lips, and teeth, and tongue. "Certainly we once were," she said. "And perhaps we still are."

"You changed yourselves," Horace said. "With the power of the Tanu."

"Yes."

Chloe held up her hands. "Wait, wait . . . so you used to be a *human*?"

Falo laughed again. "Not me personally. I am not quite so old as you imagine. The changes the Altari made to themselves happened long before I was born. And they came in the usual fashion of such endeavors—not within living individuals, but within the traits passed on from parent to child."

"Like breeding dogs," Horace said. "Or plants." Then he made a nervous face of apology. "I'm sorry. That probably sounds terrible."

Falo shrugged. "You are not wrong. Among the early Altari—those who bonded with the first Tan'ji—there were certain traits that were desired. One of the early Makers devised an instrument, now long lost, that allowed them to alter the physical appearance of their offspring. Understand that there were very few of us then. Small changes that they managed to make spread quickly through our population." Falo looked down into her open palm. "It began with the hands. We were Makers, after all. Our hands were everything."

Horace wasn't sure he liked what he was hearing. "But what about the rest? Your size, and your . . ." He didn't want to be rude. He gestured at Falo's whole body, indicating everything about her.

"I make no apologies," Falo said. "I wasn't there, and can't say what I would have thought or done if I had been. But this is the story I was told: our powers made us gods. Ordinary humans feared us, worshipped us, treasured the gifts we gave them."

"The Tan'kindi," said Chloe.

"Yes. Tanu that required no Keeper. Such devices were weak compared to the Tan'ji that the Altari kept to themselves, but this only added to the sense that we were gods indeed. And there were some among us who reasoned that if we were to play the part of gods, we should look the part as well."

Slowly, fluidly, Sil'falo Teneves stood, looming over them. She spread her splendid arms wide. "Our great height," she sang, her majestic voice filling the room like a chorus of vengeful angels. "Our beauty, if you'll allow me to say it. Our eyes. Our voices. All of these things made us unhuman. More than human. And with the powers we wielded, we *were* gods. Ordinary humans gave us names, some of which live on in stories even today. Prometheus. Hephaestus. Odin. Clíodhna. Freyja."

Horace reeled. Legends. Gods. And of course they would be. But his mind raced on. "What about the Riven?" he asked.

"Yeah," Chloe said. "They used to be Altari, so that means they used to be human, too. But why do they look so . . ."

"Different?" Falo asked.

"I was going to say butt-ugly."

"The Tanu that allowed the Altari to transform as they did was lost long ago. Lost or destroyed. But in the years after the Kesh'kiri separated from the Altari, they attempted to re-create it. That re-creation—call it a failure, or call it a manifestation of the shadow that lay in their hearts—turned them into what they are today."

"Okay, okay," Horace said. "But all this started with the Starlit Loom."

"Yes."

"And it just . . . what? Fell from the sky?"

"No one knows. Or at least, *I* do not know."

"The multiverse," Horace said. "It's like a branching tree. The paths split and split again. But if you go *backward* along those paths, you eventually come to a single place. A single universe. The one universe where Hiraethel first appeared. Am I right?"

Falo's eyes were shining now, as if calling him forward down this line of thought. "Yes," she said.

"And that means—it must mean—that the Loom started this all. A single Starlit Loom, in a single universe."

"It stands to reason," Falo said.

Suddenly a figure appeared in the hallway, emerging from deeper in Falo's quarters. April, looking lost and dreamy, a little bit faded herself. In her hand she held a large, clear bowl filled with water. Something was moving inside it, darting in a circle.

A fish.

"It's more than reason," April said. "It's true."

Horace stood up. "April," he said. "What is that? What are you doing?"

And then he understood. This was the fish from the Warren. April had released it from its prison. It was speaking to her still, and she'd been listening.

"You want to know who made Hiraethel," April said. "I still can't tell you that. Even Uroboros doesn't know. But I can tell you how it got *here*, how it got to that first universe from which all the tangled universes then sprang. The Mother universe. The seed."

"And how did it get there?" Chloe asked softly.

"It was sent there." She looked up and around, swept her arm across the room, indicating everything. Indicating the entire world. "Sent from a place like this."

CHAPTER TWENTY

A Traveler's Tale

CHLOE WAS CREEPED OUT.

The Aerary was crowded. All the Wardens from the Warren were here except Neptune. Joshua sat between Mr. Meister and Mrs. Hapsteade, looking surprised to have been invited. Brian had brought Tunraden with him. It sat at his feet looking bigger and more powerful than ever. Shockingly, he was wearing a button-down white shirt with absolutely nothing on it. It seemed ominous.

Teokas and Dailen were here too, looking magnificent as always.

They were all here to listen to April's tale. Her fish tale. And maybe she was doing a good job of it, but it was hard to tell because the tale was a world flipper. An insane thing, really. And it frightened Chloe half to death. It didn't help that April seemed frightened too. She'd taken off the Ravenvine, something she almost never did. It lay in her lap, a curling golden maze with a black flower at the center.

Overhead, the upside-down blue flames danced faintly. Everything was upside down here, it seemed. The uprooted tree in the middle of the room grew down into the floor and spread, crawling up the walls, dividing and dividing again. Just like the multiverse. And the stump from which everything grew, she knew, was the source of every path. It was like what April had called the Mother universe, the universe in which the Starlit Loom had first appeared. Everything else branched out from there—or at least, all the tangled universes had. All branching out from that first moment when the Starlit Loom arrived.

Chloe could keep it in her head, mostly. But it was hard, because on that stump sat April's glass bowl, and inside that bowl the long, finless fish circled. Black and probably slimy. Around and around, its tail in its mouth. If it had anything smart to say, it was hard to imagine what it was. This was why April had taken off the Ravenvine, Chloe knew. She didn't want to listen to it anymore.

Uroboros. Chloe might not be great with the physics stuff, but she had heard that name before. The serpent that ate its own tail. The eternity of time. Cycles of life and death. Creation and destruction.

No wonder April didn't want to listen to it.

"Uroboros is blind and deaf," April explained. "It can't sense anything. Its mind is almost entirely memory. And that memory is the story of Hiraethel, and the fish, being sent here."

"Sent from a place like this, you said," Horace prompted.

"Another world." He was getting it, as usual, in a way that Chloe either couldn't or wouldn't understand. And there was something else brewing in his brain, she knew, something he'd latched on to back in the little library. Something about fading. But he obviously hadn't worked it all through yet, because he hadn't explained a bit of it. She could be patient. You had to be patient with Horace. Big things moved slow, and sometimes Horace's thought were huge.

"Another world, yes," said April.

Brian was keyed up too, leaning forward. "What other world? Where?"

"First, let us consider the multiverse," said Falo. "You should think of the universes where the Tanu exist—the tangled universes—as being a single branch on a much larger tree. The branch itself has many splittings, many paths, each path a separate evolving universe. But those can all be traced back to a single point, at the base of the branch."

"The Mother universe," Horace said.

"Yes," Falo replied. "The single universe in which the Starlit Loom first appeared. Technically, it is *our* universe— but all the other universes that sprang from it over time can make the same claim."

"Just like the way many different humans can claim the same ancient ancestor," April offered.

374

"Precisely," said Falo.

"And you're saying Hiraethel—carrying Uroboros inside it—came into the Mother universe from a different universe," said Teokas. "A different branch, somewhere else on the tree. That was the seed for everything."

"Yes," Falo said.

"But how do you know?" Teokas asked.

Falo nodded at April, encouraging her.

"When I broke open Uroboros's cage," April said, "I could hear it. I won't try to tell you what that was like. It was . . ." She shuddered. "I won't tell you what it was like. I'm not sure I can. It was pure memory. Story. I didn't understand the images, or the words. It was foreign. Not just foreign—alien. But I understood the bones of it, the arc of it." She gestured at Uroboros, spinning her finger in a circle. "It's a traveler. It was brought here."

"But how?" said Horace, just as Brian said, "Why?"

"I don't know how," April said. "I told you, the memories were thick and confusing and . . . I couldn't even begin to translate them for you." She shuddered again. "But the why? I think I understand now. I needed help to make sense of it. And luckily I had that help." She reached into her pocket and pulled out the small sphere with the perpetually growing tree. She held it out for all to see.

"A tiny tree," said Brian, squinting.

Suddenly, Chloe got it. Maybe it was knowing that name, Uroboros. Maybe it was because she was busier listening than she was talking. But she understood. And she knew what they were going to have to do.

"Not *a* tree," said April. "A series of trees, each one different." As she spoke, the tree inside withered and collapsed. A new one sprang up in its place almost at once.

"So it's a cycle," Brian said.

"Yes. A cycle not so different from the one we're in now."

Mr. Meister cleared his throat. "Forgive me, Keeper," he said. "But are you suggesting that everything that has happened here in our world—the Mothergates, and the Tanu, and the tangling of universes—has happened before?"

Hearing Mr. Meister ask the question was a revelation. Kind of a thrill, actually. Watching the old man trying to navigate a new territory of thinking he'd apparently never considered before made Chloe feel wise.

And old. And unmoored.

"The same basic things have happened before, yes," April said. "In another place, another time, and called by different names. But the story was basically the same. Hiraethel arrived in a single universe. That universe began to split into many universes as time passed, and in many of them, instruments were created. Tan'ji. And the power of those instruments began to tangle all of the universes on that branch, just like they are now. The crisis was the same as ours is now."

"And it was solved by sending the Starlit Loom into another universe?" asked Brian.

"Into *our* universe," said Chloe, unable to stay silent

anymore. "And now we have to send it on into another."

"Yes," said April, smiling at her gratefully. "This is the end of a cycle, and the cycle has to repeat."

"You're blowing my mind right now," said Brian.

April went on. "There's a reason the Mothergate here didn't close when Horace sent the astrolabe. It was because of that effort itself. Because we're trying. But there's only one way we can make our own fate, only one way we can ensure our safety, and the safety of the tangled universes." She took a breath. "Hiraethel must go. Now."

Every eye turned to Falo. She inhaled deeply, her eyes locked on Uroboros as it swam round and round.

"Yes," she said quietly at last, her voice like low woodwinds. "When the Mothergate failed to close, I wondered. And now I realize—my wondering has become a part of the story the multiverse tells itself." She bent her head toward April's. "Perhaps that is why its urgency has waned, for the moment."

April nodded like that made any kind of sense at all.

"I am sorry, Keepers," said Falo. "I feel that I should have reached this understanding on my own. Perhaps I did not *want* to reach it."

"You owe us no apologies, Falo," Mr. Meister said. "We all walked a shared path, a difficult path. You walked it better than any of us—how were you to know that part of that path belonged to you alone?"

"But the path is still shared, right?" said Brian. "I mean,

even if we get rid of the Starlit Loom, the Mothergates will still close. We still die. Am I right?" No one answered him. "Someone tell me I'm not right."

And then Horace stirred. "I think, maybe," he said slowly, "there's a way we could make you be wrong. A way we don't have to die."

Beside him, leaning back against the wall and utterly silent so far, his mother pressed her fists to her mouth. The blue fire from above glimmered in her wet eyes like little skies.

"Go on, Horace," Falo said.

"Well, I was thinking about Neptune. About the faded. And I was trying to imagine if there was a way *we* could all fade too, without inciting the multiverse to erase all the tangled universes. A way to keep the Medium flowing, maybe slower and slower over time."

It sounded crazy. But no one said it was crazy, and now Chloe could see him really settling into the idea, gaining confidence.

"Look," he said, "the only way to remove Hiraethel from our world is to take her through the Mothergate, right? I'm assuming she can't be destroyed."

Falo wrinkled her nose faintly in disgust, but then said, "That is correct."

"So once we remove her, maybe the multiverse won't really care so much about the Mothergate itself."

"But it will close anyway," April said. "In fact, the only reason the Mothergates exist is because Hiraethel is here. Its presence has opened those cracks in the consciousness of the universe. Once Hiraethel is no longer here, those cracks will close. The Mothergates will collapse, unless . . ." She looked pointedly at Falo for some reason, and Falo inhaled deeply through her nose.

"Unless what?" Chloe said.

"Unless Falo weaves it open," said April. "She was going to weave it open when you sent the astrolabe, Horace, but then didn't need to."

Mr. Meister's bushy eyebrows went up at that one. And Chloe, for once, didn't blame him. Forcing the Mothergates to remain open was exactly what they'd been trying to stop Isabel from doing!

Falo bent over, thick with thought. "It seems like madness," she said.

"But a mad thing you can do," said Brian.

"It can be done. A weave that slowly fades, letting the Mothergate ease closed."

"How slowly?" Horace said.

"Years," said Falo. "Twenty years, perhaps? There are powerful Tan'ji among us, with bonds that will not wither in days, or even months."

"No," said Mr. Meister. "It is madness. The tangles between the universes will still exist. The multiverse will still erase that branch of itself—a branch of which we will still be a part. We will be destroyed."

"I don't believe that," April told him. "I've been listening to the multiverse for days. Sitting in the Medium, listening. You talk like the multiverse is a thing out to get us. But it isn't. It's *us*. It's our consciousness made real. Consciousness is more then what we do—it's what we *intend*. And we intend to set things right. If not for every universe, at least for ours. The multiverse will know us, because it *is* us. We will not be destroyed, not once the Starlit Loom is gone."

Chloe's head was spinning. Hope struggled in her chest, lurching, but she wouldn't let it grow. No one spoke for a long time. Mr. Meister fumed worriedly for a while, but then his face began to soften thoughtfully, slowly. He was considering it.

"April is right," Falo said at last. "Our intentions matter. We make the universe in which we live, and the multiverse that houses it. We will do this thing."

Brian clapped his hands together, eyeing Horace goofily. He looked terrified.

"But when we do it," said Gabriel softly, "Falo will die."

The room fell silent once more. Falo rose swiftly into it, towering above them. "Let us speak of life, not death," she said. The blue flames above her crackled and slid wildly as she lifted the Starlit Loom from her chest. She caught fire, blazing, becoming the elemental thing she'd been the other day, here in this very room. A Dorvala, a Maker, rippling with power. Chloe actually leaned away. Horace's mother gasped.

"We will do this thing," Falo said again. "There is a way. But when we send Hiraethel, we must send the message with her, just as it was sent to us. We're passing our troubles on to a new universe—a new blooming cluster of universes—and we need to send the solution, too. We need to send Uroboros, so that its memories will live on. Memories of how to fix what will inevitably go wrong, just like it went wrong for us."

She bent over the glass bowl, Hiraethel in hand. She dipped it slowly into the water and then—though Chloe knew it had nothing to do with the water itself—the Loom expanded. The water seemed to turn black as the Loom filled it, swallowing the creepy black fish, which appeared utterly unaware of what was happening to it.

"Don't hurt it," April said, and for a second it seemed like such a silly thing to say, considering that Falo had basically just volunteered to sacrifice herself in the hopes of saving them all.

But Falo seemed not to notice. "I would never," she said gravely. She reached into the bowl, and as she touched the Loom, it began to shrink again in her hand. In no time at all, it was back to its usual shape and size. She held it up for all to see.

A circling shadow of black rippled beneath the surface. April made a face, squeezing the Ravenvine in her lap. Chloe reckoned she was glad she hadn't put it back on.

"How did you know how to do that?" Brian said.

Falo shrugged. "I've just always known it." She flexed her hand, as if testing it. The image of a golden clockwork sphere materialized in her palm, woven from the Medium, and then vanished into vapor. "All is well," she said. "And now we must—"

Suddenly a great bell tolled, shaking the ground, as if Ka'hoka itself was a giant gong. For a moment, Chloe thought Falo had done it.

But no. She had heard the sound before. An alarm.

Teokas and Dailen were on their feet at once. "*Kesh'kiri nala*," Dailen spat. "The Riven are here."

"Those who can fight, fight," said Falo. "You must hold Isabel off until I can do what must be done."

Teokas reached out and clasped Falo's hand briefly. "*Tel tu'vra fal raethen, Falo.*"

"*Tel tu'vra fal raethen,*" Falo replied. "Give me the time I need."

"You'll have it," said Dailen, and he and Teokas sprinted from the room.

The bell sounded again. Mrs. Hapsteade hesitated, eyeing Mr. Meister worriedly.

"Go," he told her. "You have the phalanx."

She nodded at him grimly, pulling the phalanx out of her pocket—a long, wandlike instrument made from the finger-bone of a Mordin. "Joshua, will you join me?" she asked. "A well-timed portal can be a fine weapon, you know. Invaders can't fight us if they suddenly find themselves halfway around the world."

Joshua was clearly petrified. He hugged the Laithe like a life preserver. "I don't know what to do," he said.

382

April took his hand. "I'll show you," she said. "We'll do it together. Gabriel will keep us safe. Right, Gabriel?"

"Yes," Gabriel said, thumping the tip of his staff against the floor. "We will be the eye of the storm. Stay with me in the battle, and I'll keep you safe." He stalked nimbly from the room, with Joshua, April, and Mrs. Hapsteade in tow.

The alarm bell tolled again. Falo scooped Mr. Meister out of his seat with ease. "Horace and Jessica, come with me, please," she said. "Brian, bring Tunraden. I may need assistance."

She loped out of the room without a word, taking Mr. Meister with her. Horace's mother followed her more slowly, saying nothing but looking Chloe firmly and warmly in the eye as she passed. Brian sighed, then bent and stuck his hands into the stone surface of Tunraden. He lifted the Loomdaughter easily from the floor and shuffled awkwardly after Falo and the others. "Work, work, work," he muttered.

Horace and Chloe were alone now. Chloe realized the Alvalaithen was ablaze, its song like a storm inside her. She was ready, angry—startled by how angry she was.

Horace was watching her, his face so full of worry. She had no idea what to say to him, or what she wanted to hear.

"Gotta go," she told him at last. "My mom's here."

"It's a good thing you're funny," he said.

"It's a good thing you think so," she replied, and she dove into the floor.

The alarm bell tolled a fourth time, vibrating through

the rock as she flew. She'd been in Ka'hoka long enough to have her bearings, and she sped through the ground. Out into the huge white hall beyond, breaching. On she went, until in no time at all she arrived in the great entrance chamber to Ka'hoka, where the mighty Nevren of Goth en'Sethra lay in the yawning shaft directly overhead.

An army had already gathered, nearly a hundred Altari, by the looks of it. Many bore weapons, others strange Tan'ji both large and small, with functions Chloe could not divine. Near the wide glass circle in the middle of the room, through which new arrivals would emerge after falling through the Nevren above, she spied the hulking green mass of the mal'gama. She went under again, speeding over to it in a matter of moments. She emerged to find Dailen waiting, watching the floor before him, Teokas by his side.

He was so grim and focused that he didn't even startle at the sight of her.

"Chloe," he said. "The Riven are above. They're testing the Well."

Goth en'Sethra, the Well of Giving, was the only way in or out of Ka'hoka. Passing through the Well wasn't a pleasant experience. Inside it, the Keepers who'd fused themselves to create the Nevren within were strung up along the shaft, left visible. To enter Ka'hoka, one had to fall from high above, plunging past those inert forms and through the Nevren. Past that, falling visitors were teleported into a second shaft far below, rising now instead of falling, until they emerged through the one-way barrier in the floor Dailen stared at now.

A lean Altari that Chloe had never seen before laughed. "Let them test the Well. They'll come up corpses. No Kesh'kiri can make it through Goth en'Sethra alive."

Chloe looked up at Dailen sharply. "Have they not been told what Isabel can do?" she hissed. "That she tore down the Nevren at Ulu'ru?"

"They've been told," Dailen said. "They do not believe."

"And do you?"

"The Nevren is a comfort, not a cure," he said. "Those who rely on sacrifices made by others are rarely prepared to make their own."

A great crash shook the room, thunder rolling out of the gaping mouth of the Well a hundred feet above them. A moment later, a shower of golden sparks rained down from the hole. Chloe thought she heard faint screams. A murmur went up among the gathered Altari.

And then faintly, creepily, the distant strains of a flute. The murmur grew louder as the searching notes fell on every ear in the place. The music played for a few suspended moments and then abruptly faded.

"They're coming," Chloe said. "And now they know how many we are."

"Then we'll be more," said Dailen. And then he doubled, and doubled again. The Dailens spread themselves wide, waiting.

"If you see my mother, stay away," Chloe told Teokas.

"She's dangerous. I'm going to try and get to her first."

Teokas nodded, lovely and strong. She reached into her robe and pulled out a thin blade, a foot long and thinner than a human pinky. To Chloe's great surprise, she handed it over. "I brought this in case we met. It will not be enough this day to simply survive. We must win."

Chloe took the blade, testing the point. It was as dull as a crayon. "It's not sharp."

"The blade of a stonewalker does not need to be sharp, does it?" Teokas said.

Chloe had no words for that. Instead the only words she could think of spilled from her mouth.

"*Tel tu'vra fal raethen.*"

Teokas grinned and gave her a deep elegant bow that took Chloe's breath away. "And yours, my friend," she said.

Chloe tucked the thin blade into a belt loop and went to ground. She wanted to get high, to see the battle from above. She had to find Isabel as fast as she could, before the wretched woman could start cleaving. She wished she could say she was heartened by the brave show of force on display here, but instead she felt only dread. She knew what Isabel could do.

She found a thick column and went up it the inside. She emerged high above the scene onto a cornice. And just as she did, three great black serpents' heads rose out of the glass circle below, writhing high into the air. Golems.

And on their heels, an army.

Riven popped out of Goth en'Sethra like crickets out of grass. Mordin by the dozen. Ravids teeming in a swarm so thick Chloe knew the Altari would be overrun at once. Two hundred Riven or more.

But the Altari roared into battle, undaunted. Go'nesh was out front, swinging his mighty blade, carving sheets of blue that hung in the air. A dozen Dailens danced through the chaos, vanishing and doubling. The mal'gama swooned and curled around them like a moving hill, a shield made of earth, fending off the golems. And there were other mighty warriors here too. She saw a flashing broadsword that struck and broke, leaving a shard of steel buried in a Mordin. The sword forged itself anew and struck once more. A burly Altari, nearly as thick as Go'nesh but not nearly so tall, pounded at the ground with a hammer the size of a barrel, opening brutal cracks in the floor beneath his enemies.

To Chloe's immense surprise, she caught the flicker of a portal blasting open every so often. Joshua was helping, just as Mrs. Hapsteade had said, protected by a trio of Dailens. As she watched, a portal snapped open onto a wide expanse of snow. Two Dailens hurled a Mordin through it, and the portal winked out of existence. A second later, Joshua himself vanished in a flicker—swallowed by the humour. Chloe practically burst imagining it, the portal surging open inside that gray, Gabriel grappling blind and hapless Riven through it, into distant lands from which they wouldn't return. And then a black bird sailed right past her, squawking. Chloe almost laughed—Arthur! April was no doubt guiding Gabriel from inside the humour.

The crack of phalanxes sounded again and again, pinning Riven and Ravids. Chloe spotted Mrs. Hapsteade firing her strange weapon. An Auditor was among the invaders, her pale hair gleaming, and for a moment Chloe's heart seemed to stop. But the Auditor scarcely moved, caught in the white glow of the Moondoor. Teokas glided before her, wrist extended, two Dailens fighting at her side.

But there was no sign of Isabel. Or Dr. Jericho. And gradually Chloe realized that no Altari were being severed, none being cleaved. Where was Isabel? What was her plan?

And then she saw. A golem, snaking swiftly outside the main part of the fray, edging past the battle like a moving mound of coal. She understood at once. The battle was only a distraction—Isabel was trying to reach the Mothergate alone.

Chloe leapt. She fell, plunging into the ground far below like water. Bottoming out and rising to the surface again at speed, she made for the golem.

Two quick dolphin leaps, right through the heart of the battle, and within seconds she came up just where she meant to, inside the body of the golem. It arced over her like a dome, a hollow space beneath it.

And in that space—Isabel, and Dr. Jericho at her side.

They froze when they saw her, Dr. Jericho's face spreading in a grin of rage.

Chloe threw her arms wide. "Mom!" she said, mustering

all the cruel cheer she could.

Isabel recoiled, scowling. "Don't follow us, Chloe," she said. "I'm going to fix it. I'm going to set it right."

"That's a nice gesture," Chloe said, "but we're already fixing it." A confused rage roiled through her, seeing her mother here now with the hated Dr. Jericho. Half of Chloe wanted to reason with Isabel, to explain that everything was going to be okay. The other half fumed furiously at the idea that she owed the woman any explanation whatsoever.

"Fixing it." Dr. Jericho laughed, sneering. "What has Sil'falo Teneves promised you now, I wonder?"

"More than either of you ever did," Chloe said. She took a deep breath, searching for calm, struggling to find reason. "I'm telling you, we don't need you. Thanks for coming, but we've got it under control. Falo is—"

And then Isabel severed her.

The Alvalaithen's song snuffed out. Chloe collapsed. The thin blade at her belt jabbed her in the leg and her face smacked the floor, but she scarcely felt it. Dimly she understood that this severing was bad. Not cleaving, no, she'd already be dead if she'd been cleaved. But Isabel's severing came with a brambly tangle of confusion, as if all Chloe's powers had been tied in knots.

She began to drift. She couldn't find her Tan'ji. What was it again? How could she have forgotten so fast? Something white. A predator.

Heavy footsteps, and a foul smell. A bad smell meant bad

things. Something ugly and savage bent to look her in the eyes. Why couldn't she see her eyes?

No love lost, then, the voice said. A rotten voice, a rotten thing. *I hope you'll find forgiveness on the other side.*

A hand around her. And now she was being carried. Or maybe she was flying. The Earthwing, yes, but the earth was darker than this, and that was where the flying was.

Come and see, said the voice. *Let us show you.*

You'll see, she said, or tried to say. *They're fixing it and we'll all see. I see the moon and the moon sees me.*

Cruel laughter. And then another voice, a woman, a voice she'd always known. *The Alvalaithen,* it said. *The Fel'Daera.* She hated that voice and the voice hated her. The voice had hurt her and hurt was bad. Bad little girl. Little boy. Little boy blue, a true blue moon.

Whatever it is they're planning, the cruel voice said, *sooner or later it will fail.*

Still flying, still voices. Where were they taking her again? *Sooner or later a moon elevator.* But that wasn't true.

The Fel'Daera. The Alvalaithen. One into the other. One into every other. She grabbed at the thought because the thought meant something. Something about a plan. One into every other was how it worked, it turned out. And that meant the plan wouldn't work.

She tried to cling to the thought, but thoughts were so slippery here. Something was happening. Something was wrong. Not these voices, no, some other happening. A plan for someone, yes. An important one.

One into every other everything. What did it mean? She had questions, lots of them, and there had to be answers.

The answers to everything.

CHAPTER TWENTY-ONE

The Story Told

HORACE WALKED WITH BRIAN, SLOWLY CROSSING THE GREAT empty vault toward the distant Mothergate. The gate looked stark and ominous now that the Veil was gone. Falo was already beside the Mothergate, studying it carefully. Horace's mother stood a little ways back, watching Horace and Brian approach, Mr. Meister lying on the floor at her side.

The alarm bells had stopped ringing.

"I guess it's good I wore a subtle shirt today," Brian said. "Nobody likes a skeptic."

"Why is it subtle?" asked Horace.

Brian grinned. "Look in my pocket." Horace pulled Brian's breast pocket open and peeked inside. On the fabric within, he'd written:

BYE!

"You won't be needing that," Horace said. "Not today."

"I could almost believe you," said Brian.

When they reached the Mothergate, Brian set Tunraden down, and Falo began talking at once.

"Let us assume that Brian and I can do what we have suggested," she said. "That we can weave a hold on the Mothergate, a hold that will gradually fade over twenty years. What then?"

"We take Hiraethel inside," Horace said. "Away from here."

"And yet the realms inside the Mothergate are not a place," said Falo. "They are neither here nor there. You cannot simply leave Hiraethel inside."

Horace thought hard. He thought about portals, and the Fel'Daera. How the two were interconnected. "Chloe said the space inside the Mothergate is full of doors," he said. "Doors everywhere. Billions of doors. Maybe I can send Hiraethel through the box, through one of those doors. After all, sending the Loom was the reason you made the Fel'Daera in the first place."

"Wait, what?" said Brian.

Horace ignored him. "It'll go. It'll be gone."

Falo studied him for a long, somber moment. She still burned like a ghost, rippling with energy. It wasn't exactly soothing. "And you think that will work."

"I think the Riven are coming. Isabel is coming. I think if the Starlit Loom is still here, there's nothing to stop her from cleaving you."

Falo drew back. "Very well. You have quite the logical mind, Horace Andrews."

"Thank you."

"Don't thank me," she said. "Thank your mother." She turned to the Mothergate. She lifted her hands. "Brian, I may need your help. Watch me as I begin, please."

"Like I could ever not," Brian said.

Falo began.

A golden nest of tendrils snaked from the Mothergate, thin as reeds. They came gently, coaxed, and then more came by the bushel. The snaking lines thickened and reached out gently, not as if they were being pulled, but as if they wanted to be in this place. They grew longer and longer, grew strong and thick, radiating out of the mouth of the Mothergate in every direction. Falo's hands swooped like birds, her marvelous fingers working like the leaves of a tree in the wind. The tendrils of the Medium fanned out a hundred feet in every direction, thinning into nothing as they went, though Horace knew they went much farther, into places and shapes he could not see.

"Oh my god," his mother said, staring. And she fell to her knees, her Tuner's eyes wide and glowing. Mr. Meister sat on the floor beside her, mouth open in wonder, the threads of the Medium reflected on his glasses like shooting stars. The spokes kept coming, kept growing, angling and lacing over one another.

"Do you see, Keeper?" Falo roared, looking down at Brian. "Do you understand?"

Brian nodded. "I see. I can help." He bent down to Tunraden and plunged his hands into the stone. It erupted into a fountain of light, and he pulled great clumps of it into the air.

Brian's way of weaving was nothing like Falo's, but as he sent laceworks of glowing Medium out into what Falo had done, they meshed seamlessly with hers, complementing them like the cross trusses of a magnificent spiral bridge. They worked in tandem, Falo pulling more and more threads from the Mothergate, Brian wrapping them tight with immaculate, easy precision.

Although Horace could barely follow what they were doing, he slowly began to understand that there was a pattern at play. A symmetry. Though the threads and spokes were far too numerous to count, they were regimented in a way that looked oddly familiar. Or if not familiar, at least translatable. And suddenly Horace realized.

It was a clock. Not a clock that counted hours or days, but years. Twenty years. Time was Falo's specialty, after all, and whether the great decade-spanning clock shape she and Brian wove now was a necessity or an indulgence, he hardly cared. It was beautiful. Orderly. Logical.

They wove for what felt like hours, but it was only minutes. Tens of thousands of strands now emerged from the black mass of the Mothergate, each one a gentle anchor, plus thousands more woven crosswise and spiraling.

"Henry," his mother said. "Do you see it? This is going to work."

"I see it," Mr. Meister said grimly.

And it would work. It had to. But Horace felt helpless watching them. There was nothing he could do to help them. Was there?

The Mothergate began to rumble. A swath of golden strands near the top trembled.

"Do not fear," Falo said. "It fights us now, but the weavings will hold. We must finish. We must send Hiraethel far from here. All will be well." Her tone was light, but Horace could hear the strain in her voice.

"How much longer?" Horace asked.

"A few minutes. We have to hope the others hold Isabel off long enough."

Hope. A hope for a future that was nearly here.

"I hear something," his mother said suddenly. She was looking back across the room toward the entrance.

Now Horace heard it too. A distant grate and rumble, growing nearer.

The golem.

"Faster," said Falo. "Keep weaving. Let us hope there is time."

And when Horace heard those words, suddenly he knew. He knew what he had to do.

They didn't have to hope.

He pulled the box from its pouch. He gathered his thoughts swiftly, clearing his mind. The Mothergate shook, quivering.

Falo looked back at him, apparently sensing what he was about to do. "Now is not the time, Keeper," she said. "Everything hangs in a fine balance, and the Fel'Daera—"

"You have to trust me," said Horace. "Keep weaving." With an ease that astonished him, he set the breach to one minute and pinned it in place. Looking across the vast room to the faraway entrance, he opened the box.

He lifted it to his eyes, ignoring the shuddering Mothergate behind him. This *was* the time. Isabel was coming. This was the moment that mattered, here at the end of everything.

And through the glass—*two figures, drawing closer, one large and one small, the larger figure flickering and bristling like a ghoul; Dr. Jericho, Isabel at his side; the black mass of the golem sliding behind them.*

Horace felt no surprise whatsoever. Instead of fear, a kind of blessed relief flooded him. This was knowing. This was seeing. This was what he could do.

He kept his eyes on the glass, watching the future unfold. *Dr. Jericho, coming closer; a limp figure in his arms.*

Chloe.

He choked back a gasp.

"Don't tell me what you see, Horace Andrews," Falo said, still weaving.

"I'll second that," said Brian, his voice wrinkling with effort.

But Horace had no intention of telling them. What he saw now was not for them, not at all.

Dr. Jericho in their midst now, walking up to the Mothergate; pausing briefly to stare straight into the Fel'Daera from the other side of the glass; now moving to the Mothergate, depositing Chloe heavily onto the floor. Dead? Alive? Alive, it had to be, because Isabel was still here. Isabel wouldn't hurt Chloe. Whatever else she might do, she wouldn't do that. Horace believed it, knew it.

He kept watching. Ever so gently, he slid the breech ahead, fast-forwarding into the future, trying to see everything he could while he still had the chance. Falo and Dr. Jericho were talking. Isabel was standing far back from the Mothergate, the golem looming behind her. Falo's golden clock shone like streaks of golden starlight.

Forward and forward, into the near future. A future so close he could almost touch it. Through the box, everything was sharp, crystalline. Meanwhile, in the present, the sounds of the golem grew nearer, and a few seconds later the beast itself emerged into the room. It unfolded, revealing Isabel and Dr. Jericho within.

Horace ignored them. He tried not to wonder how close Isabel would have to get before she could sever him. Sever him, or worse. In the future, through the glass: *Horace himself, moving to Chloe's side, talking to someone—Isabel; Chloe stirring, looking around.* His heart leapt. Not dead, only severed. But why had Isabel released her? His mind raced. He turned the box to look at look at Isabel in the future, but saw nothing that meant anything clear. And when he turned back to Dr. Jericho . . .

He nearly dropped the box. *The Mordin, crumpled lifeless on the floor, Chloe and Horace standing over him.*

Dead.

This was what death looked like, Horace was sure of it.

But how? And then he realized Chloe held something in her hand. A dagger, thin as a pencil.

Here in the present, Dr. Jericho stalked triumphantly toward them, aware that Horace was watching the future, but with no idea what that future held for him. The Mordin was apparently in no hurry, shoulders high and bristling. Isabel walked beside him, silent and glowing. Chloe was a limp bundle in Dr. Jericho's arms, her short dark hair hanging loose.

"Stop," the Mordin called out. "Stop now or we'll end you."

Falo stepped back, dropping the strands of the Medium. Brian straightened, groaning, Tunraden winking out as he withdrew his hands. Horace took one last look around through the Fel'Daera—he'd never kept the Fel'Daera open before while the events it had revealed were beginning to unfold, and it didn't seem wise to start now. Just before he closed it, he fast-forwarded swiftly a little way further into the future. Two minutes in two seconds. *The golden clock, continuing to grow, all the strands falling into place; flickers of movement, comically fast; Horace and Chloe, standing in front of the Mothergate together.* Horace pinned the breech in place, squinting through the glass at Chloe's face—

"Stop," Dr. Jericho bellowed again.

"She's getting close, Horace," his mother murmured. "She'll cleave you."

Horace slammed the box closed, breathing hard. No one moved as the awful pair approached, the golem rumbling forward behind them. Horace held his breath, steeling himself for what had to happen next, for everything he might say. And what would he say? What would it matter? All he knew from what he'd seen was that these next few minutes belonged to words, not action. And only the right words would do, if he could find them.

Mr. Meister glared at Dr. Jericho with an almost audible hatred. Horace's mother took Horace by the shoulder, pulling him close. As the new arrivals drew nearer, Isabel slowed. Her wild eyes roved over Falo's web, growing wide. She stopped well back, just as Horace had foreseen, staring. The golem coiled behind her like a great black snake.

Dr. Jericho kept coming. He slowed as he passed in front of Horace, his beady black eyes lighting briefly on the Fel'Daera. Horace's mom squeezed his shoulder. Horace knew very well that Dr. Jericho hadn't needed to witness Horace using the box to know that Horace had been watching. Thanks to his Tan'ji, the Mordin would be able to sense the Fel'Daera open in the past even now. But Dr. Jericho said nothing.

Instead, he stepped right up to the Mothergate. He dumped Chloe unceremoniously onto the ground. She groaned, wrapped deep in Isabel's nasty knots. Horace ached for her even as the profound satisfaction of walking the willed path flowed through him. So far, this was the future just as he had seen it.

The Mordin leaned back, examining the exquisite spread of golden strands that spread from the quivering black. "What joke is this?" he purred sinisterly. "What trick?"

"Not a trick," said Falo. "We are fixing what you could not. And you still stand because of it. We all still stand."

"Have you seen the light, then?" he seemed to tease. "You admit that the Mothergates need not die?"

"No," said Isabel dreamily, still transfixed by the unfinished golden web. "What she's doing here isn't meant to last forever."

"Then tear it down," Dr. Jericho said. "Tear it down and begin again. Make it last."

Falo laughed. "You fool. Living in the shadows, fretting and raging over the wrong fear. The Mothergates must die, Ja'raka Sevlo, even if we die along with them. If we do not allow them to collapse—if we force them to remain open forever—the entire universe will cease to be. The multiverse will erase all the tangled universes from its memory, as if we never existed. You Riven cling to your petty fears while ignoring the greater danger by far."

"Nonsense."

Falo turned her attention to Isabel. She gestured to the grand woven clock. "We are buying time, Isabel. Time for all Keepers, time enough to live. There is a way the Keepers can survive the collapse of the final Mothergate. Your daughter could have told you as much, if only you'd listened. When the weaving is done, we will take Hiraethel from this place. Take her out of this world and into another. What went wrong will be set right. Our universe will be saved. Chloe will be saved."

Although he had seen these events unfold, Horace hadn't heard them. He was stunned to hear Falo revealing their plan to Dr. Jericho. Not that it mattered. Not if the future he'd seen held true.

Dr. Jericho was chuckling softly under his breath now. "More nonsense," he said. He shook his head sadly at Falo, as if in bewildered sympathy. "In your monstrous arrogance, Sil'falo Teneves, you imagine this sacrifice of yours will save us all. Save us from a danger that never existed." He turned to Isabel, tipping his chin. "Enough of this foolishness," he said, pointing back at Falo. "Cleave her."

"No," Horace said. He stepped forward, slipping out from under his mother's hand. "No. That's not what happens."

Dr. Jericho scoffed—a cruel, snarling bark. "Horace Andrews, Keeper of the Fel'Daera. You'll tell us the story of what does happen, I suppose. Another story we have no reason to believe."

"It doesn't matter whether you believe me or not," Horace

replied, choosing his words carefully. "All that matters is that you know I've witnessed this future. I know everything that's about to occur."

Isabel stirred, frowning at him. "And why should that matter?" she asked.

"This is the last Mothergate," Horace said. "It wouldn't take much to push it over the edge, to force it to collapse. And when it does, every Keeper will die. Chloe will die."

Dr. Jericho growled warily. Horace knew the Mordin could see the fear and doubt that crept now into Isabel's face.

"Do you know about thrall-blight, Isabel?" Horace asked, pressing. This was the moment. "The Fel'Daera should never have been made, you know. I know that now. No other instrument has done more to tangle the multiverse, to hasten the deaths of the Mothergates. Every time we deny the future the box reveals—every time we willingly disobey it—the Mothergates die a little more." He paused, letting his words sink in, and then he said, "I wonder how much disobedience it would take in the next two minutes to make the Mothergate collapse completely?"

"Lies," Dr. Jericho spat. "Fables and fantasies."

"If you say so," Horace said. But he wasn't lying. He couldn't lie. Everything depended utterly on the truth. He was conscious of all the eyes on him, trembling and waiting, afraid to act. His own mother. Mr. Meister. The Maker of the Fel'Daera herself.

"You won't believe Falo's story, but sooner or later you'll

have to believe mine," Horace said. "The future is coming and it can't be stopped. It'll either be the future I witnessed, or one I did not." His inner clock was ticking smoothly. Everything was happening just as he had foreseen. But it wasn't enough. Isabel had to know the future too, so that she would be bound to it.

He began moving slowly toward Chloe, just as the Fel'Daera had revealed. This was the willed path. He said, "In thirty seconds, Isabel, you're going to release Chloe. You're going to undo your severing, and all your knots. I'm going to take her by the hand and help her to her feet. This is the future I saw. The willed path. Will you walk it with me, or will you disobey the box and ruin us all?"

Dr. Jericho threw a savage gesture at Isabel. "Don't listen to him. Never trust the Keeper of the Fel'Daera to speak the truth."

But Isabel was listening. Horace could see that. "Fifteen seconds," he said. He kept moving, shocked at his own confidence, at the power that spilled from him now, as if he had taken the entire world hostage. Dr. Jericho was afraid, too. The Mothergate trembled, grumbling.

"He lies," Dr. Jericho roared.

"But what if he doesn't?" said Isabel. "What if they're right?"

Horace held his breath. Had he told the proper story after all? Was the truth really all that was needed?

Dr. Jericho reared back in anger. The spines on his

shoulders bristled, quavering. He thrust out a hideous hand, pointing at the web. "This? This is a trick. A desperate attempt to lead us astray, to make us believe all their damage has been undone. Only you can repair the Mothergates, Isabel."

"You're wrong," Isabel said. "This work is beyond me. It was always beyond me. But I see now. I see. This was what needed to be done." Her voice was dreamy and sad. And then she seemed to see Chloe's limp form for the first time, and her voice broke. "My daughter," she said.

Miraculously, Chloe grumbled and stirred. Isabel had released her. Horace's heart leapt. He reached down for her, helping her slowly to her feet. He spotted the strange silver blade, tucked into her belt loop

"You fool!" Dr. Jericho cried. "You've fallen for their lies again, just as you did at the start." He whirled on Horace and Chloe, fuming, towering over them, burning with rage. Beyond Isabel, the golem roared to life. It reared up high over Isabel, poised to strike. Chloe blinked, finding herself more swiftly than Horace could have dared hope. She reached for the silver blade just as Dr. Jericho lunged at them, grasping for Horace. Brian cried out. The wings of the Alvalaithen whirred to life as Dr. Jericho leapt. Chloe raised her blade.

And then the Mordin crumpled.

He fell to the floor with a sickening crunch, his thick jaw cracking against the stone. Behind Isabel, the golem fell apart, clattering to the floor like a sudden shower of heavy hail.

405

Chloe stood there staring, heaving, the blade unused in her hand. No one spoke. No one moved. The only sound was the grating rumble of the Mothergate.

Isabel had cleaved Dr. Jericho.

Not the blade, not at all. Words, turned into action. Slowly, every eye turned toward Isabel. She stood there amid the ruin of the golem, frozen. "So many lies," she said quietly. "All my life, all these lies. I think I don't need to hear any more."

"He's dead," Chloe said. "You killed him."

"Yes," said Isabel at last. "I think . . . I think now it was long overdue."

"Amen to that," Brian said.

Isabel looked around. Her eyes fell on Horace. "You knew this would happen."

"I knew it would happen," he said. "I didn't know how."

"I walked the willed path."

"Yes. You did."

Now Isabel looked to Horace's mother and she tipped her head, tears welling up. "Jess," she said. "Jessica. Do you know what they did to me?"

His mother went to her, kicking through the stones of the golem. "I know," she said, wrapping her up. "I know what they did."

Chloe poked at Dr. Jericho's lifeless form with her toe. She looked around, saw the radiant web of light spread out from the Mothergate behind her, Falo's magnificent clock.

"If anyone tells me I'm dreaming, I'll pinch them," she said.

"You're dreaming," said Brian.

Chloe scowled. "Anyone sensible, I mean."

Gently she knelt down before Dr. Jericho. She laid a hand on him, as the Alvalaithen's wings continued to whir. Steadily the Mordin's body began to sink into the ground. She let him drift slowly under. She guided him down until her arm was in past her elbow, and then stood up. She left him there, buried. Only then did she glance up at Falo.

"I hope you don't mind," she said. "I didn't really want that lying there."

"Nor did I," said Falo.

Isabel pulled away from Horace's mom. "Chloe," she said, starting toward her. "Chloe, I—"

"No," Chloe said, not even looking at her. "Not now. Not yet." The Mothergate groaned crunchily behind her, rumbling.

"It is time to finish what we began," Falo said.

The Starlit Loom blazed to life. Brian bent down before Tunraden, setting it aglow. They resumed their weaving, the final strands falling into place swiftly now.

The chamber was alight, as if by the sun, from the sheer volume of threads that stretched across the open expanse. Falo seemed to be slowing, tiring, and Brian's arms drooped. And then finally, blessedly, just when Horace thought the entire effort might fail, Falo dropped her arms. Tunraden swallowed its shower of light, and Brian all but collapsed across it.

"It is done," Falo said, and she dimmed from the ethereal being she had been back to herself, pale and solid. "It will hold. It will hold while we do what we must do."

Horace didn't doubt her, even though the Mothergate still seemed to strain around the edges, even though the magnificent webbed clock still shivered. Falo turned to Horace, Hiraethel in her hands. "Are you ready?" she asked.

For an answer, Horace turned to his friend. His great friend, the only friend that mattered. He needed her help now, even if he didn't know how.

"Are we ready?" he asked her.

CHAPTER TWENTY-TWO

The Answers to Everything

CHLOE'S EYES WERE LOCKED ON HORACE. SHE CROSSED TO HIM, and he recognized the moment, recognized the look on her face. The same look he'd seen through the box earlier—she knew something. She'd figured something out. "Tell me your plan," she said. "Inside the Mothergate."

"I'm going to send Hiraethel."

"And what's that going to do?"

"I'm not sure, but I think I can send her through one of those doors you were talking about. Into some other universe. Some other future."

Chloe nodded. "And you felt those doors?"

"No, but—"

"When I was severed," she said, interrupting him, "while they were dragging me here, I was thinking about when you talked me into sending the Alvalaithen."

"Yeah."

"I never thanked you for that."

He drew back, surprised. "Why would you thank me for that? Sending the Alvalaithen was completely mental. You almost died."

"But I didn't. And it was the right thing to do. You told me to be brave, and I was, and now I'm . . ."

"You're, like, a better person because of it," Horace said.

"Don't be a jerk."

"I was being serious."

"Yeah, well, so was I."

Falo approached them. Hiraethel was in her hand, Uroboros a circling shadow within. "It is time to make our intentions known."

The Mothergate was rumbling constantly now. The woven clock rippled like a spiderweb in the wind.

Horace opened the Fel'Daera. Slowly, smoothly, Falo slipped the Starlit Loom inside. So perfect. Such purpose. The creator inside its creation, for the last time.

"I don't have the astrolabe," Horace said. "What if I get lost?"

"You won't get lost," his mother said. "You're the Keeper of the Fel'Daera."

He had no idea if that was true. He stepped up to the Mothergate. This was not the way things were supposed to be, not yet, and the Mothergate was straining to resist. But he was about to fix that. Fix it for good.

Suddenly Chloe was at his side. She looked up at him, the dragonfly's wings blurring.

"I'm coming with you," she said.

And he knew that already. He'd seen it. He didn't understand why and was terrified to ask. "Okay," he said.

Even though he hadn't asked why, she gave him a reason. "To show you the way," she said. She looked over at Isabel. She frowned. "Isabel, congratulations on doing the right thing today," she said. "I don't remember you thanking me for being right."

And then she took Horace's hand, and led him into the Mothergate.

They broke through the blaze of white glass and into the chaos beyond. And suddenly they were falling. Or rising. Or both at the same time.

But no, the kaleidoscope of worlds around them heaved up on all sides and rolled into them, passing through them, going under. When they'd entered the Mothergate before, the churning space inside had taken no notice of them. But not now. Now they were at the center of a storm that crashed against them from all sides.

"It's the Loom!" Chloe cried.

And she was right. Hiraethel was causing this, as if it had an immense gravity that the storyscapes of the multiverse could not resist. Cities and glaciers and seas roared up high overhead, only to pound down around them.

"We can't stay," Horace said. "I'm sending it. We have to hope I do it right."

Chloe laid a hand on his wrist. "There is no right way for you to do it, Horace," she said. "I think you know that." Her face shifted through a swift series of Chloes, young and old, all of them somber, all of them wise.

"Do I?" said Horace, but he did know. This was the look on her face. She'd figured something out, something he didn't yet understand. His heart pounded heavy but slow, like it was pumping mud. The Mothergate boiled around them like a volcano. "Tell me," he said.

"No, you tell me. Tell me where the doors are."

He cast about for some sense of a door. Other than the patch of emptiness at his feet that led out through the Mothergate, he had no clue. And he knew this was not the kind of door Chloe meant. He shook his head, embarrassed and frightened.

Chloe stepped away from him, into a cascading field of purple flowers, into a billowing sea of fog, into a tumbling precipice of stone. As she moved, and the worlds moved around her, she laid her hands into the air again and again, left and right, high and low, like she was clutching at ghosts. "Here. Here. And here and here. Here." Horace could see nothing, sense nothing. She turned to him, still reaching out. "Here and here and here. They're moving fast, gone in a second, but there are so many that they're everywhere."

"So I'll just send the Loom," said Horace. "If the doors are everywhere, then it's bound to go through one of them."

"Not just one of them, Horace. Remember what Falo told us. Remember what she said about sending the Alvalaithen."

He stopped himself, his mind seizing. This wasn't going to work. It was never going to work. Or if it did, it would be a disaster. "Whatever I send goes into every future," he said flatly.

Chloe came back to him, her face flickering. "Yes."

"If it even works at all, it'll backfire. I'll be sending Hiraethel into every universe. Hiraethel has to go to just one future. Or one universe, anyway—one seed. But if I send Hiraethel here, I'll just be spreading the problem into *every other universe.*"

"I think so," said Chloe.

Horace clutched the open box. "But we'll be fine. Our universe will be okay."

"Yes," she said, "but that wasn't our intent. We intended to do much more." And the way she said it told him that he could not do this thing. It wasn't good enough. It wasn't what they'd come here to do.

"We can't fix it then," he said. "We can't do it." The words tore at his throat. Not because the plan was going to fail, but because he knew what the words meant, knew what Chloe was going to say next. He could barely bring himself to hear her.

"We can't fix it," she said. "But I can."

He shook his head. "No," he said. "No."

But Chloe only spread her arms. "All these doors, Horace. I told you I can feel them. Doors into every world there is. And I only need one." The Alvalaithen began to flutter, becoming a shimmer of white.

"I'll go with you," he said, even though he knew he couldn't.

"You can't. I wish you could. I would take you with me everywhere." She was crying. She reached up and touched the Alvalaithen. "The Earthwing," she said. "I can fly between worlds." She held out her hands. Wrinkled and smooth. Bony and weathered. "Give me the Loom, Horace."

The mind of the Mothergate swirled around them, tumbling over them. The ground shook below. "I can't," he said.

"You can. You will. You already have."

He looked down. The Fel'Daera was empty. In Chloe's hands, Hiraethel lay like a black pool, pulsing and gleaming and bottomless, Uroboros swimming within. At Chloe's throat, the Alvalaithen was an unseeable white song, glimmering.

"What if you get lost?" he said.

"I've always been lost."

"Not with me," said Horace, his voice cracking. "You were never lost with me. Promise me you'll come back."

"Promise me I can," Chloe said. "You're the one that can see the future."

He took a step toward her. He put his hand inside the

ghost of hers and made a fist. She squeezed her eyes closed for a moment and then made a fist inside his. Blood mingling. Skin inside skin. The song of the Alvalaithen poured through them both. Somehow, she snagged him there, gently, bone crossing bone. She tugged at him. She held him. He couldn't have let her go if he tried.

She was going. She would take the Starlit Loom through some door he couldn't see. Into another world that they could or could not imagine. She would leave it there. Elsewhere. Elsewhen.

Horace looked down. At his feet, in the midst of this tumbling chaos, the patch of sturdy blankness still gleamed. The way back. He pointed at it. "Remember this door, Chloe. Remember it. Come back. In twenty years this door will start to collapse, and you'll find it. You'll come back and go through, out of the Mothergate again, back the way you came. That's the story's end."

She nodded. "I will."

"Promise me," he said again.

She lifted her chin high, blinking fast, her eyes wet. She was Chloe now. His Chloe, the only Chloe he knew. She nodded. She looked at him. "I promise," she said.

And then she released him. His arm fell to his side, the Alvalaithen's song snuffed out. "Go back," she said. "Go out and tell them what I did."

His chest felt like it would tear in two. And maybe it was.

Chloe turned away. She looked around, searching. She

took a step into the seething body of the Mothergate.

And then she didn't exist.

He barely knew what came after. An agony of sadness. A fall into white. The churning fugue forgotten, left behind. A trip through a blaze of colorless light, through a barrier of sound. A stumble into a great stone hall. Dozens of waiting eyes upon him, and gasps of surprise all around. He hated every one of them for it.

Sil'falo Teneves was there. She swooped toward him, scooped him from the ground like a child. And he *was* a child.

Someone was crying out. A woman, shouting at him. Asking questions full of Chloe's name. Isabel fell to her knees.

"She's taking it where it needed to go," Horace said to Falo. "She had to. She had the best intentions."

"She always did," Falo said.

They walked. Gradually Horace became aware that a small crowd walked with them, Altari and humans alike. April was here, Arthur riding her shoulder like a wave. And Gabriel, and Joshua. Brian.

"How long was I in there?" he asked.

"Scarcely an hour," said Falo. "You did well."

"Where's Mrs. Hapsteade?"

"Gone," said a silky voice, rippling with sadness. Beautiful Teokas walked behind them, head hung low. Go'nesh loomed behind her, carrying Mr. Meister. The old man's face was blank and pale, his eyes fixed on a faraway place. And then Horace noticed a bloody gash on Teokas's arm.

"Gone," Horace repeated, and only when he spoke the word aloud did he understand what it meant.

"The battle was hard," Teokas said. "We lose even when we win. But win we did."

Horace scanned the little group, searching desperately for other missing faces. "What about Dailen?" he said.

Teokas dropped her eyes. Go'nesh stared straight ahead.

Gabriel stabbed softly at the floor with his staff. "There are no more Dailens," he said.

Horace looked past them, cold and hollow, at the Mothergate still standing among Falo's weaves. It was an island of steady black, holding fast, a sleeping spider in the center of a marvelous golden web. A web that would stand for years. That was something. That was everything. It was all they had.

Only then did he remember the Fel'Daera. He reached for it in his mind, and it was there. Still there, though he could think nothing in particular he wanted to see. Nothing within his reach, anyway.

"It worked," he said, mostly to himself, maybe for a comfort he wasn't sure he could believe in. "We did it."

"It worked," April said. Arthur bobbed and nibbled at her hair.

They walked. They went back to Falo's quarters. Most of the little group stayed behind as Falo carried Horace through the sitting room, and down the hall where hundreds of caged birds sang.

"The tunnel of birds," he murmured.

Falo brought him to a thick bed that smelled of leaves. Such a strange smell, here in this place, and as Falo laid him down he had a sudden, aching urge to see the sun, to walk barefoot in the grass under open skies.

April was with them, and his mother too. Go'nesh came and went, laying Mr. Meister gently in a chair by the door.

"I'm sorry," Horace said to him. When the old man didn't reply, still staring at the floor, he said it again louder. "Mrs. Hapsteade . . . Dorothy. I'm sorry."

Mr. Meister looked up, as if he'd thought he was alone. He took off his glasses and then bent slightly, as Horace had seen him do a hundred times before, clearly meaning to clean them on the corner of his vest. But there was no vest.

"I'm sorry," Horace said for a third time.

Mr. Meister smiled, thin and aching. "I struggle to imagine what debt you could possibly owe me, Keeper," he said. "I am the one who is sorry."

Horace looked up at Falo. She looked pained, sallow. A sudden sweep of embarrassed horror swept over him as he remembered.

"Falo," he said. "You're severed. How are you . . ."

She shook her head kindly. "I am severed, yes. Or something like it. And this time Hiraethel will not return."

So much lost, so fast. This was victory? He wanted to weep. "How long will you last?"

"Isn't it funny how fixated on time the Keeper of the Fel'Daera is?" Falo took a hearty breath like she was considering a long walk outdoors. "It does not matter. It is good. It is good to be released in this way. Life has been long, and full of wonder. But my work is done. All our work is done."

"But not for the new universe," said April. "Wherever Chloe finds it, wherever she takes the Starlit Loom. Their work is just beginning."

Falo shrugged, considering it. "And their wonder."

Horace's mother sat on the bed. She took his hand in hers. She was crying magnificently, her face and mouth smooth and bright and strong, tears pouring freely from her.

"Sometimes I wish I'd warned you," she said. Her voice was strong, too.

"Warned me about what?"

"About everything. That first day you came home with the Fel'Daera—I knew so much, and you knew so little. And I didn't tell you anything. I didn't warn you. And now Chloe . . ."

He squeezed her hand, shook his head. "I can't imagine a warning you could have given me that I wouldn't have mostly ignored."

She laughed, blinking up at the ceiling. "Dammit, Horace, that makes me so furious and proud."

"*Mostly*, I said."

"I thought you were going to die, you know," his mother said. "From that very first day, I had to prepare myself for the worst."

"I know. But the worst didn't happen."

"No. You saved us. You and Chloe both."

"We did what we had to," Horace said. "We all did. But what happens now?"

She stroked his forehead gently. "What a question for the Keeper of the Fel'Daera to ask," she said. "But the answer is always the same. Life, Horace. Life happens now." She laughed again, jostling loose a sprinkle of tears. "Life even with all we lose."

He nodded, crying now too. "And find," he said.

The Boy Who Knew Tomorrow

SHE CAME TO HIM IN THE PARK ONE DAY. NOT JUST ANY PARK. Not just any day.

This was the park with the wobble horses, near his childhood home, where no one Horace knew lived anymore. The wobble horses were long gone. There was a tedious plastic playground here now, like the sterile dream of a machine. This was the park he'd chased her to that first night. *Two* nights, really—at least for Horace. One on each side of the glass. This right here was the tree she'd buried herself in, hiding from Dr. Jericho until Horace had lured him away. Which night had that been, again? And maybe after all it was *that* tree, there. Horace frowned. Maybe the tree was gone by now too. It was hard to say how long things lived.

Catching her hadn't been easy. How could it be? Chloe had been the girl who walked through walls. But Horace had

421

been the boy who knew tomorrow. She couldn't escape him. She still hadn't escaped him. He knew it, just like he knew that he hadn't really saved her. Not that night or any night. Not any of the thousands of nights since. Seven thousand three hundred and eighty-nine. But who was counting?

He held the Fel'Daera in his hands, turning it over and over. How small it was, how simple. It was hard to imagine it had always been so small. He didn't bother to hide it now as he sat on the bench, waiting. There was no one to keep it from, and nothing to hide. It was just a box. It had been becoming just a box for twenty years now, bit by bit and day by day, and he had been becoming . . . what? A boy who did not know tomorrow. A man who knew the future only as a tangle of tasks to manage, aspirations to move toward, changes to tackle or embrace.

Horace realized that he had been imagining—not consciously, but playing the image out in some poorly lit, youthful corner of his mind—that Chloe would step out of a tree. This one or that one.

But she didn't. She stepped out of a cab.

She wore a plaid woolen coat. The hood of a green sweatshirt hung over the back collar. She looked like Isabel looked when last Horace saw her—the same small frame, the same wary-cat posture, the chin held high. And Chloe was about that same age now, he realized. But her hair was black and straight, and long, as long as it had been before the fire, strands of it lifting in the wind.

She'd seen him already. He started toward her, waved at her. She rolled her eyes at the wave. She just stood there, bouncing atop bent knees, like her feet were melded to the ground.

He understood. He would close the distance now. She'd come so far.

She was crying. So was he. She looked beautiful and tired and wise in a way he did not know a human could be. She waited for him, her throat working, her shoulders seizing, her eyes as fierce as fires.

He stepped into her. He pressed his foot against hers. "It's you," he said.

She nodded. Then her mouth broke into an anguished frown and she shook her head desperately, her eyes thick with wet. She pressed her foot hard against his. She grabbed his jacket and let it go. Her coat fell open. The Alvalaithen wasn't there. She nodded again, smiling, shrugging. Horace thought his chest would break apart. He had felt this before.

"I missed you," he said.

Chloe opened her mouth. She let out a great, ragged breath. She blinked into the blue sky, clouds in her eyes. The faint scars around her throat were faded now, had become whispers.

"Yeah, well," she said, "who wouldn't?"

They walked then. They didn't know to where. The world turned beneath them, becoming whatever worlds it would. Horace left the Fel'Daera behind, sitting on the bench. He did not know that he had done this. He would not realize it until tomorrow.

And when he did remember it, he would be sitting on the train to St. Louis with this most fantastic friend, a friend who had returned to this place in flesh and blood after all this time, all this life, the girl who saved everyone, the girl who had promised him. He would remember the box then, yes.

But he would not go back.

GLOSSARY

Aerary

a small chamber in Falo's quarters where she works with the Starlit Loom

Altari (all-TAR-ee)

the Makers of the Tanu, and the ancestors of the Riven

Alvalaithen (al-vuh-LAYTH-en)

Chloe's Tan'ji, the dragonfly, the Earthwing; with it, she can become incorporeal

Aored (a-OAR-ed)

Grooma's Tan'ji, a Loomdaughter

Auditor

a type of Riven; though not Tan'ji, Auditors can imitate the powers of nearby instruments

backjack

a small silver Tan'kindi whose location can be tracked with a paired, compass-like device

425

breach	the gap in time across which the Fel'Daera sees the future
cleave	to forcibly and permanently rip apart the bond between a Keeper and his or her Tan'ji
dispossessed	term for a Keeper who is permanently cut off from his or her instrument, usually by cleaving or being severed for too long
Dorvala (dor-VAH-la)	a Maker
dumin (DOO-min)	a shield of force through which almost nothing can pass; created using a dumindar
empath	a Keeper whose power is listening to the thoughts of animals and others
Fairfrost Blade	a Tan'ji belonging to Go'nesh; this weapon carves nearly impenetrable swaths of frozen blue through the air
Fel'Daera (fel-DARE-ah)	Horace's Tan'ji, the Box of Promises; with it, he can see a short distance into the future
Find, the	the solitary period during which a new Keeper discovers and then masters his or her instrument
Floriel	Dailen's Tan'ji, granting him the

	power to create multiple versions of himself
Gallery, the	a corridor deep in the Warren whose doorways will only appear by the light of certain jithandras
golem	a massive swarm of moving stones, a powerful Tan'kindi controlled by the Riven
golm'ruun (golm-RUNE)	a ring that allows the wearer to control the golem
harps	instruments used by Tuners to alter the Medium; only Tuners can operate them, but they are not Tan'ji
Hiraethel (hih-RAY-thul)	the Starlit Loom
humour, the	the blinding, invisible cloud of gray Gabriel releases from the Staff of Obro
jithandra (jih-THAHN-drah)	small Tan'kindi used for light, identification, and entry into the Wardens' sanctuaries
Ka'hoka (kah-HO-kah)	a major sanctuary of the Altari, at Cahokia Mounds in western Illinois
kaitan (ky-TAHN)	a device used to bind two potential Keepers together, turning them into Tuners instead
Keeper	one who has bonded with an

	instrument, thus becoming Tan'ji
Kesh'kiri (kesh-KEER-ee)	the name the Riven use for themselves (see "Riven")
Laithe of Teneves (TEN-eevs)	Joshua's Tan'ji, a miniature globe that grants the power to open portals anywhere on earth
Loomdaughters	the first Tan'ji made with the Starlit Loom; there were nine in total
mal'gama (mahl-GAH-ma)	similar to the golem, a Tan'kindi comprised of thousands of green stones, capable of flight
Medium, the	the energy that flows from the Mothergates and powers all Tanu
Mordin	tall, ferocious Riven who are particularly skilled at hunting down Tan'ji
Mothergates	the three enigmatic structures through which the Medium flows before reaching out to power all Tanu in the world
Nevren	a field of influence that temporarily severs the bond between a Keeper and his or her Tan'ji; Nevrens protect the Wardens' strongholds
Nlon'ka (n-LAWN-ka)	an abandoned Altari stronghold in Crete; home to a Mothergate

nul'duna (nul-DOO-nah)   a Keeper who is rendered expendable because another potential Keeper for his or her Tan'ji has been found

oraculum   a Tan'ji belonging to Mr. Meister, a lens that allows him to see the Medium

phalanx   a small Tan'kindi, made from the fingerbone of a Mordin; it fires a blast of energy that pins Tan'ji in place

polymath's ring   a Tan'kindi that allows its wearer to bond with more than one Tan'ji; shaped like a Möbius strip

Ravenvine   April's Tan'ji, a silver vine she wears around her left ear; it grants her the power to empathically absorb the thoughts of nearby animals

Ravids   small, quick Riven with the ability to teleport short distances

Riven   a hidden race of beings who hunger to reclaim all the Tanu for their own; they call themselves the Kesh'kiri

sa'halvasa (sah-hahl-VAH-sah)   related to the golem, a swarm of tiny insect-like Tanu with razor-sharp wings

Sanguine Hall	the back entrance to the Warren, once home to the sa'halvasa
sever	to temporarily cut a Keeper off from his or her Tan'ji
Staff of Obro	Gabriel's Tan'ji, a wooden staff with a silver tip; it releases the humour, which blinds others but gives him an acute awareness of his surroundings
Starlit Loom	Hiraethel, the very first Tanu, a Tan'ji that gives its Keeper the power to make new Tanu; Sil'falo Teneves (sil-FAY-lo TEN-eevs), called Falo (FAY-lo), is its Keeper
Tan'ji (tahn-JEE)	a special class of Tanu that will only work when bonded with a Keeper who has a specific talent; Tan'ji also describes the Keeper himself or herself as well as the state of that bond—a kind of belonging or being
Tan'kindi (tahn-KIN-dee)	a simpler category of Tanu that will work for anyone, without requiring a special talent or a bond (raven's eyes, dumindars, etc.)
Tanu (TAH-noo)	the universal term for all of the mysterious devices created by

the Makers; the function of these instruments is all but unknown to most (two main kinds of Tanu are Tan'ji and Tan'kindi)

Thailadun (thail-a-DOON) the Moondoor, a Tan'ji controlled by Teokas; it has a limited ability to freeze time

tourminda (tour-MIN-dah) a fairly common kind of Tan'ji that allows its Keeper to defy gravity; Neptune is the Keeper of the Devlin tourminda

Tuner though not Tan'ji, Tuners can use instruments called harps to cleanse and tune other Tanu

Tunraden (toon-RAH-den) Brian's Tan'ji, a Loomdaughter; with it, he can create and repair Tanu

Ulu'ru (ul-OO-roo) an abandoned Altari stronghold in Australia; home to a Mothergate

Uroboros (oo-RO-bur-ose) an ancient and mysterious fishlike creature trapped in a glass cylinder

Veil of Lura (LOOR-ah) a shimmering curtain of light that hides and protects the Mothergates

Vithra's Eye the name of the Nevren that guards the Warren

Wardens	the secret group of Keepers devoted to protecting the Tanu from the Riven
Warren	the Wardens' headquarters beneath the streets of Chicago, deep underground
Well of Giving	Goth en'Sethra, the massively powerful Nevren at Ka'hoka

Acknowledgments

THERE ARE SO MANY PEOPLE TO THANK, NOW THAT *The Keepers* has come to an end.

Toni Markiet, my editor, who has been with this project since the beginning and has worked harder than anyone ought to have to. Thank you, Toni, for all your guidance. Also everyone else at HarperCollins, past and present, who helped get these books out into the world: Jenny Sheridan, Phoebe Yeh, Abbe Goldberg, Megan Ilnitzki, Amy Ryan, Tessa Meischeid, Gina Rizzo, and many others. And of course Kate Morgan Jackson and Suzanne Murphy for seeing this project through to the end.

Miriam Altshuler, my agent, who has been so steady and strong through the years, and who never lets me get lost. I'm so grateful for your presence. And also Reiko Davis, for all her competence and assistance.

Iacopo Bruno, whose amazing art I genuinely treasure. I'm so honored to have had your work gracing the covers and pages of these books.

Liz Howey. I'm not exaggerating when I say I could not have finished this final book without your incredible work cataloging the people, places, creatures, and mysteries of the Keepers. I asked for your help and you sent back a miracle. Thank you for making my life so much easier.

My friends, supporters, and colleagues. Matt Minicucci, Laura Koritz, Russell Evatt, Kathy Skwarczek, Jeff & Rosita Durbin, Michele Whisenhunt, Elizabeth Tavares, Janice Harrington, Antonia Leotsakos, Tom Seals, Cara Baiocchi, Matt Mullholland.

My teachers. Philip Graham, Rick Powers, Mike Madonick, and many others—especially Neil Archer, who shocked me and changed me by hating the first real story I wrote. Your belief that I could, and should, do better was the best lesson I ever learned.

My parents, who made me a reader.

My children, Rowan, Bridget, and Milo.

My wife Jodee, who has given me so much room and support, and who has had to listen to me brag, complain, and fret for years now. Thank you endlessly for your love and patience.

And finally, all my readers, and all the fans of *The Keepers*. It's been so gratifying meeting so many of you. Your passion for these books has been the best reward a writer could ask for. Thank you all, big and small.

DON'T MISS THESE BOOKS BY
TED SANDERS!

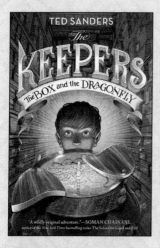

Go to thekeepersbooks.com for videos and other cool extras!